Divine Solace

Joey W. Hill

ELLORA'S CAVE
ROMANTICA®
ELLORASCAVE.COM

An Ellora's Cave Publication

www.ellorascave.com

Divine Solace

ISBN 9781419971389
ALL RIGHTS RESERVED
Divine Solace Copyright © 2014 Joey W. Hill
Edited by Briana St. James.
Cover design by Kelly Martin.
Cover photography by Valentin Agapov/ShutterstockArtem Furman/Shutterstock, sakkmesterke/Fotolia,mingius/Shutterstock/laschi/Shuterstock

Electronic book publication March 2014
Trade paperback publication 2014

With the exception of quotes used in reviews, this book may not be reproduced or used in whole or in part by any means existing without written permission from the publisher, Ellora's Cave Publishing, Inc.® 1056 Home Avenue, Akron OH 44310-3502.

Warning: The unauthorized reproduction or distribution of this copyrighted work is illegal. Criminal copyright infringement, including infringement without monetary gain, is investigated by the FBI and is punishable by up to 5 years in federal prison and a fine of $250,000. (http://www.fbi.gov/ipr/)

This book is a work of fiction and any resemblance to persons, living or dead, or places, events or locales is purely coincidental. The characters are productions of the author's imagination and used fictitiously.

The publisher and author(s) acknowledge the trademark status and trademark ownership of all trademarks, service marks and word marks mentioned in this book.

The publisher does not have any control over and does not assume any responsibility for author or third-party Web sites or their content.

Acknowledgements

My great thanks to Trish (aka Lord Mason's Mistress), for her invaluable knowledge and insights as a surgical nurse, and for her continued support of my work. I will always be so glad I had the chance to meet you at RAW! And not just because you hold a revered spot as the first person I knew who had a tattoo inspired by my books (grin).

I also send out a cheer of appreciation and gratitude to the lovely author Trista Michaels, for daring to ride the Sky Lift in Gatlinburg, Tennessee and being willing to share that experience with me. Because of that, I could give Lyda, Gen and Noah that adventure—with my feet remaining firmly on the ground. Gen and I feel the same way about heights!

As always, my great thanks to my critique partners, my editor, and all the staff at Ellora's Cave who work together to make my books shine. And a huge thanks to my readers for their continued leaps of faith, taking the journey with my characters. Hope you enjoy this one with Lyda, Gen and Noah.

Divine Solace

Chapter One

Disconcerting.

Unsettling, perplexing or perturbing might mean the same thing according to her thesaurus, but Gen decided disconcerting was the best word for the woman sitting at Table Seven in Tea Leaves. Disconcerting rolled off the tongue a certain way the other words didn't. Emotions and people were like that. Put the same emotion inside ten people, and it would look different on each one of them.

Disconcerting required an object to impact. Someone couldn't be disconcerting without being disconcerting *to* someone. In this case, that object was Gen, even though Gen worked for Marguerite Winterman. Marguerite had Margaret Thatcher's aura of command, Marilyn Monroe's ability to mesmerize, and a liontamer's touch with dangerous creatures. Maybe because Marguerite *was* one of those dangerous creatures and understood them all too well. It was part of the reason Gen had given her the nickname "M", because Marguerite had the intimidating air of the Bond movie female director of MI-6, in spades.

Yet, despite all that, their newest customer disconcerted Gen in a way Marguerite never had.

As she checked on other customers, Gen tried to pinpoint what it was about the woman. Her appearance gave mixed messages. She was beautiful, yet not wearing anything to enhance that beauty. Her pale-green bill cap had *Growing Things Nursery* logo embroidered on it, a match for the breast pocket of the babydoll T-shirt she wore over snug, stressed jeans and work shoes. When she removed the cap to run the point of her wrist along her damp brow, Gen saw her braided hair was a dark red with some gold highlights, evident from the loose wisps around her face.

Like a lot of true redheads, she had milk-white skin, despite her outdoor job. The T-shirt showed off generous breasts, large enough to swell out the sides of the cotton against her biceps. Her arms displayed smooth muscle definition. The way she moved made it clear the body beneath the clothes was equally fit.

Not butch. Nor diet-obsessed, where there was no meat on her. Just toned and strong, curved in all the ways that drew male eyes. As well as female eyes, given the way Gen was checking her out.

It wasn't the first time Gen had noticed a woman was attractive. She defined herself as hetero, since she'd been married twice and had always dated the opposite sex. Sure, she'd experimented with friends in high school, but what girl didn't? Women weren't as defined by straight and gay as the guys were. As she got older, she knew she had a bi-curious side to her, but it wasn't anything she'd ever been tempted to explore, beyond idle fantasy and pleasuring the eye. Yet when she looked at this woman, the dormant temptation wasn't dormant at all. Sensation fluttered against her thighs like butterfly wings and caused a tightness in her chest.

Maybe it was the woman's air of authority that made her distracting. She was probably the owner of the nursery, because it was clear she was used to directing things, not being directed. When she'd first walked in, those gunmetal-gray eyes had pinned Gen in place behind the counter.

"I'm here to see Marguerite."

"She's coming in around nine, about fifteen minutes from now. Is there something I can help you with, ma'am?"

That unsettling gaze ran over every visible part of Gen, the top of her head to her hips. "Who are you?"

"I'm Gen," Gen said politely.

"I'll wait." The redhead looked up at the board. "Do you have regular coffee, Gen?"

At one time, the answer to that would have been a resounding no, but since she'd married Tyler, Marguerite had capitulated to having at least one coffee option on the menu. No cappuccinos or anything fancy. A good Colombian blend.

When Gen told the woman what they had, she nodded. "A cup of that."

"All right. If you want to take a seat, it will be just a moment. I have a batch brewing now."

Marguerite's visitor had then taken her seat at Table Seven. Gen had felt her regard while she busied herself behind the counter, even when she left it and made the rounds to the other tables to ensure no one needed anything. Though Gen smiled and chatted with the regulars as usual, that scrutiny was a living thing teasing the hairs on her nape.

How did she tell a customer, a friend or associate of Marguerite's, to stop staring at her? She wished Chloe were here to help with opening. But with Chloe and Marguerite both now married, Gen tried to do it solo at least a couple times a week, giving the women time with their husbands. Some mornings, the solo opening underscored her permanent single status, but she usually squelched that blue thought pretty fast in favor of the sense of accomplishment running the business by herself gave her.

Since Gen had finished those accounting courses at the community college, Marguerite had even let her take over the bookkeeping. She might have been born trailer-park trash, but how a person was born didn't dictate how they lived. That was up to them.

I told you, Momma.

The thought inspired Gen to meet the woman's gaze. Ms. Disconcerting didn't even blink those long-lashed eyes. Gen gave her a dignified nod, not willing to simply duck her head, and returned to the counter. She'd never been the subject of such intent scrutiny. Not since her first day on the job, when Marguerite had watched her in a similar way. As if every movement Gen made, everything she said, every smile, meant something far deeper, Gen emitting signals she didn't even realize she was sending. She'd really needed that job, so she'd managed to stay cool, professional, asking questions about what she didn't know, and making up for her mistakes quickly.

If Chloe had been here, her nonstop comfortable chatter would have helped. Her irrepressible friend would have turned so no one but Gen could see her expression as she rolled her eyes about the mysterious visitor and mouthed a *what the hell's her problem?* at Gen.

At least the low rumble of conversation from other customers kept silence from becoming a taut, awkward bridge Gen might have tried to fill with inane small talk. Couldn't the intimidating woman pull out a cell phone to check her messages, the way most people did?

The coffee was done. Gen poured it, picked up napkin, spoon and condiments, and left the sanctuary of the counter. The woman's work clothes and sweaty appearance should have put Gen more at ease. Instead, she came off like Red Sonja showing up in bloodstained battle armor, making Gen think about her own appearance. Today she wore a Tea Leaves staff shirt. Not a shaped babydoll, just a medium T-shirt that didn't highlight her figure at all, though she did knot it at the hip of her fashionably frayed jeans over rhinestone sandals. She had her hair pulled up and held with sticks, and though it framed her face attractively enough, she was overdue to dye her roots.

She looked like a comfortable, pleasant thirtysomething, as sexless as a spayed cocker spaniel. This woman, around the same age as Gen, could don a ball gown and walk the red carpet at the Oscars. She was a woman who still considered herself a sexual being, not one who lacked the energy or hope to pursue the idea anymore.

Gen set the coffee in front of her. The redhead tapped the table. "Spoon on my right," she said. "Napkin on the left. No sugar or cream. I drink it straight."

"So does Tyler. Anything different, he says you might as well be a girl in frilly pink at a tea party."

The customer's mouth made a sinuous twist. What was probably a sunblock lip balm made her lips soft, gave them a faint sheen. That butterfly fluttering became the stroke of a long, firm-stemmed seagull feather up Gen's thighs, teasing her navel, her sternum.

"He said that to get a rise out of Marguerite," the woman said.

She spoke as if her tongue caressed her teeth when she spoke, the syllables coming out with a touch of breath. During sex, Gen wondered if that sighing sound was more pronounced, spinning the words with sugar and giving them a sweet heat, like cookies from the oven.

Had she woken up on the wrong side of her sexual orientation this morning? Was that even possible? Chloe would know.

"Yes." Gen cleared her throat. "He only said it once, though. She salted his coffee."

"Marriage has mellowed her. The Marguerite I know would have used a strong laxative."

"Well, they do live together. Maybe it was enlightened self-interest."

Gen colored when the woman's gaze remained on her, though she noticed the corners of her lips twitched. As Gen followed her direction about the napkin and spoon, the redhead watched her, not what she was doing. It was the first time she'd been instructed on table setting by a customer, but Gen prided herself on her customer service. It was an odd though not unreasonable demand. As she laid the folded napkin on the opposite side of the cup, the woman reached up and touched Gen's hair.

Her fingertips slid beneath the strands at her temple and brushed against her scalp. "Your hair is a beautiful color," she observed. "Golden brown, like honey straight from the hive. Why do you have it in this god-awful scraped-up mess?"

If the woman was being catty, Gen could have broken the spell and set her in her place, quick and sharp. She was far past being put down by another female. But the woman's expression and tone were merely thoughtful. She caught a wisp between her knuckles, her firm, assured touch holding Gen still. Nerves tingled along Gen's cheekbone and down her throat like a trail of breadcrumbs, begging those fingers to follow them.

"I...it's quick to put up in the morning with the sticks."

"Hmm." The woman's other elbow propped on the table as she leaned forward and plucked out the sticks. Gen's hair tumbled to her shoulders in a thick twist.

What the hell are you doing? Those were the words that should have come from her mouth. Instead, she stood there, mesmerized by the woman's gall or something else. Probably the way she was stroking through Gen's hair, those tiny caresses of her scalp. As if there were no such things as personal space boundaries, or other customers. Maybe they'd think the woman was just admiring her hair. Gen wasn't sure what to do or say. Her knees were quivering in an odd way under the woman's direct gaze.

"That feels good, Gen," the woman murmured. "Doesn't it?"

Gen nodded, a quick jerk.

"Sometimes it's that way, first thing in the morning. A need for touch, to dispel the night's loneliness. Something to connect us to the world, something that says the world notices us. And likes what it sees." Her lips curved.

The redhead's faint scent of female sweat was overlaid by earth and summer leaves. Beneath all of it was a light body spray, an aroma Gen recognized, because working for M had given her a very well-developed sense of smell. It was a blend intended to soothe the senses. Chamomile, lavender. What would Red Sonja need to soothe herself about? The day's body count? The fact she broke her nail gutting her enemies?

What would happen if she reached out and touched *her* hair? Gen got only as far as imagining her hand lifting. It seemed inappropriate.

Like this wasn't? *Yes, M, I started the day by letting a customer play with my hair. Then Table Six wanted to give me a foot massage and I had to be fair to them…*

The woman's nails scraped her scalp. For a brief moment her hand tightened, pulling on the hair beneath in such strong contrast to the lighter touch Gen's full attention snapped back to her. An incredible sensation arrowed right down her center. She swallowed, and the woman's gaze followed the movement, though Gen wondered if what she was really following was the direction of the other invisible but very significant reaction.

Gen felt a trickle of panic, the reaction to a situation where she was over her head and might end up doing something really wrong to extricate herself from it. She didn't react to women like this. But then, no woman had ever actually touched her like this.

That was when Red Sonja let her go.

"Thank you, Gen." Laying the sticks down next to her coffee, she lifted the cup to her lips. "My name is Lyda Coltrane, if you need to let Marguerite know who her visitor is. You can return to your duties."

Now her voice reminded Gen of early autumn, the advance of cool weather and lingering heat of summer mixing, neither season willing to be denied.

Her gray eyes flickered past Gen, a dismissal, before they focused on the display wall where Marguerite kept her special collection of tea sets and memorabilia. The panicked feeling morphed into something else. This woman was screwing with her. This was a *friend* of Marguerite's?

"I...no offense, Ms. Coltrane, but touching...inappropriate touching, isn't allowed here."

It wasn't written up in policy, but tea drinkers usually didn't molest the staff. Gen had to assert some kind of defense. She wasn't a teenager, so easily intimidated.

"It didn't feel inappropriate to me. How about to you?" Lyda blew on the contents of the coffee cup.

"I'm not...I've been married. Twice."

Lyda's penetrating gaze lifted to hers. "Your point?"

"Let me know if you need a refill on the coffee." Pivoting, Gen moved with stiff purpose to the other tables. No one gave her odd looks, so her customers must have missed the hair incident. Or they chalked it up to one woman asking another woman about her hair, right? Maybe she was overreacting.

Disconcerting. That fit Lyda Coltrane, for sure.

The phone rang, giving her an excuse to retreat behind the counter. As she bent over her pad to take a phone order, she had to hold her hair back on one side to see. Damn it, Lyda had her sticks. It had been awhile since she'd worn her hair down. Feeling the strands tumble forward made her feel...girlish. Pretty. Something she'd rethink if she saw a mirror. She probably looked like she had a limp dish mop on her head.

As she hung up, the side door opened, flooding her with relief. Glancing down the access hallway to Marguerite's office, she saw her boss come up the two stairs, her heels tapping against the old wood floor. "Good morning."

Lyda Coltrane might come off as scary in the right circumstances, but Marguerite Winterman was that way 24/7. Tall, with moonlight-colored hair and direct, pale-blue eyes that could laser through steel if needed, she was a woman who commanded attention and compliance from everyone around her. While she could be so calm it was eerie—Chloe's words, but they fit—they knew the loving and generous spirit beneath that reserve. The three of them had been through a lot together. As a result, no matter how intimidating M was, Gen and Chloe were as protective of her as she was of them. She was friend, confidante and family, all rolled up in one. The world would balance again. Marguerite was here.

As Marguerite snapped on the light in her office, Gen moved out of view of the public floor to stand in her doorway. "You have a visitor. Lyda Coltrane?"

Marguerite's gaze became marginally warmer, which said Lyda was a friendly acquaintance, not close friend. No surprise there, since Marguerite didn't have a great many in that inner circle.

"All right. Will you bring in some of the new Ceylon from the storeroom? I'll cover things here while Lyda and I talk."

"Sure. We have a phone order for six. It's written up on the counter and I've gotten it started. They said it would be about thirty minutes."

"All right." Marguerite put her purse in the bottom drawer of her desk. "I like your hair down. You haven't worn it that way in a while. And you're flushed, eyes bright as spring leaves." Her silken brow rose. "New love interest?"

"No," Gen said emphatically. "Lyda took it down. She—"

Marguerite's lips firmed, her blue eyes getting a less friendly look, hastening Gen to explain further. "She was checking the color, said she liked it." She'd actually said it was beautiful, but it was clear Gen shouldn't have said anything. "I—"

Marguerite held up a finger. "It's not your fault, Gen. Lyda is like that. You've done nothing wrong. Ceylon?"

At a loss, Gen chose to escape. Heading out the side door, she made the turn into Marguerite's private garden, stopping to put her hands to her cheeks. She *was* flushed. And she'd just stood there while Lyda was touching her. What the hell…

A walk in Marguerite's gardens tended to calm the mind. Taking a couple breaths, Gen inhaled the scents from the herb garden, trailed her fingers through the fountain as a good morning to the circling koi, then followed the stepping stones to the storage building. Just before she reached it, a thought brought her up short.

Lyda is like that. Of course. It should have been obvious.

Less than a couple years ago, a break-in at Tea Leaves, a terrible event connected to M's past and one that nearly lost her both M and Chloe, had taught Gen what lay beneath Marguerite's formidable calm. During that time, she'd also found out some pretty eye-opening things about her boss. Marguerite was a sexual Dominant, a Mistress. Tyler, was also one—a Master that is.

Chloe's husband Brendan was a submissive who inhabited that world.

Eventually, Chloe had revealed to Gen the shocking fact Marguerite had been Brendan's Mistress of choice before meeting Chloe. While Chloe wasn't a Mistress, she was a sexually adventurous young woman. Somehow, she and Brendan were making it work, but there was an undeniably strong bond between them, more than the usual overt affection of newlyweds.

Before those revelations, Gen hadn't known anything about the BDSM world except the distortions of pop culture, but once she learned — again through Chloe — more about what a Mistress was, it had certainly explained a lot about the effortless power Marguerite seemed to exercise over everyone in her world, though Chloe said that Dominants were as diverse as any other group. Not all Mistresses were like Marguerite.

Actually, I think there's no one like Marguerite, Chloe had said, with a twinkle in her eye.

Lyda exuded similar qualities. Obviously. So it made sense. She was a Mistress. Maybe she had trouble containing those boundaries within a proper environment, and Gen was just inexperienced in dealing with that kind of thing.

Even though Chloe frequently encouraged Gen to join them at The Zone, the BDSM club they frequented, and in which Tyler had an ownership interest, Gen had always declined. It wasn't her world. She wasn't drawn to that. Or rather, by not exposing herself, she was making sure she wasn't. She'd been down the sexually adventurous road in her early twenties. Two marriages had pretty much burned her out on all of it.

She had gone as far as looking up the club online. It was a classy, high-end establishment, the membership fee making her blanch. Marguerite had never encouraged her to visit it the way Chloe had, but that didn't mean anything. Marguerite really wasn't the "C'mon, girlfriend, let's get our freak on at the BDSM club tonight" type.

Gen grinned, equilibrium restored. *This* was her world. It was comfortable, quiet, what she knew. Things made sense. She amused herself by imagining Lyda in stereotypical dominatrix gear. Sleek, form-fitting black latex that clung to hips and trim waist. Those generous breasts would swell out the top of a corset, her long red hair loose and caressing pale shoulders. She'd be wearing gloves, the kind that fit like a second skin and went past a woman's elbows. Gen had a black, silky pair she'd picked up at a yard sale. She wore them at home sometimes for no reason, since she had nowhere to wear them.

She imagined Lyda reaching out, black-clad fingers touching Gen's face, then sliding up to her temple, into her hair, tightening there. Gen would sink to her knees, right in front of those sleek, latex-covered thighs. Would she put her lips on one and stay there, eyes closed, as Lyda stroked her hair?

She'd moved into the storeroom, was measuring out tea, but that thought brought her to a halt. Arousal dampened her panties. Weird. Another word for bizarre, peculiar and uncanny. Uncanny. She liked that one. She'd become addicted to the thesaurus as part of her collage hobby, trading out words for the patterns she created, preferring the aesthetic look of one word over another because of its combination of consonant tails and fat vowels. Other times she just liked how it fit the tone of the picture she was making. Earth instead of dirt… Rain instead of water… A choice of one versus the other made a different impression on the senses.

She was spending too much time daydreaming. The phone was going to start ringing with more orders, the door opening on the midmorning rush. She shouldn't be dallying, not when Marguerite was handling customers and a visitor.

She laid a light towel over the container holding the Ceylon, seeing no need to seal it for a quick dash. Until it was too late. She came out of the storeroom at the quick march and ran smack up against another human being.

Tea leaves did a tsunami wave over the dislodged towel, the fruit-and-molasses smell clouding the air. *Oh, shit.* She should have put a lid on the bowl, should have…

A pair of strong male hands caught hold of Gen to keep her from tumbling, but in so doing, the kind stranger was unable to defend himself from the onslaught and took the shower of leaves square in the face. Now he was sneezing.

"Oh God. I'm so sorry. Are you all right?" She snatched a paper towel from the storeroom, wet it down in the utility sink and came back out with it, bending down to insert it in his field of view. He had his hands on his knees, his head down. "Here, wipe this under your nose and on your face."

He managed a quick grin between another couple hard sneezes. "Sorry." He complied with her direction, took another paper towel from her to blow his nose, then one more damp one to finish things off. As he straightened, she saw he was a handsome mid-twenties, slim but charismatic, his sleek dark hair pulled back to show sharply sculpted facial features. He wore black-and-silver braided bracelets double-wrapped on his wrists, black jeans and a white T-shirt. A matching choker was wrapped around his throat, completing a somewhat Goth look. No eye makeup or black nails, though.

"Subdued Goth?" she ventured, seeking something to say other than apologies.

Brown eyes like rich cocoa sparkled at her, setting off those butterflies again. She must be going through some weird hormone surge today.

"I teach sailing at the community college," he explained. "Runny black eye liner scares the students."

"But you are a Goth?"

He shrugged, cleared his throat. "When I go to a club, I might trick myself out with the full regalia, but not so much on a day-to-day basis anymore. I'm evolving. I was never much of a music-inspired Goth anyhow."

This was the kind of eccentric conversation Chloe loved. She'd jump with both feet into someone's head, ferret out every intriguing thing about them. Usually Gen had a sideline seat to enjoy the show, but maybe today she'd try something different. Maybe she'd be the one daring to find out more.

"Is there another type of Goth?" Stepping back into the storeroom, she began to measure out more Ceylon, trying not to think of the gimlet eye Marguerite would level upon her for her carelessness. It wasn't cheap, one of the Sri Lanka teas that came from the highest elevations.

"I'm inspired by movie and literary geniuses of the genre," he said, leaning in the door, entirely comfortable. Of course, trying to asphyxiate someone with tea did bring down social barriers. "Like Edgar Allan Poe."

"I really don't know much about Goths," she admitted. "I didn't know there were different...sects."

"That's all right." He grinned again. "My perspective isn't that common. I tend to do my own thing. I was born in the wrong time period."

She replaced the lid, sealed the container and efficiently swept the counter. As she moved to the doorway and he straightened, she saw he was probably close to six feet. Not quite as tall as Marguerite's Tyler, but still a nice height.

"Maybe you weren't born in the wrong time period," she suggested. "Maybe you were alive then, and now you're here, reincarnated. You can't stay in the same time period forever."

Good God, Chloe was rubbing off on her. Not only was she talking like her, she was finding the topic engaging.

"Except during sex," he observed. "That's the only way you can make time stop, during any lifetime."

She gave him a sharp look, prepared to say something a little more distancing, but his serious expression said he wasn't flirting, just making a simple observation. "Spoken like a guy," she responded lightly.

"No," he said. "It's not like that. Everyone knows about that kind of sex. Or they should."

He met her gaze as directly as Lyda did, but there was a different tone to it. Whereas Lyda's gaze could hold her like a restraint, his drew her to him like the offer of a young satyr to dance with him on a moonlit night. She'd done a collage of a fairy ring recently, a birthday gift for a friend in her book club who loved fairies. That was the only reason she could think why such an impractical idea had jumped into her mind.

She decided to take it back to safer footing. "Favorite Edgar Allan Poe quote?"

"'Deep into that darkness peering, long I stood there, wondering, fearing, doubting, dreaming dreams no mortal ever dared to dream before.'" His lips quirked. "My favorite partly because I liked the quote, partly because it taught me the dangers of academic pretentiousness."

A college grad. Of course. Usually she had an aversion to that type, knowing how little she'd have in common with them and not really wanting to be reminded of her comparative lack of education, but the comment made her curious. "How so?"

He sighed. "I wrote it up on the board for a class, a visual aid for a presentation on Poe. Couldn't figure out what all the snickering was about until the end. I had left the 'r' out of peering."

"'Deep into that darkness, peeing...'" She chuckled. "Well, conceivably, one could pee into the darkness and experience fear, doubt and wonder at the same time."

It was stupid to get uptight about it. Lots of people hadn't attended college. She hadn't done well in school, too busy living up to low expectations while her single mother worked. Gen had become a hairdresser to make ends meet and found she did that well enough, but she didn't have any real flair or passion for it. Her life was littered with mediocre attempts at a lot of things. She'd liked writing poetry in middle school, until she read one to her mother and Momma made it clear girls from trailer parks didn't write poetry. They found a guy who, if they were lucky, didn't drink to excess and beat them, and settled down to have babies.

It had probably been very bad poetry. She'd thrown it away, but in the past few years she'd thought about going back to school to get an English degree, just for the pleasure of learning. Which was ridiculous. Not only because she didn't have the money to waste on "fun" classes, but because she'd made so many mistakes early on in her life, with education *and* men, learning a practical skill like accounting had made more sense. She channeled her creative side into her crafts. Collages required only access to discarded magazines, newspapers and other recycled paper sources, and a healthy supply of glue. She loved her monthly book club, though.

"Oh." She realized she was shirking another responsibility. She really was off her game today. "This is a private area. The main entrance to Tea Leaves is on the front porch. Did you get lost?" She asked it kindly but firmly.

He didn't seem offended. "Mrs. Winterman said I could check out her new garden additions, to get ideas for the nursery. I think she was trying to get rid of me while she and my...Ms. Coltrane talked.

"Oh. Okay."

"I...work for Lyda," he supplied. "When not doing the sailing."

She noted the pause, as if the answer wasn't as straightforward as that, but he'd moved on to introductions. "I'm Noah. Can I help you carry that?"

"Gen. Pleasure to meet you. No, I sealed it this time. We could dropkick it back to the kitchen if needed. In my own defense, I wasn't expecting a tree to spring up right in front of the door."

When she earned another easygoing grin, she couldn't help but note he was *really* handsome. It wasn't exactly his looks, which were a ten on any scale, but what lay beneath them, a compelling quality that kept drawing the eye back to his face, those distracting lips. "Do you know Brendan? He teaches drama at the college."

"He helped me get the sailing gig when I moved down here for my grandmother a few months ago. I came from New Orleans."

"From New Orleans to Tampa. I can't imagine. New Orleans seems so exotic."

"You guys have Miami and the Keys. Disney World."

"The first two are a bit of a drive from here. But I'll give you Disney World." As she came out of the storeroom, he reached past her, closed the door so she didn't have to do it while balancing the tea. "Did you meet Brendan in college?"

"No. He was visiting New Orleans a few years back and he and I met in one of the clubs there. We hit it off, had a lot of common interests."

A club. And he worked for Lyda. Should she just ask outright if it was a BDSM club? Chloe would. But she wasn't Chloe, no matter how she was trying to channel her. It had been her problem all her life. Always feeling out of sync, no matter where she ended up. Except Tea Leaves. She fit here. She didn't have to prove anything here, be anything she wasn't.

Noah followed her to the side entrance, apparently comfortable not saying anything further, which was good, because she wasn't sure where to go from there. He held the screen door for her, reaching out to steady her on the steps. Her nerve endings reacted with tingling pleasure to the long, strong fingers that briefly gripped her side, brushed her lower back. As she glanced back at him, she noticed his lips were red, shaped nicely. She wanted to run a fingertip over them, see what they felt like.

He was on the step right below her, which put them at eye level, his one arm stretched out to hold the door behind her, the other on the rail, making their bodies form an intimate circle, one of those inadvertent things that could happen between two strangers with chemistry. A dark brow lifted at her pause, and in that moment she reached out and touched his mouth.

It was soft and giving, a potential for wet heat that firmed under her touch as he parted his lips, let her stroke over them. His sinfully sweet gaze remained on her the whole time. Unlike Lyda's, his wasn't penetrating. It felt more like he was…waiting.

"I'm sorry," she said, drawing back. "I'm not sure why I did that."

"Because you wanted to," he said simply. "The best reason to do anything."

Chapter Two

The only answer to that was retreat. She moved back into Tea Leaves, cognizant of him following behind her. It really was turning into a peculiar day.

She put the Ceylon in its proper spot and finished up the order for six. Marguerite was at Lyda's table, keeping an eye on the customers as they spoke. Noah moved into the room, nodding deferentially to Marguerite and Lyda before he took a seat by the door. The several chairs lined against the wall there were intended for waiting to-go customers, or for those who needed an extra seat at their table. When the nearest table of customers, a group of three women dressed for the office, looked toward Noah, he gave them a pleasant, guileless smile they seemed to appreciate.

Gen didn't blame them. He wasn't beefcake hunky, but the direct gaze, the lean strength of his body, the compelling face and eyes, made a nice package. She remembered the give of his mouth beneath her fingertips, could easily imagine his tongue teasing her fingertips, those brown eyes studying her, gauging what would give her pleasure.

If Noah was "with" Lyda, not just an employee, did that mean he was like Brendan, a submissive? Did he "belong" to Lyda? As Gen imagined having someone like him at her command, submitting to anything she desired, her knees weakened a little. She'd never given a lot of thought to tying a man up. She'd barely gotten out of missionary position with the two mistakes she'd married, both of them into the traditional male-on-top scenario.

She made a face at herself. For all she knew, Noah just worked for Lyda, and Lyda was merely a very imperious person, neither one of them part of the BDSM lifestyle. Best not to let her imagination run away with her, but there was no harm in it. The racetrack was in the privacy of her mind.

When her name caught her attention, she tuned into the conversation between Marguerite and her visitor. The context put a hard brake on her thoughts, both feet hitting them with a *what the hell?*

"Gen has purchased tile for her kitchen, but hasn't yet hired someone to do the labor," Marguerite was saying. "She could use an extra pair of hands to do that."

Marguerite glanced her way. "Gen, Lyda is looking for somewhere for Noah to stay for the weekend. He has excellent handyman skills. Would you be interested in his labor in return for giving him room and board?"

If M was making the suggestion, she knew enough about Noah that he could be trusted in Gen's home. Which left Gen more worried about whether *she* could be trusted.

She glanced his way. The intent quality to his expression clogged her breath in her throat.

"He refuses to allow me to pay for his accommodations elsewhere," Lyda was saying to Marguerite. "He can be stubborn about that. He prefers to pay his own way. Besides the renovating, he'll do whatever maintenance or housekeeping chores are needed while he's there. Laundry, cleaning, yard mowing. No task too big or small."

"Sounds like I may not want to give him up." Gen meant it as a joke, but the way Lyda's gaze turned to her strangled Gen's nervous half chuckle.

"He has that effect. I'll be having some college friends visiting, but it's a girls' weekend. No boys allowed. He could crash at a friend's house, but I prefer making his arrangements for him, so I know where he is, and that he's properly occupied."

Marguerite and Lyda exchanged a cryptic glance at that. Gen turned her attention to Noah, wanting to know his reaction to such an audacious statement. His gaze was fixed on Lyda. In it she recognized a hint of what she'd felt when Lyda had gripped her hair so hard. Hunger. The kind that moved low in the belly, that had to do with sex, with longing, with a question waiting to be answered.

When Lyda's glance flickered toward him, Noah's attention dropped to the floor, so deliberately Gen felt the jolt. Okay, her Nancy Drew skills were on target. But she didn't know anything about this kind of thing. Was she supposed to treat him the way

Lyda would? No, of course not. He'd just be a house guest helping her out with the kitchen.

"Gen?" Marguerite was asking for a decision. "Would you like Noah's help? I guarantee he'll be helpful and as nonintrusive as you wish. But there's no obligation at all on your part. He can stay with Tyler and me."

Which would make more sense, really. Gen's entire house was the size of Marguerite and Tyler's living room. But Marguerite also knew that Gen's funds were limited, and she really did want to get the kitchen finished…

"No. I'd appreciate the help." She heard the words exit her mouth. Noah's expression warmed, and another wave of nervousness had her looking away.

"When you don't have need of him, just send him to his room," Lyda said. A spark in Noah's eyes, which Lyda answered with one in her own gaze, told Gen he knew when his chain was being yanked. It was amusing…and intriguing.

"I'm sure that won't be a problem." Gen said. "Thank you, Ms. Coltrane. And thank you, Noah." Marguerite gave Lyda a significant look, tapping her fingers on the table cloth. It was a gesture Lyda answered with an irritated glance, but then she met Gen's gaze. "I apologize for the presumption earlier. I wasn't trying to play with your head."

"Yes you were," Marguerite said. Lyda shot her a cool look and rose.

"If you don't want your toys played with, Marguerite, don't leave them unattended." She glanced at Gen. "You should clean up those roots. You're a beautiful woman. You need to remind yourself of it. Noah is good for that as well."

At that outrageous comment, she moved toward the door. Pausing by Noah, Lyda put her hand on his shoulder. She murmured to him and he answered in the same quiet tone. Giving him a searching look, she leaned down, brushed his mouth with her own, holding the kiss. Noah kept both hands on his knees, though it was obvious by the way he met the kiss full on, he wanted to do more.

"Be good. Else you'll wish you could stay away from me for far longer than a weekend."

His gaze burned into her face. "I'd never wish that."

She stroked his face, a brief touch. A glance her way told Gen Lyda had intended her to hear that last exchange, regardless of whether the other customers did. Gen noticed Marguerite's jaw tighten. Then Lyda left, the screen door creaking behind her. As she crossed the porch of the nineteenth-century house Marguerite had converted into her business, Gen shifted to see her climb into a pickup with the nursery logo.

"She's leaving him here now?" Was she supposed to let him sit in the corner all day, like a patient pet?

"He has a ride picking him up for his class at the college," Marguerite explained, rising and coming around the counter. "They'll bring him back in time to go home with you at the end of the work day."

"Oh. Well I haven't..." The guestroom was clean, of course, because no one had been in it for a while, but it was all pretty sudden.

Marguerite laid a hand on top of hers. She wasn't inclined to casual affection, so Gen took it for a deliberate reassurance. "I apologize on Lyda's behalf. She can be...unpredictable."

She suspected Marguerite had some other problems with her, but the matter right now was what problems she'd presented for Gen. Or problematic opportunities.

Marguerite's voice lowered. "You know enough about my world, the one beyond Tea Leaves, to understand what he is, right? What Lyda is?"

Those blue eyes were measuring her response, trying to make sure she could handle whatever this was. Gen knew without asking she could withdraw her agreement, that Marguerite would handle things for her. She didn't like that idea, though. Not after she'd said she could handle it.

"Yes. I'm not sure. Does he need...anything different?"

"No." Marguerite's expression showed gentle amusement, but not in a way that made Gen feel foolish. "If you feel uncertain about anything, simply ask him. He will tell you the absolute truth. Otherwise, he's a houseguest helping you tile your floor and paint your walls. He's very much like Brendan in that way."

"Just don't get him wet, let bright light touch him, or give him food after midnight."

That bright interjection came from Chloe, of course. The other member of the Tea Leaves staff delivered the comment while hanging up her purse on the coat rack. Chloe was barely five feet tall, with sharp blue eyes and a lovely cap of brown hair currently dyed with a blue streak. She also had a figure like a pocket Venus. She gave Gen her usual morning hug and Marguerite a smile that could compete with the sun. "Oh my God, Gen, you get Noah for a few days. I'm so jealous. I saw Lyda at the end of the street and she said she was loaning him to you."

Chloe turned her attention to the male in question. Bounding across the room, she plopped herself in his lap and hugged him. As he disappeared behind the clasp of her lush body, his arms circled her. Obviously, Noah knew Chloe well.

"Better?" Marguerite asked Gen.

Gen gave her a rueful look, but she couldn't help but smile. All the worries she could harbor about such an unexpected turn of events couldn't hold against Chloe's infusion of normalcy into a far-from-normal situation.

"Will Lyda be coming by to see him? Or coming to pick him up?" And why did the thought fluster her so?

Marguerite's attention sharpened on her. Her boss missed very little. "I expect she's already worked that out with Noah. He doesn't have a car, but he knows how to get where he needs to be. Disappointed?"

"No." *Yes.* "I mean, it doesn't matter. Whatever's easiest. I can drop him off at her place. Maybe get some plants for the yard."

Though Gen turned away as more customers arrived, she felt Marguerite's attention. She could handle that, at least better than the lingering feel of Lyda's hand on her scalp. As if that wasn't distracting enough, Lyda's lithe body, the way denim creased with the movement of her ass as she walked away, stayed with Gen throughout most of the day as well, mixing with the memory of Noah's eyes and lips, the touch of his hands. What had she gotten herself into?

* * * * *

As Marguerite had indicated, Noah returned at closing time. He came from his sailing class with damp hair and the smell of sea water. He'd also changed from his earlier clothes into a dark ribbed tank and worn blue jeans.

When he volunteered to do whatever they needed, closing became a half-the-time affair. Marguerite had shocked her by allowing Noah to do the hand washing of the cups, something she was so particular about that Gen and Chloe considered it a sacred act.

While cleaning the brewing equipment, Gen was dangerously entranced, watching his long fingers swish the disposable cloth into each cup, the way he placed the delicate porcelain in the dish drainer, his attention never leaving his task. Except once.

He stopped, his fingers tented on a cup, eyes swiveling back to meet hers. He held her gaze, acknowledging he knew she was watching him, then he returned to the task, not another word spoken. A tremor went through her fingers.

The closer they came to going home together, just the two of them, the more his slightest gesture sent sexual signals to her. That was wrong. He was Lyda's. But it was too late to back out. Or was she just unwilling to do so?

He offered to drive her car on the way home, giving her a break from Tampa traffic. She was agreeable to that. As they maneuvered out of the older downtown area of Tampa and headed for the suburbs, they morphed from a relaxed chat about their respective workdays into Gen looking for more information about him. Yes, she trusted Marguerite, but she took care of herself. She wanted some more info about the person who was going to be spending time in her home.

"So why don't you have a car?" she asked.

"I don't have a driver's license."

She blinked. "Guess I should have asked you that before you took the wheel. But you obviously know how to drive." He negotiated the Tampa rush-hour traffic far more capably than she ever had.

She found that wry curl of his lip very appealing. "Sorry. I should have qualified that. I've had one, you know, when I was first old enough to drive. Just haven't been back to renew it. I don't do a lot of paperwork stuff."

"Okay."

She didn't press on that one, but it made her think of Chloe's cryptic comment when the two of them had taken some supplies back to the storeroom.

"Did Marguerite tell you much about how Noah is?" The girl rolled her eyes, answering her own question before Gen could. "Of course not. She'd consider basic information being overly chatty."

"I know he's a...submissive. Like Brendan?"

"Like Brendan, but not. They're all so different." Chloe considered. "It probably doesn't matter. You're not going to be relating to him that way anyway."

"He's helping me with my kitchen. I don't need to know private things about him, Chloe." But she mentally willed Chloe to tell her everything she knew. For once, surprisingly, Chloe didn't oblige.

"Okay. Sure. But if you change your mind, you know my cell number."

It made sense. Those who inhabited the D/s world were probably very private about their preferences, not wanting them discussed among the uninitiated. For all her uninhibited nature, Chloe was sensitive to discretion, else she wouldn't be working for Marguerite. For instance, while she was pretty open about her relationship with Brendan, if Chloe saw things in the club that revealed more about that type of relationship between Marguerite and Tyler, two Dominants, she never spoke of it.

Coming back to the present, the thought helped Gen rein herself in. *Keep it separate. Not your world.* Of course Marguerite had said he'd be absolutely honest...

Before knowing Brendan's orientation, Gen had accepted the same BDSM stereotypes as most people did. She'd assumed a man who wanted to be ground under a woman's stiletto was a pushover, or nothing better than a child. Noah defined himself as under the control of a woman, but he refused to let Lyda pay for his accommodations and he'd jumped right in to help with closing. Then there'd been that spark as he'd met Gen's gaze over the teacup.

So even if she couldn't form any definite conclusions about Noah, she could about Brendan. Watching him with Chloe, it was clear he defined his primary job as caring for his wife. Yet Tyler had the same opinion toward Marguerite, and he was clearly the top Dominant in their unusual relationship.

Gen had married two men who, by any standard definition, would be considered testosterone-laden alpha males, and all they'd wanted her to do was take care of them. Domestically, sexually, financially.

Chloe had said they were all different, but it still made Gen's head spin. Unfortunately, not in a way that turned off her curiosity. The idea of a man wanting to take care of a woman, in the ways she truly needed his care, wasn't her typical experience with men. If she tried to idealize something she knew nothing about, she'd be doomed to disappointment. Yes, Noah was helping her with her kitchen, but if he put his feet up on her coffee table and had a beer afterward while she cleaned up the mess caused by tiling, that was fine. She'd be content with the donation of physical labor.

Though he really didn't really look like the beer type.

"Anyone else would have said something by now," she observed, shifting in her seat. "Filling the silence."

"I figured if you wanted to talk, you would have."

"Maybe I can't think of anything to say and am hoping you will."

Noah gave her a sidelong glance. "I don't know about that. The silence felt pretty comfortable, both sides. What do you usually do on the drive home?"

"Listen to music, think about the day, think about what I'm going to do that night."

"Which is? If it's not too private."

She was kind of pleased he'd asked, though she knew the truth was probably yawn-city to most people. "I can't tell you about my second job as an international spy, but I can tell you what I do when I'm not needed for top-secret missions."

She was rewarded with the full, toe-curling grin. "Okay. Tell me what you're doing when you're not chasing down terrorists or defusing bombs."

"I read, watch TV. I like to do crafts." She could tell him about her collages, but she bit that back. Did she want to sound any less exciting? "How about you?"

"Is it okay if we talk more about you first? I'm interested in what you read and watch."

"Nothing you'd like. Romances. Biographies. Poetry."

He shifted lanes, checking the mirrors with a quick flick of his gaze. "I get why you think I wouldn't like romances, but why wouldn't I like biographies or poetry?"

"Well, I guess I meant the type of biographies and poetry I read. Stories about strong women, the kind that came from hard situations and still managed to do great things with themselves. The poetry is more romantic, girl stuff. Not Edgar Allan Poe."

He gave her an ironic look. "I like strong women, Gen. My...Lyda has me read to her. I'd be happy to read to you if you like. She says I have a good voice for it."

He did. He had a masculine tenor, infused with inflections that would make him a good dramatic speaker. Underneath all that was a lazy touch of Southern. Listening to him talk was like listening to smooth jazz.

"If you want to call her whatever it is you normally call her, that's fine." At his quizzical glance, she added, "You keep hesitating over it. I do know about Marguerite and Brendan, the kind of things...people, they are. Sorry, I'm not really sure what the correct thing is to say. I don't want to offend you."

"You couldn't possibly," he said, with a genuine kindness that made her feel better. "My Mistress likes me to read...romances to her."

At his hesitation, she lifted a brow. "Erotic romances? Spicy stuff?"

He chuckled. "Yeah."

She thought about Noah reading a steamy sex scene to Lyda. Would she lounge in the bed with him, her wearing nothing but a filmy negligee that revealed all that fair skin? Or maybe, given their relationship, she'd have Noah in a chair across the room, out of touching distance. She'd tell him he couldn't lift his eyes from the page and, as he read, she'd put her hand between her legs, stroke herself...

Up until today, Gen hadn't asked many questions about all this, not wanting to encourage Chloe. Yet though she'd always told herself BDSM wasn't her thing in reality, Gen had imagined quite a few scenarios about Marguerite and Chloe with their respective husbands. It made it way too easy to get caught up in fascinating visions now of the gorgeous, intimidating woman and undeniably hot male next to her, both of whom had more than a few intriguing layers. A Mistress and a submissive. Her mind ping-ponged, considering them separately, together. As a threesome...

Leaning forward, she adjusted the air to a cooler setting. "So, are you sure you're okay with helping me out with this for no pay? I was budgeting for a laborer to do the tilework." In another month, she'd meet that goal, so she could pay one. If Noah was as good as M implied, she had no problem with him getting the money.

He shook his head. "You're giving me a place to stay. This is my way of paying for it."

"For what tile guys are paid, you could stay in a suite at the Marriott for a week."

"Yeah, but the company wouldn't be as good."

"I've never had someone try to charm me into letting them do my home improvement." She could accuse him of indulging his masochistic tendencies with the hard and tedious task, but she wasn't sure what was appropriate teasing when it came to BDSM. Plus, she didn't know if all of it was about pain. She couldn't imagine Chloe beating Brendan.

Noah eased up on the brake, accelerated through a light, changing lanes with a hairsbreadth between him and the cars fore and aft in the heavy traffic. He did it so smoothly, she didn't feel nervous in the least. She wondered where he'd acquired his urban driving skills.

"Better not thank me yet," he said. "I haven't done tilework in a while. You may have to pay someone to fix what I screw up."

She sincerely doubted that, since Marguerite wouldn't have recommended him otherwise. "I'll report you to Lyda if you do a shoddy job. She seems like the type to demand perfection."

His eyes slid over her face before they returned to the road. "She has a way of demanding a lot from everyone around her. Things you don't think you have inside of you, but it makes you a better person to find out they're there, if that makes sense."

She thought about the way her day had gone since Lyda had crossed her path. How Gen had reached out and touched Noah in a way she'd never spontaneously touched a man. When he'd been washing cups and busing tables, she'd felt a thrill every time she thought about him coming home with her. But that had connected to Lyda as well. It was as if, by letting Noah stay with Gen, Lyda was sending her some kind of secret message. Gen couldn't deny it gave her a tiny yet equally strong thrill, like being passed a note at school by a secret crush.

I'm being an idiot. "Does she always come off so overwhelming?"

That grin reappeared. "Actually, that was Lyda way toned down. Her inside voice, if you will."

"Geez."

He laughed, a pleasant sound that caressed her senses. Then he gave her a thoughtful glance. "You know, if you want to ask things about being a Dom or sub, it's okay. I'm used to talking about it. If you don't want to talk about it, that's okay too. I just don't want you to feel like you can't ask. You seem like you maybe want to ask some things."

Great. She'd been able to rein herself back under the illusion of respecting his privacy, but he'd just removed that barrier.

"Oh, that's okay. I can always ask Marguerite and Chloe that kind of thing."

He changed lanes, a quick glance over his shoulder and at the mirrors. She liked watching him drive. His focus on the road let her study him at her leisure, those attractive details that a woman didn't get to study as closely when a man's attention was on her. The flex of his forearms as he adjusted his hold on the wheel, the shift of thigh when going from gas to brake. When she next sat in the driver's seat, her backside would be nestled where his nice tight one had been. Crazy, silly thoughts. That was why it was safer not to talk about these things. She was only foolish to herself, so the pleasure was undiluted.

"Chloe said you haven't ever asked anything. She figured that either meant you aren't comfortable with BDSM and prefer not to talk about it, or you have Family Syndrome." At her look of puzzlement, he elaborated. "You're like family, so you don't really want to know about each other's sex lives. The *Ewww* factor. Chloe's term and description."

"I guess it could be that," she hedged. "I don't know enough about BDSM to be intolerant of it, so I've never really had that issue. I knew Marguerite quite a while before I knew the other stuff about her, but she's the type of person, once you find out she's a Mistress, it's like…"

"So incredibly obvious it's a 'well, duh'." His eyes sparkled. "Another Chloe term."

"She has her own language." Fondness for the girl welled up in Gen. "And even if I did have a problem with BDSM, it wouldn't matter. M and Chloe could bury bodies in the garden, and all the good things I know about them would outweigh that. I'd just assume the *True Lies* Arnold line."

"'They were *all* bad'," Noah supplied, making her chuckle. "You're loyal. That's a nice quality. One of the best, no matter what people think."

An odd note entered his voice, defensive. She decided to leave that alone, since she was still teetering on the line of how intimate she wanted the conversation to go. But she supposed some basic, less personal information would be okay.

"It's not so much because of the family thing," she admitted. "Asking Marguerite personal questions is always…problematic, and if I asked Chloe the questions I want to ask, she'd start pushing me to put on a corset, come check out a club, see it all firsthand. I'm more cautious about things."

They were idling in another snarl of rush-hour traffic, backed up at a series of lights. He looked at her. "I'm sorry."

"For what?"

"For whatever happened to you that made you more cautious about things."

She stared at him. "I didn't say anything did."

He let a fingertip whisper over the outer corner of her right eye, following a track to the corner of her lips. "I saw a flash of it, in how you held your mouth, the way the lines along your eyes creased."

His tone was gentle, his eyes even more so, delving into her and cradling her heart. So much for less personal.

Fortunately, traffic started to move and he returned his attention to the road. The person who assumed not a whole lot was going on with this one because of his age or easygoing manner would be making a mistake. She reached out, touched his jaw.

"When you said that, I saw it here too. You get it because you understand it. Yet you're not cautious. You don't seem that way."

He shrugged. "I know what it's like for things not to turn out the way you want them to. We all do. We just handle it differently. That's a good thing, because if we were all dysfunctional in the same way, it would be a pretty boring party."

"I feel pretty boring, next to Chloe and Marguerite. But I've felt safe that way, because they love me."

She couldn't believe she'd said something that honest out loud. But he merely nodded. "Being accepted for who you are, there's nothing better. If you have that, everything else is possible." He hit the brake for a light and gave her a significant glance, one that wasn't easygoing at all. It swept her face, her throat, down over breasts to the nip of her waist, highlighted by his regard, even under the shapeless T-shirt. Then his gaze came back to her face, lingered there.

"I don't find you boring at all. And neither did my Mistress."

* * * * *

Wow. That was news. If he'd left it at his opinion only, she might have retreated behind false cynicism, assuming he was positioning himself for a booty call, holed up as he would be at her place. But a woman having a blatant sexual interest in her was a new idea. On top of that, it was the first time someone had suggested — as if it was the most natural thing in the world — that *two* people might be interested in her that way. Not competitively. She got the impression — and maybe she was crazy — that he was implying they both wanted her. At the same time.

She'd likely read way too much into those two sentences. As a result, she didn't say much the rest of the trip and Noah didn't push her for more, though he made affable comments about the traffic and their surroundings in a way that let her retreat back to her comfort zone, which worked for her.

She had a little patio home in a neighborhood of five hundred houses that looked just the same. Hers was on a cul-de-sac, backing up to woods, which she liked since the developer had stripped most of the forest to put up the cookie cutter houses faster. Her small fenced backyard was shaded by pines and palms, a few oaks.

In a three-bedroom, two-bath with small rooms, the two of them would be very aware of one another's presence, since her bedroom was across the hall from the guest one. She used the third bedroom as her craft room and kept a TV in there. There was a little one in the guest bedroom for the occasional overnight visitors, but her combination kitchen and living room had only a bookshelf and a French-door view of the comings and goings of the neighborhood for visual entertainment. Seeing it through the eyes of a relative stranger, a man, she worried he might be glad he'd only be here a weekend.

But it was her place, her sanctuary, bought under good financing terms with her own money. It wasn't a rusted trailer with garbage in the backyard and a scrawny mother cat having litter after litter of kittens under the stoop until disease took her. The kittens always disappeared eventually. As a child, she'd pretended they found good homes, rather than getting sick, hit by cars or eaten up by the nearby marsh alligators.

Her mother said getting the mama cat fixed was too much money and animals were meant to fend for themselves anyway. She'd felt much the same way about children. It gave Gen a quick flash of herself at seven, standing on a stepstool to fix oatmeal for herself at the old stove, reading the package to figure out how to do it.

"What a great place," Noah said. The sincerity caught her off guard, pulled her out of such memories. He'd brought in a duffle and placed it by the door so he could wander down the narrow hallway to look at the collages she'd placed on the walls. They were enhanced by the eggshell-colored paint, and she'd found good frames at yard sales. When she snapped on a light for him, the small track lights she'd placed over each picture provided enough illumination to navigate the hall, but turned the focus to the walls rather than the beige carpet she hadn't yet replaced with hardwood, as she intended to do one of these days. The kitchen was her first order of business.

"This is awesome," he said. The collage he was studying was a garden of flowers, created with different scraps of paper, some solid colors, some patterns. Tiny knots of newsprint made up the background, as if the flowers were peering up from the colorless dark earth. She wondered if the earth ever resented being the womb, never the creation. Probably not. Even if the earth nursed such a petty thought, a look at what it had created would dispel it. At least that was the way it should be.

"I made it after I bought the house." Her own personal celebration.

"You made this? All of these?" At her nod, he gripped her hand as if he'd made a delightful discovery. It made her blush.

Fortunately, he turned his attention back to the wall before she could embarrass herself further. The next one showed the silhouette of a sitting cat, the body formed by various images of a cat playing, sleeping. She'd interspersed those images with simple colors, making her into a calico.

"Do you have a cat?"

"Not yet. One day."

He glanced at her. "A life still evolving. I like that."

"You're a strange one," she responded, but she smiled. He made her smile. She liked that.

He picked up his duffle bag. "Where am I at?"

She pointed to the guest bedroom. "It's a full-size." She hoped his feet wouldn't hang off the end. "There's a small TV in there. I have basic cable."

He waved a hand. "Doesn't matter. Lyda doesn't let me do TV. It makes my head hurt. Do you want to get started on anything tonight on the kitchen floor, or should I just fix you dinner?"

She blinked at him. "I wasn't expecting you to—"

"I'm here for you, Gen," he said seriously. "Let me make you dinner."

While she was searching for something to say, he disappeared into the guestroom, returning without the bag. "No matter what, we need dinner first. Any particular requests?"

"I have some leftover lasagna. There's enough for two, and some salad." She hoped there was enough for two, but he was a man. They could always order a pizza.

"Sounds good. Why don't you do whatever your evening routine is, and I'll get dinner ready? If you do collaging after dinner, I can hang out with a book and watch, if you're okay with that. I'd love to see how you do this."

He took her silence for assent, pressing her arm before he headed up her hallway. As she stepped into the kitchen and living area, she saw him give the latter a quick glance, then he disappeared left.

Not sure how she was feeling about all of this, she went into her room to freshen up for dinner. She was used to men taking charge in the "I'm Tarzan, you Jane" way, not the "Okay, I'm going to take care of all your domestic needs, so you just relax, find your paper and put your feet up" kind of way. It didn't feel like a role reversal, like he was trying to be a woman. Nothing about Noah said woman to her. In fact, she was a little turned on by how he'd done it, not taking no for an answer, determined in an relaxed way that made it pretty much impossible not to follow his direction.

The weekend was going to be an experience.

* * * * *

She'd gone into her craft room and spent a little time setting up what she'd do after dinner. It was an exercise in self-restraint, since what she really wanted to do was hang over the kitchen counter and watch him doing whatever he was doing. Eventually that desire, and appetizing dinner smells, won out.

Working for the tea room had given Gen such an educated and sensitive nose, she noticed aromas far more acutely, and it was impossible to ignore the olfactory temptation of spiced tomato sauce and bubbling cheese. When she came to the kitchen, she found more than one temptation waiting there.

He'd set the table and was taking the lasagna out of the oven. The ribbed fabric of his dark tank showed his lean, muscled physique, as well as the bump of his nipples. When he bent to pull the lasagna out of the oven, she got a distracting view of his ass flexing under worn denim, his shoulders doing the same as he put the tray on the stove, turned it off, transferred the two pieces to plates.

"You could have used the microwave."

"Oven keeps it warm longer. Makes it bubble better."

Yes, it did. She preferred to do it that way herself. He'd put the salad in a bowl with tongs, arranged the dressing options next to that. He'd even toasted some of her sliced bread. The smell suggested he'd added a light layer of garlic and butter to them.

"I'll gain weight with you around."

He gave her an amused glance. "My Mistress makes me work out with her sometimes, though it pisses her off that I can bench press more than she can. Claims God is an insecure, sexist bastard. I tell her she's too competitive."

He pulled out a chair and gestured to Gen to take a seat in it. As she approached, she caught his scent, distinct from the dinner aromas. Some of the molasses-wood Ceylon tea fragrance had lingered, but it was mixed with that seawater smell and his own unique blend, something that made her want to inhale deeper, press her nose against that pocket between his collarbones, the base of his throat. Some of it might be Lyda, an intriguing mix. She remembered that combination of female sweat, soothing moisturizer, lip balm.

Maybe Noah wore one of those male body sprays that included pheromones. That was the excuse Gen gave herself when, instead of putting her hand on the chair, she put it on him.

It was just his side, beneath his arm, but when she felt the firm flesh beneath the thin tank, her fingers tightened on him. Her gaze fluttered up to his, and suddenly her throat was tight. What was she doing? This man…technically he belonged to another woman, right? Yet the signals they both sent…it was confusing.

A hell of a rationalization, wasn't it? All she had to do was open her mouth and ask the question, but asking the question meant she had a reason for asking it. Caution first. Always. She didn't want to ask anything. She wanted to touch. Just touch. That was okay, right? It wasn't like she was touching anything…wrong.

Okay, another rationalization.

One he allowed her, because as her hand tightened on him, he straightened, squaring his body more with hers. Studying her face, he reached down, retrieved her other hand, and placed it on his other side. She stared at her hands, resting on his upper abdomen. She spread out her fingers, her thumb following the line of the lowest bone on his rib cage, then up to the one above it. Cotton fabric, so soft and thin, molded his shape. She could gather it up in her fingers, touch bare flesh.

As if he could read everything in her face—or maybe he wanted to be touched—he put his hands between them, took the hem of the shirt up and over his head, getting rid of it. A simple movement, no excessive flare to startle her into thinking this was about to accelerate to an act she didn't want to commit. It just gave her more access to what she wanted to touch. Now she was staring at his chest. He was about half a head taller than her, but she kept her chin tilted down, still looking at her hands, resting on bare skin. He had no tattoos on his front, but she expected he had them somewhere. All men under the age of thirty seemed to these days.

He had a light mat of brown chest hair that tapered to a bold arrow between his defined abs, headed for his groin. She didn't let her eyes go that far. She couldn't believe she was doing this.

"Noah, I shouldn't... Lyda."

"I'm here for you, Gen. She gave me to you for the weekend."

Whoa. Stop. Back up.

She did so literally, stepping away from him, though her palms itched with irritation at her, wanting to be right back where they'd been. "What?"

"There's no obligation to it, Gen," he said carefully. "I'm here to be whatever you need. Tile your floors, paint your walls. But if you need me other ways...I'm willing to be that as well."

"She just...loans you out?" Gen's shock turned into something far different. "You don't even know me."

"No. It's not like that." His voice was instantly resolute, eyes reflecting the spark she'd seen when he and Lyda had their exchange about his stubbornness. It reassured her, somewhat. He paused, sighed. "I'm sorry, Gen. I'm used to being around Dommes. Mistresses. Those who understand the boundaries, the way this works. I should have brought it up earlier, maybe in the car when it was more neutral, but until you reached out to touch me like this, I wasn't sure if it was going to be an issue. But I could feel...something, when you looked at me. You intrigue me, as much as you do my Mistress. Like I said."

The sudden, very male look of awareness coursed through her blood, but Gen pushed it away, trying to get a handle on this. She wasn't sure why she was so agitated, but she was. "So you're her Welcome Wagon? Or her bait? Works out well for you, doesn't it? I mean, what guy turns down getting laid as often as possible?" She took another step back. The lasagna was likely getting cold. They should eat.

His flash of chagrin made her wince at herself. He'd been nothing but kind and respectful. But she had no frame of reference for this except a history of men who looked out for their own interests, especially when it came to sex.

"I'm sorry, Gen. I'll go. The last thing I want is to make you uncomfortable." He spread his hands, a conciliatory motion. She sensed no resentment or passive aggressiveness in his tone, nothing but a sincere apology. "If you want, I'll come back tomorrow and help you with your kitchen. I'll just stay somewhere else."

"You can just switch it on and off. Nice for you."

In response he stepped forward, snagged her wrist. She tried to back up a step, but he followed her. The stove was warm against the backs of her legs. She shook her head at him, but then he put her hand right below his belt. Beneath the jeans where she hadn't allowed herself to look, she felt a very substantial erection.

Her gaze shot up to his face. Immediately, he moved her hand to rest in a half curl on his bare chest, his own fingers loosely clasping hers before he let her go and stepped back to the other side of the table, as if he thought she might perceive what he'd just done as a threat, since he was a stranger in her home.

Yet she hadn't perceived it that way. Just a very confusing signal that fired up her already aroused libido.

"No. I can't switch it on and off," he said. "But I'm a submissive, Gen. It means that no matter how aroused I become, I act only on the commands of my Mistress. Or the woman she is allowing to command me. You can touch me however, whenever you wish. You can make me walk around your house naked the entire weekend. I might be literally dying to fuck you, but until you want that, demand that from me, I am only what you want me to be."

Whatever he saw in her face started him back around the table. She watched him come, emotions warring inside her. His voice had become huskier during the explanation, and now his breath was warm on her face, his mouth close to hers again. "The more you deny me, hold yourself back, the hotter I get, the harder I work to please you. I want to please you."

Like all women, she'd been the recipient of creative come-ons, where the male tried the "this is really all about you" kind of lines when they all knew it was about getting himself off. This wasn't that. This was beyond description, the way Noah's body canted toward her, yet she could feel the aura of self-restraint. Her will alone held him back.

"How many…" She had to lick dry lips to talk. Leaning away from her, he snagged one of the glasses of wine he'd poured and offered it to her. She took a sip, then a swallow. Three of them. When she set it aside, her hand went back to his chest, the other resting on his hip. Her fingers hooked on his jeans waistband. She told herself it was just a place to put her hands while he waited for what she'd say. "Is it just any woman she cares to share you with? How do your feelings figure into it?"

"Rather significantly." He seemed relieved she'd gone from attack mode to wary curiosity. "Mistress Lyda has never shared me outside of a club setting, Gen. Even inside it, it's directly under her supervision, and mostly foreplay type stuff." He met her gaze. "Sometimes I'll take a strap-on from one of them, but since I've belonged to her, she's never wanted me to actually fuck, I mean, have sex, with another woman."

She should have brought Chloe and Brendan home with her as well. She could have said the kitchen was a two-man job and Brendan would have been happy to pitch in. The three of them could have had a slumber party on her living room floor, with her as a safe fly on the wall, listening and learning. Rather than being right in the crosshairs of this discussion, expected to respond intelligently to things she knew nothing about.

"Sorry. I handled this badly." He was watching her face. "We can rewind all the way back to you coming into the kitchen and start over if you like."

She shook her head. His distress over upsetting her was enough to bring some balance back. That and his forthrightness about it. She had no doubt he was telling her the truth. In fact, she suspected when Marguerite had told her he would answer anything honestly, she'd meant he was incapable of lying. Pushing away an uneasy feeling about that, she got a grip on herself.

"Okay, so she's never given you to anyone else. Why me? Why this weekend?"

He gave her a searching look, as if ensuring she was okay with the conversation, not just placating him. "I'm okay," she told him. "I want to know. You just took me off guard. You didn't do anything wrong. But more wine might be good."

His eyes twinkled, and that made things feel better. When he pressed the glass into her hand, she dared herself to follow her feelings on that. She wrapped her fingers over his, holding them to the glass so he didn't draw away. She wanted to know what he would do.

A peculiar stillness took over his expression, a look that stole some of her breath, such that she had to find it again to sip the wine. He adjusted his movements to her, so she could raise the glass to her lips with her fingers still overlapping his. His gaze was on her face as she lowered her eyes to what she was doing, took a reassuring gulp. When she loosened her fingers, he took the glass away, set it aside. Reached out and brushed a drop of the wine from the corner of her mouth.

"You didn't answer my question," she said. "Why me?"

"Lyda asked me how I felt about you," he said. "I said I would be anything she agreed to let me be for you this weekend." He gave her an amused look. "It was the Goth discussion. It made me hot."

She snorted at that, then made herself push him away. His proximity made it hard to think. She *really* needed to think. "Can we just...ease back? Please? This isn't my world, and to say I'm over my head is an understatement."

"Sure. Why don't we eat?" He moved back to the chair, pulled it out for her. In answer, she pointed him to his chair.

"As much as I appreciate the gentleman routine, I'm safer getting my own self seated."

He grinned at that and complied, moving to his chair, though she noted he waited until she was seated to take his own chair. Her little dining set was a four-seater, small enough that his foot brushed hers before he adjusted his legs out of her way.

She was thinking of something else he'd revealed, close up to her like that. "Do you have a tongue piercing?"

"I do." Fortunately, he didn't open his mouth to waggle it at her, something she found quite non-appealing. When she remarked on that, he made a face of agreement. "Yeah. Women enjoy what I can do with it more than the looks of it. Not so different from another part of the male anatomy, right?"

His comical look toward his lap made her chuckle. "I think women tend to find it more exciting...aesthetically, when they're aroused," she agreed. "When they're not, it does look a little odd. But that's not casting stones. I'd say the same about female genitalia. Wouldn't you?"

"Absolutely not." He used the tongs to dish salad into a smaller bowl for her. "I could stare at close-ups of pussy all day long."

"Which explains a great deal about cinematography in the porn industry," she said dryly.

He winked. "True."

They worked on the salads. After finishing most of her wine, she felt ready to dip her toe back into more uncertain waters. It was helpful that Noah didn't push, staying with general discussion of her plans for the kitchen, questions about the neighborhood, her collages. She sat back.

"How did Lyda react to you saying you'd be anything I wanted?"

"She agreed." Noah rose to get the plates of lasagna, which he'd put back in the oven to stay warm. "You might think of me as bait, Gen, but I'm thinking Lyda was considering me a less intimidating tour guide. She suspected you'd like to learn more about us."

"You didn't call her Mistress that time."

"She's not completely hung up on that. She always says I'll know exactly when to call her Mistress. She's right about that."

The statement was fraught with images Gen could bring into focus far too easily. As Noah put the plates on the table, her gaze coursed up his body, back to the base of his throat, the part of his body that seemed to be her particular obsession. "You know, I really have no idea what to think. Whether to feel appalled, intrigued, nervous...or send you away."

"The most important thing to remember is you're in charge, Gen. You can do whatever makes you feel best."

"But I don't know how to do that, how to ignore your feelings."

"You're not." That emphatic note entered his voice again, commanding her attention. He met her gaze. "When you touched me at the chair, why did you do that? Only because you felt like it?"

"No. The way you looked at me, I thought..."

"I wanted you to touch me. I did. I do. You may not think of yourself as a Domme, Gen, but here's the thing about them. They only do what the submissive truly wants or needs, even though sometimes they have to help us understand what that is, because we bury it under a lot of other crap. My crap's been excavated for quite a while." His gaze flickered, making her wonder what that meant for him. "I'm not confused about how I feel, and I don't want you to think my reaction to you is some kind of generic program that happens for every woman who crosses my radar."

"I didn't mean to be cruel," she said hastily. "I—"

He shook his head, covered her hand. "I wasn't criticizing you. Just making it clear because, like you said, you don't know much about it. Sometimes even Doms and subs get it fucked up. So maybe we should talk about it some, answer those questions you've wanted to ask Chloe and Marguerite but haven't. Okay? Kind of like I'm a live search engine."

While she appreciated the encouragement and understood he was obviously at ease being grilled about it, they both already knew that wasn't the problem.

"Yes. But maybe later. I need to breathe. And eat."

He gave her hand a squeeze. "Fair enough. Will you tell me more about the craft room? It looks like a major studio in there, a little bit of everything. Do you do more than collages?"

"Yes. I do beading, scrapbooking…"

Chapter Three

ʚɷ

After the earlier intensity, dinner was surprisingly low key. He got her talking about her collage projects, how she started doing them, the local craft and bookclub groups she socialized with. She and a dozen other women rotated responsibility for hosting crafting parties the first Thursday of every month. Everyone brought a current project and they chatted, ate a potluck dinner. She tried to take one course from the community college every semester. She also volunteered for an animal shelter, walking the dogs and cleaning out the cat cages a couple Sundays each month. She told him about a lean, black-and-white, seven-year-old tomcat who had come in recently, with scarred face and a bad attitude.

"I'm thinking I may adopt him. He's starting to like me. But I wanted to get the kitchen done first. I figured he wouldn't appreciate all the noise and dust."

In turn, she found out Noah had an eclectic employment history. In New Orleans, he'd worked multiple jobs, sometimes holding as many as three at a time. Stocking at grocery stores, park cleanup, mowing right of ways, construction. But his last job had been as a waiter in an upscale New Orleans restaurant. The tips he'd earned there were substantial enough he'd dropped to one job. He'd done that for about a year before coming to Florida to be near his grandmother.

"Dot's still pretty spry and determined to live alone. She's far more likely to offer help to a neighbor than ask for it in return, but she has to use a motorized chair to get around. She and I have always been close, so now that I'm nearby, if she's not feeling well or needs something done at the house, she'll call me. I've built her ramps and helped fix things in the house so it's easier for her to navigate and get things done in the chair."

His fondness for her was obvious. On the flipside, when he asked Gen about her job at Tea Leaves, she could tell he registered how much she loved working with Marguerite and Chloe.

"It's funny about Chloe," he said. "We all know she's not a Domme, even Brendan, but she's adapted herself to him in so many right ways, even Lyda's come around about it. At first she was sure they were going to crash and burn."

"Has she seen the two of them together?" Gen was offended for her friend. "Who could possibly think that?"

"That's part of why she's come around," Noah explained. "Seeing them together more often. But Lyda's witnessed relationships where someone without a true Dom/sub orientation hooks up with someone who has a strong one, and Brendan is a down-to-the-bone sub. Those relationships have a hard go of it, long term. But the way he and Chloe feel about each other, it's obvious there's something there, above, beyond and below the Dom/sub thing. That gives it a far better chance of survival."

He smiled. "Beyond that, it's impossible not to love Chloe. Brendan would ride a bicycle to the moon for her."

Gen thought about how Chloe had thrown herself in Noah's lap, his easy affection with her. She wondered if Noah defined himself as a down-to-the-bone submissive.

At this point she'd moved into the living room and was curled up on the couch, watching him clean up the kitchen. He'd shooed her out, refused to let her help.

He'd left the shirt off. When he made motions to put it back on for dinner, she'd asked him not to do so. He hadn't said anything about that, but the flicker of his gaze as he complied had made her focus on her lasagna intently for the first few minutes of their dinner. Now she studied the smooth expanse of his back. As she expected, he did have tattoos. Between his shoulder blades was a blood-colored heart with a Celtic triquetra overlay done in black. Below it was the infinity sign, the sideways figure eight, intertwined with a rendering of handcuffs. Below that was script.

Yours, unconditionally.

When she'd indicated he was merely a tool for his Mistress, not genuinely interested in Gen for her own sake, his negative reaction had been emphatic. And yet it niggled at Gen, his level of compliance to...everything. *Yours, unconditionally.* For herself, it was a highly alien concept, agreeing to give oneself to a complete stranger, just because someone else ordered it.

"What if I wanted to tie you up and drown you in my bathtub?"

"You have a shower."

She made a face at him. "You know what I mean. Smartass."

He grinned, pulling ice cream from the freezer. "I draw the line at being murdered. Unless my Mistress convinced me I'd done something that really deserved that. I hope that won't be the case this weekend."

She couldn't tell when he was joking. Holding off on further questions for the moment, she indulged herself in a study of the taper of his waist, how his jeans rode his hips, the shift of his buttocks. He'd shed shoes and socks, so he was barefoot. He'd taken off the silver-and-black double-wrapped choker before dinner, though he still wore one of the bracelets.

He brought her a small dish of sherbet, decorated with a couple vanilla wafers. Taking a seat on the floor next to the couch, he braced his back against the foot of her easy chair and drew his knees up into a bent position, his body angled so he could see her. She was willing to make room for him next to her, but he indicated he was good where he was.

"Is sitting on the floor a sub thing? Or you just like the floor?"

He lifted a shoulder. "Habit is part of it. At home or in a club setting, my Mistress often requires me to kneel or sit on the floor, so my head isn't higher than hers."

"That seems really egotistical."

"Not in that context. She's honoring what I am by letting me act as her submissive in every way. When she makes me act like her equal, often she's punishing me."

She digested that. "You don't strike me as a cringing slave type."

"It's not like that, either." He gestured with the spoon. "It's hard to explain. You sort of have to feel it, or have a sense of it."

"So you could explain all night long and I wouldn't get it." That gave her in inexplicable sinking feeling, but Noah touched her foot.

"No, not necessarily. You don't have to be as deep in it as Brendan or Lyda to figure it out. All of us have Dom and sub tendencies. Think about your job. Who would you say is the alpha dog there?"

"Marguerite," she said without hesitation.

"Yeah, no brainer. Okay, how about between you and Chloe? When push comes to shove, who defers to who? And why?"

She was about to say neither, but then she gave it some thought. "I guess...me. I don't know if that's an age thing, since I'm older than she is, and I'm not saying she does everything I say—I'd fall over dead in shock if that happened—but..."

"But you have an intuitive sense of authority over her that you both accept." He shrugged. "We're animals, and we organize ourselves in a pack mentality, whether it's in a family setting, work setting, even in social groups."

She shifted. This was starting to feel like an academic discussion, where the verbiage might get above her head, but he defused her tension about that by bringing it back to specifics. "That's the day-to-day, vanilla side of it. High level and general. If you want to understand the way it happens specifically between people like Lyda and me, or Chloe and Brendan, you do kind of have to see it in action. But I'm not pushing you to go to a club or anything."

"It's like being in the ocean versus standing on shore, looking at it," she guessed.

"Exactly." He looked relieved that she understood, hadn't become defensive. "But there are different grades to us. Like Lyda. She's pretty much all Domme. Even when she's interacting in the vanilla world, you see it, feel it."

"I hadn't noticed," Gen said dryly.

He grinned. "Other Dommes are only that way at the club or in their own bedrooms. In the real world, they might hold what you'd consider more subservient roles. Secretaries, convenience store clerks, things like that. Being a Domme in the bedroom balances that with a power shift. You see that with men as well. It's why the stereotype exists about the CEOs wanting to be tied up and spanked. There's a lot of truth to the idea of powerful men wanting to be subs in the bedroom. Whereas the guy who picks up your trash might be a hell of a Dom.

"But you can't paint everyone with the same brush," he added. "Sometimes what you see on the outside reflects the inside as well. A powerful CEO might be a powerful Dom, and the garbage guy might like being tied up." His lips twisted wryly. "And I obviously fall in the latter category. I have been a garbage man once or twice."

"I bet that can get confusing. Or cause conflict. People like being able to classify things, keep them neat."

"Yeah. Sometimes people have trouble accepting something as truth, when it's different from what they expect...or want it to be." A shadow crossed his countenance.

"Like Lyda about Brendan and Chloe." Gen ventured the comment when he didn't say anything else. "You okay?"

"Yeah." He shrugged it off and addressed her comment instead. "Lyda can be pretty black and white on certain things. She knew Brendan was a hardcore sub, and couldn't see how Chloe, who's basically vanilla adventurous, could make that work. The answer was she couldn't. Not by herself, and not under the terms Lyda defines being a Domme. But Brendan and Chloe bring a lot of things to one another that enhance and define the Dom/sub side, and that makes it work. Sorry. I'm probably going too deep here."

"No. I'm following." This was really what she'd been seeking. An in-depth exploration without the self-consciousness of the spotlight. "It's like Chloe and me. She loves me and she's afraid my life is boring, humdrum. She thinks she needs to save me from it. Her life is so vibrant, it's hard for her to realize most of the time I'm happy with mine not being that way. My experiences...have made me value quietness."

She told herself to be honest, despite the worry she was coming off as colorless as her beige carpet. "I don't need to travel the world or jump out of a plane. To me, working in my craft room, listening to music and knowing, for the next few hours, nothing's going to disturb that, that's a gift."

He'd set aside his empty ice cream dish, had his fingers linked over his knees as he listened to her. "I need to take you sailing sometime. Have you ever been?"

"I went on a big boat one time. One of those tall sailing ships."

"Those are cool, but there's a quiet on a smaller craft I think you'd like. Will you go with me sometime?"

He'd understood, and made her viewpoint, who she was, feel right. "If you don't do something that makes Lyda murder you this weekend," she managed.

He chuckled at that, dipped his finger into her dish and stole some of her ice cream. "Lesser miracles."

"Hey." She fenced him away with her spoon, making that grin wreath his face once more as he licked his finger clean. When she was done with her dish, he took it and returned to the kitchen to finish cleanup. Since he'd encouraged her to do her usual things, she went to her craft room. Once there, though, she quickly realized she wanted to hang out with him. So she called out, encouraged him to join her after he finished, if he still wanted to see how she did the collages. To her great pleasure, he did.

She showed him how she collected paper and employed different mediums to give the collages textures. She particularly liked using colors and patterns to create smaller pictures and patterns inside larger ones, like the cat in the hallway.

"I went through a religious phase. One of my first collages was of Jesus' face. I had this great idea of putting together a bunch of faces. Young, old, different races, sexes, species, and that would become the shape of his head, the crown of thorns."

"So how did it turn out?" His brow arched, eyes fixed on her face.

"Close up, it was interesting enough. But unfortunately, two steps away it turned into a man with a lot of tumors on his face. Not the effect I was seeking." She laughed at herself. "I'm babbling, I'm sorry. I'm sure this isn't anywhere near as fascinating to you as it is to me."

"On the contrary. Your face lights up when you talk about the things that interest you. It's like watching a garden bloom in moonlight." He nodded to the corner, where she had a guitar propped. "You play."

When his gaze slid back to her, expecting her answer, she was still trying to untie her tongue. "What was your major at college?" she asked at last.

"Horticulture, poetry. Philosophy. Mechanical engineering for a semester or two." He gave her a wry look. "I only had the money for the first couple years, and then I shifted to auditing classes or paying for them one at a time. I like reading just about anything, learning anything new."

"Okay." That explained how he'd been able to deliver such a beautiful line as if it was commonplace talk. "As far as the guitar, no, I don't play. I bought that for five dollars at a yard sale and then took a couple lessons, but it didn't grab me. I should probably sell it, but I haven't given up on the idea of starting my own bluegrass band yet."

He chuckled. He was on the floor again, his back against her chair, shoulder blades comfortably pressed against her thigh and hip, the position he'd assumed when she started handing him different papers to examine. She'd also given him a pair of scissors to assemble his own ideas. It was an experience she'd never thought she'd share with a date. Though Noah wasn't really a date. Not one like she'd ever experienced.

Under normal circumstances, she would have been flustered, having a handsome man in her home whose intentions were so...undefined. Instead, he was proving to be a relaxing and attentive companion on every level, anticipating things that might make her uncomfortable or self-conscious and putting her at ease before they could take too firm a grip on her psyche.

Chloe had told her that Brendan opened himself up to a wider range of experiences because he didn't try to control the path chosen for him. *He doesn't think in terms of "I'm not interested in that", unless it's something he's already experienced and really disliked. He'll try anything once, as long as he knows it's something that interests me or the people we're with.*

Did Noah accommodate what she wanted for that reason? Though she'd remained on high alert for any flicker of boredom from him, she'd come up empty.

At length, it was getting close to her bedtime. Noah agreed they needed to be up early tomorrow to get a good start on the floor, if she was going to maximize the time she had his labor at her disposal.

"The good thing is we're already going to save some time," he told her. "The floor beneath the linoleum is in good shape. I can lay the plywood foundation right over it."

She'd noted him checking the kitchen floor earlier, and now she knew he'd been testing for rot. She made an agreeable noise as he rose to help her clean up. In the small space, they brushed against one another quite often, his bare skin and male scent so close.

When they were done, it seemed very natural for him to be gazing down at her. Before she could think of what to do, he'd slid his arms around her, drawing her against him for a light embrace. A hug. "Thanks for dinner and the place to sleep."

"I feel like I should be thanking you. You made dinner, and tomorrow you're helping me tile." She gave a nervous laugh as her palms slid over his shoulders, down his back. He was roped muscle, as firm and resilient as he looked, and his hug was a far stronger, more reassuring feeling than she'd expected, such that she held on for an extra moment or two. He didn't pull away, waiting until she did. Her thighs brushed against his. She felt like a teenager, her eyes lowering because she was embarrassed by her bright cheeks. His lips brushed her temple.

"Good night, Gen."

* * * * *

She closed her door to change into her nightgown, but once she turned off the light, she opened it again. She'd told him to do the same, since the small house circulated air better with the doors open. When she slid into bed, she was facing the hallway, and she saw he was lying in bed, under the sheet. He was reading a book about landscaping. It looked like an older book, the hardback cover worn, and she wondered if he'd borrowed it from Lyda.

She didn't really care what he was reading, all in all. It was nice just to lie in the anonymous dark, beyond the thrown light of his lamp, watching him. He'd taken the tie off his hair, so it spilled over his shoulders, enhancing the chiseled features. His attractive mouth had a firm set to it when at rest, his eyes focused. His long fingers stroked the pages as they turned them. Her gaze slid down the creases of the sheet, how it outlined his legs. His groin area was hidden behind the prop of the book on his upper thighs.

"Will the lamp bother you?" His voice was quiet, in case she was already asleep. She could pretend she was.

"No." She could hear the thickness in her voice. He was so close, right across the hall. It wasn't sex she wanted. God, no. Just the thought of him touching her like that made her quake. But he wasn't a stuffed animal. She wasn't going to humiliate him or herself by treating him like one. *Come curl around me, make me feel like that hug did.*

Plus that hug had produced far more than cuddly feelings. She'd wanted to keep sliding her hands down his back until she tucked her fingers beneath the waistband of his jeans. She wanted to touch without being touched. She wanted to have all the control, none of the obligations. She was sure that wasn't what being a Domme was, but the control issue was part of it, wasn't it?

He spoke again. "May I ask…what you're thinking?"

She could be completely honest, without repercussions. And she was here in the dark, where he couldn't see her face. "Earlier today…I thought about you reading to Lyda."

"One of those erotic novels she likes to torture me with?"

So maybe Lyda had actually done what she imagined, taunting him at a distance. Things curled low in her belly. "Yes."

He was staring into the darkness of her bedroom. Setting aside his book, he turned on his hip, propping his head on his hand. When he did, the sheet moved with him, getting trapped between his thighs, sliding down a little lower. She gulped as it became apparent he wasn't wearing anything beneath it, the upper curve of one buttock haloed by the lamp behind him. If she was standing behind him, she could let her fingers slide along that curve, up over his tattoos.

"I imagined you—" She stopped, cleared her throat. "I imagined her in a short negligee, nothing else. Lying on her bed, touching herself while you read to her. She had you sitting in a chair across the room. She wasn't letting you touch her."

"She'd tell me to keep my eyes on the page, and punish me once a day for every time I stole a glance at her. Which means I'd probably be punished for a month." His lips curved, but his eyes remained serious.

"How does she punish you?"

"Various ways. What were you going to say, at the first?" He prompted her. "'I imagined you…'"

She didn't say anything, and he shifted to his back. She bit her lip as he stretched out an arm, his upper body arching as he turned off the lamp, putting them both in darkness. She could see his silhouette from the street lamps outside his window. He turned back on his hip toward her. "What do you want, Gen? Anything."

His voice was encouraging, but also male and intent. Lust pulsed on the air currents between them.

"I want you to bring yourself to climax while I watch. I don't want you to look at me while you do it. Pretend I'm not here."

"All right. Do you want the light on?"

"Yes. The lamp's a three way. Could you turn it on to the dimmest setting?" Things needed to stay hazy, dreamlike. Else she might chicken out. "And...I want to see all of you."

She bit her lip, almost saying he didn't need to do that, but he was complying. He switched the light on the dim setting, then pushed the sheet to the side, adjusting his legs over it. Her gaze coursed over the arches of his feet, over light sprinkles of brown hair on calves and the long lengths of his thighs, then paused over his testicles and the cock rising above them, a thick stalk curving over sectioned stomach muscles. He had his thighs spread so she could see all of it. Propped up on the pillows, he rested one hand on his thigh, the other curled over his head.

Liquid heat pooled in the folds of flesh between her thighs. She wanted to tuck her fingers down there, give herself that pressure, but even though she was in darkness, she was too self-conscious for that. Right now.

"I've been with a Dominant for so long, off and on, I don't really do this by myself without permission anymore. But I think I remember how it's done." Another of his charming, self-deprecating looks. He grasped his cock, gave himself a firm stroke. Her breath caught in her throat, a contraction of hard need between her thighs.

"I wish I could see you," he said. "Are you...will you tell me if you're wet?" His voice was husky, telling her—as if his cock didn't—that he wasn't detached in the least.

"Yes. I am."

A muscle flexed in his jaw and he stroked himself some more. She wrapped her arms around her pillow, shifting so she was staring a straight line to him, her breasts full and aching against the pressure of the cushion.

"Tell me what you're imagining." She whispered it, but he heard her.

"You...naked. Sitting on my legs, just staring down at me doing this. You're breathing fast, shallow, so your breasts are quivering a little...bit." He gave a groan, tightening his hand on himself. "Your thighs are spread so I can see your pussy all wet, and I want to taste it. Want to just...fucking bury myself between your legs..."

She'd expected him to talk about Lyda. "Where is Lyda?"

"She's watching. She's always watching... And when I put my face between your legs, she's there, behind me...fuck..."

Would she be wearing one of those strap-ons that allowed a woman to fuck a man? Gen imagined Noah between her legs while Lyda thrust into him, her silver eyes holding Gen's gaze, making her feel as if Lyda was thrusting into her even as she had the dual pleasure of feeling Noah's tongue penetrating her own folds.

"Slow down," she said unsteadily. He did, easing back the speed at which they were approaching his climax. As he squeezed and stroked himself with careful movements, his body was taut, quivering.

"Why didn't you want to tell me about how she punished you?"

"Because I felt like you really wanted to talk about me doing this for you."

"Do you anticipate like that...a lot?"

"Yeah. Lyda says it's part of what gets me in trouble half the time. But only half." He grunted then. "I wish my hand was your cunt, Gen. I want to give you pleasure."

"You are. Shut up."

She slipped out of bed, padded across the hallway. When she emerged from the shadows, his dark, burning eyes were fixed on her, the sensuous mouth tight. She circled around the bed, her gaze sliding down his body. His cock had leaked semen onto his belly. She marked it in her mind as she reached for the lamp. He reached for her with the hand above his head, circling her wrist gently.

"Just one more moment, like that," he said. "You brushed your hair, and it's all curled around your face. And I can see your body through your nightgown."

It was a thin cotton one with a little embroidery at the V-neck. Not outrageously sexy, but pretty. She hadn't worn anything beneath it tonight, more of that same compulsion to be daring. As his gaze coursed down, the light was showing him the shape of hip and breast, the juncture between her legs.

"That's enough," she whispered, disengaging her hand. She turned off the light and caught her hair back, bending down to put her mouth on those few drops on his stomach. "Don't touch me," she added, another quiet instruction. A thrill of power went through her as he became incredibly still, his hand motionless on his cock. As she licked the drops off the muscled terrain, he quivered harder, but he obeyed her. She reveled in the freedom of it, of touching him how she wished without the worry of him trying to take the reins from her, moving too fast or in a direction she didn't want. He tasted slick and salty. Male.

The wrist of the hand holding her hair back brushed the head of his cock, an incidental contact, one she didn't expand further. She finished suckling those drops, then backed off, standing by the dresser. The street lights outside illuminated him enough she could see the pale line of his body. In contrast, she was mostly in shadow again. The fierce desire in his gaze speared her.

"I want to fuck you."

She shuddered at the animal demand. "No. Keep going."

He began to stroke himself, more functional and down to business, the way a man did it to bring himself to the desired goal, just as she'd requested. Though she was mostly in darkness, his gaze stayed on her, stripping her bare, making her quiver and arousal trickle down her leg. He'd said it had been a long time since he'd masturbated solely for his own pleasure. That made two of them. For a lonely woman, sometimes the empty aftermath was too painful to bear.

He was working himself harder, faster. Her gaze clung to the way he held himself, that loose curl, the push-pull of the velvet skin up and down the steel shaft, the thrust of his hips. His throat arched, the loose mane of dark hair spread over her guestroom pillow, where his scent would linger. His muscles were drawn tight, a powerful male animal bringing himself to climax.

"I don't…do this…without permission."

"You can this time. Please." Her voice was quiet, hoarse.

A quick jerk of his head, an acknowledgment, and then his balls drew up, his cock jumping in his hand as ropes of come started to spill forth, painting his abdomen, his chest. His face reflected that rictus that happened during such a moment, and she drank it all in, her palms damp, body locked by the dresser, every nerve ending aware of the touch of the air, his harsh grunts, his musky odor filling the room.

Finally, all that was left were her shallow breaths, his deep ones. As he settled down, she pushed herself into motion. Going into the hallway bathroom, she dampened a washcloth and brought it and a dry hand towel to the corner of the bed. She put them there, neatly folded, within his reach.

"Thank you," she said.

"Gen…" He was trying to see her in the dark. He started to lift his upper body. Fearing he was going to reach for her hand, she backed toward the door. She couldn't bear to be touched. Not right now.

"Thank you," she said again. "Good night."

She fled back to her room, closing the door behind her. If she left it open, he might come to her. He wouldn't initiate sex, not unless she'd given a clear invitation, but in this instance, him curling around her to give her comfort or just hold her would be even worse. Far, far worse.

She crawled back into her bed, holding the pillow hard to her chest with both arms, willing the throbbing between her legs to subside, hoping the ache in her throat and heart could do the same.

She *was* happy with her life. But deep in her heart, in the place she'd allowed Noah to be tonight, she had an unbearable longing to share it with someone.

* * * * *

Because it had taken her so long to fall asleep, it took longer to rise. What woke her was the smell of breakfast tea and frying eggs, potatoes and onions. He must have brought some coffee with him, because she smelled that as well.

Out of deference to vanity, she brushed her teeth and washed her face, pulled her hair back in a tail and added a touch of makeup before she came out of her room, even though she was wearing a pair of paint-stained jeans and a man's T-shirt in size small. Unlike what she'd worn at Tea Leaves yesterday, this shirt was a worn, thin cloth that clung, with a deep V-neck that showed off quite a bit of cleavage. She hadn't bought the shirt for those reasons, but because of its softness and usefulness for dirty house projects. However, when his gaze slid over her, she wasn't unhappy with her choice.

He'd made her a breakfast casserole topped with fresh tomatoes from her potted plant. A glance out the French doors showed he'd moved the tiles she'd stored in the back shed onto the patio and set up the Skil saw, along with grout and other tools.

"I'm late," she said.

Turning from the stove, he smiled and slid the casserole into a bowl he had waiting for it. "Breakfast is a better wakeup call than an alarm clock. I'm glad you grabbed some extra sleep."

She hadn't been sure what kind of awkwardness to expect, but obviously any felt was all on her side. He wore his jeans and a community college T-shirt with a sailboat printed on it.

"I get it now. You really have outgrown the Goth thing. You just wear the jewelry so the kids you teach think you're cool."

He snorted, poured them both a glass of juice and held out her chair. She slid into it, trying not to think about how that same maneuver had gone last night. Taking a seat across from her, he nudged salt and ketchup her way. "My students range from eighteen to fifty, so there's no way I can convince all of them I'm cool. I gave up. Hope you don't mind that I started setting up."

"Not at all. Did you sleep?"

"Quite well." His eyes caressed her in a way that made her flush. "Though I wish I could have given you the same experience."

"I slept well enough," she said quickly, making it clear she didn't want to talk about that. A puzzled look crossed his face, but he respected the boundary, backed off. The conversation stayed relaxed and general over breakfast, and then they got started.

She helped him lay the plywood and he put it down with the nail gun she'd borrowed from Tyler and Marguerite. However, the kitchen space was small. It became clear he made more progress without her being underfoot, so she soon shifted to being a gofer and keeping him company. Finding a radio station he liked, she sat on a stool in the living room, discussing music and watching him when he didn't have a task for her.

Once the tile placement started she was busy again. He initially proposed doing the tile cuts with the wet saw while she laid the tile, but he was the one with the tiling experience. When she showed him she was more than capable of making straight cuts with the saw, he pursed his lips in a gratifyingly impressed expression and agreed to let her do the cutting while he laid out the floor.

She thought she could watch him work all day long. As he'd hefted plywood, denim had creased and stretched in a pleasing way, the Florida heat outside quickly dampening his shirt with sweat. When he used the nail gun, she was entranced by the grip of his long brown fingers, the way his biceps rippled with each shot. She studied the intentness of his expression as he measured and judged the distance of the tiles.

They talked about this and that—the music on the radio, anecdotes about his students or her customers at the tea room. Depending on the topic, his lips would curve or eyes sharpen. As he worked on his knees, placing tiles, she thought of him stretched out in her guest bed, hand on his erection, his eyes seeking her in the shadows.

In the bright light of day she wasn't sure she should have done what she'd done last night. Nighttime was when everyone was more vulnerable to foolishness. But she recalled something Marguerite had told her, on a day Gen had snapped at Chloe for trying one too many times to set up a blind date for her.

You're comfortable being alone, Gen, but you're also lonely. Unlike many women, you don't let that lead you. You don't act only on emotional impulse. But don't forget you can also trust yourself to make choices to alleviate that loneliness, if and when you desire to do so.

She thought of what Noah had said last night, about how to understand a Dom/sub relationship. "Can you come to a club just to watch? To learn? Do they frown on that?"

"Not at The Zone. It's as much a nightclub as a BDSM club." He was squatting, putting spacers between the next group of tiles. Glancing up at her, he wiped his forehead with his wrist. His long hair, braided in a tail, had fallen forward over his right shoulder. "You'd be welcome to come with me and Lyda one night as a guest. No pressure. The Zone is one of the best clubs around, both for checking things out and playing."

Since Tyler was a part owner, she had no doubt of that. "We'll see." She nodded to the floor. "I feel like you're doing all the work. You really should let me pay you."

"You're doing plenty. Having to get up and cut tile and do other stuff is half the labor time. You handle that Skil saw like a pro. Most women wouldn't have both the muscle and the light touch to cut the tile without breaking it."

She shrugged, though the compliment pleased her. "My first husband and I renovated our house together. I learned from him. He was a contractor."

"I'm sorry it didn't work out." Noah's eyes met hers.

"A lot of people have the same story." She wanted to move off that topic, fast. "Have you been married?"

She told herself it wasn't a dumb question. She'd met plenty of twentysomethings who'd been married and divorced a couple times before hitting thirty. She'd been one of them.

He shook his head. "No. Only been collared once."

At her quizzical look, he elaborated. "To a lot of submissives, being collared is as serious as being married. The Master or Mistress is accepting permanent ownership."

Marguerite often wore a delicate choker, a double helix of pearls with an angel pendant. She'd given it to Tyler at their wedding. At the time, Gen had thought it odd, a bride presenting a necklace for herself to the groom. Yet when Tyler fastened it around Marguerite's neck, the surfeit of emotion in his expression, and the hushed demeanor of friends Gen now knew were also part of the BDSM world, had told her he'd considered it an immeasurable gift. The gift Marguerite must have been offering him was her willing submission, promised to him forever. A collar.

Finding out Marguerite was a Mistress hadn't been a huge shock. Finding she submitted to Tyler was initially harder to understand. Yet just like Chloe and Brendan, if a person spent any time around Marguerite and Tyler, it made sense. Marguerite could rule the world with a look, but it was Tyler's possession of her heart and soul that had brought the reserved woman true happiness, peace with her past demons.

Maybe that was the mature woman's true Cinderella story. Not that the prince came on his white horse and swooped her away from all her problems, but he got off the horse and stood by her, helped her deal with all of it through an entire lifetime. The thought gave her a wistful twinge. She turned her mind back to the safer, more hypothetical discussion of collars.

"You get a vote, don't you?" she asked. "I mean, a Mistress doesn't just slap it on you without your say-so? And you can take it off when you don't want that anymore, right?"

"Or the Dom takes it off when he doesn't want the sub anymore." The tightness in Noah's voice told her that had been his experience. *He?* Noah hadn't given her the vibe of being bi. Though obviously he was, if he'd been willing to be "married" to a man, according to the terms of the BDSM world.

"I'm sorry," she said.

He kept his gaze on the row of tiles he was placing. "It was probably a good thing. Least that's what Lyda says. And Tyler, and anyone who wants to give me an opinion on it." He threw her an attempt at a smile, but it didn't detract from the hardness in his eyes. She thought of that *Yours, unconditionally* on his back. Had that been something he'd done for his Master?

"If I'm asking inappropriate questions, please tell me," she said. "Your world is so different to me. I don't want to be rude."

"You're fine. Actually, I think our worlds are pretty close to the same when it comes to this. Whether they end it or you do, a broken heart's a broken heart, right?"

His bald statement made it hard for her to turn away from the subject this time. "Yeah. I asked for the divorce, both times. The first one, Guy, he was an alcoholic. His drinking got worse as our marriage progressed. I tried to work it out with him, but it was too one-sided. He hit me one night, broke my nose. That was the final straw, but it wasn't the worst thing. The worst thing was him choosing the bottle over me."

Over and over again, after the first year of their six-year marriage. She wondered if a woman's self-esteem every recovered from that, no matter how many times she told herself it wasn't her, it was an illness, all the stuff they said on TV and in the Al-Anon meetings.

Noah sat back on his heels. Rising, he came to her, ran his finger along the uneven line of her nose. His expression held her still as he leaned down, pressed his lips to it. Then he straightened and went back to the tile placement, leaving her with a curious ache in her chest.

"And your second husband?" he asked, eyes back on what he was doing.

She shook her head. She'd taken this as far as she wanted to go with it right now. "My past is the past. At least I only made the mistake twice."

"Sounds to me like they made the mistake." He'd marked another trio of tiles and now pushed them toward her. "Can you cut these? It turns me on, watching you use that saw. Plus I get to look down your shirt when you pick them up."

It pulled a chuckle from her, as she was sure he'd intended. "Perv," she said. But she bent extra low and shimmied her chest at him before picking up the tiles and sashaying out the door with a lot of hip swivel. His wolf whistle drove the other, darker thoughts away.

Once all the tiles were placed, he mixed the grout and slathered it into the cracks, scraping off the excess. After that, she treated him to a Subway run. They sat in the back yard at her picnic table, feasting on foot longs and chips. She broke the third of a three-for-a-dollar cookie deal with him. Very magnanimous of her, since the food would disappear in his lean frame and be absorbed by his male metabolism, while she'd have to increase her daily walks to keep the fat at bay. Yet he pushed his half of the cookie at her, teasing her into finishing it before they returned to the kitchen to wipe down tiles.

"Lyda is a workout fiend," he said as they moved around one another on hands and knees, polishing the tiles with shop rags. "She does one of those basic training type classes a few times a week. She's the instructor."

"Which explains why she has the killer body."

"Yeah. But the nice thing about women is there are all types of bodies." He gave her that once-over look he did so well. "You've got a lot of nice curves. But see, you just rolled your eyes, the way women do. You don't realize how nice it is, to have a soft ass pressed up against your dick while you sleep, sliding your hands around a great set of tits first thing in the morning…

He stopped at the look on her face. "Sorry. That was a little crude. Doing tilework reminds me of being back on the construction crew, which was all guys."

Actually, his blunt observation underscored his sincerity, which she appreciated. As a result, the rough language turned her on more than she wanted to admit.

He'd turned away from her, allowing her gaze to linger. Thank all the gods for Florida sunlight, he'd removed the T-shirt a couple hours ago. The way his jeans worked with his body while he was on all fours made her have a few crude thoughts herself. "You're not as housetrained as you first appear. It...intrigues me."

His head swung back toward her. The hair at his temples was slick with sweat. Not allowing herself to think too much, she gestured. "Come here."

She was sitting on her heels. He pivoted toward her, abandoning the cloth and putting his knuckles to the tile, staying on his knees. She watched his shoulders and hips roll with the movement. He stopped within inches of her face, the flicker in his eyes suggesting what "not housetrained" could mean. She backed up and rose onto her knees, bringing her head above his. Gripping the edge of her T-shirt, she lifted it to wipe his brow, giving him an up-close look at her breasts cradled in white lace. She'd worn a bra with more push and lift today, because being around him made her feel more sexual, more female. His breath on her cleavage was a slow, measured burn.

Whoa, girl. But she didn't want to *whoa*. Maybe it wasn't just at night that strong desires could rise to the top.

Scooting behind him, she nudged his calf. He looked back at her, his braided tail of sleek hair falling over his shoulder as he adjusted his stance so his knees were shoulder width apart. Moving between them, she removed her T-shirt entirely, sliding it down the damp valley of his spine, absorbing an appealing sheen of perspiration. There actually were good things about Florida humidity.

As she traced the individual bones beneath the thin layer of cloth, she leaned forward, which pressed her hips against his ass. His buttocks flexed beneath the pressure as he braced against her weight. She thought of what he'd said, about strap-ons. What would it feel like, to do that to a man? The firm shape of his testicles pressed against her thigh when she bent, put her lips between his shoulder blades.

"Gen."

"Shh." She brushed her cheek against damp male skin, squeezed her eyes shut. Then she drew back, rose to her feet. "So maybe I was wrong about the housetraining thing," she said. "You follow commands pretty well."

Her voice was thick, heart pumping hard. Was she taunting him? She wasn't sure. She retreated to the sink, her T-shirt in hand, pressed beneath her breasts. She stared out into the backyard, at her pretty groupings of potted plants, the privacy fence and small plot of grass.

"Would you like to see the less housetrained side of me, Gen? On your terms?"

She looked over her shoulder at him. He'd risen to his feet. A delicious shiver ran through her. His tone was rough, male, not boyish at all. She'd met men in their twenties who weren't much beyond high school when it came to maturity. Noah wasn't one of them. He was as versatile and timeless as a Fae sprite. Or an incubus. Maybe a vampire.

That fit. She imagined him as a vampire, forever young in appearance, yet looking at the world through the eyes of an old soul. Other times he had an emotional vulnerability that summoned her protective instincts. He was unpredictable, intriguing. And Lyda had given him to her for the weekend. He'd said so. Her first reaction to that had been disbelief, amusement, rejection. Then she'd moved so quickly toward the desire to touch, to experiment, it had frightened her into a quick retreat last night. But now the feeling was back, thicker, richer. She was far less willing to run away.

She looked at the wall clock. "Five minutes," she said. "For the next five minutes…show me." Five minutes had to be safe, right?

It was the last coherent thought she had. At least for the next five minutes.

He moved like sunlight, bringing heat to her flesh, his erection pressed against her backside. Banding his arm around her waist, he put his teeth to her throat and bit down, hard, giving life to her brief fantasy. When she gasped and arched, he used the movement to slip the button of her jeans and tunnel down. He captured her clit over the silk of her panties, providing a friction that had her writhing, all the desire she'd suppressed last night surging against his hand.

"Fuck, your clit's so swollen, so needy. You should have let me take care of that for you." He muttered it against her throat and bit her again, sucking hard, making her shudder at his obvious marking. He'd taste the salt of her perspiration from their exertions, the flavor of her skin beneath. The smooth metal of the tongue piercing slid along her carotid, the unexpected sensation intensifying everything else.

He brought his other hand over her shoulder, across her chest, clever fingers sliding into her left bra cup to cradle her flesh. He stroked the full curve all around the nipple, but not actually making contact until all the nerve endings in the peak were vibrating and begging for it. She'd never been handled with such care and skill. If either Guy or Amos had known how to do this, she might have considered her time with them far less of a waste.

But this was about more than skill. You had to care about someone, think they were the most special thing on earth, to touch them like this. As crazy as it was, with every caress he made her believe that.

As he stroked her through the panties, she was rotating her hips against him, her arousal increasing at a rate she couldn't contain. He growled in response. He knew just how to stroke her cunt, how to circle, pinch and tease at the right moments, in the right places. He was a quick learner, adapting and recognizing what would pleasure her the most.

"Noah..."

He slid his hand from her breast to her throat, holding her against his bare upper body, her pulse crashing against his palm as he stroked her there, put his mouth beneath his grip, teased and bit again, even as his other fingers pulled on her clit, plucking at it, tapping it, an excruciating technique that had her hips beating against the counter and thrusting back against his cock, trying to get more. She felt the rise of the climax, taking her toward a sweet freefall.

Their movements and the pressure of his forearm had brought her jeans halfway off her hips. In an impatient, uncoordinated move, she pushed them down, out of the way, and groaned as the hard bar beneath his jeans pressed intimately between her cheeks. She wanted his fingers inside her. She never wanted that. She wanted...

The orgasm hit her, unexpected, no time for her to grab anything in her mind to stop its hurtling force. She shrieked as he kept up that same crazy light patter rather than a strong milking stroke. Only when she thought she was on the downside of the climax did he adjust to a clamping, squeezing touch, catapulting her into the clouds once again. Latching onto his forearm where it was bent against her chest, his hand still holding her throat, she dug her nails into him, needing to draw blood, a desperate, needy creature, overwhelmed by what he'd done to her so effortlessly.

When she turned her head, he released her throat, pressed his mouth against her jaw. He held the intimate gesture as he kneaded her clit, bringing several screaming aftershocks rocketing through her body.

She was jerking against him, making little needy noises as he nuzzled her, soothed, brought her down slow. When she eventually released his arm, she dropped her head over the sink as she tried to regain her breath and balance. She was vaguely aware of his hands moving over her. He brought her jeans back up on her hips, zipped and fastened them. Passing his hand over the juncture between her thighs, he pressed down on the outside of the denim, sending a nice vibration of feeling through her, a pleasing finish most men wouldn't have thought to do. She leaned back against him as he adjusted her bra so the cup he'd disturbed cradled the occupant as intended.

He was still hard against her backside, and when she moved against him experimentally, he let out a short breath, a huff of a half-laugh. He didn't seem as though he planned to demand anything for himself. She should offer, shouldn't she? Yes, she felt like a dishrag, and other uncertain emotions were swirling in her, but fair was fair.

When she opened her mouth to try for reciprocal courtesy, he spoke first. "I owe you an apology. I exceeded your set time. Five and a half minutes."

"I'm still giving you a gold star on your report card." She gave a weak chuckle, then an edge of despair cut into her. "Oh God, Noah…"

"Sssh." He turned her so she could put her cheek against his chest, head tucked under his. "Don't. It's just a nice, sunny day, and we're tiling your kitchen. I know you're working through stuff. Just let it go for now and feel this moment."

Divine Solace

She let out a sigh, nodded. "Okay."

Chapter Four

◈

"So...how was your weekend? Did your floor get tiled, so to speak?"

Gen sent Chloe a look. "Have you worked on that one all weekend?"

"Oh, no. That's nowhere near my best stuff." Chloe nudged her. "Come on, I have to give you some crap, knowing you were spending the weekend with a hot guy. Seriously, how is the floor looking?"

"He did a great job." She was delighted with the updated look of the marbleized earth tones that had replaced the dingy white linoleum beneath. "He said he'll come back if I want and paint the walls. I think he figured out I hate painting."

"Yeah, Noah's crazy intuitive. I told him he should join the circus as one of those fortune tellers. The ones who don't really have any psychic ability, but are good at reading tells. Of course, that would be a waste of his best skills." Chloe bounced her eyebrows, pure lecherous insinuation.

"And what would you know about those?" Gen tried to keep her tone just as teasing. She was *not* going to get possessive about the guy who'd been loaned to her by a Mistress for a weekend.

She'd told him she'd drop him off at the marina Sunday morning. He had an adult class to teach that day, and Lyda would be picking him up from there. He'd agreed, but offered to drive. She'd taken him up on that, as it gave her the opportunity to stare at him and wonder if the last two days had been an odd dream.

Despite the temptation of that embrace in her kitchen, she hadn't orchestrated a repeat of Friday night with him. Instead she'd closed her door and taken a couple of sleep aids to be sure she didn't get restless in the middle of the night and do anything regrettable. Fortunately, Saturday's exertions—tilework and an orgasm way off the charts, unlike anything she'd experienced— had helped get her to sleep.

When he pulled into a parking space at the marina, she'd exited on her side, circling around the bumper, ready to take his place behind the wheel. She found herself self-conscious before the knot of students waiting for him close by. Tucking a lock of hair behind her ear, she wondered if this was the kind of farewell that involved kisses. Probably just a hug and buss on the cheek. That was okay. A hug would let her be close to his firm body once more.

He'd held open the door for her so she could slip in behind the wheel. When he closed it, he squatted and crossed his forearms on the open window. "Come to the club next weekend," he said. "Saturday night. Chloe and Marguerite won't be there, if you're worried about that. Lyda will put you down for a guest membership and I'll meet you at the door. You can just watch, and you can leave whenever you want."

"Will Lyda be there?"

"Yes. She wants to get to know you better as well. And you can see the wildlife in their natural environment." When she gave a half-laugh at that, he touched her arm. "Come be with us, Gen. I promise you won't be pressured in any way. We respect caution."

She looked down at the connection between their bodies. "If I decide to come, it would probably be at eight."

"Ok. Don't talk yourself out of it. I'll wait at the door from eight to nine, but even if you come later, all you have to do is ask for me up front and I'll come. We're usually there for a good four hours."

She studied the way his forearms overlapped. "You should head for your class. It starts in five minutes."

He touched her chin, but she wouldn't look up. She hadn't kissed him this weekend, she realized. Nor had he pushed that agenda. She found she wanted to taste his lips. But that was way too intimate. The things crowding into her head right now, into her heart, might explode wide open. "I need to go," she said.

His touch withdrew. "All right. I really had a good time this weekend. Thanks for having me."

"Anytime you want to spend a weekend slaving away over home improvement projects, feel free."

He didn't laugh at the weak joke, though he might have smiled. She didn't know, because she kept her head down. He gave her hair a quick stroke.

"Please come this weekend, Gen. I'd like to see you again."

She gave an ambiguous nod. One more light touch, and then he was gone. Lifting her head, she watched him stride away. Some of the students met up with him, started talking. Because of that, as he walked toward the docks, she was able to watch him undisturbed until he passed out of sight. As well as hold onto the sincere urgency in his voice and regret the trace of hurt there she knew she'd caused.

She was a bitch. But her trip down a path less travelled should probably end with this weekend. Her "safe" dose of Noah had been enough to fry her circuits. She should have asked him for a cell number, but she hadn't noticed him carrying a phone, an unusual thing for anyone these days. She could always call the nursery and leave a message that she wasn't coming. If that's what she decided to do.

She tuned back into the present at Tea Leaves. She was already missing him, which was a crazy schoolgirl feeling she hadn't had…well, since she was a schoolgirl.

Chloe had brought one of her fresh pound cakes this morning, as well as strawberry preserves made from the fruits of her garden. When she and Brendan married, they'd decided to give up Brendan's apartment and stay in the house Chloe was renting. They were now on a lease-to-own plan. In a rural area outside Tampa, the run-down cottage surrounded by a wild tangle of nature had always been a good fit for Chloe. Brendan meshed with it the way he meshed with Chloe herself.

That couldn't be as simple as it appeared. How had Chloe, not a Mistress per Noah's description, made it work with a male who was as devoted to the submissive role as Noah himself? She thought of how Noah had adapted to her this weekend. True, it was a limited interaction, and she certainly wasn't a Mistress of Lyda's caliber—she didn't think of herself as a Mistress at all. Yet taking the lead with him had felt so…refreshing. If that was how it worked with Chloe, was that enough for Brendan, or was there more to it?

It didn't really matter, did it? Why was she even thinking about it?

"Earth to Gen…"

Chloe was standing at her side. Her coworker was switching out the teas Gen had put in the brewer, because she'd been about to make the wrong flavor for the morning special. Though Chloe had her trying moments, far more often she picked up on Gen's moods perfectly, like now. Chloe squeezed her hand. "Want some pound cake for breakfast?"

"Love some." They still had about fifteen minutes before opening and everything was ready. Marguerite was in early today, but currently on the phone in her office. Chloe had already parked a piece of the cake at her elbow, along with a cup of Marguerite's preferred morning brew. Now Chloe snagged herself a fork and she and Gen shared a piece while leaning against either side of the counter, something they'd done often enough it was a foregone conclusion they'd split the calories.

It was a good reminder of why Gen felt so accepted here. She shouldn't be doing anything to rock that boat, but that missing-Noah feeling was putting pressure beneath her ribs, making her stomach all swirly.

She should have kissed him. He would have kissed her if she'd lifted her head. Since she'd denied herself that, she'd let herself indulge some idle curiosity along with the pound cake.

"So what do you think is his best skill? I'm just wanting to know some more about him," she qualified. "About...that side of him."

"At the club, we call him the Pussy Whisperer."

Gen choked, set down her fork. "What?"

"Thought that would get you to lighten up." Chloe pressed the tines of her fork against the top of Gen's hand, a gentle tease. "But it is true. Mind you, I haven't experienced it directly. Brendan would absolutely flip."

Chloe beamed at her absent husband's possessiveness. "At first, he tried to be the way he was with other Mistresses before me. Like whatever, whoever I wanted, it was all the same to him, but he left that bullshit behind pretty fast. Especially when I made it clear it hurt my feelings, him thinking it was okay for me to be with other guys. Even if it was a club sub in a structured session. Sometimes it's how things go both ways in a relationship that locks it in, makes it a stronger bond, if that makes sense."

It did, but Gen's focus was on one particular submissive. "Do a lot of them have that kind of arrangement? Multiple partners? Are Lyda and Noah that way?"

Noah had made it clear that Lyda's decision to share him with Gen, without Lyda present, wasn't their usual thing. So it wasn't really the same as a completely open relationship. Did they call it a relationship at all?

"Not really. Before Lyda took temporary ownership of him, Noah was picked up by different Mistresses for sessions. But it's been only him and her for a few months now."

"Hmm." Gen stole a quick look at Marguerite. Their boss was still on the phone. "So how did he get his nickname?"

"Can't say it, can you? Pussy. Puuusssy..." Chloe fenced forks with Gen and Gen stabbed the last bite of cake in retaliation. "Say it. Here, kitty, kitty..."

"Stop it. Tell me."

"If you say it."

"I won't." Gen studiously scraped together the crumbs on the plate, then sighed as Chloe wet her finger and pressed them against the pile of crumbs, popping the finger in her mouth.

"Oh, fine. Pussywhisperer." Gen said it fast, mashing the words together.

"Close enough. Noah has this weird inner focus thing. All the Mistresses—as well as the subs they've had him play with—say he touches a woman like he's listening to something inside of her, figuring out what works uniquely for her. It's not just about him getting to touch a woman's naughty bits, which is of course where most guys screw up. You know how they are."

"Like babies with new toys," Gen said dryly. "They gurgle, drool and grope, forgetting that what they're squeezing is actually attached to sensitive nerve endings."

"Exactly. Brendan says Noah recognizes a woman's body is an orchestra and when he touches her, he finds the perfect soundtrack for her."

It was an entirely accurate description. In those five moments at her sink, Noah had let her body lead him, her gyrations and tiny jerks guiding his fingers. No. Deeper than that. He'd understood her unique emotional grid and matched it to what she needed physically. And he'd used that to take her to that amazing orgasm. The man was scary good. Just thinking about it made her warmer.

Chloe was watching her face. "Okay, if I didn't have my own maestro to have and to hold forever, I'd be feeling pretty damn jealous. He really did tile your floor."

"No, not like that. He did some things."

"Noah is very good at doing things."

Gen found herself grinning at her coworker. She flicked Chloe's arm. "You twit." But she felt comfortable enough now to ask more questions. "What do you mean, temporary ownership?"

"There are times a Dom and sub might hook up exclusively for a while. It's similar to being in a vanilla relationship, seeing where it takes you, but they might put in place more structured stipulations that keep it from being as uncharted as a relationship. I don't know if Lyda and Noah have any of that, but I do know they've been together as an exclusive item for a few months. At first she'd play with him with other Mistresses, but over time, she's even eased back from that."

Which matched what Noah had told her. Not that she'd doubted his honesty, or was in deep enough with him to trigger her trust issues, but it was always good to hear a corroborated story.

"When Noah first came here from New Orleans, Tyler was watching over him. Not in a sex way, of course, but you could tell Noah reported to him."

Gen's brow furrowed. "Are subs controlled by a Dom at all times?"

"No." An uncomfortable look crossed Chloe's face, and she glanced toward Marguerite. Their boss was off the phone and working on her laptop. Marguerite wasn't a big talker, but when she wasn't on the phone, she didn't miss a word of their conversations, even if it appeared she was otherwise occupied. Sometimes she'd insert a comment while Gen and Chloe chatted. It was another familiar ritual.

"I'm wondering if she should talk to Lyda about him, M. I'm not sure what's okay to say or not."

Marguerite lifted her attention from her keyboard, her pale-blue eyes meeting Chloe's with her unblinking regard. Gen looked between them. "What am I missing?"

"It's hard to explain." Chloe collected residual strawberry preserves off the rim of the open jar with a spoon and tasted it. "Most submissives go to work, watch TV at night, whatever. They let the sub side come out in the club or maybe in other structured ways with their significant others, like me and Brendan, but they're still really sort of like everyone else. They run their own lives. Then there are those like Noah. He's...fully subservient. I don't know if that's the right term to use or not."

"It's accurate, to a point," Marguerite said. "Noah is very independent in some ways, Gen. I'm sure you've experienced his self-determined side."

Gen had a hard time not flushing at that. Marguerite didn't miss the reaction, but she didn't remark on it, thankfully. "In other ways," she continued, "Noah requires protection. He has no use for money. Everything that belongs to him is in that duffle he carries. I expect he has a couple sets of clothes so that, when and if a Domme releases him, he can take his leave with more than the clothes on his back. However, whatever his Domme chooses to purchase for him he views as her property. Much like himself. Even if she's buying those items with the money he turns over to her."

"Wait. You mean Lyda..."

"Whatever money he earns, he gives to her," Marguerite confirmed. "Noah makes very few demands, but he's adamant about that. He doesn't want anyone paying for his upkeep. When he doesn't have a Master or Mistress, I expect he uses his money for food or to give himself a place to stay. Someone's extra room, or a place that accepts cash. He thinks about what his Master or Mistress may need from him and acquires the appropriate skills, but when it comes to the structure most of us have—bank accounts, bills—he doesn't do those things."

"So he's like a homeless person, in a sense." Gen was seeing him in an uncomfortable new light.

Marguerite lifted a shoulder. "It's tempting to define someone on your own terms rather than understanding who and what they are. Noah's free will is a very elusive thing. It tends to be like a chameleon, adapting to whoever has possession of him."

She'd fought so hard for her independence, to own her own home, car—to regain control of her life. She couldn't understand someone who turned their back on such things. It sent up all sorts of red flags. But those protective instincts she'd felt around him were also back in an unexpectedly strong way. "Can't that be dangerous to him?"

Marguerite's blue gaze flickered, telling her she'd said something her boss had hoped she'd understand. Gen didn't claim to comprehend any of it, but Marguerite's approbation was always enough to steady her in any situation. "Yes, it can. Certain submissives are so immersed in their orientation that it defines everything about them. It makes them a prize to a certain kind of sexual Dominant. Unfortunately there are good and bad ones. Once Noah commits to a Dom, he is everything that Master or Mistress desires him to be, because that challenge fulfills his soul. Even that doesn't fully describe it, because there are many things about Noah that are unclassifiable. He is a special young man."

"M's hitting the nail on the head," Chloe agreed. "He's incredible, and yet a little scary as well. If he was part of one of those cultures with arranged marriages, he'd accept the choice given him without question, and serve his wife with utter devotion. Even if she was a hideous bitch."

"But how could that make him happy?"

"Happiness isn't the primary priority to this type of submissive, Gen," Marguerite said. "Or rather, their definition of happiness lies in their service. To a point. For Noah, that point is much further along the spectrum than most."

"So how would you know if you were special to him at all? If you could be a hideous bitch, and he'd be just the same way with you as he'd be with a generous lover…"

Marguerite nodded. "It's the dilemma any Mistress who lets herself care for him faces."

Did she mean Lyda? The way M held her gaze an extra moment made her think that was the case.

"Some subs get it mixed up in their head," Chloe added. "The ones whose craving for that fantasy, the idea that their wants and needs are secondary to the Domme's, is so strong. But the healthy reality is they have to work it out where it's more of a give and take. Even Brendan has some of that problem, and I had to learn to understand it the right way, not think he was being some kind of whore."

Gen winced, remembering her initial agitation, her accusation that Noah was being used as Lyda's bait. Seeing it, Chloe made an understanding face.

"Sometimes you have to have a come-to-Jesus moment to get it cleared up. We did, even before we were married. Remember what I said about the whole possessiveness thing, when Brendan was acting like it was okay for me to make the decision to pick another sub at the club?"

The sudden bemused look on Chloe's face, the light flush to her fair skin, told Gen a great deal about the graphic nature of the memory. "I forced the issue by doing exactly that, poking his inner Hulk," Chloe continued. "And yes, believe you me, he does have one. Once we reached the green skin stage, I made it clear I only wanted to be with him, and I damn well expected him to *want* that from me."

Gen closed her eyes, rubbing her forehead. "So sometimes you have to convince a certain type of sub that they have to get in touch with their own wants and needs, because that's what you want, as their Domme."

"Yeah. Gives you a headache, doesn't it? Like a snake biting its own tail." Chloe shrugged. "Don't get bogged down in it. What you were asking, about how do you know if he even likes you? That's something you can feel in your gut, no matter what signals he puts out or what he says. So much of this is about intuition, not words. Yet in some ways Dom/sub stuff is more straightforward than the vanilla relationships. A lot less games about what they're feeling, because it's about being honest or nothing. So think about it. Did you get the feeling he likes you?"

She thought of the moment at her car, the tone in his voice when he said, *Come this weekend*. She remembered the way he'd held her, soothed her. As if he understood what it was to be hurt so deeply, to feel so lonely and afraid of her own needs…

"It was just a weekend," she said. "He belongs to her."

Chloe exchanged a glance with Marguerite, then looked back at Gen. "You were kind of interested in her too, weren't you? Things aren't always about couples."

"I…" The automatic assertion she was straight came to her lips, but she was already figuring out things weren't that clear cut in the BDSM world. "I told Noah I might meet them at The Zone this weekend."

The unexpected admission jumped out of her mouth, but fortunately Chloe didn't explode with unfettered joy, something that would have sent Gen into full retreat. Instead the girl merely said, "If you do, be sure and try the bourbon brownies in their coffee bar. They're awesome."

Gen couldn't read M's expression. Giving Gen a brief nod, she went back to focusing on her computer.

"What should I wear?" She turned to a safer topic. Or so she thought.

"You definitely need the proper gear," Chloe said immediately. "We'll hit the Naughty Kitty on the main drag this week. Four inch stilettos are SOP, and as much leather as you can slap onto yourself and still show off your tits. A corset is perfect for that. Relax, I'm messing with you."

Gen closed her dropped jaw, shoved Chloe as her friend burst into laughter. "You should see how horrified you look. You can wear whatever you want. People wear everything from street clothes to full bondage gear. There are locker rooms so you can change inside the club too. For some people, that helps them shift mindset. But if you're going mainly to check things out, I'd say go with clubwear. Jeans and a sparkly sexy top. Stay away from weekend sweats and sneakers."

"So my Eeyore slippers and flannel pajamas would be too casual?" Gen eyed her.

"Big yes. It's not a midnight Walmart ice cream run."

The faint smile playing about Marguerite's lips, a response to their exchange, gave Gen the fortitude to clear her throat, draw those pale-blue eyes back to her. "I'm getting a warning vibe off you, M, but I can't figure it out. Would you tell me what it is, so I don't mess up?"

Marguerite could be cryptic, but she never dodged a straightforward question. She stopped typing. "If you're going to a new country," she said, "go with an open mind. Learn the culture and determine if you can appreciate it. Don't impose your own or be influenced in the wrong way by the experiences of your own life. You understand?"

"I do," Gen said slowly. "I just don't know how to keep my own baggage out of it."

Marguerite knew her history, as did Chloe. Gen had never dumped it on them, but both had ways of ferreting out information. Particularly Marguerite. Gen was pretty sure their boss knew things about her and Chloe they didn't know about themselves.

"There's a difference between withholding who you are, keeping it separate, and letting who you are integrate with their world, broadening both parties as a result. My point is, if you can't accept the basic foundation of what makes them who they are, then you have to accept you're taking a vacation there, not making a permanent move."

"Are you telling me that more in relation to Lyda or Noah?" With that question, Gen knew she'd essentially answered Chloe's. Both Mistress and sub interested her, even though she had no idea how to process the Lyda side of that equation.

"Either," Marguerite replied. "Also remember the difference between trying to change someone to your way of thinking and renovating a few rooms to make moving in together more comfortable. It's always a two-way street." Her gaze flickered. "In every good relationship, everyone evolves. Follow your intuition, Gen. It's far better than you realize."

* * * * *

Gen had grimaced at the thought of herself in ankle-breaking stilettos and sweat-trapping leather. Even so, when she flipped through her wardrobe, she'd been unsatisfied. She had a basic black cocktail dress and some cute things she'd worn for dates or quick crushes that hadn't turned into anything. Nothing felt right for this.

She told herself buying something super special would doom her expectations to disappointment because of the height to which a new outfit could propel them. Despite that, she'd stopped at her favorite outlet store Wednesday and visited the discount rack. She'd found a dress she liked, and the price had talked her into it.

Thursday night, she made a late night run to Walmart—sans Eeyore pajamas—and she had what she needed to touch up her color, giving her brown hair shiny highlights and making the roots vanish.

So here she was on Saturday night, going overboard for her unlikely adventure at a BDSM club. The dress was a pine-colored green like her eyes, with cap sleeves and vee neckline. The fabric of the dress was gathered in tiny folds at the waistline, an hourglass-shaping design that ran down to the mid-thigh hem, scalloping away to reveal her thighs. That same tight fold pattern was in back as well, flattering the shape of her ass.

Bringing out her airbrush kit, a keeper from her days as a beautician, she did a nighttime makeup application so her green eyes glowed from a frame of thick lashes, enhanced by the brown eye shadow she used. She brushed and curled her hair, clipping it high in back, and pulled some of those lighter-streaked pieces out from the brown, letting them curl around her face, soften it.

It had been a long time since she'd dressed up. Had the last time been Chloe's wedding? Even then, she hadn't really focused on being sexy. Tonight, she felt sexy, female. Young. She wasn't old, yet she'd gotten in the habit of feeling that way. She tried to remember the last time she'd let herself get infatuated with the possibilities of a date. She couldn't. As each candle had been snuffed out by incompatibility, her glow for it had dimmed further, until a hot bath, book and hanging out with crafting friends had sounded more appealing. Safer. What a depressing thought.

Despite her reservations about getting so dolled up, she couldn't deny it helped fuel her excitement about tonight. This wasn't about romance, not exactly, but it was sexual in an exciting way. Her escort was a male who definitely fascinated her. And then there was the woman who "temporarily" owned him. Thinking about a range of possible reactions from either one of them, Gen thought she was like a Coca-Cola, a tingly, fizzy feeling coursing through her blood. Executing a slow turn, she looked at herself from all angles in the floor-length mirror. She'd worn two-inch black pumps on her feet. No stockings. Her legs were good enough not to need them. She'd forgotten she had good legs. And *really* nice breasts.

Her ass could use work, but most women thought that. She blamed that on Chloe's baked goods, but thinking of what Noah had said about waking up against a soft ass drove any self-denigration away. All in all, she thought she looked pretty damn good. At least here in her bedroom, where she wouldn't suffer in comparison to anyone else.

This was foolish. Too much. She needed to change into jeans and a spangly top, just like Chloe had implied. But that would be wasted money on the dress, and Gen felt strongly about wasting money.

Noah would be there, and so would Lyda. As much as she told herself this wasn't a typical date, and definitely not a three-way date, her mind was churning over the possibilities. She was going to a BDSM club, where sex would be up front and foremost in everyone's mind.

"All right. Enough. This is what they're getting. Tonight will be whatever I want it to be. Nothing I don't want. I'm in control."

Flipping off the bathroom light, she went to hunt up her purse and keys before she lost her nerve.

* * * * *

She'd never been to The Zone. Typical of many adult clubs, it wasn't in the best area of town, but she saw Tyler's influence in the ownership. Security personnel patrolled the parking lot, and a complimentary shuttle circled through to offer rides to the door, a boon to women in icepick heels. She saw plenty of those, and the women wore clothes to match the shoes, which made her glad she'd worn what she'd worn. While she saw some casual street garb, the place had that festive, dress-up feeling classy clubs emanated after sunset.

She hadn't expected to see anyone wearing scanty bondage wear in the parking lot, but plenty of the members carried purses or totes large enough to contain a change of clothes, or other things her wild imagination couldn't help but entertain. Whips, chains…

Some only carried a small handbag, however, reassuring her that she wouldn't be the only one here just to watch. For them, the BDSM might be merely a titillating floor show. She expected that provided a good balance, since some of those who actively participated might like having an audience.

Did Noah like being on display while his Mistress was dominating him? Did Lyda get off on people watching her do that? When she imagined Lyda binding Noah and doing a wide variety of sexual things to him, Gen wasn't sure how she felt about it, mind-wise, but her body obviously had no problem with the idea.

The thump of music coming from within reminded her that there was a great dance floor and DJ, according to Chloe. Another clue that the activities inside weren't all about the D/s games. It made her feel a little better, a little less self-conscious. She shouldn't feel self-conscious, though. That was for people who cared what other people thought about them, and she was supposed to be way past that.

Yet this was what happened when a cautious person left her comfort zone and tried something so freaking brand new it might just change her entire life. A car horn beeped, startling her back to the here and now. She'd stopped just short of the curb, the car owner reminding her she was standing in the flow of incoming traffic. She gave a startled hop up onto the curb, touching her hair self-consciously and staring at the red carpet leading into the double doors. Silver lettering slashed across the smoky glass. The Zone.

She propelled herself into motion. The two security people at the entrance, one female and one male, opened the doors for her with polite efficiency and watchful eyes. The woman gave her a reassuring look, though, telling Gen she must look nervous.

Noah had said he'd be watching for her between eight and nine. It was a few minutes after nine, so she thought she'd have to page him. Instead, she saw him right away. There was a lounge just beyond the hostess' station, and he was in a small booth by himself. He rose the moment she crossed the threshold.

He'd waited for her. One part of her felt guilty for being late, but the look on his face when he saw her flattered her beyond description. There was no mistaking the expression of a man who felt every minute he'd waited had been worth it.

On her side of that equation, he made her pulse accelerate to the urgent beat of the dance floor music. He was wearing some type of slick leather pants. No shirt. The silver and black thin braided cord was double-wrapped around his throat, and the matching ones were back on his wrists. His long hair was in a sexy tousle, loose on his shoulders, his brown eyes fastened on hers like a sleepy wolf who'd just woken up.

She was a thirty-something woman who could handle all this in a mature manner. Yet when she clung to that gaze, she was reminded of a film she'd watched where a teenaged hero had touched the young heroine's jaw in a key moment. He'd stilled her fears by drawing her attention to his eyes, to the assurance there that all would be well. He'd done it with such surety, making it clear all his attention was on her care. Their youth hadn't really mattered. It was a simple heart-to-heart, soul-to-soul communication, recognized and desired by all ages.

She followed her more carnal desires now, letting her gaze course downward. The pants were low on his waist, below his hip bones. He had the lithe rock-star build to pull off such a look well. From the glances that followed him when he passed other tables, his ass must look irresistible in the tight pants. The front view was nothing to be sneezed at, his groin nicely substantial. Yet he seemed neither self-conscious nor like he was flaunting it. As he approached, his gaze was traveling over every inch of her. She wanted to touch him too, and so a breath caught in her throat as he kept coming, right into the grasp of her eager hands.

He curved a hand alongside her neck, under her hair, and lowered his mouth to hers. She leaned into him, letting his strength support her as his other arm circled her waist. Sliding her hands around him, she hooked her thumbs in the low ride of the pants. Then she couldn't help herself. She cupped his ass and found yes, the people who'd sent him covetous looks were absolutely right. His ass felt awesome. And of course there was nothing under that thin, slick covering but him. Her abdomen was pressed against the decidedly firm package of cock and testicles.

He hadn't kissed her this weekend, and she hadn't given him the opportunity when she dropped him off. She wasn't making that mistake twice. When she lifted on her toes, he took it as the invitation it was. His tongue teased her lips open and delved in to play, the pierced stud caressing her moist flesh as his fingers tightened in her hair. She wasn't thinking, wasn't planning, anticipating, worrying. She hadn't realized how getting dressed up in a sexy dress, being in an environment like this, would prep her for a state where inhibition was clearly less important than letting oneself *feel*.

"You look incredible," he said against her mouth. "Lyda's going to eat you in three bites."

Sensation shuddered through her, awaking nerve endings like the sweep of a gusty summer rain. His fingers trailed down her spine, back up, teasing her bra strap. She tried to breathe, to slow things down, but she didn't stop holding onto him. She was grabbing a guy's ass in the middle of a crowded place, and no one seemed to think it was unusual, but it was unusual for her. Trying to prove she could control her own impulses, she adjusted her grip to his waist, his lower back. He wrapped his arms lightly around her shoulders. His skin was slightly damp, as if he'd been dancing or exerting himself some other way.

"Want the tour?" he asked. "Or do you want to grab a quiet corner and make out until Lyda finds us?"

His eyes were intent, aroused, but playful. He always seemed to know how to help her handle her mixed feelings. "Yes, to both. But take me on the tour first."

"Your wish is my command." When he tucked her hand underneath his arm, she clasped his firm biceps. He leaned down to speak into her ear, so she could hear him over the crowd noise. "Lyda will join us in her own time. She's with some other Mistresses right now, probably swapping favorite CBT stories. Or talking about shoes. Girl stuff."

She glanced up at him. "What's CBT?"

"Cock-and-ball torture." He gave her an apologetic look. "Sorry, didn't mean to be that blatant right off the bat. Don't want to scare you."

"It would have scared me more if it applied to me. Just don't tell me if there's a version of that which does."

He grinned, leading her away from the foyer and pointing out the high points as he explained them. "The Zone has three levels now. On the top floor, there's a sound-buffered glass-bottom bar and restaurant where you can watch the dance floor or public play areas from above and have normal conversations without screaming. This middle level has a big dance floor with a perimeter mezzanine to hang out and talk, if you can manage it over the music, and another couple sections for public play. There are a few sitting areas like the lounge area where I was waiting for you, and some of them have noise buffers. The bottom floor has the private playrooms and changing areas."

As they moved through a wide walkway that split off toward different areas, she saw a carpeted stairwell leading to the lower level. Erotic art, chandeliers and elaborate moldings captured her gaze and added to the ambiance. "Watch the signs." He nodded toward one. "They tell you where drinking is allowed. See that archway over there? That's an extreme play zone, where they do anything from advanced suspension to heavy pain stuff. The security guy at that door administers a breathalyzer on whoever passes through, even if you're just going to watch. You score over the legal limit, you can't go in. There's a mezzanine viewing area." He glanced at her. "You want to go take a look from there? If you start with the scariest stuff, the rest will seem totally normal."

She gave a nervous laugh. "Okay. Why not?"

As the crowd heading onto the mezzanine area got thicker, he slipped his grip to her hand to move single file up the stairs and onto the walkway. Watching the club lights play over the tattoos on his back, she reached forward with her free hand and slid her fingers over them. He gave her another of those sleepy wolf looks over his shoulder.

He found them a small spot at the crowded railing, where she was secure between his body behind her and the rail in front, such that she could put her hand on either to steady herself. His breath was on her neck, voice against her ear to compete with the backbeat of the not-too-distant dance floor music. "If it gets to be too much," he said, "just let me know. We can go dance or look at some of the less hardcore play. Just remember, everything happening is consensual and okay. You'll see staff circling whose job is to step in if they think otherwise. They're really good at that."

When she was a teenager, she'd been the person who liked to jump in the deep end of the pool and work back to the shallow, as if she was challenging herself to face the most difficult part first. Tonight she felt like she was that more daring girl again, and Noah was helping her enjoy that long forgotten side of herself.

Then she looked down at the floor. She felt her eyes go wide, her hand dropping to curl around Noah's on her hip. A woman was suspended like a spider's prey in a web of ropes. She'd been bound like a ballerina leaping, one leg bent beneath her, the other stretched out behind her. Her arms were up to her sides like a bird, her back arched and held that way with an array of ropes fastened to a metal circle against the small of her back. The ropes looked like a sunburst, all the "beams" tied to her thighs, arms and torso in a way that kept her in that position.

As Gen looked closer, it was clear the Dom in charge of her suspension had tied her so her joints, while strained from the position, were bearing none of her weight. Even so, she was completely helpless.

He was a tall black man with dreadlocks, wearing jeans and black mesh tank. He was in the process of pinching her nipples repeatedly. In a smooth movement, he added clamps to them. The woman cried out at the stimulation, writhing as much as the bonds allowed, which wasn't much. He stroked her face, her mouth. Gen thought she heard him call her his beautiful bird. Then he started to attach glittering weights to the clamps.

The weights were metallic colors, so as she shuddered, the light sparkled off them. The white noise of the crowd swallowed some of her response, but Gen could still see her lips part with moans at the stimulation. He'd bound her breasts so they were constricted, her nipples enlarged. Her own tingled in sympathetic response.

Hearing a raucous shout, she turned her attention to another scene, a few feet away from the suspended woman. A man was bound on a large X-shaped upright frame, being struck by a woman with a long whip. Unlike the women coming in from the parking lot on their slender heels, she wore sturdy block-heeled boots. Gen surmised it was necessary to maintain the steady, squared stance as she threw the whip. She placed the popper precisely on his shoulders, his ass, and the inside of his wide-spread thighs. Her movement was like continuous ripples on water. His raw groans built with every strike, as if he was experiencing an overload of sensation. Gen saw red marks on his back, like straight pieces of straw.

"Did the whip do that?"

"No, she caned him first. Or it might have been a switch."

Noticing Noah's voice had a hoarse note as well, Gen glanced up at him. He was studying the scenario with an intent expression. His fingers were curled over hers, and the tight, coiled feeling she was experiencing in her stomach seemed to match the grip he had on her. Was he imagining himself where that man was, Lyda on the other end of the whip? What about herself? Which side fascinated her more?

When the Mistress rotated the cross to face another direction, Gen drew in a breath. The restrained man's cock was locked in a steel cagelike device that clamped at the base of that and his balls.

"Is that...CBT?"

"Yeah, one kind. If he starts to get erect, the chastity cage contains it, makes it painful enough that it subsides."

Did Chloe do things like this to Brendan? She had no idea how Marguerite's submission played out between her and Tyler.

Actually, she wasn't sure she was ready to see any of them doing these types of things. She was glad Noah had been sensitive enough to arrange for her to come here on a night they weren't present.

Her gaze shifted left, where a heavyset woman was bound naked over a bench. She had two tattoos, one on either shoulder. One said "Delia" and the other said "David". Perhaps her children, because Gen saw stretch marks. Looking around the play area, Gen realized then there were all ages and body types, and what was striking was the lack of self-consciousness by the submissives exposing themselves at their Master or Mistress's demand. Only their approval appeared necessary, and what she saw in the faces of those Dominants suggested the degree of submission was the attraction, not an arbitrary physical standard of beauty.

Another woman around the same age and body type began paddling the tattooed woman, landing blow after blow. After a time, she gripped the bound woman's hair, lifting her head to kiss her. The submissive kissed her back with yearning greediness, her hips jerking in aroused response on the bench. As her hips lifted, Gen saw she had a plug in her cunt, one with a jeweled base and prongs that spread out and clamped on the labia, pressing into the skin. Gen tightened her own thighs, her fingers tangled with Noah's. The hard spanking, the woman's grunts of pain, made her flinch, but that kiss did other things to her.

Needing a break, she lifted her gaze, deciding she'd watch the people on the facing mezzanine level, see how they were reacting to the performances. She found herself looking directly across the open area at Lyda.

Noah's Mistress was standing at the rail, close enough Gen saw the frosted gloss on her lips, the dusting of glitter across the top of her high bosom. She wore a silver gray corset and tight gray leggings tucked into black boots. A jet pendant nestled in her deep cleavage. She'd done something to her red-gold hair that turned it into crimson flame, the waving locks forming a lush swirl around her face.

The woman was overwhelming in jeans and T-shirt, wearing sweat and a bill cap. Seeing her like this set off electric impulses in every part of Gen's body and got her heart jumping like a frog on a hot plate.

When her silver gaze met Gen's, it held. With Noah holding her from behind, and Lyda's attention pinned upon her, Gen felt as surrounded as if Lyda was right up against her front. Noah's hands had shifted to her upper arms and Gen imagined he was holding her still for the Mistress's touch, her mouth...whatever she willed.

Yikes. This environment and these clothes could be more than a little dangerous. She reminded herself she'd never felt an attraction this overt to a woman, let alone to a man and woman at the same time. Hell, even though she'd nursed a curiosity about the world Marguerite and now Chloe inhabited, it hadn't motivated her to join the world of whips and chains. Not until she'd been exposed to it by these two people. They made her consider things she'd never considered before. The startling thing was realizing they hadn't planted the seeds. It was more like they were the sunlight and rain that had finally made them grow.

Noah had implied everyone had Dominant and submissive cravings to a certain extent. Though Gen wasn't sure everyone wanted to carry them out to the degree she saw in this club, she couldn't deny the things that surged up in her when she was around them felt...familiar.

Lyda tilted her head, and Noah lifted a hand in acknowledgment. "She wants us to meet her downstairs. It'll be quieter there and we can talk."

In her current state, Gen didn't think she was going to be capable of much coherent conversation, but she let him lead her back out of the crowd. As they followed the perimeter of the dance floor, which was quite impressive, Noah made her smile when he took advantage of an open space to propel her into a turn, waltzing her along the edge of the wooden floor with smooth grace. "It's all right," he said into her ear. "You're just here to watch. Remember? Nothing you don't want to do."

Her body language had communicated her tension. Lyda introduced a more demanding dynamic, and she'd reacted to it. Noah, bless his intuition, was reminding her it was no different with either of them. It was all her choice.

Their destination was a sitting area buffered from sound by glass walls, such that the groupings of chairs and couches encouraged intimate conversations. An efficient staff and well-stocked bar provided refreshments. Gen noted the furniture was a mix of antique and retro furniture, including the swan fainting couch on which Lyda waited. She was sitting with her back against the cushioned side, her hand resting on the carved swan's neck, which emphasized the grace of her arm stretched along the slope of the wood. One knee was bent to rest on the seat.

Up close, Lyda was even more captivating, her hair soft and touchable, eyes vivid. The wetness of her lips made Gen moisten her own. Lyda's attention slid over Gen, marking her appearance in much the same way Noah had. Only this time, there was an undeniable predatory intent in the scrutiny. It didn't make Lyda less tempting at all. More like the opposite.

She'd stopped a few feet from Lyda. Glancing between them, Noah released her to step aside, leaving the view clear for his Mistress. Gen flushed as Lyda continued to study her from head to toe. Would she realize Gen had bought pretty new underwear for this, fixed up her hair? Misted body spray on her throat and inner thighs, just in case?

When Lyda lifted a hand, Gen saw she'd polished her short nails tonight. One of those fingers made a rotating movement. She wanted Gen to turn, to see her from all angles. She did it, strangling back another nervy chuckle. She could have been a puppet, Lyda's finger executing an idle spin of the string. She felt the woman's eyes on her bare back, her legs exposed by the short hem of the dress. Her ankles trembled.

When she finished the full turn, Lyda crooked that finger at her. Aware of Noah's regard as she stepped past him, Gen wanted to reach out, graze his bare abdomen with her fingers, but she didn't. She closed the distance between her and Lyda until she was inches away from her bent knee.

She should say something. *Hi, how's it going? Great turnout tonight. Love your outfit.* She didn't.

Lyda rose. In her boot heels, Lyda had about an inch on Gen. That meant on bare soles, Gen was slightly taller, but she didn't presume that gave her an advantage. What emanated from Lyda had nothing to do with size. It was all about confidence, a blood-deep understanding of what she was, and the many faces that identity took as she executed the day-to-day of her world. Like this moment. She slid a hand under Gen's hair, much as Noah had done, but she gripped it tight, just as she'd done at Tea Leaves.

Gen wondered what would happen if her quivering knees buckled. Then she felt Noah shifting behind her and knew.

"Stay still," Lyda said, and moved close enough her lips were within touching distance of Gen's. Another inch and she'd be kissing her. A woman had never kissed her on the lips, not even the quick family brush thing. Gen couldn't hold her gaze. She had to look down, which meant she was looking at the way Lyda's corset displayed her breasts, the quiver of them as she breathed. The pendant looked like an oblong river stone, polished as if still wet from rushing water. What would Lyda do if she bent her head, brushed her lips over the top of one breast? It was so close, right there. She wanted to see what it felt like, a woman's breast against her mouth.

As if anticipating the move, Lyda's grip on her hair constricted, holding her still. Then she molded her other hand around Gen's right breast. It was a matter-of-fact, exploratory touch, as if she had every right to touch Gen so intimately. Lyda wrapped her fingers around the full curve, Gen's nipple stabbing into her palm through the satin of the bra. Lyda's thumb passed over it once, twice…three times. Slow, even strokes, as Gen's body hollowed, pressing into that touch, her breath uneven. Pleasure pumped through her as Noah's hands closed on her shoulders. His body was a column of support, a prop holding her in place for Lyda.

"You're beautiful, Gen," Lyda said, touching her chin to draw her gaze. "I'm glad you dressed up for us. And for yourself."

Marguerite had that kind of touch. Sparing, but something in it that made everything ache and need at once. Chloe called it the benevolent goddess touch, containing protection and kick-ass scariness together. Lyda's touch compelled that vital, indefinable want from Gen. As well as blatant, pulsing sexual desire.

Lyda nodded to Noah. "He sees the beauty, the sexiness you've let out of the box for the night. He senses this is exciting for you, different, and his energy will fuel yours. But a woman sees the deeper side. The fragility, the uncertainty beneath, especially when you've locked it down for so long. As you were getting ready tonight, it felt like the first time you ever dressed up, like for a high school dance. Right?"

"I'm not sure what you mean." Gen cleared a thick throat.

"Back then, you wondered if anyone would think you're pretty. It's even possible that giddiness in front of your mirror was swallowed as soon as you arrived at the school. But maybe it came back when your friends validated your appearance and boys were looking at you. You were still nervous, but you felt better. You were willing to explore the feeling. Time passes, and you lose that confidence. But you hoped for that feeling tonight, hoped enough to try. I'm very proud of you."

Gen had learned the dangers of seeking approval from the wrong places, had learned to stand on her own without any at all. Yet Lyda reached into her soul and plucked out feelings like flowers from a field. The bouquet she arranged confused Gen, but she couldn't deny Lyda's approval was like sunlight. It spread heat through her, while Noah's presence at her back was the vital force of a summer storm.

"You are very, very pretty, Gen." Lyda stroked her cheek, her lips. "And you're watching me like a forest animal. Wondering if I'll cause you harm."

"Will you?" Despite the desire of her lips to tremble under that touch, Gen firmed her chin, lifted it.

"If I do, it will be because you've begged me for the pain." Lyda's eyes glimmered like a frost queen's, hinting of magical, mysterious things.

Releasing Gen, she moved back to the fainting couch. "Come sit with me."

Chapter Five

ஐ

Noah nudged her forward. Gen began to sink down on the sofa facing Lyda, two women prepared to have a chat, but Lyda extended her hand, clasped it around Gen's. "Come here."

Gen was reminded of how one walked a tightrope, keeping eyes on the end goal, not on the feet. Lyda's grip told Gen what she wanted. What Gen herself wanted.

Lyda was against the arm rest of the couch again, and this time she had one leg up on the seat, knee bent and propped against the couch's back. Her other booted foot was braced on the floor. It made an open triangle between her legs, and that was where she brought Gen, pulling her down to sit face forward so her back rested against Lyda's bent knee and supple boot, her hip inches from the juncture between Lyda's thighs. Lifting her other leg onto the sofa, Lyda stretched it across Gen's lap. She kept her knee bent enough the weight of her leg wasn't resting on Gen's thighs.

Gen noted that the antique furniture had either been reupholstered or it was a modernized replica, because instead of the plush velvet or brocade expected on such a piece, it was covered in a nonporous but butter-soft vinyl, comfortable but resilient to puncture and easy to clean. It gave her vivid ideas of what happened on it to justify that practical design. Lyda shifted her grip to Gen's other hand, holding it loosely between them as she reached out with her free hand, played with a curl at Gen's temple.

"Beautiful color. Much better." Her fingertips slid along Gen's throat. "Fast pulse. Am I making you nervous, Gen?"

"I think that's your plan."

Lyda flashed a smile. "Does that upset you?"

Gen shook her head. She was out of her element, but she didn't want to move. She was hyperaware of Lyda's leg stretched over her thighs, her bent one against Gen's back. She wanted to touch Lyda and be touched by her, and the woman had delivered on that wish.

"Close your eyes."

"Why?"

"Do it and find out. Don't be a chicken."

Gen hedged. "Were you a cheerleader? A popular girl who got whatever you wanted?"

"No." Lyda traced Gen's cheek bone and the soft skin beneath her eye with a fingernail, her thumb following behind to caress the track of the sharp edge. "I was working two jobs to earn money for college. I did think once or twice about bringing a machine gun to the pep rallies, but the narrow-minded college I wanted to attend didn't consider shooting fish in a barrel a commendable school activity, even if it did show individual initiative. Do you think I expect you to obey me without earning your trust?"

"I don't know why you expect me to obey you at all. Do you act like that toward anyone who isn't...like you?"

"Who isn't a Domme, you mean?"

When Gen made a noise of agreement, Lyda stroked her temple, working her way down. Gen lifted her chin, an instinctive desire for Lyda's hand to follow the line of her jaw, down to her throat, tease her collarbone. Lyda did it, bringing the other hand up to cup Gen's face on the opposite side, holding her there as she stroked her windpipe, all the sensitive pulse points around it.

"I expect you to obey me because you want to do it," the woman said. "You want to see where I'm going to take you, Gen. You want someone you can trust to take you nice places. Close your eyes, and I'll do that."

It plucked a heartstring, disturbing layers of emotional sediment. Since Gen wanted to keep the focus on waking her body, not her past, she let her eyes fall shut. Her body was even more attuned to Lyda's touch without the distraction of sight. Gen wanted Lyda to keep touching her this way, all night. But she wanted to do the same, find out what it was like to touch this fascinating woman. Her hands had initially been on her lap, but part defense mechanism, part following her own wants, they'd drifted to the leg in her lap, one resting on Lyda's shin, the other on her thigh. Gen's fingers curled into the thin, stretched fabric of the tight leggings as she closed her eyes and Lyda made an approving murmur at her compliance.

"What did you want me to do when you saw me, Gen? What did you want to do? First thing that comes to mind."

"I wanted to kiss you. Be kissed by you."

"Two different things, aren't they? Which one did you want more?"

"Too hard to choose. Do I have to?"

Lyda chuckled, an erogenous sound. "Keep very, very still. Eyes stay closed. Face turned toward me. If you move, or open your eyes, I'll draw back."

She held her breath as Lyda shifted. The woman's palm slid across her abdomen, curving around her waist, just above her hip. She adjusted the leg behind Gen so it was bowed around her buttocks and hip, and moved the other one off her lap to the floor so Lyda's foot was braced between Gen's, her calf pressed against her shin. It left Gen's hands empty and on her lap again.

Gen held her breath as Lyda's mint-tinged breath teased her lips, her mouth brushing over hers. Her lips were already parted. She felt a touch of Lyda's tongue, tracing her lips, darting inside to caress Gen's tongue. That held breath caught in her throat. Lyda's fingers dug into her hip, and her other hand locked against Gen's jaw, holding her still as she played with her.

A tiny, needy noise came from Gen's lips, spoken into the other woman's mouth. Lyda answered with an incoherent reassurance, one that had a firm note to it, reinforcing the order to stay still. Then she eased back, though she stayed close enough her arm was still around Gen's waist, hand kneading her nape beneath her hair line.

"Let's talk about your weekend with Noah," Lyda said. "I understand you let him give you pleasure this weekend."

She couldn't claim that wasn't Lyda's business, right? In the context of this world, Noah was "hers". Gen nodded.

"Did you like having him come for you? You can open your eyes."

Gen felt Noah's attention in her peripheral vision, even though she couldn't pull away from Lyda's irresistible stare. "I liked everything about him. He's a pleasure to have around."

"He is, isn't he?" Lyda allowed her to look toward the subject of their conversation. Noah shifted into view from behind the couch, where he'd been standing in quiet attendance. He had that absorbed look men always seemed to have when two women were touching one another. Seeing him after having her eyes closed, all of her now quivering from Lyda's attention and kiss, was like the well-timed stroke of a vibrator against her pussy.

Gen bit back a murmur of want as her gaze slid over all the bare skin, the way he looked in the laced pants. She wanted to tug on those wrapped bracelets, let her hands glide up his forearms, spread her palms out over his chest, tangle her fingers in the choker at his throat.

Lyda twisted one of Gen's curls around her fingers and leaned forward. Gen saw the delicate flare of Lyda's nostrils as she inhaled, rubbed her lips over the thick lock.

"I wondered if he smells like you."

Lyda drew back enough to arch a brow. "Pardon?"

Gen swallowed. "Everyone carries a certain combination of scents, natural as well as soap or perfume, that kind of thing. I wondered if your scent is on him."

Lyda's eyes glowed like burnished metal, her glossy lips pursing. "I might just let you get close enough to both of us tonight to find out."

Gen couldn't help taking another look at the distracting size of Noah's genitals beneath the hold of the pants. It hadn't abated since he'd met her at the door.

"On your knees, Noah," Lyda purred. "Keep your eyes on the floor until I say otherwise. Put your hand inside those pants that have all the women creaming themselves and stroke yourself."

Gen's heart fluttered up, not just at the direct order, but at Noah's instant compliance. He dropped with lithe masculine grace. No hesitation. The pants had the provocative flexibility of a condom as he slid beneath the waistband, found himself. She could see the outline of his knuckles, the thickness of his cock as he gripped himself.

"Her pulse just rabbited." Lyda had her thumb alongside Gen's neck as she fondled her hair. "Her pussy's getting wet, the more she thinks about your cock ramming into her."

"No, I..." She didn't think of it that blatantly. Couldn't. Too fraught with potential disappointment. Lyda pushed her hair aside, put her mouth to Gen's ear. Gen let out an unsteady breath as Lyda nibbled and teased the shell, nipped the tender skin beneath.

"What are you thinking then, fierce rabbit?"

"I think about…touching myself while he does that. The other's…too much. Too soon."

"Like this weekend." Lyda lifted her head. Gen kept her eyes on Noah, not sure she could face Lyda's intense scrutiny, but Lyda delved into her guarded consciousness anyway. "Someone's made you gun shy. You have trouble getting out of the way of your own head, don't you?"

Gen guessed that was part of it. She wanted to look at Noah. Doing that, not thinking, was so much easier. He was stroking himself nice and slow, that gorgeous upper body rolling with the movement. Though it captivated anyone looking their way, he didn't seem aware of any other audience. When he dared to flick his gaze up, she saw a male desiring only to pleasure the two of them. The jolt that came from such concentrated attention beat the hell out of a hundred female self-empowerment books.

"You can tell he's stripped for a living once or twice, can't you? He's done a little of everything. But that's not where he belongs. Is it, Noah?"

The sharpness of Lyda's tone pulled Gen out of her head. This time as Noah's gaze rose, Gen saw more than just desire. When he shook his head, Lyda's muscles tensed against her.

"You'll answer me, Noah."

"I only want to pleasure you both, Mistress. Please." The rough plea was a clear request to stay away from whatever gate Lyda was crashing. Lyda considered, pressing her lips together.

"You get a pass for now. But we'll come back to it." Sliding her hand down the side of Gen's throat to her shoulder, Lyda hooked her bra strap beneath the dress's neckline. The pure sexual intent yanked Gen's attention away from the puzzle of that exchange. "Did you buy something nice to wear beneath this dress?"

"Yes." On a normal date, it would be an outrageous question. In this environment, such questions seemed normal. Though Gen wasn't sure what she would do if Lyda told her to strip, right here, right now.

"Turn around. Lean against me and stretch out. Noah is going to give you a foot massage."

"Oh...well, he doesn't need to do that."

"Don't deny him, or yourself, the pleasure."

Noah removed his hand from its distracting task and rose to help. Gen couldn't resist them both. He lifted her legs, helped Lyda turn her so her upper body was settled back against Lyda and she felt Lyda's breasts, molded and held up by the corset, press into her shoulder blades. Lyda's thighs spread to accommodate Gen's hips.

Her arm slid around Gen's waist, her jaw pressed against Gen's temple. Lyda feathered her fingers over Gen's cheek. It started out as gentle as before, but then the pressure on her jaw firmed, turning Gen's cheek toward Lyda's shoulder. This time when Lyda's lips touched Gen's neck pulse, she gave her the edge of her teeth.

Arousal surged within Gen, but panic as well, caused by her lack of control over her own responses. "This feels strange to me."

"This isn't being done for you, but for me, Gen." Lyda spoke against her flesh. "It pleases me to hold you like this, to explore your body while you're stretched out in front of me." She traced the neckline of Gen's dress and played in the valley between her breasts, causing ripples of sensation that ran across them and made Gen shift restlessly.

"When it's not about you, but what I want, what I demand, it becomes easier. Does it feel good, pleasing me?"

It did. But Gen wasn't sure what strings were attached to such a question, so she didn't know what to say.

"Simple truth, Gen. No analysis." Lyda held her chin, her mouth so close to Gen's she couldn't think beyond the thought of how Lyda had kissed her. "Does pleasing me feel good?"

"Yes."

A brush of Lyda's mouth rewarded her, but since the woman was holding her head, it was controlled, Lyda sipping from Gen's mouth while Gen became parched with the desire to return the favor.

In the meantime, Noah had been removing her shoes. He dropped to one knee, his strong hands caressing her arches. When he closed his palms over them and began to massage, it was instant Nirvana, a paradise mix of intimacy, comfort and sensual pleasure.

"Oh...wow."

"Exactly." Lyda said, her tone full of feline satisfaction. "Have you noticed Noah has a tongue stud?"

She began an idle tracing of Gen's sternum, making wider circles, finding the curves of her breasts beneath the neckline of the dress. When Noah kneaded her arches, a thrum of reaction ran up Gen's inner thighs from the dual sensation.

"I asked you a question, Gen."

"Yes. Yes, I noticed it."

"He's very skilled in its use. He said you didn't avail yourself of it very much this weekend. I like that you exercised restraint because you weren't sure of his relationship with me. I also think you held yourself back because things like this aren't casual for you. I particularly like that. Noah, come up here."

He knelt at Gen's side, put his arm on the other side of her hip, corralling her between him and Lyda. His hip pressed against Gen, and her gaze strayed down to his cock, causing a mouthwatering stretch against the pants. "You want to touch him somewhere, Gen? Touch him there, one fingertip only."

As tempting as his cock was, her attention had moved to the lacings on the sides of the pants. She could see his bare skin beneath them, all the way from waist to ankle. Thinking about the impressions that would be on his skin when he finally took off the pants, she caught a fingertip underneath the lacing on the nearer side, a tiny stroke of the visible inch of skin.

"A nice choice. You notice the little things. Make her smile, Noah. She's getting too worried about things."

Noah leaned forward, blew on Gen's lips, which did make her smile, but he wasn't done. As her lips parted, he pressed the advantage, bringing them together in a kiss, his tongue entering to tease hers. Then she jumped as a tickling vibration skated along her tongue, the inside of her lip.

He drew back as she caught herself in a startled chuckle, a near giggle and squirm. His devilish look made her laugh outright, her body moving against Lyda's hold. Lyda held her in her lap, her palm flat on her abdomen right below her breasts, her other hand playing in her hair. It was intoxicating to have her vision taken up by them both.

"Yes, it vibrates," Lyda said. "Which doesn't seem much different from what you can buy in a novelty shop, until you experience what he can do with it."

The part-threat, part-tease transformed Gen's amusement into anticipation. As Noah shifted back to the end of the couch, Lyda held her body more securely. "You relaxed a little more. Progress." Lyda spoke against her ear. "Do I make you feel safe, rabbit?"

Yes. And no. Again she recognized the echo of the feeling as something she often experienced in Marguerite's presence. With Lyda, the core of it included a craving to get even closer, physically, not just stand under the shade of that canopy. "I keep myself safe," Gen said.

"I'm getting that. But there's a difference between being safe in a panic room and feeling safe in the sunshine. We'll talk about that another time, though. Right now, I'm going to make you lose your mind."

"Ah…" Gen didn't have to come up with an answer for that. Noah was back to giving her a foot massage, but not with his hands. He'd started to tease her bare feet with his mouth, running that tongue stud up the arch. It wasn't vibrating, which was probably good, because she had very ticklish feet. Yet the feelings he was evoking weren't ticklish. The aroused strumming up her legs during his massage had been gentle waves. Now they sharpened into direct lines of sensation, shooting up her inner thighs, behind her knees. As he moved to her ankles, Gen let out an unsteady breath.

"That dress is short enough I bet Noah can see your panties. You're nice and wet aren't you? He'll smell it as he gets closer."

Gen had paid little attention to the surrounding people since Lyda had sat her down on the couch, but realizing where this was heading, she became aware of interested glances, and not just in the sitting area. Since she was in a position to look up, she saw what Noah had pointed out earlier. Both the second and third floor of The Zone allowed for mezzanine galleries to view what was happening below, even in a seemingly casual area like this. Noah and Lyda were striking enough to attract attention, even if they'd been doing this to a mannequin. She saw faces above, studying them.

"They don't matter. All that matters is how you feel, and what I want."

Lyda leaned forward, taking up more of Gen's vision. She also moved her fingertips beneath the vee of the dress to caress Gen's breast more intimately. "Spread your legs, Gen."

Lyda said it in a low voice, but it was her first direct order to Gen, no mistaking it for what it was. By obeying, Gen would be doing what felt right at the moment, but how did that commit her future actions? If she let go of the anchor of her own will, she could be swept away on the tide of Lyda's. She caught Lyda's leg in one hand, white knuckled.

"Ssshh...close your eyes. Just listen to my voice."

Gen shut her eyes. Was she really doing this, in the middle of a public room, voices all around her? Though the room was buffered, it wasn't completely soundproof. With her eyes closed, she heard other things, as if they were conspiring with Lyda to gain her compliance. Cries of pain from one direction, underscored by a rhythmic noise like the slap of a flogger, a counterbeat to the distant dance floor music. A shriek of ecstasy, as someone else reached climax.

When Gen inhaled, she was inundated with perfumes and colognes, everything from jasmine to lavender to sandalwood to the overwhelming smell of sexual desire, which overlaid everything else. What had Noah said? Everything here was consensual, what people wanted. Craved. Needed. One of those aroused scents was hers.

Noah had reached her knees, that clever mouth making wet patterns on her flesh, his teeth adding marks from short nips. When he curled his tongue around the crease of her knee, teasing the back, she shifted restlessly. She'd spread her legs a little at Lyda's command, but now Noah's strong hands gripped her thighs, spread her wider. Enough that one knee was bent and pushed against the back of the couch, the other positioned so her foot was flat on the floor. Lyda adjusted her so her back and hips accommodated the change. She wanted Gen to let go of the anchor, trusting Lyda to be the vessel.

Noah's upper body was stretched over the couch, one hand braced against her bent leg to hold it in place, the other curved over the upper thigh of her other leg to hold it down. Uncertainty returned at the restraint, but Lyda used the nylon content of the dress Gen wore to stretch the neckline of the dress open and down, revealing and framing the satin bra.

"Very pretty," she confirmed. "And thin, so I can see when your nipples are hard. You're already dressing for a Mistress's pleasure." She slid her hands inside the bra, her knuckles pushing back the cups to keep them out of the way. The open air touched Gen's taut nipples. Now anyone could see. But when Noah lifted his lashes to give them a lingering stare, she couldn't look beyond his expression or Lyda's reaction.

"You have gorgeous breasts," Lyda said. Noah made a noise of fervent agreement. He dipped his head, returning to licking, kissing, nuzzling her inner thighs. Occasionally she felt a tiny thrum as he let the tongue stud vibrate, then he cut it back again, its stimulation unpredictable. His hands had slid up her thighs, pushed back the skirt, his thumbs so close to her pussy they pressed against the elastic of the panties.

"Noah is going to go down on you." Lyda leaned forward further, her beautiful hair curtaining Gen's face. Reaching up, Gen threaded her fingers through it, pleased with the thick softness. Lyda studied Gen's fingers on her hair. The look on her face was pleasure, laced with a reserve that told Gen she'd considered ordering her to put her hands down. But Gen wasn't here as a sub or a Domme. Certain liberties would be allowed. At least right now.

"Noah is going to eat your pussy, drive you to insanity," Lyda continued in that melted-sugar voice. "But he's not going to let you come. Not until you beg me to take you home with me tonight."

That was blackmail. Extortion. Something nefarious. Before she could argue, though, Noah's tongue slid over the crotch of Gen's panties, teasing her pussy through the silk fabric.

"He's a master at this. He compares it to martial arts positions, giving names to different strokes, positions, rhythms. Hummingbird, Flowing Water... He'll tell you all that nonsense sometime when his mouth isn't otherwise occupied."

Noah had a finger occupied as well, because he'd caught the edge of the panties, eased them aside, so that metal stud was sliding up her bare labia. It made her thigh muscles strain. Lyda's thumbs and forefingers captured Gen's nipples. It started as a light hold, but then became an increasingly firmer pinch. As the discomfort increased, the coil low in her belly got tighter, and she found she didn't want Lyda to ease off, as if the pain was feeding into the pleasure, making it bittersweet. Gen arched into her touch.

"That's it. Thrust those lovely tits up at me." Lyda tugged harder on her nipples, as if she was pulling Gen up by that hold. Gen gasped, her head pressing against the firm pillow of Lyda's breasts, Lyda's shoulder. Which also pushed her pussy against Noah's face, increasing the sensation there. Noah shifted his position. It was as if he was teasing her with light fingers, only this was his tongue against flesh, wet heat.

She moaned. "That first sweet taste," he murmured. He slid his hands under her buttocks, digging into the satin of the panties as he pressed his thumbs on either side of the labia, a compression she felt in her clit. When he spoke again, she strained to hear him, even as everything he did made it more difficult to focus her senses.

"This is called…bee on a flower. Following the stem, every petal, to the center, where your honey is sweetest…" The tongue stud pressed one single point, and sensation exploded in her core, bucking her up against him in an unexpected flow of motion he nevertheless anticipated, his sure hands holding her. The stud began making a light buzz, and that sensation skyrocketed. A desperate sound broke from her lips. Now she found just how strong Noah was, because his hands held her fast, didn't let her move more than an inch as he played with her.

"Hold there. Ssshh. Just ride it." Lyda's hair brushed her face again, and Gen's wild gaze flicked up to her. Lyda looked as caught up in Gen's pleasure as she herself was, in a different way. Gen panted, attention latched onto Lyda's mouth, the moist lips, the gloss there.

"Do you need a kiss, Gen?"

Gen nodded and then her body twisted hard as Noah's tongue slid right up beneath the clit. He swirled a tight circle there, then pushed deep into her cunt. The rate of vibration had become more intense. She felt it everywhere, through all the delicate tissues and veins, those layers of flesh like the juicy inside of a ripe fruit when like this. That was probably what he called this maneuver…ripe fruit…

"Ask me nicely." Lyda's intent face was over her, eyes demanding.

"Please..." She couldn't call her Mistress. Could she? She wasn't sure. Fortunately the please was enough.

Lyda bent, and Gen kept her eyes open, wanting to see this time. Lyda's lips pressed against hers, an exploratory caress, soft but not too soft. A woman's kiss wasn't as girly as Gen had expected. Maybe because Lyda didn't kiss the way Gen did, a yielding of her lips to the pressure of the lover's. Lyda held her mouth firm, so it was Gen's mouth that became more pliant, gave way, trembled, as Lyda's tongue slid along her lips, entered her mouth, and then her lips sealed over Gen's, making the kiss strong and sure, sweeping her away. Seeking an anchor, Gen tangled her fingers in Lyda's silky red locks. Lyda's hand locked over her wrist, holding her there.

It was an amazing mix, Lyda's female beauty so close, her hair brushing Gen's cheeks and temples, her lips on her own, while Noah's five o'clock shadow rasped against Gen's inner thighs. Male and female, integrated. Noah wasn't the type of male Gen knew, the kind she treated with wariness. Even so, she didn't think Noah alone could have coaxed her into this position, for the simple reason that Gen's vulnerabilities had been past prey for male attentions, not female. Noah was under Lyda's command. Somewhat. Was that why it was easier for her to let go like this?

Any intelligent thoughts were driven away as Noah shifted once more, flattening his upper body on the loveseat. His chin scraped her perineum as he flicked and worried her clit, making her hips gyrate like a carnival ride, her hand clamped on Lyda's thigh. Lyda curved her fingers into the spaces between, unlatching Gen from her leg to form a hard knot. She did it with the other hand as well. But as Noah continued his torturous magic, Lyda shifted her grip to Gen's wrists. She drew her arms back past Lyda's hips until her knuckles were pressed against the couch arm, as if Gen's hands were being restrained behind Lyda's back. Lyda's upper body pressed more firmly into her shoulder blades, arching Gen further.

She was soaked, Noah likely getting a wealth of the honey he'd described on his tongue and lips as he drove her higher. How wet was Lyda? What would happen if Gen turned over, pressed Lyda back on the sofa, buried her face in Lyda's pussy the way Noah was buried in hers?

"Ahhh..." Gen let out another cry as Noah did a new amazing thing between her legs. Lyda remained bent attentively over Gen's face. Her lips were moist from kissing Gen.

She was so close...or not. Her body thrashed on the couch as Noah teased her. Her hips lifted again, pussy wet and begging. The arch of her body displayed her naked breasts, the stiff tips, for Lyda, Noah, anyone watching. It didn't matter. Seeing Lyda study them with proprietary detachment was a hungry thrill she couldn't explain.

I'll keep you safe...

Everything Noah was doing to her, Lyda saw as something she had the right to command, Gen's body her possession. Gen could see it in her intent look, feel it in Lyda's touch. Maybe it was just a feeling-of-the-moment, but it had an overwhelming effect on Gen's senses.

The climax coiled like an unhappy, frantic snake, thwarted in its strike. She tried to follow Noah's mouth, to force the issue. He held her down, teasing her labia with dragging strokes of his tongue, creating patterns with the tongue stud, here, there. When he lifted her up enough to trace a firm line up her perineum, such that she felt the vibration of the tongue stud in her rim, a scream tore from her throat.

"Please..."

"Please, what, Gen? Beg me for what I want, or you won't come."

"Please..." She tossed her head back and forth. Noah's fingers bit into her thighs, his hair brushing them as he nipped them then went back to her pussy, tonguing her deep once more, a thrusting penetration, a swirling lick inside. He made a slow excavation, sliding up toward her clit, under the hood, putting pressure there. Oh God, she was going to die from all the sensation. That tongue stud vibrated, lashed over her clit, making her crazy. Spots came into her vision, but he had the skill to hold everything else out of reach. Until Lyda got what she wanted.

What Gen wanted.

"Please...I want to come home with you. You and Noah. Please."

"That's your pussy talking. You just want to come."

Noah did something then that took her so close to orgasm tears threatened. Her throat worked, fingers clawing at the side of the couch. Christ, the woman was strong. Gen was straining against her grip on her wrists with all her might, not to get away, but just in reaction to what Noah was doing, and making no headway at all. Her agitated gaze rolled over Lyda's smooth biceps. They were firm, unyielding, like the woman herself. Gen wanted to put her mouth on them, on Lyda's neck, on the rise of those beautiful breasts above the corset. She was so beautiful. To feel like this all night, to be beyond thought, lost in whatever Lyda demanded, in Noah's touch...

"No...please. I want to be with you...both."

"What will you call me when you're in my home?" Lyda's grip constricted enough to leave bruises. Gen felt a thrill shoot through her with the pain. When her lips parted in aroused response, Lyda's eyes flashed triumph. "Tell me, right now."

"Mistress. Oh God. *Please.*"

It came out a wail. Lyda gave the barest of nods, and Noah changed rhythms once more. Not a frantic devouring that matched the chaos of Gen's mind. Instead, he began a slow stroke around her clit, a circling motion combined with the press of his tongue, the sucking of his lips she could hear. It only took three such rotations and she was like a stone fired out over Niagara Falls. Experiencing a crazy, stomach-rolling rush, tumbling over and over, buffeted by sheets of water, blinded by the glittering diamond flow, the mist and foam.

He maintained that deliberate rhythm as her climax pulsed through her tissues, as her pussy gushed its release. He made a surprised, pleased noise, suckling the flood of juices. She was making a thin sound, strangled from a deep part of her that wanted release on so much more than a physical level. Something just out of reach, but oh so close. So much closer than she'd been in a really long time. It was terrifying.

When she was gasping, limp in their hold, she trembled under Noah's kisses along her thighs, the brush of Lyda's knuckles along her damp face, against her breasts as she readjusted Gen's bra, the neckline of the dress. Gen kept her eyes shut, face pressed against Lyda's upper arm. Not thinking was a conscious choice, because to think would be to evaluate what she'd done and reach a serious *WTF*.

But it was inevitable. The bitch of such an incredible experience was how it resurrected lost dreams and hopes, unleashed a soul-deep yearning. She was clinging to the bittersweet moment as long as she could, a slippery rock face in whitewater.

"She's going to crash," Lyda said. "It's where she is right now, who she is. Bring her, Noah. We'll see what we can do about that. We're going home."

It was too soon. She couldn't get up. Her legs were noodles. But Noah lifted her, taking her out of Lyda's arms. Lyda stayed close, giving Gen's hair another stroke. "Take her to my car. I'll follow in a few moments."

No one had ever carried her as an adult. Noah brushed a kiss over her temple. "Sshh," he murmured. "I've got you, baby. It's all right."

No one except her first husband had called her baby, and that had only been when they were dating and he wanted to have sex. The first time she'd heard him say it, her heart made a tiny leap, like now. She hadn't realized then the implied promises behind the endearment—care and protection—were empty.

Her head felt like a bowling ball, so she kept it on Noah's shoulder. "I'm older than you, you know. Calling me baby seems...weird."

"Does it really seem weird, or is the weirdness because it doesn't?"

Yes. Because it felt exactly like what she wanted him to call her at this moment. It stroked her nerves, calmed her. And that agitated her. She couldn't explain that, even to herself, so she said nothing.

He took her through the club, back to the crowded main foyer. She kept her eyes closed, even when the hostess stopped them. "Oh, it's you, Noah. That's fine. Go ahead. Have a good night."

In the relative quiet of the parking lot, she wondered if she was getting heavy to him. Yes, he was strong, but he was lean. She didn't consider herself overweight, but she wasn't skinny. He didn't seem to be tiring, though. He hadn't even adjusted his grip. He still held her in a secure cradle.

"Why did they stop you?" Her speech was sluggish.

"Security stops anyone not leaving under their own steam. They don't take chances on someone using a date rape drug or letting subspace disorientation cause a nonconsensual situation. But the owners here know I'd never endanger anyone else, no matter what a Master or Mistress ordered me to do."

When he let her feet down, she was standing by a black Escalade with all the trappings. Apparently, Lyda working those two jobs in high school had paid off. The nursery must be a successful venture, and she obviously hadn't made poor choices in men, like Gen had. Her corset was probably custom made, not underwear bought off the discount rack.

She realized abruptly she'd put her car key in her bra, and it wasn't there. "My key…"

"Lyda has it. She put it into her bag so you wouldn't lose it."

It also made a cowardly escape impossible. Not that she would do that. Maybe. "What about yourself?"

"Hmm?" He had his arm around her waist, so she could lean against him, get her bearings. He was nuzzling her temple, long fingers stroking her hip. He was an irresistible blend of nurturer and utter temptation.

"You said you wouldn't put anyone *else* in danger. It was a weird way to word it. What if they put *you* in danger? You said no murder, unless you deserved it, but there are a lot of awful things that don't result in death."

"She doesn't miss much, does she? Even when she's a little fuzzy." Lyda strode toward them. She was wearing an embroidered silk tunic over her corset, belted with a silver and black sash. A tote bag was slung over one shoulder. The Escalade chirped as she unlocked it and opened the passenger door. "Put her in the front seat with me."

Noah slid Gen onto the seat and leaned in to pull the belt across her. Gen laid her hand on his back, tracing the *Yours Unconditionally* tattoo, sliding up over the Celtic heart as he shifted to buckle the belt. Catching her hand, he kissed her knuckles before laying the hand in her lap.

"I could have done my own seat belt," she informed him. "It was more fun to let you do it."

Amusement captured his expression at her slurred tone. "I bet you're a sexy, adorable drunk," he said.

"Not drunk. Just lost. Confused." She wanted to ask him if she should be doing this, and that disturbed her. She could ask herself. If she'd made a wrong choice, she could back away from it. Even now, her mind wasn't that scrambled, even if her physical coordination was.

What had Lyda said? *She's going to crash.* Was that what this sudden despairing feeling was?

"Hey." Lyda slid in front of Noah, framing Gen's face in her hands. Noah was right behind her, his hand resting on Gen's leg. "You're not going to be alone tonight, Gen. You're with us. Okay?"

"Okay."

Lyda slipped out from between them and Noah closed the door. Lyda tossed him the key to Gen's car and a T-shirt from the bag slung on her shoulder. As he caught them, she pointed to Gen's car, parked further down the same row. "Follow us home."

* * * * *

Lyda had the radio on a satellite station that played oldies. The late hour and her post-climactic lassitude should have made Gen as mellow as the music. But those weird feelings kept cycling in her mind. Past baggage, disappointments and worries, twining with current concerns. What would she be doing with Noah and Lyda the rest of the night? What would Lyda demand of her? Gen had called her Mistress. Only once, but had that set up certain expectations? Things she should rectify?

"I'm not sure if I want to do anything else tonight. Maybe we should pull over and I can head for home. I had a really good time, though..." God, she sounded stupid. "I'm not sure if what I did was just the situation, hormones, whatever. You and Noah...you two could convince Mother Teresa to go home with you. I don't want to be a disappointment."

"Or get too deep. Take too many risks?"

Lyda's tone was even, neutral, making it impossible for Gen to bristle. Much. "I'm not good at this kind of stuff."

"One-night stands? Relationships? Sex?" Lyda glanced at her. The sudden trace of warmth in her eyes made her seem more approachable.

"Yes," Gen said bluntly. "I suck at it. All of it. You seem like a decent person, and I have no idea of your expectations in this situation. I don't want to be rude to a friend of Marguerite's."

Lyda's visage sharpened. "Did you do what you did tonight because you think you owe sexual favors to Marguerite's friends?"

"No." Gen blanched. "God, no. I didn't mean it like that."

"So why did you bring Marguerite's name into it at all?" Lyda gave her a shrewd look. "Do you feel an obligation to her?"

"I...she's been very good to me. She's a friend. Family, really. I love her. I just...I don't know. You have a connection to her, and I didn't want to screw with that. Screw it up. That's all. Give me a break. You fried my brain."

It was a relief to see amusement return to Lyda's face, but she didn't say anything for the next few intersections. She was an aggressive driver, one who drove with the speed of traffic rather than the speed limit, and maneuvered through congestion like a Tijuana taxi driver. It didn't unsettle Gen, though, because Lyda projected the same poise she seemed to bring to every situation.

In the heat of a sexual moment, it was clear how liberating that confidence could be to whoever was under Lyda's command. Outside that moment, it left Gen feeling uncertain, on quicksand. Not worthy. She didn't care for the feeling, especially since she knew it was self imposed. She straightened in the seat. When she did, Lyda was slowing down for a traffic light. After a glance at Gen, she slid a finger beneath the neckline of Gen's dress, straightening the curled fabric. Her knuckle brushed Gen's breast, leaving a tingling wake as she withdrew.

"You're not going to screw anything up, Gen. I have no expectations of you except what you've promised. To come spend the night in my home. I'll let you know what I want when we're there, but the choices you make are yours, and none are wrong."

"I need to get up early. Go home and do some things."

"I had some things left over today from the nursery I need to do tomorrow as well. Of course, if I don't lock him up, Noah will probably handle them by dawn."

"I noticed he's a night owl." Despite him saying he'd slept well at her house, Gen had woken a couple times that night and the subsequent one to find Noah reading by a book light. Yet he'd been up well before her both days.

"He doesn't sleep well at night, unless he's completely wrung out." Lyda shifted lanes. "What did you think about being in charge of him for the weekend?"

"I didn't really think of it that way. He was a guest."

"I mean when you told him to come for you. You gave me somewhat of an answer in the club, but I want to hear more."

"Oh." Gen focused on passing Tampa traffic. At just after ten o'clock, the town was still wide awake. She took a steadying breath. "I liked how he was willing to let me take the lead on certain things, but that's not really the same thing as what you do. The way he took care of things, took care of me...that's more about what he is than me acting like a Domme, right?"

"Much of it is instinct, and you seem to have good instincts." Lyda glanced at her. "Fierce rabbit. Soft fur. Haven't seen much of your teeth and claws yet, but they're there, once you're less worried about being careful."

"I've been less careful. It doesn't work out." Gen brushed her hair back, glancing down to confirm that seam was still straight. She could still feel the lingering effect of Lyda's touch. She wanted to stroke her fingers over it, reignite those nerve endings. She should be done with sex for the night, but her simmering body told her otherwise.

"Depends on whether you're with people you can trust." Lyda looked in the rearview mirror. "Noah pulled off. He must be picking up drive-through. He didn't eat dinner yet."

Gen thought it more likely Noah had found her ancient compact car wasn't capable of keeping up with Lyda. "So, what will we be doing for the rest of the night?" she asked. Trying to sound casual.

Lyda turned off the main road. "I'm not going to tell you. That's part of the anticipation. As I said, the choices will be yours, Gen, but I view you as mine for the night. I'll treat you accordingly. The things I'll do with you are more light handed than what I do with Noah, but what's light handed for him will push your limits to the max."

That pretty much tangled up Gen's brain and took care of any attempts at idle chitchat for a few minutes. They turned off on a road with a big sign for Growing Things Nursery. Apparently Lyda lived on the same property as her business. "Are you ever light handed with Noah?"

"Never. It doesn't work for him, because that's not what he needs. If and when I get more demanding with you, it will be different, because your needs are different."

Lyda pulled up to the house, which looked like a 1920s clapboard farmhouse. Moonlight glinted off several large greenhouses beyond it. A line of solar lights etched out the front walkway. Removing the key from the ignition, Lyda put her wrist on the wheel. She slid a finger along Gen's knee, playing under the hem of the dress. "You're a very sexy woman, Gen. The more you believe that, the more people will feel it when you're around them. They'll see it in the way you walk and dress, the way you present yourself to the world. You're a woman who, if you were truly owned and cherished, would set the world on its ear."

Gen had never thought of herself as any of that. Up until that last part, she would have said that Lyda was describing herself. But Lyda would never be owned.

"If you were treating me...heavy handed, what would you do? Unless it's revealing your diabolical master plan. Or mistress."

Lyda's lips curved. "Don't taunt me, rabbit. It's not a place you're ready to go." Her gaze swept Gen again. "As we were driving home, I would have ordered you to spread your legs and put two fingers inside yourself, your thumb on your clit. No movement of those fingers, no playing with yourself. Just your hand on and inside your pussy while I was driving, to remind you I'm in charge, that your body belongs to me. It's my plaything tonight. I'd want you to feel how wet you were getting, not from the stimulation of your hand, but from the thought of how I'm controlling you, commanding your arousal."

Her gaze shifted. "Once we pulled into my driveway, I'd have you pull your fingers out of yourself, show them to me. I would tell you to suck on them, clean them with your mouth. Then I'd kiss you, taste your pussy on your lips, and think about what I'm going to do with that tasty little cunt to keep it wet for me. You're a squirter and—"

"Don't. I hate that word."

She hadn't meant to cut Lyda off, as much because it revealed too much about herself as to avoid being rude. "Guy, my first husband, laughed about it. It made me feel dirty. Gross."

"Asshole." Lyda stroked her thigh, tugged on the hem of her dress. "Look at me, Gen. I loved watching you do it. Do you remember the noise Noah made? It turns him on three ways to Sunday. He'll work his ass off to earn the right to fuck you, feel that happen around his cock."

"That would be my choice, not yours."

"You're right about that. But if we go down a road where you give yourself to me, at times it becomes one and the same."

She should disagree with that, but the way Lyda said it, the sensuous inflection, her fingers still drifting over Gen's thighs, made it difficult to articulate the reasons it wasn't true. She struggled to get back on track. "What else…would you make me do?"

"I have no close neighbors." Lyda drew her attention to their surroundings. The white house had one outside spotlight, showing Gen a small yard with a variety of flowers and potted plants. A stepping stone walkway was illuminated by the solar lights. "I'd tell you to take off the dress, walk up to the door in that cute bra and panty set and your heels. That's all you'd be wearing for the rest of the night. Or less."

"What does that give you?" Closing nerveless fingers on her thighs, Gen cleared the rasp out of her throat.

"There's a sweet vulnerability to a woman who submits to another woman. The way she kneels at my feet, wearing nothing but her underwear. I like looking at the line of her spine, the nape of her neck when her hair drapes forward because I've made her lower her head, raise her ass in the air, spread her legs. It's exciting you, isn't it? Hearing me describe it to you."

Gen gave a spare nod.

"Spread your legs, baby." Lyda said it so softly, and she used that same endearment Noah had. Like the two people themselves, it elicited different reactions from her, both of them intense. Pleasurable. Gen loosened her thighs, throat working as Lyda slid a finger beneath the panties, stroked her cunt. "There you are, so wet and hot for me."

"I don't know anything about you," Gen said desperately. "Except you worked two jobs in high school."

They hadn't had any of the normal discussions for a date. Background, family. She knew Lyda's profession only by happenstance, not inquiry.

"I'm a Mistress, Gen. For tonight, your Mistress, by your own choice. There will be time to learn more, but there's a difference between asking because you want to know me better, and trying to hold onto control." Lyda withdrew her finger, touched it to Gen's mouth, a gentle but inexorable probe that had Gen tasting herself.

"Sweet, sweet honey. I want to fuck you into oblivion, Gen. Until I'm the only thing you can hold onto to keep your world sane." Her gaze ran over Gen's flesh, encompassing the dress and shoes, the hair curling around her face. "You've given me hints of who you are, enough that I want to pull you out of that chrysalis and see what you become when you let go of the shit you don't need anymore."

Light flooded the vehicle as Noah pulled in behind them. Gen, snared in a look that had become more steel than liquid silver, was released as Lyda glanced in the mirror. "Let's go inside." Opening her door, she exited the vehicle without Gen's response.

Gen stared after her. Her car was right here. She could ask Noah for the key, leave. She wasn't a prisoner. Lyda was trying to unbalance her, and it was working. She'd done something she'd never done before tonight. She wasn't up to a whole night of that. It was time to step back, retreat. If Lyda didn't like that, well, she'd just have to pull someone else out of their "chrysalis". Maybe over-the-top, charismatic Dommes had tried-and-true pickup lines, just like anyone else in the vanilla dating game.

If so, it was a doozy. Gen would give her that.

Lyda had denied Gen any personal information, claiming that Gen was trying to hold onto control. Well, yeah. That was what normal people did, right? Tried to figure each other out, balance the scales, keep things on an even keel so one didn't feel so out of her element she might drown.

She opened the door, slid out. As she did, she was arrested by what was happening at her car. What Lyda had described was apparently a standard requirement for Noah. He'd changed into jeans, maybe when he'd stopped to grab the quick drive-thru meal. He'd put the McDonald's bag on her hood because he needed both hands free to remove the T-shirt Lyda had tossed him. While Gen watched, he shucked off the jeans. Beneath he wore charcoal-gray cotton shorts-styled briefs that made the most of his legs and hugged the appealing package at his groin. He toed off his shoes as well, his bare body a pale blur illuminated by the solar lights.

Gen looked toward the house. Lyda had gone inside and left the door open, a screen door keeping out bugs. Gen could see her tossing her keys onto an entranceway table, unconcerned about when and how they might follow her.

She thought about walking from the truck in only her panties, bra and heels, like Lyda had described. She imagined Lyda walking next to her, fingertips trailing over the valley of Gen's spine. It gave her a shiver.

No. She wasn't ready for that tonight. Wasn't even sure how much of this submissive stuff she was into doing, outside of the structured club environment. It felt more real here, less like a game.

When Noah touched her back where she'd imagined Lyda touching her, she twitched. He had his clothes folded over one arm and extended the other with a reassuring look, offering his hand. "Like Hansel and Gretel," he teased her.

Going into the home of a powerful, scary witch. It wasn't entirely off the mark, though the danger of this one was in the desire to be eaten, not the fear of it. She gazed up into his face. He was relaxed. This was normal to him. Whereas she wondered if she was going to Crazytown, because she took his hand and felt a bit steadier from his firm clasp. But Lyda had made it clear all choices were hers, and so far she hadn't asked Gen to do anything she'd refuse. The desire for escape had passed, for now.

She was carrying her shoes, and Noah nudged her onto the stepping stones, keeping her out of the vegetation that might prick her feet. The slate still held some of the heat of the humid day. She heard the faint pops of bug zappers.

At the top of the steps, Noah opened the door for her. Thinking of what Lyda said about Noah working his ass off for the right to fuck Gen sent a ripple through her. She had a difficult time not staring at the heavy weight filling the charcoal-gray knit shorts.

Gen managed not to stumble over the threshold as Noah gestured her to precede him. Lyda leaned against the wall at the end of the hall, arms crossed beneath her breasts, one booted foot hooked over the opposite ankle. Her perusal made Gen feel as undressed as Noah. A female glancing at her in a dressing room was just curiosity. *Are her thighs fat as mine?* Lyda was evaluating her as a sexual being, someone from whom she intended to make sexual demands. The difference was astronomical.

Lyda took off the tunic covering her corset. The latex leggings molded her sex, the tantalizing crease between thigh and hip. As Gen watched, Lyda unfastened the first several hooks of the corset, exposing a deeper plunge between her breasts.

"You're not in the position I require when you enter my house."

She was talking to Noah, because he immediately dropped to one knee. He kept his grip on Gen's hand. Lyda's gaze remained cool, dispassionate. When she arched a slim brow, Gen wondered if she expected her to kneel.

That wasn't the scary thing. The scary thing was Gen had to lock her knees to keep herself from doing it. A big part of her wanted to tumble down that rabbit hole, see what adventures lay in wait for her.

This isn't me. Be cautious.

Better to be safe, even if it made her sorry.

Chapter Six

She'd been so close to doing it, her heart hammered in her throat as if she had. Did Noah feel it? His grip had tightened, his thumb sliding over her palm, a reassurance.

Lyda moved down the hall, her body sexual poetry in motion. "Eyes on the floor. Let go of her hand."

Gen alone had the pleasure of seeing the latex crease around Lyda's sex, the way her breasts quivered as she sauntered toward them. She had a thin silver chain wrapped around one hand.

"You knew to kneel when you first entered. You were being polite, trying not to make our guest feel self-conscious. But who do you obey, first and foremost?"

"You, Mistress." Noah's voice was respectful.

"Take off your underwear."

He did so, with more grace than Gen could have managed if she'd been on her knees the way he was. She saw a bare haunch emerge, the seam of his buttocks. When he sat back, she bit back a surprised noise. His cock was locked in a curved, form-fitting metal sheath. His testicles were swollen beneath its steel collar.

She'd thought he'd been erect tonight, and instead it had been the frame of that chastity cage. When he'd been stroking himself, he'd been gripping that sheath, the entire purpose to titillate Gen's senses. But God... He'd said the pain of getting hard in such a device kept the cock from getting erect, but in that environment, saturated in sex...God, performing oral sex on Gen... Lyda was a sadist.

Lyda let the chain unwind from her hand, dangling a key in front of him. "You may release yourself, now that I know your cock will only be getting stiff from what I do to it. Or what I allow Gen to do to it."

"Yes Mistress." When she dropped the key to the floor in front of him, he unlocked a small padlock that rested in the valley provided by his testicles. Gen watched, fascinated, as he parted the two pieces of the sheath. There'd been a thin steel rod inserted into the slit, about an inch long. *Jesus.*

The tip had milky-white pre-cum collected around it. Even as he removed it, blood was starting to fill his cock. It was clear the organ would soon be standing proud between his thighs. Wearing it only restricted his physical state of arousal, not the mental one.

"As soon as the beast is out of the cage, it's ready to play." When Lyda caressed his hair, he pressed his temple to her thigh, brushing his lips there. "Let's see if you've been as good as you're supposed to be." She crooned it, but Gen saw the measuring look in her eyes. Squatting, Lyda clasped his cock in a functional grip, probed the slit. Muscles rippled across his back, his body tightening at the stimulation. "Good boy. You didn't wear it too long."

She looked at Gen. "He earned himself a severe punishment the night it started to hurt and he didn't tell me. Taking care of his cock so I have use of it whenever I wish is an important priority for a male sub."

"What did you do to him?" Having this conversation while Noah kept silent, his eyes down, was odd, but Gen was too curious not to ask. Lyda's hand remained on his neck as she rose, thumb tapping his main artery in an idle caress that had his fingers curling and uncurling on his thighs.

"I shamed him by doing the cleanings and flushings myself. He took the prescribed antibiotics from my hand. On top of that, he was allowed to do nothing for me, as his Mistress, for a week. If I couldn't trust him to care for something as precious to me as his dick, I couldn't trust him to care for me. It did the trick. For now."

Noah's cheeks had a dull flush from that exchange. Gen noticed a flex of his jaw muscle. Lyda saw it too. "You have something to say, Noah?" she said sharply.

"No Mistress."

"Hmm. Gen, are you hungry?"

"A little."

"Noah, go fix us a snack and a drink. Something with carbs and protein. Gen will need her energy and so will you. Bring it to us in the living room."

Taking Gen's hand, Lyda turned and moved up the hallway, leaving Noah there. Gen heard the sound of him rising, his bare feet padding behind them. She wanted to look back, but Lyda kept a brisk pace. As they passed the kitchen, Gen glimpsed an open space with gleaming pots and pans.

The living room had designer furniture and beautiful, bold prints of exotic plants. A flat screen TV was mounted on the wall. Lyda took a seat on the sofa, propping an arm on the back of the couch, her legs curled up beneath her. She patted the cushion in front of her. "Facing me, one leg bent on the seat cushion in front of you, the sole of your foot against your opposite knee, forming a triangle. Other foot on the floor."

The position stretched the thin crotch of Gen's panties over her plump sex. It was clear from Lyda's appreciative glance that the short skirt revealed it. "You blush when I look at your pussy. It's charming. Noah only blushes if I embarrass him."

"Why did you? Just now. All of it seemed…mean."

"Remember what I said about Noah needing the more heavy-handed methods? The cock sheath might seem cruel, but it's part of what he craves, Gen. A good Domme never does what a sub doesn't truly, deeply want." Lyda pursed her lips. "As far as telling you about the infection, a submissive's top priority is self-care. There's no failure a good Mistress punishes more harshly and, with a sub like Noah, you have to remind him, over and over. He's an excessive nurturer, to the point he could be mistaken for a Dom. His form of submission is like an ocean wave, holding you down. Which makes him an excellent partner to work with a Mistress. It also makes him insanely indifferent to himself."

She paused, as if she'd say more, but then she shook her head. "Tonight is not about that."

She reached out, stroked Gen's hair some more, but when Gen began to lift her own hand to return the favor, Lyda's look stilled her. "Hands stay at your sides, Gen."

"I don't get to touch you?"

"Not unless I give permission."

That had been easier to accept in the club environment. Here, she found herself more uncomfortable with the messages being sent. Toward her, Noah. "Why is that?"

"Because I said so." Humor flitted through Lyda's gaze at the parental dictate, even as her expression remained set, telling Gen that the teasing didn't change her orders. "As children, we may resent hearing that, but it shuts down the argument, makes us focus on simple obedience. It's a reminder of structure and boundaries, of who holds the reins. At its root, it's a feeling of security."

"Do I seem like someone who needs that?"

"You tell me." Those silver eyes pinned her. "There's a part of you that's thinking you should pull back, tell me to get over myself. You're telling yourself you need to do something to reestablish us as equals. But another part of you wants to submit, and the why of that has you confused.

"There are submissives who need to resist to achieve that sense of security, and they'll challenge a Dom more or less to get it. Then there are those who'll play for the fun and novelty of it, but when you tap into the deeper levels, they simply draw away, a clear message that true submission, that craving, isn't their thing."

Gen wet her lips. "How do you tell the difference?"

"Practice. Intuition. Trial and error. This is a consensual game, Gen. No matter what I do to you, you can end it with a single word. We call it a safeword. However, I always rely on unconscious signals first and foremost, because they're more truthful, and often come into play long before the safeword."

"You think I'm a submissive, not just someone indulging a sexual adventure."

"Being a submissive is a wide, wide range. At this point, I'd rather not slap a label on you, and not just because it would spook you. I think it would limit us both. Whatever you are...it's interesting." One of those slim brows arched. "The fact you did what you did at the club, and how you respond to soft commands, like keeping your hands at your sides now, tells me you want to explore this more yourself."

It was hard to argue with that. But since she seemed amenable to questions, Gen had plenty. "Say all that's true tomorrow. How does this work going forward? Do we set up appointments...dates? Is it a relationship or like going to a carnival every once in a while?" Realizing she might sound like a clingy first date, she added, awkwardly, "This isn't my world. I don't know how it works."

"I wouldn't say it's not your world. It's not a world you've chosen to enter until now." Lyda lifted a hand, ticking off points on her fingers. "Your boss is a very strong female Dominant, but you defer to her on a personal level as well as a professional one. Are you friends?"

When Gen hesitated over it, Lyda nodded. "The question gives you pause because yes, she is a friend, but there's something more there too. Like family, but not. She provides a certain direction to your life, a stability to your core, that you've never examined all that closely."

Lyda slid her fingertips over Gen's knee, a stroke that sent the nerve endings around it rippling. Then she resumed her count. "Your best friend chose a man fully immersed in the Dom/sub world for her husband. You took Noah into your home for the weekend, and when you learned what he was, you took steps toward exploring the limits of that. In the shallow end, yes, but you did. And tonight, you surrendered yourself to me publicly, almost without hesitation."

"It was the environment. When in Rome…" Gen trailed off before that keen glance, one that brooked no lying. Jesus, just like Marguerite. "But I have no idea what I'm doing or why I'm doing it. That's not like me. I don't like uncertainty."

"This is entirely different from anything you've ever done, but don't assume it's alien, Gen. Haven't you ever visited a new place that, for reasons you can't explain, feels familiar?"

"Sounds like what cult leaders say."

Lyda chuckled at that, but it wasn't cynical or mocking. She sounded appreciative of Gen's humor. The sultry note was also very distracting. Gen found herself wanting to lay a hand on her throat, feel the vibration of it. Lyda had a beautiful neck, coaxing the fingertips to stroke the lines of it, follow that slope to the generous breasts. She was obviously not going to have clear thoughts about any of this until she was well out of range of Noah or Lyda.

Resigned to that, she shifted the topic to Lyda herself. "Was that how it worked for you? I mean…you weren't born with cuffs in one hand, a whip in the other, right?"

The lines around Lyda's eyes crinkled. "No. But as I told you in the car, stories about me will come another time."

The woman slid her nails under Gen's bra strap, caressing her collarbone, then dipped to the upper rise of her breast. Gen's skin rose in gooseflesh beneath the touch, and she drew in a breath as Lyda pushed deeper into the cup, her finger playing over her nipple as it hardened. Gen tried not to squirm on the couch in response. Her attention went back to Lyda's breasts, those few undone hooks of the corset revealing a tempting, shadowed valley.

"What are you thinking, Gen?"

"I find you...very attractive." What a stupid thing to say. Lyda probably heard things like that all the time. Was she really playing teenage mind games, trying to figure out the cool thing to say? Was she regressing that badly? *Just be an adult and say what you mean.* "I haven't ever been attracted to a woman like this. Not past the casual fantasy level."

"Then I'm flattered I've won your attention. Take off your bra, Gen."

No matter what conflicting thoughts were going through Gen's head, Lyda was right about one thing. Something about all of this worked for Gen. Maybe it wouldn't tomorrow. Maybe she'd think she'd lost her mind, but tonight, when Lyda spoke, she wanted to obey. Unhooking the bra beneath the dress, she slid the straps out the sleeves, pulled the whole garment free. At Lyda's nod, she folded it neatly and laid it on the coffee table.

Lyda straightened on the couch, putting both feet on the floor. "Stand up in front of me. Don't be worried, Gen."

When Gen complied, Lyda cupped her hands around Gen's breasts, exploring their weight and shape through the thin dress fabric. She kneaded them gently, stroked her thumbs over them. She didn't touch the nipples, even though Gen could see as well as Lyda how stiff they were, begging for the contact. Instead, Lyda dropped her hold to Gen's hips and brought her close enough her legs touched Lyda's knees. "Spread your legs so they're wider than my feet."

She did, and Lyda slipped a hand between Gen's legs, up under the short skirt. When her knuckles slid over Gen's labia, teasing her clit, Gen swayed in reaction. Lyda's other hand tightened on her hip. "Put your hand on my shoulder."

She'd take any excuse to touch the woman, and this one allowed her to twine her fingers in the silky hair that had fallen forward on the shoulder Lyda had bared. She had silky skin as well. When Gen inhaled, she got a faint whiff of perfumed powder. Gen drew in a breath as Lyda inserted a finger beneath the panties and pushed up inside her pussy. When the muscles contracted in response, Lyda let out a pleased hum. "Nice and wet."

Gen heard her pussy make a sucking sound on Lyda's fingers as she explored. She had no time to be embarrassed over that, because whatever else she did made Gen bite back a moan.

"Keep your other hand at your side, unless I direct you otherwise. You hold onto my shoulder with the one hand, I'll keep you steady with the other one. You're safe with me, Gen. Do you understand?"

She didn't understand it, but she certainly felt it in this moment. Her uneasiness about that wasn't strong enough to make Gen want to stop what was happening.

"You said you haven't really taken it past the fantasy stage." Lyda asked the casual question as her hand stayed busy. "So you've never had sex with a woman, Gen? Played with one during your teenage years?"

Gen shook her head. "A little experimenting in high school. The usual stuff. Mostly fantasy, though."

"Did you ever think about taking it past the fantasy stage?"

"Right now." Gen's throat was dry. "A lot."

Lyda's expression was capable of making Gen's cunt suck harder on her hand. She wanted that mouth on her. Her fingers tightened on Lyda's shoulder, her body yearning forward.

The woman made a pleased murmur. "You're hot for it right now, that's for certain. When you were fantasizing about it before, did you think about taking it further then?"

"No. I kept it at fantasies. I figured that was normal for most straight women."

"Straight and gay are relative terms on a normal day, but especially when it comes to Dominant and submissive behavior." Lyda took her hand away from Gen's hip to slip another several hooks. It opened the corset enough that she could fold it back, the stiff cloth holding it in that position to reveal a full, blue-veined, pale-skinned breast with a deep-mauve areola and nipple.

"Would you like to put your mouth on me here, Gen?"

Gen's mouth was too dry to swallow. Lyda gave her a sharper look. "For some things, I'll take a nonverbal response. Not for this. Ask me for what you want."

"I want to suck...put my mouth on you. Please."

Lyda's eyes glittered, her mouth firming. "Already jumping ahead in your mind, aren't you? You're going to need to be on your knees, aren't you?"

They weakened immediately, her body already telling her it wasn't going to listen to any rational arguments against this.

Lyda slid her hand free and used both hands to ease Gen back and down to her knees, widening her own to give her the ability to shift closer. "Hands still at your sides," she reminded her. "Mouth only. And get rid of the panties."

Gen bit back a protest, because her fingers were itching to touch Lyda's curves. But the denial added a sweet bolt of longing to her core. As expected, Gen couldn't remove her underwear as smoothly in a kneeling position as Noah, but she managed it under that molten stare, setting them aside. When she moistened her lips, anticipating what would happen next, Lyda didn't make her wait long.

Cupping Gen's head, Lyda brought her forward again, her other arm sliding around her shoulders, gathering her in. "Put your mouth on me, Gen. Suck my nipple. Show me if you know how to give me pleasure."

Gen parted her lips. She was barely breathing as she made contact. It felt the way her own nipple felt, crinkled roughness and soft both. She explored, sliding her tongue around it, then opened her mouth wider, wanting to taste the pale flesh beyond. She traced several of those blue veins with her tongue, then returned to the nipple and took a stronger suck on it. Lyda made a noise...pleasure. She was giving a Mistress pleasure. Her Mistress, for tonight.

Lyda molded her hand over the back of Gen's skull. Gen wanted to put both her arms around Lyda's waist and hips. Wanted to let her fingers slide over latex and feel just how tight it was molded to Lyda's ass. She couldn't be wearing anything under it.

Her hands had moved before she realized it. Lyda closed her hands around her wrists and spoke. "Noah."

Gen hadn't heard him come in, but his hands were on her shoulders, sliding down her biceps, drawing her arms back. He held her by the elbows with gentle strength, kneeling behind her as Gen continued to suckle Lyda's right breast. His rigid cock pressed against her buttock, the inside of his thigh against her hip. Her elbows brushed his upper abdomen. His scent mingled with Lyda's, and Gen had that curious sense of being surrounded by both of them again, in a very good way.

She also noticed being restrained increased her fervency, as if she was trying to prove she could give Lyda more pleasure if she gave her more freedom. Lyda's knee pressed against her other side. However, she threaded her other leg between Gen's and probably Noah's behind her. At first the leg was straight so it made no contact, but then Lyda bent it so her thigh pressed against Gen's cunt beneath the dress. Gen moaned outright this time, her lips against Lyda's flesh. Lyda's fingers tangled in her hair, tugging at her scalp in a rhythm that matched the flex of her leg muscles, both suggesting lovely, rocking sex.

She thought about what would happen if Lyda pushed Gen's face down between her legs, let her pleasure her cunt beneath the tight hold of the latex. Gen's pussy convulsed at the thought, the reaction turning into thick liquid rolling down her thigh. It would pool against Lyda's leg, dampen the latex.

"Ease back now. There you go." Lyda broke the contact, nails whispering against Gen's throat before she pushed her back into Noah's embrace. He slid his hands around Gen's waist, bringing her full against him, both of them facing Lyda.

She gazed up at Lyda, who'd risen and circled behind the couch. She folded the corset back in place, but she didn't rehook it. "I'm going to go get changed. Then I want to do a little pre-bedtime reading. Noah, feed Gen her snack. Afterward, I want the two of you lying on the floor there."

She pointed one elegant finger toward the rug laid out before the fireplace. The fire screen was stained glass, showing a tulip against multi-colored green shards. "Legs scissored together, both of you on your sides. Get comfortable, because I won't be permitting you any movement until I command it. I'll be back in a moment."

She disappeared down a hallway. Noah shifted next to Gen, putting his back against the sofa. When she collected herself enough to drag her gaze from the hallway, he was studying her unbound breasts beneath the filmy dress fabric.

"I like this look," he said.

Rallying, Gen gave his naked body a similar once over. "Same goes."

He was beautiful, all firm muscle and tanned skin. And he had a really nice cock, thick and ready to perform, the testicles a dark-plum color beneath. Her fingers got that itchy feeling again, wanting to cup and stroke. It was pretty clear the conditions tonight were not the same as when he'd been at her house. But did that restrain her? The rules were only there if she chose to accept them. If she didn't, then...

She walked her fingers up the inside of his thigh. He watched her, those dark eyes not discouraging her, but not encouraging either. He was letting her figure it out. His cock jumped, though, telling her she had its vote. Curling her fingers around the shaft, she pressed a thumb over the slit, feeling the arousal there. She brought that fluid to her lips, tasted him.

"Let's get you fed," he said. She was happy to hear an unsteady note in his voice.

She noticed then he'd placed a plate on the coffee table behind her. It contained a sandwich and chips. Next to it was a glass of soda, as well as a glass of water. He'd quartered the sandwich. Picking up a piece, he extended it toward her mouth.

Gen drew back, settling on her heels. "I can feed myself."

"She said to feed you." He cocked his head, his hair sliding forward over his shoulder. "It helps to stay in the zone, so to speak. If that's where you'd like to be."

"They immerse you in the commands, make you rely on their direction, and brainwash you so it's all about pleasure, not questions."

Noah didn't seem offended. If anything, he seemed to ponder it. "It's not really brainwashing. Wouldn't most of us like a safe way to leave all questions behind, not have to worry about anything, and just feel pleasure? In a good way?" He met her gaze. "It's all a choice. If you prefer to feed yourself, you can do that."

Gen looked at the quartered sandwich in his hand, the rest on the plate. It was one thing to follow sexual commands. But being fed like a child...it didn't appeal to her.

"Can I try something different?"

"You can do anything you want," he responded with that smile that made her want to do all sorts of things to him.

Taking the sandwich from his hand, she offered it to him. He took a bite, keeping his eyes on hers as he chewed, swallowed. She had to admit, it gave her a peculiar thrill, having him accept the food from her hand. She took a bite of the sandwich for herself and then did it again, choosing to alternate between feeding him and herself. She handed the next quarter of the sandwich to him. "Okay, I'll give it a try."

It was arousing, though not for the reason she expected. From the first bite she took from Noah's hand, she saw what Lyda had pointed out. He did enjoy this, in a way that could be mistaken for how a Domme like Lyda would enjoy it. His eyes darkened, facial muscles tightening, his entire focus on how she took food from his hand. He became even more intent when her lips and tongue teased his fingertips.

She shifted onto her knees and put her hand on his thigh, gripping it with needy fingers there as he fed her the next bite. He lifted the water glass, guided the straw between her lips. When she was done drinking, her lips were wet and cool. He leaned forward, tasted them, a sliding type of kiss that didn't linger. Yet his eyes glinted as if they'd committed a playful infraction, coconspirators.

Losing her earlier reservations, she ate every bite from his hand. Licking the oil left on his fingers by the chips allowed her to bring up both hands to cup his. She followed the creases of his palm, nipping at the base of his fingers, pleased at how they caressed her face as she did it. His cock jerked, responding to the stimulation, but she gave him credit for keeping his attention on the charge Lyda had given him, as immersed in the pleasure of it as Gen.

At length, though, he pushed the plate away and scooped her up, bringing them both to their feet. He took her hand. "Ready to do the scissor thing?" he asked.

"Maybe. If you tell me what that means."

"Easier to show you."

She gave him a narrow look. "I'm sensing ulterior motives."

He chuckled, but drew her to the rug, an ultra-soft throw meant to feel like animal fur but wasn't. Kneeling, he drew her down with him and stretched out on one hip, propping up his head with a bent arm and hand braced in front of him.

"Okay, lie down with your head at my feet and body stretched out in front of me so your feet are here." He patted the spot in front of his chest, accurately gauging the difference in their heights. "Just think erotic Twister."

That made her smile, which she was sure he intended, since she was feeling nervous again. When she complied, he adjusted her so she was turned mostly on her stomach, helping keep her comfortable as he adjusted their legs into a scissor lock. As he gripped her hips and eased the core of their bodies closer together, she realized only a few inches separated her pussy from his testicles. She expected "flush" meant closing those few inches.

He met her gaze, making sure of her state of mind as he made the intimate contact. Her thigh muscles twitched against his, an outward reaction to her inner one, feeling the weight of his balls press against her labia in such a careful, planned way, where the body wanted to move but the mind held it still. Looking down their bodies, she saw his cock hard against his belly.

"No movement now," he said. "Pillow your head on your folded arms. It's more comfortable that way." Since he was still on his hip, he folded one arm beneath his head, his palm pressed against the rug, holding them steady as much as was needed.

Lyda was moving around in the kitchen. Gen heard the microwave going. Perhaps she drank tea with her evening reading. Gen could feel the pulse in his scrotum, matched by the beat in her own cunt. What had seemed like an odd, maybe even silly position—erotic Twister indeed—was apparently up there in the list of erotic torture methods. Her breathing was shallow, her nipples tight against the rug through the thin dress. She wanted to move, wanted to rub against him. Why shouldn't she?

Because Lyda had said they were to remain still. Unlike small infractions like Gen touching Noah's cock, which hadn't been directly proscribed, Gen sensed deliberately going against something Lyda ordered would be disrespectful, like putting one's feet up on someone's coffee table when invited to a luncheon. Gen had choices, yes, but in this case she suspected she only had two approved ones. Stay in this position or back away from Noah and decide not to do this. Period.

Lyda reentered in a thin silk robe, one that stopped midthigh and showed enough provocative movement of her breasts beneath the overlapped lapels, a flash of thigh as she moved, to suggest she wore nothing under it. She carried a book and a teacup, the tag fluttering over the edge. Setting them on the side table next to a wing-backed chair close to the rug, Lyda moved to the mantle and uncovered a metronome. "These are very useful for taking things slow. Did you think I wouldn't know about that kiss, Noah?"

She didn't turn as she said it. Gen realized Lyda must have lingered to watch their mutual feeding from an unseen position.

"No Mistress." Noah didn't look disturbed, but he wasn't rebellious about it. His gaze was fixed on everything Lyda was doing, his body tight and aroused in its locked position against Gen. She found herself caught in the same thickening atmosphere, her heartbeat accelerating.

"I'll address that later. For now..." Lyda set the metronome ticking in a steady rhythm. Turning, her gaze covered Noah's naked body and Gen's, still in her dress. The skirt was rucked up so high from their position, Gen knew her ass was peeking out of the bottom, revealing the pink curves. Lyda's look of pure pleasure confirmed it.

From the pocket of her robe, she produced two scraps of cloth Gen realized were blindfolds. She squatted before Noah first, while Gen was thinking, *oh no, I don't think so*. Before Lyda put it on him, Noah caught her wrist. They locked gazes, Lyda giving him a cool stare. "Let go of me, Noah."

He nuzzled her hand with his mouth, his nose, closing his eyes as her nails lightly raked his forehead, his cheek. Her gaze softened, and she caressed the strands of hair scattered on his brow. "Behave," she murmured.

He let her go and she put the blindfold in place. When she shifted to Gen, dangling the blindfold before her, Gen smelled the tea, a chai blend, on her fingertips.

"This will intensify your pleasure," Lyda explained. "And my own."

Gen wasn't sure. But her hands weren't being tied. She could remove it at any time. So she didn't protest when Lyda put the blindfold on her, leaving only a line of light at the lower part and the weight of Lyda's proximity. She adjusted Gen's hair over and around it.

"Hear that slow click, click? That's one back-and-forth movement. During those two clicks, Gen, rub your cunt against Noah's balls and the base of his cock in a slow circle. Then you both wait another two clicks and Noah returns the favor. You alternate, never going faster or slower than the metronome. For every three times you mess up, get off rhythm, you get punished. Neither one of you is allowed to come unless I give permission. You'll do this with minimal talking. I don't want my reading disturbed."

Gen had no doubt she'd be watching them as an eagle watched prey, but the blindfolds would enforce the illusion. They'd hear the turning of pages, the shift of her body as she read, that seeming detachment only increasing the intensity of what they were doing. Hell, her pussy was already quivering with the restrained desire to move, to rub against that provocative stimulus, Noah's heat and rough-textured flesh against the petals of her cunt.

Lyda withdrew. They heard the sound of her settling, the light clink as she picked up the teacup.

"Ladies first." Noah's voice was already strained.

It was a game. Erotic twister, right? She focused on the metronome. It took a moment to get it right, and she hoped Lyda was allowing a learning curve before counting infractions. What would be the punishment? Don't Pass Go, stand in the corner for a minute? Her guesses probably weren't even close. But she wasn't into pain. Definitely not humiliation. That was a deal breaker.

"Focus," Noah murmured, a sensual invitation to play, not an admonishment.

It wasn't difficult, not from a mechanical standpoint. Rotate... Sliding her labia against the base of his cock, firmly enough the lips split over his hardness, then down... Press against his testicles, the give of them making an uneven stroke over her tissues. Then two beats and he did it to her, working himself against her cunt.

What was difficult was staying to the slow, ticktock, ticktock rhythm. Especially as they heard those pages being turned, the teacup lifting and lowering. The intensity was driven as much by

Lyda's command as the direct physical stimulus. They were performing for her, serving a Mistress's desires. As her arousal built, Gen found herself losing a grip on self-consciousness as well as her internal debate about why she was doing this. She wanted to please Lyda, wanted the chance to wrap her lips around that succulent nipple again, feel her hair being stroked and her pussy getting needier as she suckled, as she maybe got the chance to do even more, feel even more, with both of them.

Her breath started to rasp. She bit it back, then cursed as she missed the rhythm count. Again.

"That's three, Gen." Gen's stomach jumped, but after a weighted pause, Lyda merely said, "Keep going."

Okay, so punishment was going to wait for later. Maybe Lyda was enjoying her voyeurism too much to interrupt it. It was her game after all, from beginning to end.

That spurt of thrilling panic had only increased sensation, such that she had to bite back a whimper. She'd seen plenty of people tonight who not only got off on being punished, but on watching it. From the size of Noah's cock pressed against her leg, she thought he'd gotten harder, and her pussy became even more soaked, sliding her against his testicles even faster.

"On rhythm," Lyda said sharply.

The slowness became the true torture, her pussy convulsing with every rotation, her clit hardening, quivering. If she could rub even a modicum faster, she would come. She thought Noah might be reaching the same point, from how careful their movements were becoming. Her fingers dug into the carpet. She'd flattened her upper body, the rug a sweet friction against her nipples. Lift, lower, rotate.

"Fuck," Noah breathed. "Mistress…"

"Sssh…" Lyda said absently. It sounded like she was engrossed in her book, but Gen was sure she was feeding off the pleasure she was denying them. The thought only inflamed Gen more. She and Noah were writhing on the floor like wanton animals.

"Please…" Gen whispered to the carpet. Then, so softly she thought it might not be heard, she said, "Mistress."

Lyda's bare foot pressed against her buttock. Still no response, no command to come. They had to keep to that rhythm. Over and over, until Gen's body was dewed with perspiration and she'd coated Noah's balls in her juices. His leg was damp beneath hers. They were both shaking with the effort of holding back.

"Stop." Lyda's foot withdrew. "Gen, on your knees. Come toward my voice. I won't let you run into anything."

She obeyed, clumsy, uncoordinated, but when Lyda touched her, drew her closer, she made that whimpering sound again. The blindfold helped remove all inhibitions, all embarrassment. There was just lust, the need to come.

"Sit up on your heels. Hands behind your back. Lace your fingers."

She teetered forward as she did it, but Lyda held her securely, hands on Gen's shoulders. She drew her down and forward, so Gen's chin rested on the seat cushion. Lyda was sliding closer, her thighs pressing against Gen's shoulders as she hooked her heels around the back of Gen's knees. Oh...she was going to... *Yes.*

She pushed Gen's face directly into her wet, fragrant pussy. "Eat my cunt, Gen, until I tell you to stop. Serve your Mistress well, and I'll allow you and Noah to come."

She didn't have the reasoning power to worry that this was her first time doing this to a woman and how to do it. She wanted to taste Lyda's pussy, suck juices from it, tease the labia, lash at the clit, nip at her with an almost savage hunger, no finesse. Lyda pulled her head even closer, burying Gen's face and mouth against her, moving against Gen as if she was marking her.

Gen plunged her tongue inside Lyda's cunt, finding it slick and hot. The musk of it was different from a man, the strength of the smooth thighs on either side of her head tempered with the delicate scent of that floral powder. She moaned as her own empty pussy contracted, so sensitized, so close to climax, it made her work all the harder now for the reward she'd been promised. That they'd both been promised.

Noah was behind them, listening to her going down on his Mistress while he was blindfolded. Were his fingers itching to wrap around his engorged cock, jerk himself off to the sound of Lyda's heavy breathing, the moans that slipped from her lips, the aroused sounds humming in Gen's throat as she licked, thrust into and suckled Lyda's cunt?

Lyda's grip became rigid on Gen's head. As she ground herself against her face, she released with guttural cries, a hard pumping of her hips. Gen lapped up the small surges of cream that bathed her pussy, suckled her clean all while savoring the strong woman's shudders as she came down, as she twitched and quivered. Reading her body as she might read her own, Gen applied her tongue with steady pressure, slowing the swirls and teasing licks to accommodate Lyda's aftershocks, her sensitized skin. She could smell Lyda on her lips, on her face. In her current state of extreme arousal, she inhaled it like an elixir.

"Now your punishment. Turn around."

Once again, Lyda guided her like a doll. She pushed Gen down until her forehead was on the floor but she kept Gen's hips up. She was so aroused, the position was more arousing than threatening. All Gen could think of was how her exposed pussy must look, wet and ready to be fucked, tissues flushed, and how easy it would be to make that happen in a variety of ways. Noah's cock, his or Lyda's tongue, fingers, a vibrator. She had to come or she'd die.

A sharp slapping noise made her jump. She was going to be punished, and though panic surged through her, none of it translated through her lust-fogged brain as an act of refusal. Lyda's hand slid between her legs, cupped her mound. The contact alone made Gen moan, and when Lyda pushed a thumb inside her, using the other fingers to hold her up, she was shuddering.

Something hard, slim and far too flexible smacked her ass. It hurt, the sting sharp and jarring, but all the arousal swirling through her made the cry that broke from her lips sound near orgasmic.

"Thought you had that in you, with the right conditions." Lyda did it again, harder, and Gen yelped. Panted. Gripped the carpet. After the sting came a flush of heat that was hard to classify. Especially when she felt Lyda's lips brush her raised buttock. Right before the third blow, the hardest of all. She jumped, her brain saying *No, no. That hurt too much, no more...* And yet she wanted to lift her hips to ask for more.

Lyda removed her hand from her pussy, gave her throbbing buttock a light slap with her hand. "That's all you get for now, rabbit. Resume the scissor position and begin again."

Noah took over then, which was good since her mind was floating somewhere, her body too spun up to be controlled by her brain. When he eased her back into place, she let out a harsh groan. That contact between their genitals ran electricity through her body, warning her how close she was to climax.

The metronome was reset, this time to a faster pace. Lyda was trying to turn her into a lunatic. "You may work at the same time now," the woman said in her pure sex tone "but follow this rhythm. I want to see my pets come, writhing at my feet. Ask my permission right before."

With the first friction of Noah's testicles against her labia, her pussy spasmed. "God...please...I need..."

She strangled on the words, and Lyda said nothing. She was going to make her say it all. Choice or no choice, free will, wasn't even in Gen's mind now. She and Noah were Lyda's pets, owned by her entirely, able to do what she wanted to them. And that ownership was the most erotic thought Gen had ever experienced. All the independence she valued so highly, it wasn't as if this moment negated it—it was as if Lyda had called forth an alter ego from Gen, one who wanted this. Needed this as a reward for the other.

The words blurted from her, lust-infused panic. "Please, Mistress...may I come? Please..." The last word was a near scream.

"Come for me, Gen."

Vaguely, she heard Noah ask for the same privilege and Lyda give consent. His legs jerked, the two of them bucking against each other. She spurted against his testicles, soaking them with her response she was sure. She could see it just as Lyda had described it, them writhing on the floor, humping like the naked, unrestrained animals they were, giving their owner pleasure as she watched.

Their Mistress.

When Gen at last landed from her orbit of the moon, she worried she might have scrubbed all the skin off Noah's testicles. His deep breaths, the way his legs were twitching against hers, told her he was feeling no pain, however. No more than herself. Aftershocks kept rippling through her, mixed with plain old shock. She became aware that Lyda was on her knees next to them. She was stroking Gen's hair, hip pressed against Gen's backside. From the rhythmic movements, Gen suspected she was stroking Noah as well. Perhaps his hip or side. Soothing them. Expressing her pleasure.

"So you aren't really a nighttime TV watcher," Gen mumbled.

"I prefer live entertainment options when I can get them. Sshh." Lyda stroked the side of her face, coiled her fingers in Gen's hair. She kept doing that for a while, until lassitude settled over Gen's limbs and she thought she could stay this way forever.

But at length, the Mistress took off her blindfold. The intensity in Lyda's gaze, the tempting beauty of her mouth, made Gen quake helplessly. And Lyda saw it all. The power of her expression, what Gen was feeling, was too much, such that Gen's gaze lowered before she even realized she'd done it. But the gesture gave her some room to notice other things.

Lyda had her other hand braced on Noah's hip. She hadn't yet removed his blindfold, so the press of his lips, the musculature of his body delineated by the aftermath of his climax, was all Gen's to enjoy without him seeing her stare, giving her a taste of the exclusive pleasure Lyda had enjoyed. His climax had spurted over his sectioned stomach muscles, up to his chest. Despite the depletion of energy that came with her climax, Gen wanted to slide her fingers through it, paint it over his nipples. Taste it, and him.

"He's so beautiful, isn't he?" Lyda ran a hand down his side, over his buttock, back up to his shoulder. "My sweet boy. My gorgeous, lost soul. Wonderful man."

Noah turned his face to the carpet as Lyda slipped the blindfold from him. His eyes stayed closed, his face relaxed, still lost in a haze. Gen understood the feeling. The only thing tugging her toward reality was the trickle of shock at the extraordinary things she'd done tonight. Her languid state kept worry at bay. For now.

"Time for bed, for all of us." Lyda rose, offering Gen a hand. When she hauled her to her feet, she swayed. Lyda slid an arm around her waist, letting her lean.

"I..."

"Sssh. Let it all go for tonight. You did beautifully."

Relief filled her. Yet following, allowing things to happen, wasn't what she did. She never trusted anyone else in that way, but Lyda simply took control and Gen let her. Lyda was right. She didn't have the brain power to interpret that, think about it now.

As Lyda held her in one arm, she prodded Noah with her foot, a gentle tease. "On your feet, you worthless male animal."

Noah cracked an eyelid, but agreeably complied, pushing himself up onto his hip and getting his feet underneath him. When Lyda reached down to him, Gen automatically did the same. Noah paused, as if he might wave off the help, but in the end, he clasped their hands, though he used his own strength to pull himself up, tightening his grip on their fingers as a sign of connection. Despite that, Lyda watched him with her sharp eyes to ensure he had his balance before releasing him.

Gen thought she could have walked on her own as well, but having Lyda's body pressed against her side wasn't something she'd deny herself. She hadn't tied the robe, completely comfortable with exposing her breasts, the slope of her abdomen and the shaved point of her sex, her long, toned legs. Gen had tasted those breasts, that sex. She wanted to taste her everywhere, wanted to taste Noah's flesh. Though it was a low-level hum beneath the emotional and physical exhaustion from the big events of the day, it was a tone that was steady and true. A promise that she'd want more than one night of this.

Lyda took her down the hall and up a set of steep, narrow stairs smelling of old wood. Noah followed close behind them. Gen had the impression of more interesting artwork along the way. No photographs, except for a couple art pieces, not family photos. At the top of the stairs, they turned right, passing a guestroom, a bathroom, and then they were at the master bedroom.

Lyda had a tester bed with thick pillars and a carved wooden overhang. It looked like an antique, but some unusual customization had been done beneath it. Something startling enough to break Gen out of her post-coital trance. She balked, uncertain. Lyda's grip tightened on her.

"It's all right, Gen. Trust me."

Tester beds sat high enough off the floor that there were usually steps to allow shorter people easier access to the mattress. Gen remembered Chloe talking about them once, suggesting they'd been designed by adults who missed childhood bunk beds.

Nothing childish about what had been built beneath this one. A cage, as long and wide as the mattress, sturdy enough to also serve as the frame of the bed. The six-inch spaced bars looked like steel. A twin mattress inside the cage ran parallel with the long side of the bed. It was a freaking cage.

"I don't want to do that."

"It's not intended for you." Lyda said it calmly enough to soothe Gen's nerves. Until she realized the implication.

When Lyda pointed to the enclosure, Noah knelt and rolled gracefully into it. He stretched out on his stomach, bending one leg up and shifting his hips in a way that had his ass flexing as he adjusted to his preferred sleeping position on the mattress. Given that he was entirely naked and seemed to want to sleep on top of the covers, he looked like a Playgirl centerfold. She wasn't sure Playgirl got into bondage, though. She was trying to stay appalled, but when his heavy-lidded brown eyes slid over her with lazy erotic pleasure, she remembered comparing him to a sleepy wolf.

Letting go of Gen, Lyda leaned over to close the cage door. Gen noticed the latch had a padlock eye, but it didn't contain a padlock. Noah could get out on his own if needed, which made her feel somewhat better. Reaching through the bars, Lyda tousled Noah's long hair. His eyes were already closed again, and when he grunted at the attention, she snorted. "Typical post-orgasmic male. Useless."

She said it fondly, rising to face Gen. Pressing her fingers to her own lips, Lyda laid the transposed kiss on Gen's forehead. "Bathroom's down the hall. I have a guest bedroom next to it, or you can come back to bed with me."

Giving her a direct look, Lyda dropped the robe. As she stepped onto the short set of steps that led up to the bed, Gen noticed Noah's eyes opened again. He took his fill of his Mistress naked, and once she'd ascended to the bed, he slid a hand out between the bars to snag the robe. He reeled it in until he had it in a silken puddle by his pillow, close enough he could dream with her scent in his nose.

"You get any drool or other disgusting male fluids on that, I will cut off your balls with my pruning shears."

He let out a snuffled sound that could have been a chuckle.

Lyda stretched out her lithe body to turn off the bed lamp. A nightlight, shaped like a porcelain orchid, glowed by the antique dresser. Then she turned on her side, facing away from Gen. The cover was off her bare shoulder, her hair loose along the pillow.

Gen found herself several steps closer to the bed, but she wasn't sure of her intent. Her gaze went between the woman on the bed and the man beneath it. If Lyda extended her hand over edge of the mattress, Noah could reach through the bars and clasp her slim fingers, if she so desired. The appeal of that thought disturbed Gen. Then she felt Noah's fingers slide over her foot, take a loose grip on her ankle, stroke. Soothing.

"Why a cage?" she asked softly.

"Because it underscores that he's in my care," Lyda answered for him. "That he can trust my ownership, whether it's simply for a night or for a longer period. And because it fucking turns me on to see my sub locked up that way."

Noah gave that half chuckle, an amused sound of agreement. Gen turned her gaze down to him. "What does it do for…you?"

He tilted his head up, meeting her gaze with those distracting brown eyes. "Come inside and find out," he said simply.

Instead she slid her foot from his grasp and retreated, mumbling something about the bathroom.

Lyda had an appreciation for top-of-the-line fixtures. Gen had briefly glimpsed the master bath, and seen a shower with multiple sprayers and corner benches, the area large enough to double as a steam room. There was a smaller version of that in the guest bath. The walls and tile were white, but she'd highlighted the blank canvas with a spray of purple and yellow flowers over the commode. Along the side of the wide mirror, she had a trio of colorful, whimsical watercolors of mermaids.

Gen studied the pictures. Lyda's reserved humor came in sporadic flashes, but like the touches of color in this room, that gave it more of an impact.

Gen pulled a makeup wipe from the beauty products in a sample basket on the counter. Worrying about being seen without makeup seemed pointless after how vulnerable she'd made herself tonight. Lyda had come out of the bedroom to do her "reading" without makeup, dressed for bed, but of course with or without makeup, she was striking. The force of her personality overrode any embellishment.

Gen cupped her hands over her face. She inhaled Lyda's damp pussy, the fragrance lingering in her nose, on her lips, her cheeks. She was reluctant to wash it away, but she did.

Leaving the bathroom, she found the guest bedroom. The white spread had fine needlepoint depicting sprays of greenery. Well-tended house plants clustered in the corner, next to a rocker with a stuffed white bear in it. The bear was new enough to suggest it wasn't a cherished childhood memento, so she wondered how Lyda had acquired it and why she kept it, though it added a further touch of comfort to an already welcoming room. Lyda had said she could stay in here.

Or she could get her clothes, find her keys, leave. They wouldn't stop her.

Instead, she wandered down the hall, closer to the main bedroom, though she paused at Lyda's home office. A laptop on the desk, a printer and router, the usual things. There was also a TV in there, a shelf of books and a portable heater for winter, a necessity in a drafty older house to cut down on heating bills. Though it had looked as if Lyda had a main office out by the greenhouse, Gen knew running one's own business successfully was more than a nine-to-five endeavor, something she appreciated even more now that M had increased Gen's involvement in the running of Tea Leaves.

She was back at the entrance to the master bedroom. The mistress bedroom. A weak joke, underscoring her anxiety. The nightlight showed Noah sprawled on his stomach, pillow bunched under the curl of his arms, Lyda's robe a neat swirl under his elbow.

His breath seemed even. She couldn't tell if Lyda slept, but as Gen circled to the other side of the bed, she hesitated. She'd been invited earlier, but it felt wrong to simply slip in the bed with Lyda, now that her eyes were closed. She shouldn't be intimidated by her. She was just a woman, like Gen, or Chloe…

No, she wasn't like them. She was like Marguerite, a different classification. Something inside Gen recognized it and responded accordingly. That would bear some thinking about. She really should go home.

"Are you sleeping in that dress?"

Lyda's eyes were half-slits, studying her. Sliding her hand toward Gen, she hooked the covers, flipped them back. "Take it all off, rabbit. Come to bed."

Gen turned to the closet. She slipped the dress off, hesitating when she saw her thong panties hanging over the knob. Lyda must have been carrying them in her robe pocket.

Even with a handy vibrator, Gen was usually a one-orgasm-a-week kind of girl. It seemed impossible that thinking of Lyda handling her underwear, marked by her arousal, could stir her up again. Lyda was sleepy, though. There wouldn't be anything more happening tonight. *Take a breath.*

Tucking the thong inside the dress and hooking both on the closet knob, Gen turned back to the bed. She used the steps on that side to crawl onto the mattress, slide under the covers. She hadn't slept with anyone since her second husband. Well, except the night before Chloe's wedding, when Chloe and several of her early female guests had dog-piled onto Gen's bed, talking into the wee hours of the morning. Chloe had eventually fallen asleep there, arm wrapped around Gen as she slept, that fond affection that Chloe did so well. This was very different.

Lyda slid closer, propping herself on her elbow and pushing Gen to her back so she could gaze down at her. Lyda cupped the side of her face, her fingers drifting along Gen's jaw, down her throat, her sternum.

"Ass sore, rabbit?"

"A little."

"I could see the marks I left on it when you undressed. I liked that." Lyda folded back the covers so she could see all of Gen. She watched the Mistress gaze at her body, fingertips trailing Gen's rib cage below her breast, circling over her stomach, teasing her hip bones. She was being explored. Lyda stroked her knuckles over Gen's hip, her upper thigh. When she exerted pressure on it, Gen opened her legs without thought. The approving murmur made Gen tremble. Inside and out.

Lyda didn't touch cunt or nipples, barely grazed Gen's breasts at all. She stroked her arms and upper thighs, inside her thighs, high enough to caress the tender pockets on either side of her pussy. Walking her short-nailed fingers over Gen's mound, Lyda played with her navel.

Then Lyda lowered her head and put her mouth on all those same places.

Gen's breath accelerated, her body moving restlessly. She bit back a moan, not wanting to disturb the hushed charge in the air. Was Noah awake and listening to the shift of the box springs above him, wishing he could be part of this, watch? She bet he was, as much as she wagered that was a vital component of Lyda's pleasure, denying him the view to goad his arousal, while stoking Gen's.

"You thought about going into the cage, didn't you?" A seductive whisper.

"No. Yes…but it's not for me."

"But it's a nice fantasy." Lyda kissed the valley between her breasts. Gen had kept her hands at her sides, thinking Lyda would prefer that, but she couldn't resist sliding her fingers through her hair now. Lyda didn't stop her, and Gen thought nothing had ever felt so lovely as those silken locks sliding over her fingers, over her breasts. "Would you like to know how I imagine it, Gen?"

"Yes." She was whispering too. Lyda discovered more of her with mouth and fingertips, at the leisurely pace of someone getting used to a new treasured toy.

"You, captured. Here. Belonging to me, like a pet in truth. Enclosed, safe. Owned. You can sleep in peace, nothing to do, to think, no actions to take that I don't command. Not because you're helpless." Lyda lifted her head, pinned her with that intent gaze. "But because the one thing a strong submissive deserves and needs is a safe way to surrender all control."

"There is no such thing."

"Yes, there is." Lyda slid her leg over Gen's, pressing her knee against her pussy so Gen arched at the pressure. She swallowed a cry as Lyda rose on both knees and then slipped her hands under Gen's buttocks to lift her up to ride the column of her thigh.

"Hands open and above your head."

Gen complied, though it was hard to stop touching Lyda's hair. Her legs were shifting even more impatiently at the flexing pressure of Lyda's leg against her pussy.

"All nice and wet again. I want your lovely gush of come to mark my sheets, Gen. Noah will wash them tomorrow, though I'll bet our bad boy will smell them first, rub them against his body."

A needy noise broke free from Gen's throat as Lyda put her body fully between Gen's thighs, stretching out upon her to bring naked flesh to naked flesh, her breasts brushing Gen's, hips pressing her thighs wider.

"Have you wondered how two women have sex, Gen? It's not about dildos or strap-ons, though those can be plenty of fun. And no mouth between your thighs, though that's a pleasure I'll take from you again, when I wish. Tell me what you feel."

"Your legs...against my thighs. Your body, pressing mine down. Your breasts, your smell...your hair, falling against my face and shoulders. I love your hair. Everywhere you are against me...it's like I'm turning into flame."

"And there she is, a quiet, earnest poet when the world is still enough for her to whisper her sweet, tender thoughts."

The words had come without thought. Gen's moment of embarrassed regret for not suppressing them evaporated into wonder as Lyda smiled down at her, silver eyes luminescent. "Women tend to experience one another as a whole body, because it's not just about our pussies. I love feeling you squirm beneath me. Looking at your fingers, curling and uncurling, wanting to touch me. Next time I'm at Tea Leaves, watching you prepare tea or take a phone order, I'll stare at your hands and remember this moment. When you speak, I'll think of how your lips are parted now, wet like your cunt."

Her labia and clit slid against Gen's, an indescribable feeling of pleasure. Gen moaned again, her hips lifting. "It's like the metronome, only we set our own music this time. Move with me, Gen. I want you to sing for me. Lift your chin."

Gen did so, and another shuddering sigh broke from her lips as Lyda kissed her neck, nipped her breasts. Then she pressed her own against Gen's, an intriguing weight, the drag of the nipples inspiring Gen to return the favor. Lyda's hips worked against her, clit rubbing clit. Then bearing down, she slid her wet labia over Gen's with slick purpose. Gen wanted to raise her legs, lock them around Lyda.

"Keep them down. I like seeing you spread out all helpless like this. Mine to do whatever I want with. You're gorgeous."

Tangling her fingers in Gen's hair, she yanked, arching Gen's throat so she could take a harder bite out of it. Gen cried out, pure need. Lyda slid an arm beneath her shoulder blades, pulled her off the pillow enough she could keep her cunt rubbing against Gen's as she wrapped her mouth around a nipple. She gripped the curve, squeezing so she could suckle it more deeply. Gen's back bowed into an impossible crescent to help Lyda do as she wished. "Oh God…"

"You're so beautiful." Lyda lifted her upper body then, bracing her hands on either side of Gen's ribs, caging her as she began to work against her with greater purpose, her lips wet where she'd tasted Gen's flesh. Her breasts trembled with her rhythmic movement, upper body rolling in sinuous display. Gen had a flash of how she looked from behind, the heart-shaped ass pumping as if she was fucking Gen like a man. But she was, wasn't she? Lyda was drawing in every sensation through her eyes, through everywhere their bodies touched, as much as where their genitals made contact. Gen was pushing against her, no longer guided by anything but desire.

"Oh…God…I'm going to come…"

Lyda's eyes caught flame, her mouth tightening. "Come for me, Gen."

Gen clenched her hands into fists on the pillow, not able to leave them loose as the orgasm took her. Lyda's head dropped back just as Gen was coming down, and Gen felt the spasm through the Mistress's cunt as they found a climax together, hips bumping, breath sighing out in long moans, bed rocking with the force of their need.

At the height of their chorus of pleasured release, Lyda captured one of Gen's hands, guiding it down to her side, a nonverbal direction to have Gen grip her hips, press her fingers into Lyda's buttocks to add to the friction. And then, as the tide ebbed, Lyda let her stay that way a precious moment, so Gen could explore the beauty of those pale curves. God, Lyda had a wonderful ass. Gen slid her fingers over the taut flanks of a sensual female animal, tracing her upper thighs. Lyda had kept one hand tangled with hers, so Gen could also make tiny strokes of her knuckles.

Lyda kissed between Gen's breasts, to her navel and below. Gen sucked in a cry as her clit was suckled, her labia licked. Lyda pressed her palm against the sheets.

"A nice puddle there. That's my good girl."

She'd never though it erotic. Lyda made her feel like it was incredibly so. She shifted next to Gen, gathered her in her arms, spooning against Gen's back, her arm over her waist, the other tangled with her hand up near her head. "Noah," Lyda said in a conversational voice, "Is your cock hard?"

"Yes Mistress." His muffled voice was rough, sending a little ripple through Gen. In one night, these two had tripled her normal libido, with no signs of it decreasing.

"How hard?"

"Really fucking hard, Mistress."

"You wish I'd let you take care of that, don't you?"

The unspoken yes was like a primal shout, so Gen was impressed with his actual response. "Whatever my Mistress wants is what I wish."

"Remember that next time you steal a kiss without permission. Go to sleep, Noah. And if you have any wet dreams, you'll spend tomorrow watering stock with a dildo strapped up your ass."

"Yes Mistress." He sounded resigned, but still hugely aroused. Gen was beginning to realize the threats contributed to that. At least for Noah's form of submission.

She wondered how she was going to deal with thinking about this in the morning, but she was too exhausted to worry. Her mind drifted back to what Lyda had said about the cage. For just a moment, she almost understood why Lyda had described it the way she had. Enclosed, safe. Owned.

In such a state, she could just...sleep.

* * * * *

She hadn't expected to sleep so deeply in an unfamiliar place, but sexual repletion had that effect. The bed was as comfortable as a nest, and she'd fallen asleep still grasping Lyda's hand. Waking without that connection was the only thing that felt off. At least in that first moment.

Lifting her head, she saw a note tented on the side table. A water glass filled with buttonlike flowers in white and pink sat next to it. *Grab yourself a shower in the guest bath if you'd like. Breakfast is in the oven. I'm in the nursery whenever you feel up to saying good morning. I have your car key.*

"Bitch," Gen muttered without rancor. Lyda had obviously anticipated her wanting to slink away to think about all of this, discomfited about facing those with whom she'd committed the crime, so to speak.

Lyda's robe hung on the back of the bedroom door. Gen's dress was gone. While it seemed silly for her to worry about covering herself, things were always different in the light of day. After a brief hesitation, she slid the robe onto her shoulders, bemused by how Lyda's scent both eased and tightened things.

In the guest bathroom, a fluffy towel waited for her, tied with a sprig of rosemary. Her dress had been hung on a rack, and her underwear was folded on the counter on top of a nursery T-shirt. Her clothes, even her underwear, had been cleaned. She glanced at the clock. It was only eight a.m. Lyda had done all of this while she slept?

She wasn't the type comfortable with being waited upon. Still, she rubbed the rosemary, lifting her fingers to inhale the pungent, pleasant aroma. When she removed the robe, she glanced at herself in the mirror. She saw abrasions on the inside of her thighs from Noah's jaw rasping against her there. A slight turn showed her Lyda's punishment had left faint marks. She ran her fingers over them, wondering at the erotic tingle she felt.

Beyond that, she had a dozen little sensual pains to remind her that, at every turn last night, it had been one or both of them, touching her, holding her. Her hip joints were sore from Lyda being between her legs.

No surprise then, her cautious heart and soul feeling a little tentative about it all. But this was likely no more than an extraordinary one-night stand. Their world wasn't her world. She had no complaints, though. They'd given her a bucket-list kind of night. She'd never known such a thing was on her bucket list, but it was on there now. Box checked. No need to repeat.

Unless she really, really wanted it to be repeated. Which would be problematic. When Noah had waltzed her along the dance floor to help her relax, her heart had tilted at his romantic gesture, but she couldn't block how he'd gone so still behind her, watching the man be whipped. Noah slept in a cage for Lyda. Yes, he'd submitted to Gen's touch, to her request to masturbate for her...but that was nowhere near the same. He needed more extreme levels she already knew she didn't have. And then there was Lyda. What she needed, demanded, expected, wasn't even in the realm of Gen's reality.

So that was that. This was just a pleasant adventure with two fascinating people. *Stop making so much of it.*

She stepped into the shower, intending to do a fast soap and rinse, but the high-pressure spray was as good as a massage, easing rediscovered muscles. She washed herself thoroughly, smelling the reminder of her climaxes as she washed between her legs. Had Lyda done that as well? And what about Noah? She imagined him washing the jetted semen off his chest and stomach, cupping his balls, cleaning his shaft and the corona, thumbing soap into his slit.

When she left the shower, she realized why the nursery-logo T-shirt had been left. Knotting it over her dress gave her a more casual look. She noticed a pair of canvas sneakers on the floor, white ankle socks draped over them, a replacement for her heels, which were aligned next to them.

The sneakers were clean but not brand new. It was unsettling, to be with someone so observant she'd noticed Gen and she were the same shoe size. She was glad Lyda hadn't left her jeans, because she was sure she couldn't wear whatever size Lyda wore on her perfect ass. Gen slipped the clean thong beneath the skirt, mind skittering over Lyda washing her saturated underwear.

The nursery shirt was faded, comfortable and had Lyda's clean fragrance. Like all women, Gen had worn a male lover's shirt, wanting his smell surrounding her. She'd never thought of having the same urge with a female lover, but she'd wrapped Lyda's robe around herself for more than just modesty. Now that she was wearing her shirt, she hoped Lyda wouldn't want it back. It could be her souvenir, like I-went-to-the-Grand-Canyon.

I-had-a-mind-blowing-BDSM-threesome.

Shaking her head at herself, she exited the bathroom carrying her heels, the bra stuffed into one of them. Too bad she didn't know how to hotwire a car, but that would be the height of cowardice. Morning-afters could be so awkward, though. She was reluctant to destroy the pleasurable memories of it.

Despite her trepidation, she was all too aware she hadn't donned the bra, something she was full-breasted enough to normally do as a matter of practicality. She couldn't deny knowing that she'd see Lyda or Noah before she got into her car had probably contributed to the decision. She was going to avoid overthinking it. Or at least try.

The living room throw rug was gone. Lyda had probably tossed it into the wash as well, because there would certainly be fluids upon it, given Noah hadn't been wearing a condom and Gen...well, Gen tended to make a similar mess. She'd done enough internet research to know that women could learn to have such a response, but those that did it spontaneously, regularly, weren't as common. She'd considered it on par with chronic adult acne. Until last night.

That's my good girl. She remembered Lyda passing her hand over the wet spot, the smoldering look that said it made Lyda hot.

If she didn't think some mundane thoughts, this was going to be more awkward than she already anticipated it being. She pushed that aside to take in the details of the living room and kitchen she'd missed last night. Plant clippings in interesting vases were scattered through the house. Lyda's furniture choices straddled the line between good design and comfort. Everything spoke of a successful woman who knew her likes and dislikes and rarely doubted herself. Gen stopped at the mantle. She saw a few colorful prints like what was in the bathroom and a small abstract sculpture or two. Again, no personal photographs. She hadn't seen any in her brief glimpse of Lyda's home office.

She was private, a woman who didn't give away much about herself. The impressions given were those intended to be conveyed. Like a portfolio.

But... Gen fingered the shirt, lifted some of the loose fabric to smell it again. This was personal. It sent a more intimate message. Or it could simply be what Lyda had available to loan her and Gen was being an infatuated idiot.

Then there was the puzzle of Noah. Why had Lyda called him a lost soul? Gen had seen sadness in the Mistress's eyes when she said it, overlaid by a fierce protectiveness. If Gen hadn't been paying close attention to Lyda's face, she would have missed both, because the expression was gone in a flash.

Where was Noah this morning? She missed them in different ways, but with an equal measure of longing, such that she felt it in her vitals. In her wildest dreams, she'd never imagined she'd be caught up in a relationship so hard to classify or predict.

Careful, Gen. This isn't a relationship. Call it infatuation or a crush, it was still so outside her milieu it wasn't out of line to compare it to getting starry-eyed over celebrities. Noah and Lyda might as well be Orlando Bloom and... As she moved into the kitchen, she couldn't come up with a starlet comparable to Lyda.

The appetizing odors leading her to the kitchen reminded her breakfast was in the oven. A place setting—bright-red and brown pottery plate, shiny utensils arranged on a neat cloth napkin—waited at the table. The spotless juice glass picked up the sunlight from the picture window. Cracking the oven door, she found it on low heat, keeping the pancakes, eggs and sausage warm. Though she was normally a tea and toast person, it smelled heavenly. She transferred the food to the plate then opened the fridge to find a cup of juice and cut fresh fruit lined up at eye level with a note next to them. *For Gen.*

Last night, she'd been treated like a submissive, here to serve a Mistress. Yet she'd also been pleasured to the point of brain overload, and this morning, she was being cared for like an honored guest. It was a lot to think about.

As she ate at least half of the food, she gazed out the big window and wondered if Marguerite and Lyda consulted on gardening tips, because the view reminded her of Marguerite's private side garden at the tea shop. A perfect meshing of plants flowed together around conversation points, like a spiral walkway, a fountain, a meditation bench. A pair of concrete rabbits sat next to the bench, one on his hindquarters while the other burrowed among a lavender-colored sprinkle of flowers. Marguerite might have bought some of her plants from Lyda, though Gen didn't know how long they'd known one another. She didn't know much about their relationship at all, which made her wonder how much Marguerite could be coaxed to tell her.

No one coaxed Marguerite to do anything. You asked and waited for her decision. She and Lyda had that in common as well, but Gen had noted an intriguing softer side to Lyda, like the expression in her eyes when Noah had gripped her wrist. She'd issued that gentle reproof, *Behave*, but it had been laced with fondness.

Was Lyda in love with Noah? How would being in love look on Lyda?

She wrapped up the rest of her breakfast and found a bag in a stash of recycled grocery bags to tuck it away, along with heels and bra. She'd eat the remainder at lunch. Gen washed her plate and utensils, put them in the dish drainer. As she straightened, she realized there was no evidence of Noah's presence here. At Gen's house, he'd been very respectful of her space, making his bed in the morning, leaving the room exactly as he'd found it. Was that part of his submission?

Marguerite had said Noah didn't really have belongings, but was there a place here he might leave a book or two, his few clothes draped on a chair? Pocket change on the dresser. Or, given that he gave Lyda his earnings, maybe not that.

She wouldn't know unless she talked to Lyda. Gen sighed. Maybe she *could* figure out how to hotwire a car.

On that dubious thought, she left the house. Two cats, a calico female and a fluffy black male, curled up in the sunlight warming the concrete stepping stones. They gave her a lazy look, not the least concerned by a stranger possibly stepping on them. It suggested they were used to comings and goings on the property. By customers, she hoped.

In the tidy box she'd put this incredible week, she'd imagine she'd been as special an event to Lyda and Noah as they had been to her. But she was mature enough to know that would be part of the fantasy.

Bending down, she petted both felines. Maybe she'd move the cat adoption up on her timetable. It would be fun to have a cat playing with the scraps of paper in her craft room, falling asleep on the table, keeping her company.

The cats were affectionate, well-fed, healthy. Very likely spayed and neutered, otherwise the female would show signs of repeated pregnancy. Good. Nothing could disrupt her fantasy as quickly as finding Lyda was an indifferent or irresponsible pet parent. She thought about the kind of control Lyda held over the people around her and imagined all that going down the drain when it came to her cats. Did they jump up on her desk, shred paper despite her chastising? Make her laugh as they raced around the house, ignoring stern reproofs about wild behavior? She'd like to see that.

The woman was so self contained. How much could Gen invest in someone she knew so little about? How much of herself would she risk? She'd risked a lot last night.

At this rate, she'd be confronting Lyda for her car keys three days from now. Bidding the cats a reluctant farewell, she followed the gravel drive around the back of the house, back to the nursery. Since it was Sunday, the business was closed, no chance of customers or employees providing a buffer. Gen looked into the open greenhouses. Automatic misters were watering an array of plants, washing humid greenhouse air over her skin. Maybe that was why Lyda's skin was so lovely.

She located Lyda behind the third greenhouse, in front of a field of young saplings. She was wrapping the root balls of a dozen young crepe myrtle trees in burlap. They were probably being transported to new homes tomorrow.

As Gen moved toward her, Lyda's head lifted. In that one sweeping glance, Gen felt everything that had happened last night anew, including those several screaming orgasms. Lyda's gaze covered the way her T-shirt clung to Gen's body, then rose to her face, as if evaluating everything about her state of mind before one word was spoken.

When Gen's attention slid to the right, finding it hard to meet that stare, she discovered Noah taking a nap on a lush square of grass about thirty feet away. He wore jeans and a nursery T-shirt, stretched attractively over his shoulders and chest. He slept on his side, folded arm pillowing his head.

"Midmorning break?" Gen asked low, nodding toward him.

Lyda glanced his way. "He's already put in a good four hours this morning, digging up this stock. As well as making you breakfast and cleaning your clothes. He sleeps better in the daylight, so I make him take a nap midmorning. Else he gets cranky in the afternoon and I have to spank him."

Despite the humor—she assumed it was humor—Gen felt a pang of horror. "He didn't need to do all that. I'm sorry. You should have woken me."

"You're not my employee. Or my committed sub. He is. If I'd wanted you awake, Gen, I would have woken you."

Gen had plenty of bland, polite things to say, but Lyda's directness drove everything away but the thing uppermost in her mind. "I have no clue how to process what happened last night."

Lyda dropped to her haunches, wiped her brow. She had her hair pulled in a tail through the back of the bill cap. The brim shadowed her eyes, enhancing the dark lashes. "How do you want to process it, Gen? An adventure, a one-time event?"

As Gen shifted, Lyda nodded. "It's fine to rationalize it that way, if that's all you want. It's more comfortable that way, to bring closure to it. Right?"

"Yes. I guess. I mean, do you..." Gen trailed off. "It was an amazing night. Very different from what I'm used to. Thank you."

Could she sound more stiff and stupid? Maybe if she broke into song and tried a cartwheel.

"You were a pleasure to command. You should let that side of yourself rise to the top more often."

"I don't know if I'm that way, really. Like you said, I guess all of us have some of it in us, and with the right triggers... Someone like you would bring it out of a person, no matter how dormant."

As Gen spoke, Lyda pulled off a work glove. She gripped Gen's leg above the knee, beneath the hem of the short skirt. "Why are you standing above me, Gen?"

Her hand was slightly damp from the perspiration of her efforts. Gen's knee trembled under that touch. But it wasn't like last night. There was too much reality around them. She backed away a couple steps. Lyda put the glove back on, but gave Gen a frank look.

"Do you want more, Gen? Because you can have more. I'm willing to explore that."

Explore her submission? A relationship? "I don't know. I need to go home and think about it."

"A cautious approach isn't a bad idea. Just don't paralyze yourself with it. If this is something you want, you say how much or how little. You're in control of your own participation."

Again that emphasis on choice. But Gen hadn't expected Lyda to be willing to choose more time with *her*. "What do you want...I mean, do you..."

Do you really like me? It sounded so juvenile to ask it that way. But she hadn't anticipated falling short on a mature way to voice her innermost feelings about this. Maybe she could come at it from a new angle.

"You said last night I could try it from different sides. How I was with Noah that weekend…what if I wanted to be more…assertive with that?"

"Like try on the Domme hat? Where you exercise full control?" Lyda's expression was neutral, but Gen wondered if she was laughing at her. The rabbit wanting to be a wolf. She lifted her chin.

"Maybe."

"Hmm." Lyda pursed her lips. "We'll be back at The Zone Wednesday night. Can you join us? If you want to use me as a mentor, I'll walk you through some of the basics. Or I can introduce you to a club Domme, if you want a more neutral party."

Just like that. As if it wasn't a momentous decision, an explorer declaring her brave intent to seek new lands. "Would I be practicing on him?" Gen glanced at Noah.

"I'm sure he'd be happy to help you in that regard, with my permission, which I would certainly grant. But we'll see what you think once you're there. There are always more subs than Doms. You needn't limit your experience."

Gen pressed her lips together. "Are you hoping I'll fall on my face and prove that I'm really a submissive, because that's what you want me to be?"

Lyda's eyes frosted. "That's rude, Gen."

"Is it true, though?" She wasn't overwhelmed by her hormones now. She wasn't begging for punishment with her ass in the air or writhing in ecstasy beneath Lyda. What had happened last night, that didn't completely define her, as it seemed to define Noah. She needed to make that clear. Lyda wasn't Gen's Mistress. She had the right to be rude if she thought she was being patronized.

When Lyda said nothing, just continued to regard her, Gen thanked God for her interactions with Marguerite. As intimidating as Lyda's gaze was, a damn Supreme Court judge couldn't top Marguerite's pale-blue stare. Lyda's intimidation factor was close, though, especially since Gen had never made herself vulnerable to Marguerite as a lover. She literally dug the heels of the sneakers into the earth to hold fast.

"What is it you're really seeking here, Gen?" Lyda asked. "I don't think you're trying to pick a fight, but you want something that's causing you to provoke one."

"I know nothing about you," Gen pointed out. "If last night *was* just a carnival ride, then that's fine. I don't need to know anything more about you than the guy who pushes the lever of the Ferris wheel. And if that's it, then that's it. I go home, and I see you and Noah now and then when your paths cross Marguerite's, and I remember last night with this fond sort of disbelief. Maybe it was how little I knew about you that made last night possible, the intimacy-of-strangers kind of thing."

As Lyda remained silent, bottled emotions surged forth, surprising Gen with their strength. "I don't know what I want, Lyda," she blurted. "Any relationship scares me, because the plain truth is I make bad choices when it comes to all that. Maybe you'll think I'm silly and unsophisticated, but it's also all too intense, too emotional, for me to treat it like a carnival ride. If you tell me you want it to be more than that, maybe I'll find the courage to come back for another ride. But if the ride is all you're going to give me of yourself, I probably can't do it. There's a way about you...I could turn into some kind of puppy, craving every scrap you throw my way. I have enough self-respect to make the choice to stay away. I can sew up any holes you put in me last night and pretend they never happened."

She hadn't meant to go off like that. But every word was the God's honest truth. It had been a really long time since she'd made herself as vulnerable as she'd made herself last night. Lyda's charisma and personality tempted Gen to crack herself open like an egg and let it all spill out before her. She couldn't risk a deeper relationship on such unequal footing.

Lyda still hadn't said anything. Gen swallowed. Okay, ask for the car key, call it done. God, she was one of those crazy people who changed their social media status after one date. Lyda would be glad to be rid of her. She'd order Noah to avoid Gen like a plague.

"I'm not a soft woman, Gen. I don't do nurturing, unless ordering a man to take a nap counts."

Lyda's expression softened then, enough to ease the fist around Gen's chest a little. She even gave her a smile, helping Gen manage a tentative one in return. "I don't really know why. Over the years, I've found out *why* isn't always that important. But I'll give you the answer you're seeking. Yes. I'm interested in exploring more with you."

"All right." Gen tried to steady her heart rate. She wanted to match Lyda's apparent calm now. "Can I ask you a couple questions about yourself? Is that okay?"

"We'll see." Lyda shifted her squatting position so she had one knee bent and her denim-clad butt braced on the heel of her work shoe, her forearm propped on the bent knee. Gen's thigh muscles would have been screaming by now. "Go for it."

"Do you have family in the area?"

"No. I pushed them away in college, and never really found my way back. I have four siblings who've provided grandchildren. I'm not missed."

She didn't see any regrets in Lyda's face, but the woman could compete with a sphinx. "You don't have any pictures of them."

"I do. In photo albums, and on my computer. I entertain in my home. I don't care to share parts of myself I don't wish to discuss."

"Entertain...as in like last night?"

Lyda's expression flickered. "It's a little early for you to become possessive, Gen. Though I think I like that you're feeling it."

Gen flushed. The interested glitter in Lyda's eyes only deepened it. She shifted to the sleeping Noah, a safer topic. "You called him a lost soul. Can you explain?"

"Noah is too difficult to explain with words. You'll understand if you spend more time with him."

Similar to what Chloe and M had implied. Interesting. "Will he break my heart if I care too much about him?"

The woman gave her a sharp glance. It was a pretty deep question, but it seemed the best way to target the sadness she'd seen in Lyda's gaze last night.

"The heart always gets broken when it cares. That's part of caring. And he breaks the heart of anyone who does. It doesn't make him any less appealing. In some ways, it's part of what makes him so irresistible." Lyda took both her gloves off, reached out a hand. "Come down here."

It was an unmistakable order, made even clearer when Gen hesitated. "Now, Gen."

She closed those few steps between them, sank down in the cushion of dirt Lyda's efforts with the trees had wrought. Lyda took her hand, her fingers wrapping around Gen's as she knelt. Gen laid a tentative hand on Lyda's bent knee and wasn't discouraged from keeping it there. She smelled coconut and almond butter sunblock. "Do you want a kiss, Gen?" Lyda asked.

"Yes." Gen cleared her throat. "Do you?"

"Yes. A soft, pretty girl kiss, your mouth trembling because you're not certain where this is going or how much of yourself you'll risk."

As Lyda regarded her steadily, Gen realized she was inviting her to initiate. She eased forward, those mesmerizing eyes and sensual lips beckoning. Putting a hand on Lyda's arm, she followed it up to her shoulder, to her neck, shyly teasing the ponytail over Lyda's shoulder. She caressed her face, neck. The line of shoulder again. Lyda stayed still, watching her, which increased the charge. At length, Gen leaned in, pressed her lips against Lyda's.

The woman didn't respond immediately, allowing Gen to explore and coax, the tip of her tongue tracing the seam. She put her other hand on Lyda's opposite shoulder to steady herself. She played with Lyda's lips, seduced, sent yearning, unspoken messages she herself couldn't yet decipher.

When Lyda at last cupped the back of her head and took over, Gen sighed into her mouth, her lips parting. Lyda's tongue tangled with hers, her arm circling Gen's waist, pulling her between her thighs. Gen caught the belt loops of her jeans, fingers sliding along the small of Lyda's back, the delicate bones of her spine. Lyda's thighs trapped her on either side as the woman delved deep in her mouth, her hand dropping to grip Gen's ass, the bare cheek exposed by the thong beneath the skirt. As Lyda tightened her fingers enough Gen felt those flogger marks, she let out another needy breath.

Lyda raised her head. Gen was practically reclined in her arms, her knees folded beneath her. She hadn't appreciated a woman's strength before. It was different from Noah's, more sculpted and soft-skinned, but Lyda had it in good measure.

"Drop your head back. We have an audience."

Gen complied so she saw Noah from an upside-down position. He had his chin propped on a hand and was studying them with avid appreciation.

"Men are so simple," Gen said, a little shakily.

When he grinned, Lyda snorted. "Isn't that the truth?" She eased Gen back up to a sitting position. "Come to the club on Wednesday. We'll see how you do as a Domme. For now, go home. And don't think too much. It gets in the way."

"Of what you want?" Gen said, feeling a little spirited. Lyda's eyes sparked, her lips tugging.

"Of what we both want," she replied.

Chapter Seven

A straight dismissal. Lyda's brief answer to a couple questions hadn't given her much in terms of reassurance, but that kiss...well, that had given her something. Enough to keep her on this crazy course. And give her an overwhelming case of hormones.

That day when Gen came home, she considered fishing the vibrator from her sock drawer to deal with it, but in the end she held off, though she wasn't sure why. She told herself she'd do it before Wednesday, indulge a few dozen outrageous extension fantasies about Lyda and Noah so she didn't go to the club a mass of nerves. Yeah, like that would help.

Marguerite gave her a speculative look on Monday, but she didn't say anything. Fellow club members could have told M how things had gone, since it had all happened on the public floor, but the idea of M checking on Gen didn't bug her. She'd realized a long time ago Marguerite had a hawklike protectiveness of her two employees. M never pried or asked questions unless she had a specific concern, which made that trait unobtrusive most times.

Chloe was a different matter, but she wasn't there Monday, and Gen was off on Tuesday. She had time to get in the right mindset to talk to the younger girl about her club experience in a casual, fun way, rather than as a potentially life-altering experience.

She told herself she was being overly dramatic, but when she flipped through magazines in her craft room Monday night, looking for collage material, she realized she was seeking their features. Noah's mouth. Lyda's eyes. She wasn't trying to match the physical elements. It was the way Lyda looked at Gen, at Noah, that sense of expectation, control, confidence. The set of Noah's mouth, aroused, amused...or when he was in that quiet place in his head.

Closing her eyes, Gen remembered Lyda's hand closing on her nape, bringing her between Lyda's legs to taste her flesh. Directing her how to pleasure her Mistress. There was no tentative wait-and-see to Lyda. Not like Gen had been with her husbands, following their lead so as not to undermine their traditional role in the bedroom.

Now she wondered if it had really been that, something derived from the low expectations of her upbringing, or an innate personality trait. She liked the feeling of someone she could trust taking charge, though her husbands had fallen so short in the trust department, she'd turned her desire for that into a character flaw. Lyda made her look at it differently. The way she treated Noah and Gen suggested Lyda considered their submission a gift, one she took seriously. At no time during their extraordinary evening together had Lyda betrayed Gen's trust, manipulated her feelings or tried to make her feel inadequate. Anything like that had come from Gen's own insecurities — she knew enough about herself to be honest on that score.

Then there was Noah. She'd been so wary of men for so long, expecting them to be disappointments. He'd come into her world sideways. She'd been told he was a submissive male, and then been thrilled by the mix of what that meant for Noah. His sudden passion when she'd desired it, how strong he could be when she needed nurturing. His odd vulnerability, sleeping on the patch of grass near Lyda, or his chagrin for upsetting Gen, that first night in her kitchen.

She could be romanticizing all of this, based on one single night, but there was no denying the truth. When Lyda had asked "Do you want more?" Gen knew the answer was a resounding yes.

She moved to the computer. Searching for male erotic images, she weeded out the crass porn sites and focused on the more artistic venues. She studied long, lean male bodies with smooth muscles, but Noah's eyes were the challenge. She wasn't sure she'd ever met a male with eyes like his. So many different things lay in those eyes, a huge mystery waiting to be unlocked.

In erotic female images, she discovered Lyda in the build of female athletes, though fortunately not one so absent of body fat she had the hard look of a man. Lyda was all female with her full breasts, the nipples high and tight, the nice curves at hip and ass.

She imagined Lyda's lips, her cheekbones. The cascade of her hair framing her face and throat, the shining waves on her bare shoulders. Finally she found the right picture. It was a grayscale photo of a naked woman sitting in shadow, her back to the camera. Only the graceful lines of hip and back were visible, along with her vulnerable nape, because her hair was pulled forward. Gen printed the picture, cut around the outline with her razor and put it against a lavender paper.

Using a fine marker, she wrote *Lyda* across the woman's back in calligraphy script, the tail curving beneath her buttocks. She wrote the name around the form as well in tiny script, moving outward from there in a spiral. Pulling from her magazines, she pasted other words into the open spaces, creating a garden of words. Lyda's name became the blooms and the words were the green background, or different, smaller blossoms, accentuating and defining the bigger flowers.

Strength, beauty, uncertainty, challenge, control, trust...

When she turned back to the computer, she indulged a darker urge. She clicked on an image of a woman in the stereotypical dominatrix gear she'd first imagined Lyda wearing. Tight, shiny garb, thigh-high boots, whip in her hand. This model had a cruel expression, slick red lips. Gen shifted her gaze back to the naked woman, sitting unafraid in darkness, the line of her back straight, self-contained in her solitude. Beautiful. The essence of Lyda was there, not on her computer screen.

It didn't mean she couldn't wield a whip if she so chose. Gen replayed the sting when Lyda had struck her. What astounded her was how she'd taken it without protest. She wasn't ready to say she'd embraced it, but she'd definitely opened herself to the experience.

Her cell phone buzzed, making her jump. The disruption jarred her back to a less pleasant reality, because phone calls often meant collection agencies still trying to collect on unsecured loans from her ex-husband. If Marguerite hadn't helped cosign on the house, Gen never would have acquired loan approval. He'd destroyed her credit rating that badly. Seeing the nursery number, however, she relaxed. She wondered which voice she'd hear at the end of the line, knowing she'd be thrilled by either one.

"Hello?"

"Hey, Gen. It's Noah."

"I didn't know you knew how to use a phone. Chloe says you're a Fae spirit, unable to touch technology. Something like that."

His chuckle sent a ripple of pleasure from her tailbone up through her vitals. Yes, she had it bad. "That girl is a troublemaker," he said. "Do you have Tuesday off?"

"Depends. Why are you asking?"

He sighed. "I'm surrounded by suspicious females."

"Or smart, depending on how you look at it."

"True. Want to go sailing with me? It's supposed to be a great day for it."

She blinked. "Um...yeah. Remember, I don't really know much about it."

"No worries. Just bring lots of sunblock, a willingness to learn and a swimsuit. Preferably something that doesn't cover a lot. It helps with the wind shear."

"And you wonder why females are suspicious." She laughed. "Should I bring snacks?"

"I'm never averse to snacks. I have a small storage area up front that holds the life jackets, so we can stow them there. I'll have bottled water."

So this would be just her and him, not Lyda. "Did Lyda ask you to set this up?"

"She gave me permission to set it up, but the idea was mine. Is that okay?" His tone was neutral, so she couldn't tell if she'd offended him or not.

"I'm sorry, Noah. I'm not sure how this works. I wasn't trying to be snarky."

"I know that." His tone warmed instantly, reassuring her. "See you in the morning. About eight, at the marina?"

"I'll see you then."

*****

When she parked at the marina and pulled the key from the engine, she waited a couple minutes for the motor to stop rattling and cut off. Her car was doing that more frequently of late. She'd learned to ignore people's looks when it did, or crack a joke like, "he likes to complain when I leave him alone". She didn't care she had an old car. It was all hers, and it took care of her.

On the way over, she'd been enjoying the sexy tone of Kylie Minogue's version of "Can't Get You Out of My Head", which was the mood she hoped to sustain today. Seeing Noah first thing helped with that. Maybe too much, since she suppressed the urge to do a few cartwheels when she found him.

He was watching for her, sitting on top of one of the pilings that followed the marina dock. He wore a pair of swim trunks, boat shoes and nothing else. Two young women were walking past him, their gaze lingering, because it was impossible for any straight woman not to indulge in a look. His hair was tied back in a thick tail, but it draped over his tanned right shoulder.

The two girls had the bodies for their skimpy bikinis and short shorts, but Noah's gaze never left Gen's as she headed in his direction. She thought one of them made a passing flirtatious comment, but a polite, faint smile was his only response.

She shouldered her tote as he slid off the piling, walked toward her with a loose-hipped stride. She was glad she'd dared to wear her two-piece. It wasn't hugely sexy, but the top did show off her breasts well without being in constant danger of falling off. She'd worn a pair of cut-off shorts over the bottoms. She might take them off later. Maybe. It was silly to be self-conscious, since Noah had seen her naked, but somehow the focus of all that had been Lyda's reaction. This felt different, just the two of them, and he looked so good. Wouldn't it be nice to be like a guy, not measuring his looks against her own, just enjoying a full ogle of his appearance?

"Hi gorgeous," he said, making her decide right off it was going to be a nice day. He gave her car a look as it subsided. "I can fix that for you. It's just an ignition timing issue."

"Really? I might take you up on that. If you let me pay for it, of course." She pushed on before he could shrug that off, as she knew he would. "Tyler keeps threatening to buy me a new car. I'm always deathly afraid I'm going to show up for work one morning and he'll have done it. I told Marguerite I'd quit if they did something like that."

"You don't want Tyler to be your sugar daddy? In an entirely platonic, Marguerite-maybe-wouldn't-cut-up-my-body-for-shark-bait way?"

His eyes danced and she pushed at him. He caught her hand, held it against his chest, his fingers sliding over her palm and knuckles. "I'm glad you came," he said.

She took one of those unsteady breaths his touch seemed to cause, and curled her fingers to stroke the lightly furred flesh beneath them. "Me too. Are you going to teach me enough to keep me from drowning?"

"Absolutely. If you offer me food. Or sexual favors. I accept either as payment."

"Guys are so easy."

"I thought we already discussed that." He pointed down to the bulkhead, where a two-man sailing craft waited, the mast raised and sails furled, ready to go. "If you want to hit a restroom before we head off, there's one in the marina office."

"Okay."

A few minutes later, she was ready. He'd stowed her tote, and offered her a hand onto the boat. He was sitting next to it on the floating dock, his feet holding the craft, keeping it steady as she stepped into it and sat down where he directed her.

"In the beginning, I'll sail her, and talk you through the basics. Then you can start helping out. By the end of the day, you'll be able to single hand her."

"So you can sit back and do nothing."

"Except watch you."

Then he was in the boat with her, casting off. He did it all so smoothly, she didn't have a chance to feel any trepidation, though she might have if she'd realized how small their boat was and how big the channel was. But he projected such calm, not at all concerned as he navigated the motorless boat among the power boat traffic. She sucked in a breath when the boat tipped.

"Very normal," he assured her. "It's going to heel when the wind catches it. That's part of what makes it go, and the closer you can hold it to the wind, the faster we go. The trick is not letting the wind overpower it and capsize us."

"Which is not going to happen."

"No." He promised. "Let's do a tack. Move with me. One, two...now."

He did that with her a few times, until she could do it with reasonable ease, moving from side to side of the boat with him as needed. Once she fell into the rhythm, she could enjoy looking at their surroundings, which included him. Leaning out over the water, his ab muscles tight, thighs taut, bare feet braced against the opposite edge of the boat. Holding onto the boat with her other hand, she slid her fingers over those abdominal muscles, wanting to feel.

He glanced her way, but he didn't stop her. She caressed those shifting muscles, enthralled with them. Enthralled with him. Still, she wasn't sure what was allowed, so she contained herself, withdrew her hand.

He'd made her don a lifejacket, but he wasn't wearing his. While she appreciated the access that provided her questing hand, as well as his effort to make her feel more secure, she wondered if that was more of what Lyda had implied. So protective of others, but not of himself...

She was glad he'd warned her about the sunblock, because the reflection of the sun on the water which felt so good would nevertheless fry tender skin. He was so evenly tan, she expected he spent a lot of time out here with his students, but he had the faint coconut aroma of sunblock as well.

A boat went by with a black Labrador on the bow. The dog was wearing a yellow life jacket and wagging his tail. With his majestic profile, he looked like a figurehead. The lolling tongue and dancing eyes made it clear he was ready to fling himself in the water the moment his master gave the go-ahead. Noah pointed out a set of kayakers paddling closer to the shore, one of whom had a dachshund sitting on his lap. The little dog was also wearing a lifejacket.

When she asked, teasing, how Lyda's cats would react to boating, Noah gave her a slow smile. "It depends. Farclaws will lie in the birdbath on hot days. Sleep there, even. I think it just has to be their idea. They're a lot like their mistress in that regard."

After about an hour of sailing, he maneuvered them into a quiet cove and loosened the lines, letting the sails flap and slowing them to a drifting halt. "Okay, let me show you the basics of handling her yourself. When you're comfortable, we can go back out again where you can really put her through her paces. Then we can park and have some lunch. This is a nice secluded place to relax and take an afternoon nap."

"Okay." It occurred to her, the things that could happen during such a siesta, but there was no innuendo to the friendly suggestion. This time there'd been no instructions, no indication that Lyda was "giving" him to her. Caressing his abdominals was one thing, but more than that? She could ask him, of course, but felt shy about it. Maybe because if Lyda had said no, it would feel like rejection.

Noah touched her collarbone, bringing her attention back to him. "Take off the lifejacket. You need to put on some more sunblock, because you're turning red in a couple places. Lyda *and* Marguerite will have my ass if I let you get burned."

She unclipped the jacket as he retrieved the tube from stowage. When he proffered it, she met his gaze. "Will you put it on me?"

"Sure." He gave her that look that made her stomach do a somersault like a happy squirrel. "Hold your hair off your neck."

She turned her back to him. As those capable hands started smearing the block on her skin, a deep sigh welled up. Part pleasure, part other. "I don't know what's allowed, Noah."

He paused. "What do you want to be allowed?"

She looked at glittering water and green shoreline. A heron fished in the shallows of the cove. "I want to do whatever I feel like doing with you. But I don't want to do anything to offend Lyda. Or take advantage of how you are."

"And how am I?" His teasing tone reassured her. Then he slipped the back strap of her bikini top. When she caught the front, he tapped her gently between the shoulder blades. "There's no one here but us. A lot of women get burned at the edges of their swimsuit because they put the block on while they're wearing it and they don't want to get the swimsuit messy. You can do the front part if you like, or I can do it."

She shook her head. Spoke with a catch in her voice. "I want you to do it."

His breath was on the back of her neck. Without saying anything further, he released the neck strap as well. Reaching under her arm, he slid his fingers beneath her grip to give the top a gentle tug, telling her he wanted her to let it go. She did. It left her sitting in her shorts and bottoms only. She heard him squirt more of the sunblock into his hands. The faint quiver of the boat suggested he was rubbing his hands together, making it less cold. She was still holding her hair up on her neck, and now she added the other hand, moving both arms out of his way.

He slid up behind her, adjusting so one leg was aligned with her hip, the other angled so his foot dangled off the boat, though his thigh pressed against her, keeping her between his legs. When he leaned forward, his bare chest brushed her back, making her aware of the faint stickiness where the sunblock was drying.

As his hands closed over her bare breasts, she drew in a breath. They rose in his hands like bread dough responding to heat. Chloe, their passionate baker, would laugh at that comparison. Gen looked down at his brown hands against her pale flesh. He rubbed the sunblock into the area the edge of her swimsuit would follow. The deliberate omission of the area closest to her nipples made them tighten, beg for touch.

"You didn't answer my question, about 'how I am'," he murmured against her throat. She laid her head back against his shoulder, turned her face so her nose brushed his jaw. He was gazing down, eyes intent on his task, on her breasts.

"I'm still learning everything a male submissive is, and Chloe keeps insisting you're all different. My exposure has been to Brendan. Doing things Marguerite or Chloe ask him to do brings him pleasure, the service. But I think there's a tendency for a woman to think it means…that she can treat you like an unpaid prostitute."

His hands stilled. "I know that's not what you are," she added quickly. "But I would be really, *really* upset if you let me do that anyway, simply because you knew I was too ignorant or driven by my hormones to know better."

She was very cognizant of how he cradled her breasts, simply holding them, but she forced herself to focus on the importance of the topic. "Your feelings are important to me, and I can't get a grasp on them. Or Lyda's, for that matter, in a lot of things. It's hard to get a handle on anyone when you've just met them, let alone two people who are part of something I really know so little about."

"You know everything you need to know. In your head and heart. In your body." He put his mouth to her neck, shifting his grip so her nipples pushed into his palms. The contact made her moan, a soft sigh.

"Lyda thinks you're good for me, Gen," he said. "And I like being with you. All you have to do is follow your own needs and desires. You don't have to think about it more than that, because I know you have a good heart. I'm not worried about what you'll do to me, only about what you'll allow yourself."

Nothing in life was ever that simple. Yet when he resumed massaging the cream around her breasts, she couldn't think of anything else to say. Not when he occupied himself with kissing her neck, slow, sucking kisses that awoke erogenous zones all the way to her curling feet. Her backside pressed into the fiberglass in tiny, coital movements.

"If we don't start sailing, there's going to be a lot of bare places on me where you'll need to apply sunscreen," she muttered.

"You say that like it's a problem."

She chuckled and wiggled to put some space between them, despite the incredible difficulty of finding the willpower. She retrieved her swimsuit top and gave him a narrow glance. "I was promised sailing lessons."

He smiled. He also helped her put the swimsuit top back on, fastening the back and the neck piece, smoothing his hands briefly over her breasts, solemnly informing her it was to ensure everything was covered properly.

When he finally began her sailing lesson, she realized he never really had answered her question, unless deflecting it back on herself was an answer. The man was like the sunlight glittering off the water. He wasn't the water or the sun, but some sparkling reaction between the two, part illusion, part reality.

He shifted gears well, though. After about forty five minutes, thanks to his excellent teaching skills, she could handle the mainsail lines while he handled the jib of the small craft. She had them tacking well together, leading them in the duck beneath the boom. He'd been right about the privacy of the cove. They were undisturbed.

"Only shallow craft can get through here," he explained. "With it being off the main channel, a good distance from the marina, only your most experienced sailors navigate to it. Plus it's a weekday. Ready to try the channel again?" he asked.

"I'm not ready to solo yet."

"We'll do it together until you tell me you want to solo. And I'll be right next to you when you finally do that. We're going to practice capsizing as well. In here," he added at her alarmed look.

They were at rest again and he'd turned fully toward her, one leg bent, the other doused in the water up to his knee. "Aren't we supposed to avoid doing that?"

"Yes. But if it happens, you need to know how to right the boat. Say if I was hit on the head, or whoever you were sailing with was less experienced, you should be prepared. But you should never sail alone."

"You do."

He shrugged. "I've been doing this a long time. I really don't ever want you to sail alone, okay?"

"Okay." She responded to the determined look in his eye, but she couldn't help asking. "Noah, do you care what happens to you?"

For the first time since they'd met, she saw a shutter close fully behind his eyes. He lifted her hand, brushed his lips over it. "I serve my Mistress's will. I know it's important that I care for her. And you."

She didn't know how to push it further than that without ruining their day. As Lyda had warned her, he could be stubborn. Proving it, he didn't let her pursue it, instead getting them back to the sailing.

The wind had built and the tide had turned. Going out into the stronger wind and current of the channel, she discovered the exhilarating speed of a small craft, especially in the company of an incredibly experienced sailor like Noah. They made a good team, her following his direction to the letter about when to let off or draw in, shift weight. At one point they were both stretched out at a forty-five degree angle, the boat heeling enough to have them skimming over the water like a bird. She tipped her head back, her hair whipping over her shoulders, and laughed at the feeling of it. His eyes shone with the same feeling, making everything just perfect. A perfect moment, no matter what came before or after. She'd learned to treasure those rare gifts.

She loved watching his mix of concentration on the sailboat and their surroundings, his appreciation of all of it. Another cliché discarded, the idea that a submissive male avoided situations where he was completely in charge. He handled the sailboat and her direction as crew with an impressive mastery she found arousing, mixed as it was with those conflicting signals in his personality. But she loved running Tea Leaves, and yet she'd submitted so willingly to Lyda, hadn't she? What had Lyda said? *A strong sub needs and deserves to be able to surrender...*

When they finally sailed back in the cove, she was wired with the pleasure and excitement of the day, but ravenous. They disembarked on the strip of beach, setting up an impromptu picnic under the canopy of trees hanging over the bank. She'd made four thick sandwiches and brought cookies, chips and fruit. Noah provided the bottles of water and put away two and a half sandwiches easily, complimenting her between bites. He grinned when she reflected men had a relationship to food in general the way a woman did to chocolate. Yet he ate his share of the cookies too. From the discreet way he eyed the rest, she expected he was hoping she'd only want a couple.

She extended one of hers to him. "Here. I'm stuffed. At this rate, we're going to have to wait on teaching me how to right a capsized boat. I'll sink if I go into the water now. You too."

"We can take a little break." He bit into the cookie, stretching out on the wet packed sand and folding an arm behind his head to gaze up into the trees. Because she wanted to do it, she stroked his chest to his stomach, and back up again.

"I love touching you," she said. "You're so pretty."

When he gave her a pained look, she laughed. "I didn't mean that in an unmanly way. You're beautiful, Noah. It's not just a physical thing. There's something about you; it's really kind of mesmerizing. Like a drug, but not. More like a feeling of happiness. Like being out on the sailboat when everything is working right. You're a living, breathing, perfect moment."

He propped himself up on his elbows, staring at her so that she colored a little. She wasn't in the habit of stating things so out front like that. But that was part of his magic, as well. Anything could be said to him, without judgment. No games, no embarrassment. He'd simply accept it. Like talking to the trees or wind.

"Lyda was right, about your poet side. Thank you," he said with sincerity. "You're a gift, Gen. I wish everyone you've loved realized that."

He was also good at touching past scars and making them feel better, even as it also made them hurt. It pricked at tears that had never been shed, because they required the right stimulus to bring them to the surface, purge them. Stimulus she tended to avoid. "It's water under the bridge. And I'm here with you today, probably because of some of those things. So that's good, right?"

"Right." His gaze remained serious. "I want to make love to you, Gen. Right here. Okay?"

"I… Okay." She whispered it.

He put his hand on her jaw, fingers curving around the side of her neck, pressing against the tripping pulse there. Drawing her down onto his chest, he guided her hand so it spread out there, over his nipple, the firm pectoral, as their mouths met. His other hand framed her face, holding her. He focused first only on her mouth, his tongue teasing hers, his fingers sliding into her hair, releasing the clip so it spilled over his hands, down against his face and shoulders. He traced her lips with his tongue, sealed his lips over hers again, taking the kiss even deeper. He moved his mouth to caress her cheekbones, the bridge of her nose, her eyelids.

Dropping his hands to her waist, he opened the cutoff shorts, pushed them off her hips. When she kicked them away, he shifted her on top of him, his stiff cock pressed against her belly, her knees pressed into the sand between his thighs. He cupped her buttock, fingers sliding beneath the edge of the swimsuit to play as his other hand held her, keeping her still while he suckled her throat, bit. She dug her fingers into his biceps, her pussy throbbing already, needy for him. She rubbed against his hardness, transmitting her desire.

But he let the feeling build, until she didn't care if the cove was private. A cruise ship could have come through with a legion of camera-snapping tourists. Everything was Noah. His hands, his mouth, his body. Then he destroyed another idea she'd had about a submissive male. He reversed their positions, turning her so she was beneath him and he was pressed solidly between her legs.

She arched full against him, rubbing in frustrated desire against that barrier of clothing. He gave her a full stroke back, cock against cunt, but then moved down her body, getting rid of her bikini top so he could suckle her nipples. That stud in his mouth began its low level hum, stroking her there, making her writhe and gasp at the stimulation. He cradled her breasts, squeezed them together, lashed at her nipples, taking that vibration to the channel in between, while she bucked her lower body.

"Noah...God..." She raked his back with her nails, not expecting her own ferocity. She choked out an apology, but his gaze scorched her.

"Mark me however you want, Gen. I'm yours."

Yours Unconditionally. Who had he meant that tattoo for? At the moment, it felt like her, Lyda...he was a gift given to a woman, whatever woman he was with. He was everything she needed. A treasure from the gods.

He was playing at her navel now, disrupting the intensity by deliberately tickling. When she pushed at him, he sent her a wicked grin, then went lower, catching the swimsuit bottoms in his teeth, letting his vibrating tongue play beneath the edges. When he took those off her, he stood on his knees, pushed his trunks down. He'd brought a small waterproof container with him to shore, and he removed a condom from the wallet in it.

"Prepared," she observed, her voice shaky. "Take the swimsuit off, all the way."

He nodded, to both things, she assumed. Standing, he removed the swimsuit, the sun praising every line of his body. He rolled the condom on while she watched, moistening her lips.

He knelt between her legs again, met her gaze. "I was going to make you come with my mouth first, but I want inside you too much, Gen. I need to be fucking you."

In answer, she reached for him. He came down, guiding himself into her wet heat. It had been so damn long. She closed her eyes at the feeling, shuddering hard as he eased in.

"So tight..." His voice was strained. She could feel the energy of his body, the desire to thrust, and yet he took his time, concentrating on not hurting her. The care it took to do that, to step outside oneself and make someone else matter more, was something neither of her husbands had given her. Noah gave it to her in ways large and small, and the smaller things held more significance. Yes, he'd keep her from falling off a cliff, but the fact he'd give her the last cookie if he thought for a second she wanted it meant even more.

And that thought was the kind capable of unlocking those more painful memories. She didn't want them to intrude, so she lifted her upper body abruptly, shoving her hips forward and pulling him to her core in the same motion. The lancing pain of it had her sucking in a breath, her face reflecting the discomfort, but she wouldn't let him draw back. She dug her short nails into his buttocks, feeling their muscled tension as well as that in his thighs, against the inside of hers.

"No. Please stay. Stay."

"Sshh." His brow was creased, eyes concerned as he slid his arm beneath her shoulders. He kept her close to his chest, holding their upper body weight on his other braced arm. "It's all right, Gen. Don't do that to yourself. I'm right here. Ease back. I've got you."

He put her back on the towel, bringing his body down with her, so she was pinned beneath his chest. "Let me just do this." He put his hand on her thigh, a nonverbal cue to loosen her lock as he adjusted his hips, slid back a little, then back in, an easier angle.

"How do you know a woman's body like this?" Her heart and soul…

"I feel you, Gen. Everything about you is mapped right here." He held her gaze, telling her he meant her eyes. "Let me give you pleasure. Unless…do you want me to force you to accept it?"

As she stared up at him, he let his touch shift, slowly, deliberately, to her arms, down to her wrists. He moved them to her sides, held them locked to the sand. When she trembled he saw it, eyes darkening. His abdomen muscles contracted as his hips lifted, then sank back into wetness, her cunt slick and welcoming, now lubricated to take him deep, but instead of ramming in there like a hammer and nail, it was like the Creator bringing together two body parts, joint to ball socket. Something meant to fit together, move easily, capable of power, speed, flexibility. Control. Utter, blissful control. She'd given it to him.

Her clit spasmed, her inner muscles clutching him. "Noah…"

"There's some of it in you, what you see in me," he said. She appreciated the catch in his voice, since she was unraveling. "It's different, but there. Lyda really brings it out in you. It makes me crazy hard, watching you two. Listening to her make you come the other night just about killed me."

She writhed against his hold, and his grip tightened, underscoring his strength. He could make her helpless, and that turned things in her lower body to molasses, but she also wanted to explore, to experiment. Lyda had offered her that opportunity, and she wanted to start now.

"Let go of me, Noah. I want to touch you."

Her voice was hoarse. As he cocked his head, not immediately complying, she saw the challenging light in his eyes. He wasn't an automatic pleaser. He understood when *not* being so accommodating could be a huge turn-on. The man was an endless puzzle.

"Now," she said softly. "Don't make me get rough with you."

The corner of his mouth twitched, and her eyes sparked in answer. He let go of her but curled his arm beneath her again to cradle her upper body against him, half off the sand as he slid in deeper, more firmly, making her gasp.

"You may have noticed I like it rough." His eyes were much closer now, his mouth. "Do your worst."

She kissed him, and his lips opened, welcoming her into heat and demand both. She lashed at his tongue, the surge of hot, needy lust translating into her sliding her hands up over his shoulders to rake his back again as he thrust into her, setting off a rhythm she matched with the movement of her hips. The towel was rough beneath her bare buttocks, her ankles crossed over the bend of his knees, pressed into the soft sand, their mattress beneath the terry cloth. His hand tangled in her hair to tip her head back and he bit her throat, suckling. She pulled loose and returned the favor, biting his shoulder when he plunged deeper.

"God..." She shoved at him, levered herself up. She couldn't hold against his physical strength, but when she made it clear she was going to insist, he gave way, letting her roll and reverse their positions so she straddled him. He stared up at her, eyes dark with desire. She felt powerful, beautiful, dangerous. Those bikini-clad girls couldn't give him this. Noah wanted the goddess inside a woman. He hungered for that power, wanted to worship it, be lost in that wave. A woman had to have known bittersweet pain and loss, to give him that. She had to understand what love and surrender, sacrifice and pain, were all about.

Testing herself and him, Gen slid a hand up his chest, trailing over his nipple. His expression and body went still, a powerful, combustible force, as he realized her destination. She closed her hand over his throat, the pulse hammering against her grip. When he tilted his chin up, accepting the hold, her body hummed in fierce, pleased response.

"Stay still," she whispered. "Don't move."

She rose and fell. Up, tightening all along his sizeable shaft, then down, enjoying every delicious inch of friction. Her pussy was so lubricated, she heard the sucking noise on each downward stroke impact. His breath rasped in his throat.

"Fuck…Gen."

"Don't come," she said. "I want to see you fight it until I finish."

"Anything for you."

Her heart tore free a few mooring lines at that, rising higher in her chest, the thumping painful. "Don't…" she said. It wasn't an admonishment. He hadn't done anything wrong. She just couldn't do this, couldn't hold the reins if he broke her heart wide open.

He didn't disturb her hand on his throat, but he laid one hand over her wrist, coiled his strong fingers around it, his thumb rubbing her pulse, an erogenous zone that leaped at the caress. "Ride me however you want, Mistress."

She returned to that up and down movement, the pure pleasure of it. God, there was a lot of pleasure to fucking Noah. He moved with her, anticipated when she needed him to lift his hips to help her impale herself deeper. He was hard and thick, and he met her demand, the muscles of his face tightening, then all along his body. His eyes had that feral, desperate light that told her how close he was.

She pushed herself to hold out. It felt too damn good. She didn't want it to end, but more than that, she was feeding on his self-restraint, his obvious desire to please her on every level, even the deeper ones most men weren't even aware were there, let alone expended the effort to try to satisfy. She was around some of the rarities like Tyler and Brendan, but until now that had sometimes been as torturous as being stabbed daily with a dull knife. Why did Chloe and Marguerite have what had eluded her?

No, don't go there. This was about pleasure, a sun-filled day with an exciting man.

Fuck, it had caught her. She'd faltered, despite being so close to the knife-edge of release. Her body was quivering, fighting her.

"Gen." He cradled her face, drawing her attention back to him. Her hand had shifted from his throat, the heel pressed against his heart, fingers curved into a claw over his collarbone. "Stay right here. You aren't lost. I have you."

Noah pushed himself into a sitting position, adjusting her so her legs were curled around his hips and she was cinched in closer to him, his mouth near her breast, his head pressed into her neck. He had his arms banded around her, one hand curving over her buttock. He took over, working his cock into her from that more limited movement position, making the sensation overwhelming. He nuzzled her breast, her nipples pressed high against his chest.

"Lay your head back like you did when we were sailing. Close your eyes, feel the sun and wind. Feel me."

Though she was on top, the power balance had shifted back to him, easy as the flow of water. She'd needed him to be the one in charge of the boat for this to work. He'd figured it out, accepted that responsibility without a pause.

He rocked her, such that she could imagine the lift and fall of the boat on the water. As he began to do it faster, he set those delicate tissues on fire, driving everything else away. Now he unleashed his male strength, holding her, pounding into her, stroking her clit with the motion. She sealed her mouth over his again, teasing his tongue stud with her own tongue, kissing him with frenetic passion as the climax surged up. She didn't want to break the connection, so as the orgasm swept through her, she dug her claws into him once more, holding on, screaming into his mouth as he kept driving into her. She felt the impact all the way deep inside where he was rubbing against her. He sent her soaring to the freaking moon.

His hand coiled in her hair, holding her tight, fused to his mouth, his other hand spread over her back, his thumb in the valley of her spine. He held her so tight, almost bruising. He was hanging on by a determined thread. Waiting on her to release him.

She stared at him through glazed eyes. Marguerite and Tyler both loved sculpture and possessed an impressive collection. Some of it was erotic, because several of Tyler's friends specialized in that area, but she wondered if any of them had ever captured a man when he looked like this. Almost like she imagined he'd look in battle, eyes fierce, muscles rigid, cock hard. A state where killing rage and lustful need were so close, and a woman felt a thrilling desire seeing either demonstrated on her behalf.

She slid trembling fingers down his jaw, to his throat, over his shoulder. Taking her time with it as he quivered, chest rising and falling, and that look became even more dangerous.

She reached back, bracing her palms against his knees, lodging herself deeper on his cock, the angle tilting up her breasts. She loved the frustration in his expression, but also the fact he complied with her nonverbal cue to keep holding.

"Tell me what you're thinking right now. Uncensored."

"That I'd kill to fuck your cunt. That's all there is. The desire to fuck."

She trembled at the growling response. "I want to watch you come. Come for me, Noah. Don't look away." Then she braced herself.

He tightened his grip, lifted her, thrust upward. She gasped at the deep penetration, and then she had to hold onto his legs as he started pumping himself into her with that singular focus. *The desire to fuck.* She clung to his expression, to his eyes which never left hers as he hammered his cock into her, over and over, such that her post-climactic tissues clutched him, sending sweet aftershocks through her that made her moan. He devoured every reaction, and then he was coming, his face creasing with the effort, harsh grunts breaking free. His gaze shifted only once, to her breasts, quivering with erotic movement because of the power of his thrusts, but she'd forgive him that since his heated attention sent waves of pleasure over the nerve endings.

"Yes…" She encouraged him with sighing pleasure. "Yes…"

When he finally began to slow down, rather than flopping back to the sand like a grounded trout as she expected, he slid his arm around her waist, brought her to him once more. Capturing her right breast with his mouth, he sealed wet friction over her nipple, flicking her with the tongue stud. Arousal feathered through her as she coiled her arms around his shoulders. She held him to her as he nursed each breast to aching, pleasurable response again, rubbing a jaw with that afternoon sandpaper texture against her tender flesh.

At length, he laid his head there, his damp breath on her tight nipple. She kept holding him, stroking his hair, loving the feel of her arms around him, his around her.

She'd touched him how she'd desired, learning to trust herself to command him. And he'd provided her the guidance to do it.

"So…" She cleared the frogs out of her throat. "I realize it's a really convenient time to ask, but you did say Lyda was okay with this, right?"

He smiled against her breast. "Yes. Lyda commands my pleasure, Gen. She told me I was to provide you anything you desired. And before you piss me off by asking, yes, it worked out pretty well for me as well."

Now he did do the fish thing, flopping back with drama, as if she'd completely drained him. "I guess capsizing *will* have to wait for another day," she chuckled.

"Nope. Just give me a minute to recharge. A couple more of those cookies would help, if we still have any."

"I could learn to hate you," she said, eying the hard body beneath her.

He grinned. "Does that mean we still have cookies?"

With a sigh, she began to slide off him. When her muscles contracted on him, a reluctant farewell, he caught her hips. Bringing his mouth to hers, hand cradling her face, he captured her lips in one more kiss, this one deep and long, a promise of the same passion, but something more tender too.

When he drew back, she had her hand around his wrist. "What was that?"

"I just felt like you needed it. Or maybe I did. I wanted it."

With a pensive look that puzzled her, he let her slide away. He discouraged further discussion of it, helping her to her feet and then pulling on his swimsuit while she did the same with her suit and shorts. The silence was weighted, but comfortable, so she left it undisturbed as she brought the extra cookies back to the towel. They shared one and then he ate another as they passed a water bottle back and forth. A line of pelicans passed over and she closed her eyes, enjoying the sun on her still tingling skin. When Noah brushed a finger along her cheek, taking some cookie crumbs or a few grains of sand away—she wasn't sure which—she opened her eyes.

"The cage at Lyda's, there's a freedom to it," he said. "You understand?"

Her brow knit at the unexpected topic. "I didn't feel comfortable with that. For me."

"I know. But a part of you knows why it works, right? The real cage for most people is the one memories put around us." A lot of things moved behind those dark eyes. "If you were in a car crash tomorrow, every reservation or doubt you felt with me today, it would have been a waste, right? You look down the road to the future, and it paralyzes you, because you think you'll find you're still in that prison of memories, that you never left, and this is just more of the same. If there's no future for the past to mess up, there's just this moment, right?"

Whether or not it was his intention, the simple logic helped with her own doubts. But applying the words to that shadow in his makeup she kept detecting, it reminded her of a bird who'd finally escaped a cage. The bird soared, feeding on the pleasures of the air, but he refused to touch the earth for fear of that prison closing around him again. Living in the moment could also be an act of desperation.

She slid her knuckles along his sculpted cheekbone, the firm jaw, feathered a fingertip over the lashes a woman would kill to have. "I think we are who we are because of those memories. They can help us make good decisions, better decisions, for ourselves."

"It pulls you down, though," he said. "It makes you sad. Hurts you."

So he was talking about her, the near miss on the climax because she'd gotten mired in old pain. She shook her head, laying her hand on him in reassurance. "What you and Lyda unlock inside of me, I don't yet know how to reconcile that with old wounds, but so far, I'm willing to keep going down that road and figure it out. You made it easier to do that today. Let that be enough."

She thought he might say more, but she put her fingers on his lips, a mute request not to do so. He kissed them. Reassured, she pushed away to retrieve a hidden cache of cookies she'd prudently packed, anticipating his male appetite and sweet tooth. Though she could feel him watching her intently, he said nothing further about it.

That was good. It had been a wonderful day, one that made her all for living in the moment. At least until tomorrow.

Divine Solace

Chapter Eight

Gen had never been in a relationship that was like a force of nature, so beyond her control, yet so irresistibly powerful she couldn't help but want to run wild in the storm. Interacting with these two complicated people had so far been exciting, passionate, pleasurable, scary and thought provoking. Disturbing. She was doing things she'd never contemplated doing.

"New blend?" Marguerite inquired, pausing at her elbow.

Gen was preparing the order for a couple at Table Two. The man wanted coffee, the woman, the chai tea special of the day. With a start, Gen realized she'd poured them into the same cup. "Oh good grief."

Giving her an amused look, Marguerite lifted it to her lips, took an experimental sip. Grimaced. "We won't be starting a chai-coffee offering with that blend anytime soon." Dumping it down the sink, she set out a clean mug next to the one that was intended to take the tea. "I'll handle this order. Why don't you make it an early day?"

"I'm fine, M. I'm not sick, just distracted. I'll do better."

"You're doing fine, Gen. I thought you might like extra time to prepare for your evening plans."

She'd mentioned it to Chloe, so of course M knew about it. Before Gen could think of a response, Marguerite nodded toward the door. "Speaking of which."

Gen glanced over her shoulder to see Lyda coming in. Her jeans were stained with dirt, showing she'd already had a busy day. Because the heat index was in the hundreds today, her T-shirt was dark with sweat, her pale face flushed.

"Iced tea," Marguerite said, unnecessarily. Gen was already reaching for it. "Unsweetened. Lyda doesn't do sugar. Put some of that herbal energy blend in it I've been using in the sweet tea order for Todd's group," she added, referring to the construction foreman who came in regularly to get sweetened tea for his crew. "Add some raspberry to cut the bitter."

"Christ, why do I live in Florida?" Lyda grimaced, sliding onto a stool at the counter. She stripped off her gloves, tucked them into her belt.

"Because there isn't a huge demand for nursery stock and perennials in Alaska," Marguerite offered.

"I'd go up there and change that, except Noah hates the cold. That skinny boy would freeze to death the first day."

"Why isn't he or one of the others with you, helping with the deliveries?" Gen now knew Lyda had four employees other than Noah. Lyda's neck and arms were dry. Though she could have mopped them off with a towel in her truck, a lack of perspiration was precursor to heat stroke.

When Lyda raised a brow, Gen realized how sharp she'd sounded. Gen put the tea in front of her, hoping it distracted from the color now in her own cheeks. "Here, drink this. You'll dehydrate fast in this heat."

"I didn't realize," Lyda said dryly. But she laid her hand on Gen's forearm, keeping it there to run a caressing finger over her skin, oddly playful. "I'm fine, rabbit. You need to come to my fitness class to see a real workout."

"Do I have to participate?"

Lyda gave her a feral smile. "Not the first time. As I told you, I like your soft places, Gen. Keep them soft." Her gaze swept over Gen's upper body, pointedly lingering on her breasts and the nip of her waist. Unlike the first time Lyda had visited, today Gen was wearing a fitted shirt that hugged her curves over a nice pair of stressed jeans that had a white stencil of a faded rose down one thigh. She'd always dressed appropriately for work, but her choices were now being driven by new feelings. *Cue the Jon Berry song about Rosie.*

"Nice look," Lyda murmured. "I hope that's for me."

Since Marguerite was within hearing distance, Gen felt her cheeks heat anew. "You never said where all your employees are," she said hastily.

Lyda waited a beat. "They're out on deliveries as well. We have more business than we can handle lately. I'm going to have to hire more temporary help."

Marguerite drew Gen's attention. She had the coffee and chai tea ready. "Table Two."

"Oh, right. Okay." Picking up the tray, Gen maneuvered around the counter. She was not going to stumble and scald a customer. She wasn't going to act like a teenager whose boyfriend had just stopped in. Or girlfriend. No matter how true that might be.

If it had been Noah, she'd probably still be distracted, but the high, fluttery pulse beating in her throat would have a different cadence. Noah was like wading out into a gentle surf, coaxing her out further and further, because she felt safe in that tide line. Lyda made Gen feel like she was watching an approaching high wave, with only a moment to decide whether to duck beneath it, be swallowed, or take the churning, exhilarating ride to shore. Either way, the wave was going to have her.

Gen delivered the order and did a round of the other occupied tables. When she was done with that, she tidied up one of the workstations. Fortunately, M and Lyda weren't lowering their voices beyond her eavesdropping radar. She sidled closer, anticipating casual conversation, a way for her to enjoy the rise and fall of Lyda's voice, the flow of her moods.

She should have remembered Marguerite didn't do casual conversation.

"You've been stopping by a little more often lately, Lyda," her boss said. "I don't stock your usual preference."

Startled by Marguerite's cool tone, Gen turned her head from what she was doing. Lyda's silver-gray irises were comparable to a knife blade. "Do I need your blessing, Marguerite? I wasn't aware she was yours."

"You're quite aware there's an ownership question here. Which is why you're here today. You intended to broach it in exactly this fashion."

Lyda set down the tea. "What do you need to hear?"

"Nothing. Words don't impress me overly much. It's what you need to recognize that's relevant." Marguerite held her gaze.

When the women said nothing else for a weighted moment, Gen wondered if she was witnessing a Vulcan mind meld. Should she get involved? Only an idiot tried to step between two crossed swords.

Lyda nodded at last. "Understood."

Marguerite's teeth flashed. "Be mindful of it." Without turning, she spoke. "Gen, go ahead and take off. Chloe's coming in at one."

"If you're sure." She waffled, not sure how to take her leave with Lyda here, and so much in the air. "Um...Lyda, if you need an extra pair of hands, I can help."

Lyda was still holding Marguerite's gaze, but Gen's offer changed something. She projected a sense of satisfaction, as if Gen's offer had tilted the scale of whatever they were resolving toward Lyda. Marguerite's flat expression didn't change, however, which made Lyda clear her throat, then finally look Gen's way. "No. You'll need your energy for tonight. Put the tea in a to-go cup, and top it off."

Marguerite shifted, turning away. It was a deliberate gesture, transferring the responsibility to Gen. Gen wasn't clued into everything happening, but that one was clear. Lyda's order was directed to her.

She hoped her fingers didn't tremble when she closed them around the glass to take it away, but if they did, the motion was arrested when Lyda laid a single fingertip on her wrist. Gen stilled. She stared at the cup, kept holding it, didn't raise her gaze. Didn't move. She couldn't. Aroused need spread out inside her, and the reaction in her fingers manifested in her forearm, giving it a quiver beneath Lyda's finger. The woman tapped her once. Gen realized she expected an acknowledgement.

"Yes ma'am," she murmured. She'd respond that way to a customer on a normal day, but it meant something entirely different with Lyda. When Gen dared a quick look at her, Lyda's countenance reminded Gen of how the woman had looked when she demanded that "uncertain girl kiss".

Lyda drew her touch away and Gen pivoted to dump the glass contents into a to-go cup, top it off. It was probably good she hadn't requested sugar, because Gen's unsteady hand might have tipped in enough to put the woman in diabetic shock. She did add more of M's rehydration blend. That truck was way too full, and it was obvious this wasn't Lyda's first delivery of the day. Who would plant in the heat of summer? People with enough money for a huge water bill, apparently.

When she brought the cup back to Lyda, she was on her feet. Marguerite was checking on the current brew. Lyda took the cup from Gen's hand. "See you tonight."

"All right. Thanks." Gen felt awkward again. Lyda gave her a level look.

"You really should come to my class. You might enjoy it more than you think. It's the Blood, Sweat and Tears fitness center, about a mile from the nursery."

"Blood, Sweat and Tears. Seriously?"

"Planet Fitness felt I was too extreme." Lyda gave her an arch look. When Gen watched her move toward the door, she wasn't alone. Other customers watched her, that purposeful way she had of moving, the sexual energy pulsing off her. Gen wanted to lift her hair off her neck, press her lips to the perspiration that would be there. Push her T-shirt up so she could slide her lips along the valley of her spine, her buttocks.

She could imagine it, but would Lyda ever permit it? Had Lyda ever had a lover, someone not locked into a rigid submissive structure she defined? Was the answer to that question staring at Gen from her own mirror?

Lyda got into her truck, twisted to put on her seat belt, picked up her phone. She tilted her head to study the screen, probably reading a text from one of the other employees. Then she'd turned over the ignition and was gone. Gen realized then that she'd watched her until she drove out of sight.

She pivoted toward the other enigmatic female force in her life, who was working on a call-in order. "Can I ask you what that was about?"

Marguerite glanced her way. When she didn't say anything, Gen figured she might be waiting for clarification. She checked to be sure no customers were in earshot. "The ownership thing?"

"You already know the answer to that, Gen." Marguerite's tone wasn't unkind, but it was firm.

"I meant..." She struggled for the right words. "Your part of it. What were you telling her? It was like..."

Marguerite didn't often make prolonged eye contact. As a result, when she did, it was like having a railroad spike driven into both feet, keeping a person in place. "I was telling her, in a way she understood, that whether or not you are starting to think of yourself as hers, until she reciprocates the feeling sufficiently, you're mine. Which means if she fucks with your head, I will take her apart."

Her office phone started ringing. Marguerite passed Gen, touching her back.

Gen drew an unsteady breath. Was she starting to think of herself as Lyda's? *You already know the answer to that.*

Yeah, she did. It was funny how one intense club session with Lyda, and an even more intense night at her home, as well as the separate times with Noah, were starting to sharpen nebulous feelings. A few days ago, if someone had asked her if she wanted to be a part of something like this, she would have politely declined. Now she was seeking answers, wanting a deeper understanding.

She studied Marguerite. Gen hadn't ever settled into a job the way she'd settled into working at Tea Leaves. From the beginning, she'd loved working with the reserved woman, proving she could perform to her exacting standards. When she met them, gained Marguerite's confidence, trust, it had meant everything. At first she'd thought it was a weird kind of maternal transference, because her own mother had never really expected too much out of her, but she'd never thought of Marguerite as a mother figure. Yet she responded to her as an authority figure.

It wasn't like she'd needed Marguerite's approval to be whole, but it made things better, to see that look in Marguerite's eye when Gen met or—even better—exceeded her expectations. That light touch she'd just given Gen was something Gen considered a gift, whenever it happened.

Lyda had drawn that connection, pointing out how comfortable Gen was under the shelter of Marguerite's protection. Yet Gen wouldn't call the feelings she had about Lyda comfortable. She craved more from the Mistress, with an all-encompassing yearning that startled her.

Yes, she was getting involved with two complex people, but perhaps the most complicated and hard-to-decipher member of their triad was Gen herself.

* * * * *

Back to the club again. From her existing wardrobe, she assembled a short skirt and sheer black top with some sparkles across it, coordinating a lacy bra and panty set beneath. She took extra time with her hair, knowing how Lyda and Noah liked it, and slid into a pair of heels. Digging through her jewelry, she found a beaten silver anklet and put that together with a pair of silver wire earrings. She left her neck bare, thinking of Noah's mouth there, Lyda's sharp nails grazing her pulse. That thought set things pounding like she was already on a dance floor. She considered putting a liner inside the scrap of panties she was wearing, but Lyda might want to stroke between her legs. Gen knew without asking that Lyda would rather have arousal dampening Gen's flesh, soaking the crotch of the panties.

You're already learning to dress for a Mistress...

As she leaned against the bathroom counter, it put pressure against her pubic mound, sending a little zing through her nether regions. She rubbed against the edge, eyes half closing. The sensation intensified as she imagined them touching her. When she was with Noah, she was consumed by him, yet when she anticipated being with Lyda and Noah together, she always saw Lyda in the primary position. She wondered if that was how it was for Noah, when he was with other women versus his Mistress.

How long had they been together? Did they consider themselves permanent, like a boyfriend-girlfriend thing? Maybe she'd keep her head together enough tonight to ask some intelligent questions, get some real answers. Or maybe she'd figure out more by simply riding the ride.

When she arrived at the club and locked her car, she realized she wasn't even sure if Noah would be there. Lyda hadn't confirmed that, had even implied Gen could look at a wider pool of candidates to try out being a Domme. She wasn't sure how she felt about that, but she'd cross that bridge when she came to it.

Checking her appearance against that of other women entering the club she thought might be Dominants, Gen saw everything from snug designer jeans to short skirts or leather or latex. The diversity made her more comfortable about her own appearance. Hell, Lyda was able to command her wearing a sweaty T-shirt and dirty jeans. But she was just kidding herself if she thought she possessed the aura Lyda did.

Her chin firmed. If she wanted to try to be a Domme tonight, she would. It would tell her something about Lyda's character if the woman provided her real mentorship, or if she just gave it lip service, waiting for Gen to crash and burn. Was that ultimately what this was about, testing Lyda? The anxious coil tightened up, but she quelled it. She wasn't going to bolt now.

The club was quieter on a weeknight. She could hear the faint sounds of punishment, cries of pleasure and pain, mixed with the distant music beat. Her palms dampened. Her flesh was already feeling sensitive, swollen in noticeable places. She handed over her guest membership, and the hostess checked her log.

"You were here as an unclassified guest last time, Ms. Wisner. Do you prefer a bracelet tonight?" The hostess gestured to a board, which showed the different colors of bracelets that indicated Dom, sub, switch, undecided. "You can have any of those four to let people know your preference, but you can also have a second no-play bracelet, so they know if you're here merely to watch."

She had to give Tyler and his partners kudos for their employee training, because the woman had given her exactly the guidance she needed without being asked.

"The Dom bracelet, please. And one of the no-plays." She was willing to take some chances, but at her own pace.

Suitably "classified", she wandered in. She'd seek Lyda's whereabouts eventually, but Gen wanted to get her own impressions first. What would a Domme be feeling as she entered this world? Closing her eyes, she imagined herself as Lyda, then slowly opened her eyes, let her gaze trail over the scatterings of people. The dance floor had a moderate but enthusiastic group. The bracelets were done in glow-in-the-dark neon colors, and subs wore red. Her Domme bracelet glowed green, a marriage of Christmas colors she wondered if was intended for the whimsical irony. Every day is Christmas...

Speaking of which. Her gaze landed on a male leaning against the wall, arms crossed over his chest. His face was in the shadows, but he seemed familiar to her. Regardless, she saw enough of him to have her libido sitting up to take notice. Since his arms were crossed, she couldn't see his bracelet color, but him in a submissive bracelet would be pure fantasy.

Built like a brick house, he had an alert body language that said cop or military. He was more mature, somewhere in his late forties. A very fit, mouth-watering late-forties. His jeans held what he had to offer in just the right way and he was shirtless. A couple of wicked scars on his six-pack abdomen, including a round one that looked as if it had been caused by a bullet, added to the dangerous look of him. His hair was thick and curly, an intriguing mix of black, silver and white.

Reluctantly, she shifted her gaze from the pleasure of perusing him. Maybe she could bribe him to let her tie him up and spank him. *Yeah, right.* She had about thirty dollars of her carefully hoarded entertainment budget in her purse. In this place, that would buy her the two-drink minimum and a snack.

Oh, hello. The red bracelet was a distinctive glow on the next male who caught her attention. Like the cop, he was sporting the pleasing shirtless look. This one was younger, perhaps late twenties. Sprawled out across a bench in a cozy alcove that invited trysts, he had one foot on the floor, the other propped on the wall as he lay on his back. In Gen's position on the mezzanine, she was looking down at him. He was all smooth muscle, tribal tattoos on the biceps, and...*oh my.*

He was wearing the tight shorts Olympic athletes wore, the kind that stopped high on the thighs and displayed a cock ready to do whatever a woman demanded. Even in a resting state, the whole package was quite noticeable. Strands of black hair brushed carelessly across his forehead drew her attention to devil-may-care blue-gray eyes. Ones that flickered up and found hers.

Seeing her interest, his gaze went to her wrist. Though she had the no-play bracelet with the Domme one, an anticipatory look spread across his face, like a wolf seeing dinner. He had a whole Channing Tatum thing happening, a dose of hundred percent trouble, the kind that scrambled a woman's mind. He wanted her to remove that no-play bracelet.

She'd watched how all this worked the other night. If she removed it, she could explain she was a newbie, and if he was okay with that, they could set boundaries. She could tie him up, enjoy touching him the way she'd enjoyed touching Noah. Right?

She thought of Noah's hands on her, his body pressing hers into the sand, those dark eyes so close. He wasn't Noah. While her libido wasn't choosy, it was hardwired to her heart and mind, and they were far more selective. She'd told Lyda she didn't do casual. Was this really any different from a bar pickup? Would it feel just as empty, or was it more like an evening out at the movies, where you enjoyed the show and went home with a sense of satisfaction? How did a woman program her emotions for this?

He'd lifted a brow, a question. Sitting up, he stretched an arm out along the back of the bench and then, holding her widening gaze, he slid his hand down those lovely abs, down, down, and into the shorts. Gripping himself, he stroked, keeping that sinful gaze on her, even as she lowered her eyes to what he was doing. His cock responded instantly, growing longer and thicker under his stimulation, so that he stretched it out under the shorts, cupped his balls, rolled them. As he adjusted his legs to give her a better view, there was a challenge in those eyes, one that made her think of an incubus luring a maiden into a dark, secret place.

"Not that one."

Lyda's sultry voice was against her ear. Gen let out a startled breath as the woman's arm slid around her waist. When Lyda pressed her mouth against the tender skin beneath Gen's ear, her pulse leaped at the first contact. She caught that breath as Lyda cupped her breast, ran her fingers over it in an unmistakably possessive act, plucking at the lace of the bra through the shirt's thin fabric. The male's eyes sharpened, his own lips parting, but in her peripheral vision, Gen saw Lyda lock gazes with him. Whatever message she sent, he removed his hand from his shorts, lifting both palms in mock apology, but the smile he sent their way was not the least bit repentant.

Lyda nudged Gen. "Trust me, Marius is the abyss end of the pool. He'll hold you under and drown you if you show weakness. But it's a Lucifer thing. Everything you fuck up with him is your own choice. He gives you just enough rope to hang yourself. Only one Mistress has ever been able to get his number. He treats her with what little respect for authority he has in him." At Gen's look, Lyda's lips twisted. "Marguerite."

"Of course," Gen murmured.

"He's a top from the bottom *ass*, but he does it so well too many Mistresses let him get away with it. He's like overdoing the Jack Daniel's, where you have a huge good time that night, but you wake up with a what-the-fuck-did-I-do hangover the next day. He part-times as a cooler here. Ironically, he has an aptitude for defusing volatile situations. He also does wait staff, whatever handy stuff they need, since he gets no regular play because of how challenging he is. Come on. We'll find you someone fun in the Domme 101 category."

Lacing fingers with her, Lyda drew Gen toward another public gathering space, one with tables and chairs like a restaurant, rather than a living room furniture arrangement. Gen saw some submissives on their knees beside Dominants, but most of those here were informal socializing groups, regardless of the bracelets they wore. Yet there were a good number of submissive males, and she felt their eyes on her, causing her to draw closer to Lyda. They were probably looking more hopefully at her anyway. She couldn't help doing that herself.

Lyda wore a pair of ivory-colored riding breeches that zipped up the side, forming a tight, second skin fit over her ass and thighs. The pants tucked into polished riding boots. A translucent linen shirt limned her upper body, highlighting the lace bra beneath. The curves of her breasts were revealed by the open three buttons of the neckline. Lyda's flame-gold hair was pulled back in a french braid, and she wore a cameo pendant that highlighted the delicate lines of her throat. It was impossible for the woman to look anything but mesmerizing. Daunting, yes, but people would draw as close as they dared. And that daunting person was holding her hand, pulling her through the crowd as if she was hers alone.

Don't be stupid, Gen.

I'm not. It's okay to fantasize.

Lyda wasn't wearing a bracelet, but she didn't really need it. Why on earth did you have to put a "hot" sign over coffee? People that clueless wouldn't get it anyway.

"It's all right," Lyda said, sliding her arm around Gen's waist again, her fingers curving over her hip to give her a reassuring pat. "The Zone's rules are very strict, Gen. Even Marius, flirting so outrageously, wouldn't have approached you until you clearly invited him to do so. Or took off the no-play bracelet."

"Can you help me understand some things…before I do anything?"

"We can spend the whole night talking, if that's what you want to do." Lyda gestured to a table, and Gen took the chair across from her. Gen didn't detect any hedging in Lyda's tone, nothing but sincerity. To all appearances, she was respecting Gen's desire to be something different tonight. Which was even more distracting, in a perverse way.

"What do male submissives want from a Domme? Do they just want women to do everything, get them off?"

"There are some like that in both genders. A bottom might require only the loss of control and sexual release. For the Domme who wants the mirror of that, to take over and achieve sexual pleasure for both, that works. I've taken on some bottoms for one-night stands, but I've always preferred the nature of the true submissive. A true submissive, male or female, is hungering to serve at some level, even if it's just sexual."

"Like Noah?"

"Like Noah."

"Will he be here tonight?"

"Maybe. He's doing a shift at a pizza delivery place, but he gets off at nine."

"I know you've both tried to explain it to me, and maybe I should stop worrying about it, but I can't figure out you two. He said, when we went sailing..." She reddened, and Lyda's lips curved.

"You and he had sex. It was allowed."

"But don't you consider him yours?"

"Absolutely. I haven't put a collar on Noah, but we still have rules." The fiery glimmer in Lyda's gaze gave Gen thrill and reassurance both. "He has to get my permission for all of it, until I release him. Or he asks to be let go, which Noah will never do."

"Is that why you won't collar him? Because he doesn't choose?"

Lyda's expression closed down. "I'm sorry," Gen interjected. "I didn't mean..."

Lyda shook her head, waving her hand. "Let's leave that one alone for now. What other questions do you have?"

Gen remarshaled her thoughts. "Before Brendan, I thought a male sub would be...wimpy. Doormats. Not possessive at all."

Lyda snorted. "If they were only that pliable. See him?"

Gen followed Lyda's direction. The brickhouse male who'd first caught her attention was sitting at one of the tables, straddling a chair. Now that she could see his wrists, she saw he was wearing a pair of silver cuff-style bracelets that looked like overlapped angel wings. Holy crap, he *was* a submissive. And she realized why he looked familiar. "Mac."

"You know him?"

"Yes. He and his wife were guests at Marguerite and Tyler's wedding. I would never have guessed…"

"That he's a submissive? A lot of people react that way to him, but you have to look beyond the surface, see the cues. As far as a doormat…" Lyda looked amused. "If any man here put hands on Mac's Mistress, Tyler would have to install a floor drain to wash away all the blood. Mac belongs to Violet, but she's his as well. They're married, but more than that, there's a mutual soul possession. That's something different from just playing at Dom/sub games."

Gen's gaze shifted to Violet, sitting on Mac's right. Under the table, her booted foot rested on the top of his, a casually intimate pose. The woman was as petite as he was large, and even though they were talking to another woman at the table, the bond between them was obvious.

"Taking care of a baby MIT tonight, Lyda?"

A black woman, nearly six feet tall, had arrived at their table. Her long, dark-red braids were sprinkled with silver glitter. Her crimson corset and black leggings with beautifully crafted red-and-black boots made her formidable, as well as out-front sexy.

"Regina, this is Gen. Gen, Mistress Regina. Gen is still learning her place in our world," Lyda explained. "And deciding if it's her world at all."

When Regina shifted her weight to one hip, Gen expected her to pull a sword from a back harness and test the blade with a fingernail. The woman projected off Amazon warrior queen without any problem at all. "Well, child, you'll either find it's Disney World, a bunch of fun rides and then back to normal life, or you'll never want to leave. Course, Disney World can be like that too." Regina said it pleasantly enough, though her eyes were measuring. Gen wondered if every Domme she met tonight was going to make her feel like she was just pretending at what was so natural to them. Even petite Violet had that measuring look when she gazed at her husband. The tilt of her head and her posture broadcast what she was, again making the bracelet irrelevant.

"Are you playing tonight?" Lyda asked Regina.

"Hmm." Regina glanced toward Marius. He was in the same alcove, both feet up now, ankles crossed and heels propped against the wall. He had a baseball and was throwing it up in the air to catch it. He didn't look frustrated by his lack of play. He reminded Gen of an amiable snake, sunning itself on a rock while its slit eyes watched for a hapless mouse to scuttle over it.

"I told Tyler I'd whip Marius' ass for putting his feet on the walls."

"Good luck with that." Lyda chuckled as the woman gave them another cordial nod and moved off. Gen stared at the table.

"You think this is a pointless exercise. That I'm as much of a Dominant as Noah is."

Lyda's brow creased. "No. And yes. No, it's not a pointless exercise. You have the desire to top, Gen, but in a very targeted way." Lyda touched her face, drawing Gen's gaze back up. "The bull's-eye has just arrived."

Following her direction, Gen saw Noah step into view from the main hallway. A Domme in steampunk wear beckoned him over to the booth where she was sitting. As Gen watched, she slid a riding crop down his chest and used it to snag the T-shirt he was wearing, drawing him closer. Her other hand latched onto his waistband, fingers teasing his navel just above it.

"He's the one you want tonight, right?"

She looked toward Lyda. "Is it that obvious?"

"Pretty much. You were enjoying looking around the candy store, but you were waiting for him. Right?"

Gen saw no reason to deny the truth, not when relief had flooded her vitals at his appearance. She admitted she had been enjoying the fantasies she could attach to something like Marius, but when Noah had arrived, what she wanted, who she felt comfortable pursuing this with, was as clear as a glass table top. "Is that okay?"

"I think if you'd chosen differently, it would have been hard for Noah to watch. He's becoming quite attached to you." Lyda's expression remained neutral, but Gen sensed the woman was pleased by their mutual attraction.

Noah smiled at something the Domme was saying. Though his gaze never left her face, Gen was almost sure he'd already located Lyda and her. When the steampunk Mistress ran a familiar hand down his hip, she looked at Lyda. "Is *that* okay?"

"Noah is well known here," Lyda said. "The other Dommes play and flirt with him. It's harmless fun, and I allow it. Some of the Masters and Mistresses who don't have the patience or take pleasure in aftercare for their subs have him serve as an aftercare nanny. He's very nurturing."

"It doesn't bother you, to see other women touch him?"

"The boundaries are very clear here. It's outside that things can get a bit more…muddy." Lyda sent a pointed look at her hand, clenching the edge of the table. "I can tell you don't particularly like seeing him being touched by other women. How about when I touch him?"

"That's fine. I mean, he's yours." Quite frankly, watching Lyda touch Noah aroused Gen greatly. Seeing this stranger touch him provoked a far different reaction.

"It's more than that." Lyda leaned in, closing the personal space between them and pulling Gen's attention from Noah like a magnet. "What about seeing someone touch me, Gen? How would you feel about that?"

"You're playing with my head."

"I like to play with my cake before I eat it." Lyda ran a fingertip over Gen's bottom lip. "Put a bit of icing here, let it melt, tease it off with my tongue. You're such a confusing mix, Gen. It's irresistible."

"Watching me flounder? Learning my place?"

"No." Lyda's touch stilled, a warning look in her eyes. "Watching you choose your path through the woods. Seeing how brave you are. In Dominance and submission, a lot of layers come off. We get to see the soul beneath shine or bleed." Lyda gestured toward Noah. "You want to see how it works, with the lines in place? Play with him here tonight, whatever way you wish. I can help as much or as little as you want, though I will be present to guide you on safe play. When it's over, you can keep him overnight. My only condition is that everything sexual with him happens here, at the club. You can take him home as a cuddle toy, but nothing else."

That first night, Gen had resisted the urge to use him that way. A big, sexy teddy bear tempting her to do things she'd never consider with a stuffed animal. There was probably a fetish for that, one she was sure she didn't want to know about.

"Why nothing else?" She was curious, not complaining—though she expected at a certain point tonight she'd want to whine about the stipulation.

"Because it will keep you both aroused, knowing you can't touch one another until I say so. That gives me pleasure." She extended a hand. "Deal?"

Lyda was right; Gen had a confusing mix of emotions to juggle right now. The deal Lyda was offering was a clear act of submission, Gen's to her will. Yet it was the reward for "allowing" Gen to dominate Noah. Reaching out, she clasped Lyda's hand. Lyda held onto it, firm and tight.

"That prohibition goes for self-pleasuring as well," she added, her mouth getting a stern look that sent crazy thrills through Gen. "You save that sweet fountain between your legs for me."

Gen swallowed. "Deal."

* * * * *

Confirming Gen's theory of where Noah's attention really was, the instant Lyda gestured in his direction, his eyes were on them both. As he came toward them, he gave Gen his serious smile. Yet when he reached out to take her hand, Lyda lifted a palm.

"Gen is your Mistress tonight, Noah. Not your equal. You understand?"

"Yes Mistress." He stepped back, giving Gen an intriguing look before his dark eyes lowered, sending a startling bolt of anticipation through her. All the things she'd seen here or imagined flashed through her mind. Yet she honestly wasn't sure how to start. She looked toward Lyda. Fortunately, the woman did as she'd promised. She helped, becoming Gen's Domme 101 personal tour guide.

"How about a semiprivate area? One of the cubicle areas that can still be viewed from the upper levels, but feels a little more sequestered, like a corner table in a restaurant."

Gen nodded. "I like that."

Lyda scraped a nail down Noah's arm, making the same spot on Gen's arm tingle. "I'm thinking Gen would like to learn more about how pain and pleasure work. You did keep her waiting, Noah."

"Yes Mistress. My apologies."

"Oh, I…" At Lyda's look, Gen let that trail off. She took her lead from the other woman. "That's true. And you missed a spot on my stomach with the sunscreen."

The red area was the size of a penny. The evidence of how thorough he'd been everywhere else had made the spot endlessly fascinating to her.

Lyda's reaction surprised her. Reaching over, she lifted Gen's shirt. Gen shivered as that fingertip slid over the abraded area. No nail this time, just a light caress. Dropping the shirt back in place, Lyda leveled a steely gaze on Noah.

"You'll get a severe punishment from me later, Noah. I made it clear that you were to protect every inch of Gen while she was in your care."

"Yes ma'am." Noah looked genuinely chagrined. "I'm sorry."

"It's okay," Gen hastened to tell him. "It doesn't hurt at all."

His look broke her out of any role-playing, because for Noah, it clearly wasn't a game at all. Maybe this wasn't a good idea.

Lyda touched her arm, drawing her gaze with the caress. The woman's direct look was reassurance and admonition both. *Don't pussy out of this. Don't doubt yourself.*

The night at her house, Lyda had made it clear Noah needed heavy handed. Even on her best day, Gen couldn't give him that. So she really couldn't go too far. It was okay. Lyda had said she'd keep Noah safe, and Gen wanted to try being a Domme. She firmed her chin. "Can we… Let's go to the cubicle."

Lyda rose. With Noah following behind, she led Gen to the far side of the large public play area on the main floor. The cubicle area was called "The Maze". It was designed so people could walk through and see what was going on in each space, but only four or five could stand in the opening of any given cubicle. A red line was drawn at that threshold to keep them outside the space itself.

The only place for large gatherings of viewers was in the distant upper mezzanine, lacing the privacy Lyda had mentioned with the thrill of exhibitionism. Some of the cubicles only had a chair and a scattering of restraint and flogger options on the walls. Others had equipment in them, pillories, a St. Andrew's Cross, and things Gen couldn't identify but which made her intensely curious as to their purposes.

Lyda took them to a cubicle on the edge of the maze, partially hidden from above by the mezzanine overhang. A rectangular frame with a thick, padded top piece was anchored to the floor. The top piece was a few inches above Noah's head. It also had rings embedded in it. On the wall was a selection of cuffs that could be attached to them. On the floor, about two feet in front of the frame, she saw a pair of steel boots, also bolted to the floor.

"The boots can be adjusted to lock onto his calves, so he can't move his feet," Lyda explained. "You put his hands in the cuffs attached to the top of the frame. Because of the position of the boots to the frame, his forward weight rests on his palms. It helps him brace himself while you're punishing him. Or fucking him."

Fucking him? Gen followed Lyda's attention to an array of packaged strap-ons, in various sizes. "Oh. I don't know if I could…"

"You've never thought of fucking a man the way he fucks you? Feeling the power that comes from thrusting into him, taking his surrender?"

She'd just wanted a man who treated her decently. Who loved her. She hadn't given anything else a lot of thought, not until recently. Fantasizing about things like strap-ons fed her newly discovered prurient imaginings. What was even better, she was being encouraged to pursue the prurient imaginings. Gen didn't look up beyond the cubicle walls, though. She didn't want to know who might be watching on the mezzanine, didn't want to lose her courage.

"Does this work?"

At Gen's nod, Lyda touched her hand. "He's yours to command. What would you like to do first? You can tell him to kneel until you decide. He waits on your pleasure."

Noah was standing so close to Gen's back that his breath stirred her neck hairs. He'd never stand this close to Lyda without her permission. But he knew she and Lyda were different. She wasn't trying to be Lyda. She was trying to be who Gen would be in a Dominant role. That felt right to her, as did drawing reassurance from his proximity. "Noah, go to the corner and kneel until I call you. Um...take off all your clothes first."

Lyda gave her an approving nod. His fingers brushed Gen's hip, maybe because of the small space, or maybe he just took advantage of that. She didn't mind that, either. With a sinuous twist of his upper body, he pulled the T-shirt off his head, then shucked off jeans, underwear, shoes. He put it all in a neat pile under one of the two chairs and then knelt, balancing his ass on his heels, placing his hands on his knees, his eyes directed to the floor. His thighs were spread, giving her full access to a stiffening cock. From direct experience she knew the testicle sac hanging beneath was substantial and pleasing in the grip of her hand.

With an amused, conspiratorial look, Lyda drew Gen to the implements on the wall, picked up a flogger. "This is a good weight for a novice. If you hit hard with it, it will sting, but it can't do any damage, not if you're aiming at back, ass and legs. Even if you slap his testicles some, he'll jump in a pretty delightful manner, but you're still not endangering him in any way."

His genitals? "Should I have him put the cuffs on first?"

"I don't know. Should you?" Lyda gave her a teasing look, not unkind. "It's up to you, but I often like to do the cuffing. There's something about a strong man letting himself be bound that gets all the juices flowing. Literally." Her voice dropped lower, though Gen assumed Noah could still hear them, given the small area. "He'll probably behave himself tonight, but he can get feisty. He's not a brat, but it's his subtle way of asking for the noose to be tightened. Watch his cues."

Lyda nodded toward him. "He'll also pull shit if he thinks that's what you want and need. He anticipates and he's a nurturer. Sometimes he messes up that way, but he's digging deep for what you want and need from him. Like I said, he'd be a good Dom if he ran that way. But he doesn't. Watch his face, body, everything, and follow your own instincts, what you desire. I won't let you hurt him or yourself. All right?"

"Is that what you look for from a sub?" Gen asked impulsively. "Or is that what drew you to him?"

"He was given to me to protect," Lyda said.

Noah's head came up at that. Rather than his usual easy expression, or slumberous sexual promise, Gen saw a flash of something else. Offense. Anger. Here then gone, but his back had stiffened.

"You want to argue about it, Noah?" Lyda's tone went sharp.

Though Gen was still learning a lot about this world, whenever the two of them hit this area, it was clear that things moved quickly out of sensual play into a far darker realm. It caused a tense ball in her own stomach, a swirl of feelings like a fight-or-flight instinct, except it wasn't her in danger. It was the special, unexpectedly fragile connection between Mistress and sub.

Gen expected Noah to respond with a "No Mistress," in that wooden voice he used whenever Lyda touched a nerve of that enigma Gen hadn't yet deciphered. Instead he turned his gaze back to the floor and said nothing. That ball in her stomach grew spikes, because she knew Lyda wouldn't let it pass. And she didn't.

Moving across the floor, Lyda stood where her knees practically pressed against the crown of his head. "You will answer me, Noah."

He tilted his head to the right, his jaw tight. And stayed silent.

"You don't like hearing I'm your warden?" Lyda demanded. "Your babysitter?"

His gaze snapped back up to her at that. Was Lyda deliberately baiting him? Gen bit her lip. She was about to stick her nose into something she likely didn't understand. But she remembered Noah leaning over her on the beach, the tilt of his head toward the sun, that half-smile.

"He thinks that's all you consider yourself."

Now two sets of eyes came to her. Noah's showing dismay, as if he'd have preferred her not to say it, and Lyda looking like she'd stated the obvious, making Gen flush. The silver eyes had frosted at the interruption.

"It's always intriguing, how subs tend to protect one another, even when they both crave their Mistress's attention," Lyda said in a deceptively casual tone. She turned her gaze back to Noah. "She can already give voice to the preferences you can't,

Noah. Your own personal Cyrano de Bergerac. With a much nicer nose, though big enough to interfere when she can't help herself."

Lyda didn't say it in a mean way. There wasn't even any mockery in her tone, but the pain Gen saw grow more stark in Noah's face, something he couldn't seem to voice, awoke something inside her, something hard and ugly. She should retreat, leave the cubicle. This kind of behavior was likely a deal breaker for her. But she couldn't make herself move. Any more than she could stop the words that sprang to her lips.

"Have you ever told him how you feel about him?"

Lyda's gaze flickered back over to her. Gen could tell she was about to tell her to back off, and she couldn't handle that. She had to get this out, because all of a sudden it was filling up her diaphragm like an explosive device.

"It seems so little to ask, but it's everything," Gen said. "Seeing it in someone's eyes, that you matter…more. It helps everything else make sense, every other problem seem solvable." Her eyes locked with Lyda's. "You said being a Dom is about really knowing what the other person wants and needs, but what does it mean when you hold back on that, not for them, but to protect yourself? How is that different from being a cruel bastard who can't put down the cable remote and make you feel for one goddamn second like you're more special than a fucking golf match?"

Lyda shifted forward. Noah went to a half kneel, as if he might get up, but Gen stepped back, holding up a hand. "It leaves you hating yourself, you know," she told Lyda. "If he'd just done that, given me those two precious seconds, I'd have felt like the queen of Egypt. Such a little thing. Maybe that's why he didn't give me that. Because if that's all it takes, then I didn't expect a lot for myself. I was giving him permission to treat me like I was nothing." Her attention shifted to Noah, came back to Lyda. "But I don't have it in me to demand. I never thought I'd have to demand to be treated special by someone who loved me. I always thought he'd want to do that."

She swallowed. "Can you do something like that for Noah right now? Nothing elaborate. Just one gesture, so I can believe this isn't just another version of the same place I keep finding myself whenever I get pulled into a relationship?"

Lyda pressed a hand into Noah's shoulder, a nonverbal command to stay where he was as she stepped away from him. Gen backed up into the cubicle wall, but Lyda kept coming. She cupped Gen's face, drew closer until Gen's nose brushed her jaw, her forehead against Lyda's prominent cheekbone, all those sculpted angles and fragrant skin. As Lyda's fingers slipped around to the back of her neck, holding her, Gen's throat was burning with a dry-eyed pain, the worst kind, like a desert where life had been burned from it.

"Ssshh," Lyda said against her ear. "It's all right, rabbit. It's all right. Okay."

Lyda had said she wasn't a nurturer, and she wasn't, but maybe that was what made a comforting touch from her so potent. There was a strength to the woman, like a tree. Gen knew she should push away, but it felt so good to be held against her. When Lyda at last drew back, her gaze was thoughtful. "All right, Gen."

She pivoted, shifting so Gen could see Noah as well. He was still on the one knee, quivering with the effort of self-restraint. His gaze was on Gen, showing concern for her, yet still holding onto that wary pain he and Lyda had stirred up between them. Then Lyda snapped his attention back to her with one sharp question.

"Noah, would you go into my home and piss on my expensive rugs?"

He looked startled. "No Mistress."

"Set fire to items that have great sentimental value? And yes"—she shot a glance at Gen—"despite reports to the contrary about what a hardass I am, I do have those."

"No Mistress." His brow creased. "Absolutely no."

"Would you let anyone else do it?"

He shook his head. Stepping forward and catching his chin, Lyda jerked up his head, roughly enough Gen winced. "Then why do you consider yourself different from my other possessions?"

She bent down, stared into his eyes. "You are a gift. One of the finest submissives I've had the pleasure to own. Yet until I break into that flawed part of you and tear the guts out of it, I won't give you an inch, Noah. You'll get no tender moments from me. Not as long as I know you'd let someone treat my prized possession like shit. My *most* prized possession."

As she spoke, the agony in his eyes increased, but Gen saw the moment those last four words registered. Pain transformed into shock, then confusion, as if he wasn't entirely sure how to process such a statement. Lyda's delivery had been a backhanded compliment, but Gen realized there'd been a power to it that a simple, sentimental offering would have lacked. This fit the dynamic that existed between the two of them. And maybe not only the two of them. Lyda straightened, eyed her.

"Your desire to protect him makes me think you should take the punishment he's begging for, Gen."

"No." Noah spoke up, adamant.

Lyda ignored him, attention staying on Gen. She sensed a message being passed to her, something important. "What if I let you sacrifice yourself for him, protect him, then let you fuck him, while I fuck you? You'll get a taste of being both top and bottom, and maybe you'll figure out where on the scale you really want to be." A faint smile touched her lips. "Your place, as you said."

When Lyda shifted to the side, Gen saw Noah watching them both. Conflict was written on his face, his fingers curled on his knees. A moment ago, Lyda had bid him stay where he was. She'd recognized correctly that Gen could only accept comfort for this situation from Lyda herself. A Mistress. Gen touched on the idea tentatively, thinking about what Lyda had said about subs wanting to protect one another...yet both craving punishment from *their* Mistress.

The Ferris wheel lever had been pushed again, taking them up to that top, teetering point, where everything of the world fell away but the three of them. And though Gen was conflicted over the last few moments, she realized Lyda and Noah had brought her back on the ride with them. Proving it, she opened her mouth and said the words a dark and swirling part of her told her to say.

"Yes," she said. "I want to take his punishment. Then...do what you said. Try that."

Lyda cocked her head. "All right. We'll take it a step at a time. Noah, look at me. She's fine now."

Lyda ran her thumb over his bottom lip, a tender act of truce. "Get your ass up. Gen's going to chain you up exactly the way she wants, and you're going to let her do it."

Chapter Nine

Lyda extended a hand, inviting Gen to proceed. Emotional outbursts must be part and parcel of D/s sessions, since Lyda seemed to have taken Gen's in stride. Being unbalanced in a good way seemed to be contagious. Even Noah looked like he felt better.

He'd moved to the frame. Gen paused at Lyda's side, joining her in sheer female appreciation. Noah, naked, his arms bent at a ninety degree angle above his head and palms braced against the padded horizontal bar. He'd threaded his wrists into the open hold of the loose cuffs already dangling from the top padded bar. As her gaze slid down over his tattooed back, she wanted to touch, to taste. He adjusted his feet inside the boots, ass shifting in delightful counterpoint, lean muscles of his thighs flexing.

She hesitated, looked toward Lyda. Lyda brushed a knuckle over Gen's face, increasing her confidence. "Have fun with it," the Mistress murmured. "Let your mind loose to play. It's all wonderland now."

Gen could fall down the rabbit hole. Lyda had called her a rabbit, after all. At first, she'd wondered if Lyda was calling her too timid. But maybe Lyda had been a fan of *Watership Down*, where the rabbits could be fierce fighters among their own kind, as well as fleet of foot and staying alert in a world that considered them food.

Fun. Okay, good with that. Gorgeous, naked male to play with. She could just hear Chloe— *You go, girl! Go tap that fine ass!*

Suppressing a smile, she moved forward. But though things seemed smoothed out, she hadn't forgotten the distress in Noah's expression. So first she pressed herself against his back, the rise of his firm buttocks, and dropped a kiss on his shoulder. "I'm okay," she murmured. "You okay?"

He gave her a nod, bending his head so she could see a dark eye through a fall of silky hair, the tug at his mouth. "Sorry," he mumbled.

She laid another kiss on his shoulder blade. Then she straddled his thigh, giving a sinuous little wriggle as she used the extra few inches of height it allowed to reach up and cinch the first cuff tight enough around his wrist he couldn't pull free. The look he gave her then had a different tone to it, one she answered with a playful lift of her brows, a shift of mood and energy.

Lyda was right. As she buckled that first cuff around his wrist, she experienced a distinct tingle in her loins.

"Feel his cock, Gen."

No need to tell her twice. Sliding an arm around Noah, she closed her fingers over him. He was already hard. That tingle between her legs intensified and spread.

"Now do the other wrist and grip it again."

She did it, watching his fingers twitch, a ripple go through his arm muscles. When she took hold of him once more, he was noticeably thicker and harder. She stroked him, leaning against his side. His eyes were closed, internalizing what she was doing to him.

"The more you restrain him, the more aroused he gets," Lyda said. Her voice had that tone that caressed Gen's nerve endings. "Because he knows he can't stop anything you want to do to him. He has to let go of all control. Adjust the boots so he can't pull his feet out of them."

Her own breath was a little fluttery, her reaction to the proof of what Lyda was describing. With Lyda's guidance, she figured out how to adjust the steel framework so the band around the ankles and just below the knee were cinched enough he still had circulation, but he couldn't remove his feet from the boots. Lyda tested the cuffs as well, running a finger beneath them to verify they weren't too tight.

Gen had knelt next to the wall to work on the boots. Putting her hand on his thigh, she looked up the length of his body, at a very prominent, pleasing erection. He was staring at what she was doing, his brown eyes filled with an enticing fire.

"Here." Lyda tapped her shoulder with a wrapped condom. "Put this on him so he doesn't make a mess."

Gen had the additional pleasure of fitting the tip to his head, rolling it over the engorged shaft. The way his muscles tightened, she could tell he wanted to thrust into her hand. She teased him, rubbing him, squeezing him. He let out a quiet oath, closing his eyes again.

"We all have some sadist in us," Lyda observed with quiet amusement. "I think you're in for an interesting night, Noah. Two women who want to use you until you're drained dry."

"I think he's up for the challenge," Gen said. His eyes opened to half slits at that, what she saw there making her stomach jump in delicious anticipation.

"Doesn't matter if he is or isn't," Lyda said. "It's what we'll demand of him."

His cock jumped under her hand at the sensual threat. Gen felt a hard contraction between her own legs at the way the woman was looking at *her*. A potent reminder there was only one alpha bitch in this room.

"You said you wanted to take his punishment, Gen. Last chance to change your mind about that."

Lyda removed a flogger from the wall. It wasn't the soft flogger with wide straps she'd recommended to Gen. This one had thin, rolled strips. When Noah saw her choice, he shook his head.

"I'll take my punishment, Mistress. I don't want Gen to take it."

"I wasn't aware your opinion mattered," Lyda said. "So shut up while the women are talking, unless you're told to speak."

Her tone was casual, but the look she sent his way was pure ball-busting Mistress. It jolted Gen, sending a wave of uncertainty through her, mixed with a heavy dose of pure lust. For both of them. For what might happen in here.

Noah's jaw got that set to it again, but he shifted his gaze back down. The look he sent Gen first was clear, however. *Don't do this.*

It bugged him, a lot. But Gen thought of how Lyda had looked at her when she suggested that Gen take Noah's punishment. Lyda had told her to follow her instincts and they told Gen that was exactly why she *should* do it. Even though what Lyda was proposing put Gen in a subjugated position, a position of punishment, when she met the Mistress's gaze, Gen felt like the two of them were in collusion about something vital to Noah's well-being. To what he needed.

Gen wanted to give him what he needed.

There were a lot of things she didn't understand in this room, about the many ways she reacted to both of them, but the less she thought about it and the more she followed those instincts, the more *right* it all felt.

"Where do you want me?" She stroked Noah's thigh as she asked it, the light layer of dark hair.

The flare in Lyda's eyes gave Gen a thrilling sort of fear. "Face forward against his back. Take off the skirt and top first so I don't damage them. I want to see you wear that outfit again. Leave on the underwear and heels."

A purely female consideration on the clothes, and a stirring compliment. The way Lyda stroked the whip tails through her curled hand as she said it had the same effect on Gen that the cuffs had seemed to have on Noah. Gen was starting to accept that the two of them could keep her in a constant state of arousal.

Usually Gen took off her clothes in front of a lover as though she were in a dressing room, quick and functional, even a little self-conscious. Now she drew off the top in a way that arched her back, displaying her breasts and that soft skin Lyda claimed to like. Draping the sparkling top on Noah's shoulder, she turned away from both members of her immediate audience. Unzipping the skirt, she shimmied out of it, bracing herself against the wall to step out of it without snagging the heels. As she dipped down to pick up the skirt and pulled the shirt from Noah's shoulder, she could feel his stare. Placing the clothes on the seat of the chair, over Noah's clothes folded on the floor beneath, she met Lyda's eyes.

She'd seen lust in a man's eyes before, those instances where it was clear he had sex first and foremost on his mind. Seeing it in Lyda's gaze, coupled with the intent to possess the object of her desire, made Gen's stomach flip-flop in a new and exciting way. Her knees trembled.

"Bitch tease," Lyda murmured. "It's going to be a pleasure, getting a little-girl squeal out of you." Using her boot, she hooked a footstool in the corner and sent it in a controlled slide and spin across the small space, so it bumped against the back of one of Noah's metal boots. "Get up on that, put your arms around his chest, your face against his neck. Your tits should be pressed between his shoulder blades."

That knee-weakening reaction spread. No, she wasn't a submissive like Noah, but Gen wanted to be commanded by Lyda, taken over. Like taking a tandem jump out of an airplane, trusting the experienced skydiver to carry her on an exhilarating journey.

Noah started to speak. "One more word out of you," Lyda said, "and you'll be gagged. Suck it up."

Gen saw his jaw flex, the flash in the dark eyes. She wondered what he'd do if he was loose. It was a shivery thought.

Stepping up on the stool, she started to slide her arms over Noah's shoulders. Lyda stopped her.

"Under his arms, Gen. I don't want you cutting off his air and not realizing it. He'd let you strangle him if he thought it would interrupt your pleasure or mine. Dumbass."

Noah started to retort to that, and Gen dug her nails in, not wanting him and Lyda to engage again. "Fun and pleasure," she whispered.

He subsided with a grunt and she adjusted her arms as Lyda had directed, banding them around Noah's chest, the widest part right under his armpits. She stroked his chest hair as she overlapped her forearms. With the way the boots were positioned in relation to the frame, his upper body was tilted forward, allowing her to lean. She wasn't sure how much of her weight to rest against him. She also wasn't sure if Lyda wanted her to have that full contact. Those questions were quickly answered.

Lyda drew closer and rolled the flogger down Gen's thigh. Gen made a startled noise when Lyda pressed the rounded handle between her buttocks, pushing the silky fabric of her panties against her anus. Lyda rotated the handle, stimulating her rim through that thin barrier. Gen squirmed against Noah, arms constricting over his chest.

"You like having your ass played with. That's good. Are you a virgin here?"

No. But she might as well be. The experience hadn't been pleasant. She knew it was all the norm, even for teenagers these days, but it hadn't been as popular when she'd started dating, and only one husband had wanted to do it.

Lyda gripped her hair, pulled her head back. "I asked you a question."

"No, ma'am. Once." She wondered if she should say she didn't want to do it, that she hadn't enjoyed it, but maybe it would be different with Lyda. Just the whip's touch had set off an explosion of sensation she hadn't experienced during anal play before.

"All right." Lyda released her hair, removed the prodding touch of the whip. "Take your legs off the stool, wrap them over his knees. Brace your heels on the lip of the metal boots. Like you're riding him piggyback, only a little more spread out. Don't worry about his back or legs. He's strong as an ox, but I'll know when it's time for you to move off him."

There was a smooth curved lip to the front of the boots, wide enough to make the position tenable, maybe even designed for that or other restraint options. As she complied, Lyda tucked the flogger under her arm and cupped a strap under Gen's ass. Threading the ends between Gen's thighs and Noah's, Lyda wrapped it around him so when she buckled it, it cinched Gen's mound against the top of his buttocks. The seam between put friction on her clit, making her squirm the small amount the strap allowed.

Smack!

Lyda stung her ass with her palm. "You'll be moving soon enough, dancing from the whip."

She put a set of cuffs on Gen then, so her arms were locked together over Noah's chest. Lyda slid her hand between his back and Gen's front. The nonverbal cue had Gen hollowing her back so the woman could caress Gen's breast. She gave her nipple a quick flick before she descended, following the line of Noah's lower back and hips, her knuckles gliding along Gen's skin. Her body yearned toward more of that touch. However, when Lyda shifted, followed that same track to his shoulders, Gen realized she was gauging the stress on his joints and muscles.

"I'll think you'll be good for as long as she'll be able to take it." Lyda disappeared from view with a deliberate tap-tap of her boots. Gen wondered if she'd made a mistake. The woman could single-handedly unload young trees from her truck, root ball and all.

"Breathe," Noah rumbled. "Accept the pain. Don't tense. It works better that way."

He let out an oath, and Gen jumped at the pop, realizing only after the fact it hadn't touched her. Whatever Lyda had used had licked up between Noah's spread legs and sent an admonishing sting to his testicles. The passage of air beneath her own spread legs, as well as his flinch, told her the target. It also reminded her how vulnerable her own genitals were to such a strike.

"I can gag you or give you one of those every time you talk out of turn, Noah. Which will it be?" Lyda's voice was scary pleasant.

"The lash, Mistress," he gritted out.

She tsked. "Exactly why it should be the gag. But I'm in a benevolent mood."

When he let out a fierce, whispered curse at the next one, Gen squeezed him. "Sshhh," she said. "Don't talk."

"As I said, subs do tend to try to protect one another, even as they crave the pain. I'll let you use the softer flogger on him later, Gen, but here's a taste of it."

When the blow from the flogger landed, Gen had tensed, she couldn't help it. Though it stung a bit, it wasn't bad. It was almost pleasurable, the stimulation of the wide straps licking at her buttocks, her back, falling away from between her shoulder blades like a stroke from Lyda's hand.

When Noah shifted, the teasing friction from the seam of his buttocks made Gen tighten her legs, bear down to get more of that sensation against her clit.

"I like that. Let me see that ass wiggle when I hit you. It makes my pussy cream. I might let my pets take turns lapping it up later."

God. Gen squirmed even more at that, dancing under the flogger, just as Lyda had predicted. Her buttocks and thighs started to heat up and tingle. She let out a little noise as Lyda let the flogger lick up between her legs once or twice, hitting Noah's buttocks a glancing blow. Then she paused.

"Now you get his punishment, Gen. Next time you try to step between us, you remember what you're taking on."

Her skin was already tenderized from the other flogger. Lyda had wanted a little-girl squeal. She got one, within three strikes. Gen yelped, fingers digging into Noah. He had his head down, his whole body rigid against hers, as if he were fighting an invisible foe, but she wondered if he was nevertheless hard, imagining taking the lash instead.

She had some of that going on as well. Even though this pain was more than she'd expected, her mind warred between wanting Lyda to stop and wanting more of it.

The next strike was with the gentler flogger, only Lyda brought it straight up between Gen's spread legs. The tips struck her pussy. She writhed at the sensation, tightening her thighs over his hips, feeling the grind of his ass beneath her upper thighs. Then came the more painful one, a sharper blow this time. Gen's head snapped back, then pressed forward, jaw wedged between Noah's shoulder and jaw as several blows fell in succession, bringing the pain to a level that took everything else away. Lyda then started to alternate between back, ass, pussy, thighs…

"Stop, stop…" She was gasping, everything vibrating. Lyda paused. Her fingers touched Gen's back. Gen shivered as her nails scraped her flesh.

"Nice red lines. They usually take about a day to go away. I have a shirt that's all mesh in the back. I might make you wear it tomorrow so Marguerite will see those marks. She'll want to touch them. We can't help ourselves. Do you want more, Gen?"

Gen moaned as Lyda leaned against her, cupping Gen's buttock, and then lower, to do the same to Noah's, obviously enjoying her ability to play with both of them.

"Yes." She couldn't believe she said it, because those last ones had really hurt. But in the aftermath, she had a craving to feel it again. "More."

"That sounded like a demand. Ask properly."

"Please. Mistress."

"Better." A quick stroke of her hair, then Lyda's knuckles grazed her buttock. "If you want me to stop, use your safeword, Gen. 'Stop' isn't it."

She should have used it, the very next stripe. Those thin straps felt like they were slicing furrows into her flesh. But she imagined carrying Lyda's marks, imagined Marguerite's gaze on them, those cool fingertips sliding over them, acknowledging another Mistress's work. And she felt Noah's body shifting beneath her, all those lovely muscles. She thought about what

Lyda had said, that Gen would be fucking him tonight, feeling his ass flex against her pelvis…

A scream tore from her throat at the next one. God, the woman had to be drawing blood. She felt like the center of Lyda's universe, every touch, painful or not, building the bond between them.

"Diamonds," Noah snapped. "Mistress."

"A miracle," Lyda said. Gen was panting. While Lyda might not be drawing blood, Gen thought she might be, her fingers digging into Noah's chest. "The first time he's ever used it," his Mistress said. "But he used it for you. Which is good, because you've never chosen a safeword, Gen. You didn't even think about that, did you? It's why a Domme can't trust a sub to use a safeword, though you should always have one."

Gen had her head on Noah's shoulder. She couldn't speak yet, her mind whirling at the idea that she'd taken such a beating and still wanted more. When Lyda touched her hair, she closed her eyes. The woman brushed a kiss on her temple. "You've learned to take pain, no matter how bad it gets. You endure, don't you, rabbit?"

She realized she was shaking. This wasn't aroused trembling, but something emotional that had dislodged and was bouncing around loose. Lyda made a soothing sound. Her hand slid down Gen's spine, trailing between her buttocks. Gen's eyes opened, her legs jerking but unable to close as Lyda slid the whip handle into her soaked pussy. Slow, pumping the shaft like a man's cock. When Noah jumped, hips thrusting forward, Gen suspected Lyda had slid the other whip handle into him. Imagining Lyda impaling them both, working the two whip handles in their overlapped bodies, had her body's shakes turning into different kind of spasms.

"When you were fucked in the ass, Gen, did you enjoy it?"

"No."

Guy had pushed her face into the pillows, nearly suffocating her and making her neck hurt as he tried trying to adjust himself at the right angle, forcing it until she had to complain, ask him to take it slower. He did, but it still burned, and she bled afterward.

"So he did it wrong." Lyda touched Gen's lips. "Suck my finger. Get it wet."

Gen parted her lips. Lyda watched her suck on the digit, her absorbed expression whetting Gen's response. "Keep holding that whip handle in you, Noah," the Mistress said absently. "You let it drop, Gen will be wearing a much bigger dick to fuck you."

She gave Gen a feminine look of conspiracy as Noah bucked, a groan coming from his lips. "When I tell him to clench those lovely ass muscles, it makes it more pleasurable inside. Tsk, tsk. Leaking into that rubber, aren't you? Every drop of that belongs to me. You hold it in until I give you permission."

"Yes Mistress." He spoke through gritted teeth as Lyda withdrew her finger from Gen's mouth. Sliding her dry fingers down the valley of Gen's spine, she probed between her buttocks with the wet one. The quivering of her body, the way she felt inside and out, was wild, desperate. It was obvious Lyda liked that. "No clenching against me, baby girl. Let it in. There...we go."

Gen let out a surprised breath as Lyda's finger slid through the rings of muscle, moving in a way that produced an intense spiral of interest from Gen's nerve endings. "You have a fine, tight little hole. Some night when you've been a bad little girl, I might let Noah give you an ass fucking. There's an untamed beast inside him. But you know that, don't you? Would you like to see more of that?"

So Lyda knew about those precious five minutes in the kitchen, when Noah's power and ferocity had taken Gen over so that she'd nearly lost herself in it. "I'd like to see any side of him. Ah..."

Lyda had hooked her fingers back around the whip handle she had inside Gen's pussy and was working that at the same time she was working the finger in her anus. "Keep clenching on that handle for me, Noah. I want your muscles milking it like you'll be doing when Gen's fucking you."

"Yes Mistress." Noah's voice still had that strangled quality. Gen pressed her cheek hard against his back, fighting her own growing response. She was rubbing herself against his buttocks. The two whip handles knocked against each other. She could feel the impact as they made contact, the wide and thin straps brushing their legs.

"Stop moving, now. Both of you." They stilled, bound to Lyda's every wish. She removed both whip handles, a sensual pull out of Gen's engorged tissues. Lyda's finger came out of her anus with a teasing stroke of her rim. Setting the whips aside, Lyda released Gen's bonds and eased her off Noah's back. She'd pulled over one of the nearby chairs, and lowered Gen's shaking body into it. The first pressure of the vinyl seat on her aroused pussy caused a whimper. Lyda pressed her down fully, so the stripes she'd left on Gen's flesh were against the firm surface of seat and back, the flash of discomfort balancing the crazy need to rub against the chair, against anything.

"Feet flat on the floor, back against the chair, like a proper schoolgirl. I need to wash my hands and then we'll get to the next part."

Noah remained in his bound position, head down, shoulders rising and falling. Lyda had put her directly behind him, so Gen couldn't see how thick his cock was, but if his arousal was as intense as hers...it made her shudder, thinking of him thrusting into her, stretching her. His buttocks flexed again as he shifted in the boots.

Each cubicle had a small sink unit. Lyda washed her hands, then examined the selection of strap-ons on the wall. "There's a pink one," she said, with amusement. "Bright, girly, princess pink. It adds the extra dose of humiliation to the man whose ass you're fucking. But we're not about humiliation, are we, Noah?"

"No Mistress." His back vibrated, odd little shivers, his head still down. Gen looked toward Lyda. Despite her apparent focus on the strap-ons, the Mistress had an eye trained on the male as well. On them both. Gen lifted a questioning brow and mouthed *Is he okay?*

Lyda tilted her head left to right, a *sort of* kind of answer. A serious look to her eyes, she gestured to Gen, letting her know she could go to him. Though she was still riding that intense arousal, her knees were steadier now. Gen rose, circled in front of him. His body shadowed her in its angled position like a leaning tree, his arms the spread branches. When she touched his chest, his eyes opened. She thought she saw anger, arousal, fear, a deep hurricane of feeling that couldn't be separated or described. Or answered with words. She put her fingers on his mouth, and he kissed her fingers.

"Turn around," he said.

Realizing what he wanted to see, she pivoted, looked over her shoulder at him. "It's okay," she said. "It felt...good. And bad."

"Yeah." He studied the marks. "Step back? Close enough I can touch them."

She wasn't sure how he could do that with his hands bound, but he pulled against the hold of the wrist cuffs, managing to reach her shoulder with his lips. The resulting sensation activated the nerves between the mark under his mouth and the ache of the closest stripes like the strands of a charged web. "I'll kiss every one of them if you want," he said.

"Afterward." She turned to face him. A whirl of feeling rose at his tender gesture. It evoked similar ones in her. It also somehow connected to a sudden deep urge to do exactly what Lyda was going to allow her to do. She wanted to fuck him the way a man would.

* * * * *

Gen trailed her hand along his side, leaving him with the caress. Lyda was leaning against the wall, waiting on her. Moving across the room in her heels and sexy underwear, Gen didn't stop until she stood in front of Lyda. She stayed that way, letting Lyda look her fill, waiting for what she'd command. The Mistress nodded, tacit approval. "Take off the panties."

Gen stepped out of them without hesitation. She realized she'd stopped thinking about anyone on the mezzanine, and she was only vaguely aware of the voices and music outside the cubicle. Yes, there were plenty of naked people here, but it was more than that. This was a fixed spot in the universe, the only one that mattered.

Taking the panties, Lyda tossed them onto the pile of Gen's clothes on the chair. Then she lifted a flesh-colored strap-on from the wall and fitted it over Gen's hips and between her thighs. As efficient as a horsewoman saddling her mount, Lyda cinched it up against Gen's clit, closing the distance between flesh and rubber. Then she adjusted the straps at the waist and those threaded between and around Gen's thighs. When she was done, Lyda was behind Gen. She slid a finger back into Gen's pussy, putting her other hand on Gen's shoulder to hold her steady. Gen made a needy noise, her fingers clenching.

"Making sure there's still room for me," Lyda said, sliding free to pinch her ass. "Walk around in it. Feel the way it moves. Get used to it, think about where you're going to be putting it. Let him see you in it. And let's get rid of this." Unhooking Gen's bra, she slid it down her arms, and added it to the rest of the clothes. Sliding an arm around Gen's waist, she guided her to an angle where Noah could turn his head and see them.

His eyes latched onto the strap-on, then moved up. Lyda stood behind her, one arm looped around Gen's waist, her other hand sliding up to cup her bare breast, pinch a nipple as Gen leaned against her.

Lyda pushed her hair aside with her jaw, kissed her neck. "So beautiful," she said against Gen's skin. "The two of you. I can't get enough."

Gen had no will of her own, but she'd never been in a situation where it mattered so little. Everything Lyda did to her was something she wanted, and she was eager to see what she would do next. She didn't have long to wait.

"Hold out your palm," Lyda ordered.

When Gen complied, Lyda produced a tube of lube. She squirted a generous dollop of the warm, slick gel in Gen's palm. "Rub it on your cock, Gen. You're getting ready to fuck him. You want to go in easy and deep. Watch his eyes as you do it. Think about how you'd put the lube on his cock."

Gen curled her fingers around the phallus. It was a good size, thick and hard like Noah's cock, encased in latex. She could tell the inside of his condom was already streaked with his pre-cum. Though technically she wasn't stroking herself, it felt amazing, her pussy tingling under the pressure she put against her own clit. Was this what a man felt like, standing before a woman, stroking his organ, a sense of conqueror in the motion? Rousing the desire to sink deep into a wet, welcoming pussy?

Noah's expression of suffused lust made her hotter. "Oh, yeah, he likes watching you do that," Lyda said. "You can make him come, just by doing that and talking dirty to him. Telling him where you're going to stuff that, how hard you're going to make him come, pounding his ass. Watch his hands fist in the bonds. He fights it, but he wants it too. I've seen a man fuck him, and he enjoys it, but it's not the same as when a woman does it to him. It makes him come undone, and you remake him in the aftermath. You take him all the way home, and then you keep him there."

Lyda pressed herself against Gen's back again, cupping both her breasts. Gen let out a moan as Lyda ground her pubic mound against Gen's backside. Gen rolled her hips, wanting to give her Mistress pleasure. Lyda nipped her neck.

"Look at his chest, Gen. You did that." She saw it then, the crescent marks where her nails had bitten into his skin.

"He likes nothing better than to be marked by us. Maybe we'll do that permanently one day. Brand his ass when he figures out what belonging to a Mistress really means."

His gaze slid to Lyda's. Gen sensed a whisper of that conflict between them again, but Lyda didn't linger long enough to let it snag them this time. Her hands slid from Gen's breasts, and she gave her a push. "Flirt with him while I get ready."

Gen wet her lips. Keeping her hand moving on the now well-greased phallus, she moved forward, shifting closer to the wall so Noah could get a better look at her.

"No wonder a guy thinks this makes him king of the world. The weight of it makes me want to swagger."

A smile touched his lips, but it didn't dilute the intensity of his eyes. "Closer," he said, his voice a growl.

She arched a brow, but eased forward. His legs were bound, his wrists, but he still managed to emanate a sensual threat. She expected there was some primal dance of testosterone versus estrogen where the former, when whipped to a lustful frenzy like this, could set off a woman's flight instinct. Only in this case, she kept drawing closer to the threat, not away, as if she knew the danger was worth it.

When she was close enough that the tip of the dildo brushed his testicles, she reached up with her non-lubing hand. Gathering a handful of his hair, she stroked the straight silk of it over his bare shoulder, tangled her fingers in it. The other hand she put on his abdomen, leaving a slick trail down to his cock, where she closed her fingers over him. She played with the corona through the latex, wishing the barrier wasn't between them.

His head dropped, neck twisting. Before she could anticipate him, he closed his teeth on her throat. His clamp on the carotid was so firm she could feel the pump of her blood, and it accelerated as she recognized that untamed side Lyda had talked about. Her eyes closed, and she gripped his hips with both hands, pressing her upper body as close as she could, lifting upon her toes. The tip of his cock dragged against her navel, the hard length pressing against her lower abdomen.

His tongue played along her pulse, teeth tightening further. He wasn't breaking skin, but he was compressing the area enough the pulse rate started to thunder. She felt the faint buzz of the tongue stud and her whole body reacted with a gooseflesh-raising shudder.

"Noah," she breathed, her fingers scraping at his flesh. "I'm getting…dizzy."

He released her, nuzzled the bitten area. She captured his mouth, gripping the back of his neck to hold him, plunder his lips. He gave her back a kiss so intense, her toes curled in her heels. When a track of arousal ran down her leg, Lyda's fingertip slid along it. She gripped Gen's waist, drawing her back.

The Mistress had one hand on Noah's back, the other now up to her lips, tasting Gen. "Ready?" she asked, her gaze like molten steel.

When Gen made a noise of agreement, Lyda curled her fingers in the strap at her waist, gently tugged so she was shifted between him and Lyda. He adjusted his feet in the boots, getting ready for her. His fingers curled and uncurled in his cuffs.

Gen glimpsed another strap-on Lyda had laid on the chair. Lyda had chosen the princess-pink one for herself. The one she'd be fucking Gen with. Another little shudder ran through Gen, imagining Lyda driving that into her. "This is now your party," Lyda said to her. "You're lubed up good enough. You fuck him when you're ready. Take your time with it, play with him, do whatever foreplay you enjoy."

"I don't want to hurt him. I've never done it."

"Ease in, don't push," Lyda advised. "Other than that, you'll be fine. He has a nice, tight ass, but it's been well used. He's not a virgin to it."

Gen saw Noah's eye trained on her through that fall of hair along the side of his face, but then Lyda captured her attention with a firm touch on her jaw. "You command his orgasm, Gen. He doesn't go until you say so. If he does, he gets punished." Her gaze gleamed. "So you can guess which way I'm hoping things will go. I was holding back with you. I won't with him."

Gen remembered the pain of those thin straps. The same way he'd wanted to protect her, she didn't want Noah punished. Lyda was right. It was hard to reconcile those two emotions, craving the pain Gen wanted to spare another.

Lyda stepped back, picking up the pink strap-on so she could sit on the chair. "He's all yours, Gen. You own his ass, his cock, and everything attached to them. He's your property. Touch him any way you wish. Command him however you desire."

A heady thought. Wicked, politically incorrect, titillating. Irresistible. With every word Lyda spoke, Noah's breathing elevated, making those handsome shoulders and chest expand and contract, conveying arousal, anticipation. Gen's gaze riveted on the curves of his buttocks. Wetting her lips, she stepped forward. She slid one fingertip over the right cheek, and it quivered, both of them tightening in automatic reflex. Hard desire speared her.

"Do that again," she murmured. "Hold it that way."

He obeyed, tightening his ass so his thigh muscles hardened, as well as the muscles of his lower back. She ran her fingers over the pleasurable terrain, scraping him to watch those little twitches and movements. God, he had a fine ass. "Now relax it."

"I like thinking about the way it looks from behind, when a man's inside me." She wasn't sure if she was talking to herself, him or Lyda. It didn't matter. "The pumping motion as he's thrusting. I'd like to have a mirror on the ceiling, so I could watch. I think I could come from just that, no matter what else he was doing."

An image passed through her mind of Lyda lying on top of her the other night, making a similar movement. Her beautiful heart-shaped ass would have been making that flexing motion, her shoulders and slim back shifting.

Gen ran her hands over Noah's back, that vision melding into this one, both pleasurable. She caressed his shoulders, his neck, under his hair, into his hair. He rolled his head with the movement, like a horse being pleasured by her touch, and she liked that, so she did it again, exploring all of him. As she did, she moved closer, nudging him with the dildo. It slid between his legs, and she rotated her hips, rubbing the phallus against his testicles. Sliding her arms around him, she pressed herself full against his back and began to work her hips in the act of coitus she'd just described. When he let out a quiet groan of pleasure, she ran her lips along his spine, between his shoulder blades. All hers. He was all hers.

And they both belonged to Lyda. The Mistress's regard was a tangible force. She was seeing what Gen had imagined, the rise and fall, flex and release of her ass as she moved against Noah, their naked bodies pressed together. Though Gen was allowing her own desires to lead her, Lyda had directed their physical and emotional responses onto this track. Yet it wasn't all one-way. Gen loved knowing they were making Lyda wet and aroused. She was strangely humbled that Lyda was restraining her obvious natural instinct to dominate them both to let Gen explore who and what she was.

She rose on her toes to bite Noah's shoulder hard, payback. She thought again about Lyda's threat to make her wear a shirt that would show off her own marks. It made her crazy hot to think of it.

Sliding the dildo from between his thighs, Gen adjusted the stool. With a steadying breath, she stepped upon it. As she guided the lubricated tip between his buttocks, she earned a fervent oath from him and felt him bracing himself in the boots.

A well-used ass, Lyda had said. But to Gen it was all brand new.

She was careful, because she remembered how much it had hurt her. But Lyda's finger hadn't hurt. Gen had begged for more with the movement of her hips. She pressed inward, her heart high in her throat. God, it felt... She eased farther in, and those muscles gave way like open sesame, a gateway waiting just for her.

She expected it was the closest a woman could get to what sinking into someone was like. She slid deep, Noah shuddering all the way, and then she was holding him tight around the waist, the strap-on pressed against her cunt in a way that begged her to keep moving, keeping working it back and forth so she'd get that stimulation as well. But she stayed like this an extra moment. She could feel Noah's inner muscles clutching the dildo. The vibration came up the shaft, sexy, involuntary little twitches. Experimenting, she drew back, then sank back in.

Oh yeah. That was the ticket, if how his breath whistled out and he clenched his fingers in the cuffs were any indication. She did it again, small movements, spreading her hands against his chest, plucking at his nipples. She wasn't hurting him, which was a relief that spiked the pleasure, as did his rough words.

"God…fuck…Gen."

The power of it was unbelievable. Lyda had said he was her property. Hers to fuck, to possess. To keep. She'd never experienced that with any boyfriend, husband…they'd been sand passing through her fingers, even when she lay in bed next to them, even when holding them. Was it like this every time a Domme claimed a sub? Was it just an in-session kind of feeling, or could it be carried into the real world? Could it intertwine with how Gen felt about Noah and become a constant element of their relationship, as much as waking in the morning together, sharing breakfast, paying bills…

If it could, how did Lyda keep it compartmentalized the way she did? Or did she?

Gen's response was ratcheting up with every impact of the strap-on. It silenced the debate, focused her on the here and now. Then Lyda's fingers curled over her hips. On Gen's next pull-back stroke, Lyda slid deep into her cunt.

She'd stayed aware of Lyda's scrutiny, but somewhere along the way Gen had lost where she was, what she was doing. So it was an erotic shock to be suddenly impaled, her aroused tissues clutching the dildo inside her the way Noah's ass was holding onto Gen's. "Oh…Christ…"

Lyda was doing exactly what she'd threatened…promised. She pushed Gen flush against Noah and held her there, using him as a wall and not allowing Gen to move as she worked her hips, thrusting the pink phallus in and out of Gen's pussy. A slick slide against tissues already vibrating with need.

"Mistress…"

"Just take it, baby girl. I get my pleasure before you get yours. That's the way this pyramid works. Don't you move, or I'll beat you with that flogger again."

Noah was a lit cannon under Gen's grip, his body hot and hard, every muscle clenched. Her own thighs were shaking as Lyda kept driving into her. At some point, she and Noah were doing the shuddering thing together, incoherent breaths, pleas and oaths slipping from their lips. Gen dug her fingers into his chest, held on for dear life.

"Please...Mistress..."

Lyda let out a nasty chuckle. "Keep begging. You have such a sweet pussy, I might just have to keep at this for a while."

"I can't..."

"But you will. You both will." Lyda pinched her nipple, making Gen flinch. "If he gets too close to coming before you give him permission, dig your nails into the base of his cock, give his balls a twist. It works wonders to keep them focused."

She'd forgotten Noah was waiting on *her* to give the command. She'd abdicated everything to Lyda the moment she touched Gen. What did that say about her?

Lyda had said he'd be punished if he came before Gen gave the order. Noah was obviously so desperately close she followed Lyda's orders, groping for his cock. Holy fuck, he was huge. Her pussy got even wetter, if that was possible. She could hear it sucking on the phallus Lyda was thrusting into her. Lyda made a pleased noise.

Gen bit her nails into his cock, squeezed his testicles. Harder, until she heard him grunt. And Lyda slammed into her again. The woman's breath was rapid, and then it moved into a soft moan, entirely feminine, unexpected. Gen had expected her to roar like a lioness. Yet it was even more arousing to hear Lyda release with those female helpless cries of pleasure. She had her mouth pressed to Gen's shoulder, teeth on her flesh as she held Gen's hips tight, worked the dildo in her fast and furious. Gen couldn't last a second more. She barely remembered to gasp out the permission.

"Come, Noah. Please come."

He released with a snarl. With his hips pistoning and Lyda still deep inside Gen, Gen was catapulted into another universe-bending climax. When Lyda's hands gripped her breasts and tweaked her nipples this time, it shot her over a higher ledge. She was whirling, spinning, tumbling.

She clawed at Noah as if she really was falling off a cliff. Since Lyda was pressed full against her back, Gen groped behind her, latched onto her forearm. She held them both tight as she fell to earth like a stone.

Divine Solace

* * * * *

Music returned. Voices. The erratic air currents in a place occupied by a lot of people. She'd had another intense sexual experience in the middle of a club, a public forum. When she tilted her head to look up, she regretted it. The mezzanine had become standing room only, like ringside seats at a heavyweight championship. She knew without being told it was all for them. It had been a spectacular event to witness, let alone experience. God, what the hell?

"I need to move," she managed. "Please."

Lyda lifted off her, gently detaching her arm from Gen's grip when Gen couldn't uncurl her fingers on her own. Lyda guided Gen's arm under Noah's. "Hold onto him," she ordered. When Gen complied, palms pressed to his chest, Lyda withdrew. Gen's pussy contracted with the movement, a shiver running through her. She only had a moment to miss the pleasure of Lyda's body before a terrycloth robe was laid over her shaking shoulders. Lyda threaded her hands into the sleeves, one at a time, as if Gen was a doll. She didn't try to pull the robe around Gen's front, letting her draw warmth from Noah's strong back, the curve of his buttocks against her pelvis.

After Lyda ensured Gen's arms were wound securely around his chest again, she released Noah's wrists. She brought his arms down one at a time, ensuring he kept his movements gradual. She directed him to hold onto the side pieces of the frame. "Stay in this position until I get her moved."

Putting her hands on Gen's hips, Lyda eased her back, bringing the strap-on out of Noah's ass together. "Easy. Take everything slow."

The internal muscles released. Gen heard Noah's grunt at the stimulation, then the phallus was out. After Lyda removed the strap-on, she let Gen collapse against his back, her damp pussy pressed against his ass. She didn't want to think or feel beyond the simple bulwark of his body.

But Lyda insisted on moving her once more, guiding her down into the chair she'd slid up behind them. Gen blinked. The world was spinning. Though her butt was in the chair, the rest of her wanted to go topsy-turvy, like a rag doll with no bones.

While Lyda was steadying her, Noah bent and unlatched the boots. He stripped the condom off his cock, tossed it in the trash. "Let me help, Mistress," he said.

Though Lyda made a mildly annoyed sound at his disobedience, she nodded. Noah scooped Gen off the chair. Her arms circled his neck, hiding her face. When he slid down the wall of the cubicle, seating them on the floor, she realized he'd picked the side partially beneath the mezzanine, sheltering her from the watching faces above. He understood so much without being asked. No wonder Doms liked using him as an "aftercare nanny". Did Lyda ever do that, so she didn't have to do it herself? It made Gen sad to think so.

Just as before, she had a mix of desolate feelings warring with post-orgasmic euphoria. Distantly, Gen was aware of Lyda stripping the condoms from the strap-ons and putting everything they'd used into a used toy bin for sterilizing. Mess all cleaned up, at least on the outside. She needed to go home. She wanted to go home.

"You said he could go home with me." She spoke against his throat.

"Yes, I did." Lyda's voice told Gen she was across the cubicle.

"I want to go home."

"All right. We'll get you dressed—"

"I don't care. I just want to go home." Gen pushed herself up, rising on unsteady legs. Way unsteady.

"Whoa." Noah, somehow far more recovered than she was, was on his feet. He had her on one side as Lyda caught the other. "Take it slow, Gen. You need to—"

"Let go of me. I need to go home. I…stop…"

She pushed away from them, never mind how disoriented she was. She couldn't find the exit to the cubicle. It was a fucking maze. A labyrinth, just like her feelings, this sudden panic. "I'm going." She bumped into the wall like a beetle in a bottle, but started moving along it. The wall should give way to an opening.

"Gen." Lyda's snap was effective as the touch of a whip, jerking Gen around. She was pushed into a chair. "Sit until you're steadier. Sit. Down." Lyda's unshakable grip stayed on Gen's shoulders until the words penetrated. She met Lyda's silver eyes. In control. Lyda was in control.

Gen shivered. "I can't...what is this?"

"It's kind of subspace and sub-drop, all at the same time."

"Sundrop? Like the soda." A hysterical laugh bubbled up. Noah was squatting by the chair, his hand on her knee. She gripped it as if she thought she might fall off a real cliff if she let go of him. She wanted to seize Lyda's other hand, but Lyda had straightened. As a result, Gen's hand landed on the soft linen of her shirt, Gen's fingers curling into the waistband of the riding breeches, thumb fingering the zippered side. Lyda was beneath, cool flesh, a bare hip bone. No underwear. Would she ever see Lyda naked...and not just physically?

"Sub-drop, dopey. Not sundrop." Lyda stroked her hair from her cheek, then took a firm hold on her chin. "Sessions bring up a lot of shit in a submissive's subconscious, things that can overwhelm you, because you're too emotionally drained to process them. No shields to contain them. That means it's working the way it's supposed to work. Don't fight it. Just ride it out. We're here to watch over you."

Easy for Lyda to say. She'd caused that earthquake inside Gen, yet she looked unfazed, steady as a mountain. Detached. It hurt. Gen drew away, closer to Noah. She clenched his hand. "You said...I could keep him tonight."

Lyda's beautiful face became expressionless. "Yes I did. He's yours."

The way the skin pulled tight over Lyda's cheekbones bugged Gen, but her fuzzy brain couldn't process that. Lyda's gaze shifted to Noah. "Take her home, Noah. Care for her properly. I'm done with you both for the night."

Noah began to say something, but Lyda put a quelling hand on his shoulder. "Do as I say. Take care of her. That's what she needs tonight. We'll deal with the rest later."

Chapter Ten

Done for the night. That described Gen as well. She wasn't aware of the ride home, though she didn't ever let go of Noah. She kept her arms wrapped around him while he drove, his own arm circling her as he stroked her hip. He even carried her to her front door, only letting her down to unlock and open her door. When he took her into her bedroom, he undressed her, his touch a misty memory of pleasant caresses. But her bedroom, her solitary place of retreat, to think and dream, to find her center, brought some sanity back to her.

"I want you to stay, but in the guestroom. Close, but not in here. Please..." She cleared her throat, looked up at him in the direct way Lyda did, so he knew it wasn't a request. "Don't come in unless I tell you to."

Her voice quavered, draining any real authority from it, but Noah simply nodded. Brushing a kiss over her forehead, he tugged on the oversized sleeve of the Snoopy nightshirt she'd wanted to wear. "I'll be close."

The need to feel in control was overriding the euphoria. Ordering him away from her, which was against what she was sure they both wanted, felt right. She had to be sure she still had a brain, a will of her own. The things she'd done tonight were beyond what she'd ever thought herself capable of wanting, let alone experiencing, yet she'd embraced so much of it. And she wanted more, even with no idea of what lay beyond the curtain, or the end destination. She wasn't the type who took the unmarked path.

Not anymore, because when she had been that kind of person, she'd always chosen the one that had the hidden sign screaming "path of sure self-destruction".

Sliding into the bed, she burrowed herself under the covers. Her gaze slid toward the nightstand, where she had a small vase of dried flowers and a little plaque she'd bought from a secondhand store. The simple mantra *Be true to yourself* was printed on it. Had she done that tonight?

Commanding Noah under Lyda's direction had been amazing, incredible. His responses, her own. Lyda, commanding both of them. *I can't get enough.* Gen remembered Noah quivering, just the way she had, when their Mistress had said that. Lyda's desire for them had been so clear, no conflict. So why was Gen now curled up in a ball, wishing Noah was here beside her and afraid to think too much about Lyda?

She couldn't succeed at a normal guy-girl relationship. She'd picked two wrong men. They'd reduced her to poverty, stripped her self-esteem, and made her doubt her ability to find love. She'd watched Marguerite, followed by Chloe, find an amazing man any woman would want. As a result, Gen had concluded finding love wasn't magic, no *presto, I'm here*. It was something certain people had mapped in their destiny, like DNA. The rest were doomed to spend their lives seeking it like a drug, exhibiting all the irrational behavior of addicts to get and keep it. Or they compromised themselves to have merely a shadow of it. The alternative was figuring out how to be happy and enough by yourself. She'd settled on that course, hence the plaque.

Why did she keep falling into the trap of thinking she could step back, treat this as a kinky, fun adventure, no harm done? She wasn't built that way.

Lyda represented the greater risk of the two. Elusive, remote and mesmerizing, she was fully capable of destroying Gen's heart. The more she wanted Lyda, the more frightened she was of wanting her. But she couldn't discount the peril of Noah. He'd stepped into her heart the first weekend and yet, as accessible as he seemed, he was as elusive to define, in terms of a relationship, as Lyda. Gen had no doubt the two came as a package. Even if they hadn't figured that out between them yet, she could see it, feel it, whenever she was around one or both of them.

Long and short, she was a vanilla girl who was in way over her head. Wrapping her arms around herself, she started rocking. She wasn't going to call Noah to do it. She had enough respect for herself and him not to use him that way. The decision made her resent her conscience like hell. It took a long while to fall asleep.

When she did, it was a sleep punctuated by distorted memories from her past. A fist raised, hitting her in the face. It had hurt, but the shock of it, the utter betrayal of love it represented, was the true horror. She rolled away from the blow, but found herself standing, bound to the frame the way Noah had been, her feet in the boots, arms stretched up, so she had no defense as her first husband came at her again. He hit her in the face, bouncing on the balls of his feet like a boxer practicing at one of those balloon-like punching bags. Her other husband sat on the floor, tossing handfuls of money in the air and laughing like a child. God, dreams sucked.

She'd been a tool, a means to an end. No, worse. Betrayal meant you were nothing to the betrayer. Insignificant, unworthy of love. No matter how horrible the betrayer was, that was the poisonous seed they embedded in a soul, never to be dug out again.

She saw Lyda watching from the corner. She begged her for help, but why should Lyda help? Gen had turned away from her. Suddenly Gen was standing beside her, but Gen was locked in a box, invisible. Noah was chained to the frame, and Gen's first husband was hitting him. Her other ex approached, bat in hand. Though she screamed in protest inside that soundproof box, he brought it down on Noah's fingers. She heard the crunch of bone. Blood drained from Noah's face, body giving way before the blows, but his burning eyes remained on Gen and Lyda. Not asking for rescue, not asking for anything. But needing everything.

Gen kept screaming, wondering why Lyda did nothing. She was a statue, made of smooth concrete. All except her eyes. Gen saw pain there. Now, instead of being right beside Gen, Lyda was watching from a remote mountain, far away from Gen and Noah. Yet Gen could still see that pain in her face, and she wanted to ease it, take it into herself. But the only way she could help either one of them was if she could get out of the box. If she could touch them both, she'd break this nightmare, the solitary confinement into which they'd placed themselves, fighting their own personal demons alone. But she needed their help to do it.

"Help...help me...please..."

Just as she was despairing, she began to hear music. A guitar, strumming out an aimless, wistful ballad. Slowly, too slowly, it started drawing her away from the nightmare, coaxing her on a short drift through dark clouds of sleep, and floating her down into fantasy. She was in a stable. A bard sat on a hay bale in front of a horse stall. He'd been given this place to sleep, after playing for his supper in the great hall. Now his music had a much smaller audience. It had wooed the attentions of a kitchen wench and the lady of the house.

The kitchen wench sat on another bale close to him, the lady of the house in the shadows, watching. He played to their hearts, making them both long for him. Gen stared at Noah's beautiful, unbroken hands, his long fingers plucking and stroking the strings. He had the musician's irresistible lure, as if the way he sang or played telegraphed what kind of lover he would be, his ability to make music with one's body the same way.

Gen realized then she was in a hazy half-sleep, banishing the nightmare by consciously weaving more details around this preferred stage. As a teenager, she'd attended a heavy metal concert, and the tickets had put her close enough to the stage to watch the visceral way the guitarist pounded on his instrument, cradled against his leather-clad pelvis. The ultimate bad boy, who'd pound into her in the same wild, untamed way.

The bard's music was a different, spiraling, clouds-in-the-sky feeling, but no less seductive. She was the kitchen wench, in a peasant smock that barely held her breasts, pushed up by the waist cincher she wore. The bard's gaze slid over them. Often.

He'd had his supper, and was now playing for dessert. That undercurrent of male interest dampened her cunt, made her breasts ache for touch. The lady of the house came and sat next to her. When she stretched out an arm behind Gen, Gen leaned into her body, the side of her breast pressed against her Mistress's as they both listened. Her lady's long hair was already unbound for the night. She wore a velvet robe over her nightrail, which made her no less imperious yet so sexually mesmerizing it was impossible not to be drawn to her. She stroked Gen's hair, the bare line of her shoulder, as they both watched him. His eyes, the color of a dark ale, followed the movement, intensified at the implication.

Gen remembered her station then, giving her lady the hay bale, sinking down to the floor at her lady's knee. Yet her Mistress kept her hand on her. She stroked Gen's throat so she lifted her head, met her lady's mouth for a long, sweet kiss. Her slender hand caressed Gen's breast, so accessible in the blouse. It wouldn't be the first time she'd shared her lady's bed, for her Mistress had appetites as strong as any man's, but tonight it would be a threesome. The bard missed a chord. Her lady smiled against Gen's lips.

"We'll have to punish him for that, won't we, rabbit?"

Gen came out of the smoky fantasy. She had her hand between her legs. The music hadn't been part of fantasy or dream. She *was* hearing guitar music. Noah apparently had retrieved the instrument from her craft room. He'd had more music lessons than her, enough to strum out the tune that had guided her fantasy.

She wished Lyda was here, in bed with her. But it was hard to envision Lyda in Gen's simple bed. Seeing herself in Lyda's opulent tester bed was much easier. The Mistress would tie Gen's hands to the rails, move down her body, feasting on Gen's cunt while she begged for mercy the woman would wait a long time to give. Noah would be locked beneath the bed, listening to Gen's moans, his hands bound so he couldn't touch himself. Lyda wanted him to climax from nothing more than listening.

Was this part of subspace-subdrop as well, one's libido bouncing back faster than a boomerang? Gen turned on her side, listening. Just as she'd ordered, he hadn't come into her room. He was humming along with the guitar tune, sitting in the hallway, perhaps leaning against the wall next to her door. Had she cried out, such that he'd known she was having a nightmare? No. If that had happened, he would have come to her, all bets off. Maybe he'd just anticipated her sleep would be restless. As Chloe had said and Gen was learning firsthand, he excelled at anticipating a woman's needs.

She rose, padded across the floor. Opening the door to a welcome touch of air from the A/C, she looked down at him. He didn't stop the song, or his humming, though he tilted his head, gazing at her through the darkness. Sliding down the wall, she sat next to him, put her head on his bare shoulder. He brushed the crown of her head with his jaw, kept playing. His biceps flexed under her breast where it pressed against him.

"I'm not a Domme," she said at last.

"No," he agreed. "But you're great at working with one."

"You're like that too, aren't you?"

"Sometimes. I like feeling in control, under direction, if that makes sense."

It did. "Is it because it feels safer that way? Like you can't screw up or take responsibility for anything that goes wrong? Puts it all on her?"

His fingers stilled a moment, then resumed. A different tune now, but still pleasant to the ears. "No. Don't try to work it out in words. It doesn't work."

"I screwed up with her tonight, didn't I? At the end."

"You can't screw up something like that, Gen." He touched her knee, a brief caress. "She knows how crazy it gets after she scrambles your brain. It takes time to process it all, especially at first."

"But you knew. You tried to talk to her about it, and she told you to take me home, that we'd 'deal with the rest later'."

"Yeah. That's Lyda."

Now that her eyes were adjusted to the dim illumination in the hallway, she could see his hair was tousled enough to suggest he might have slept some. He wore jeans, but when her hand crept beneath his arm, slid across his rib cage and down, her questing fingers found the top button had been left open and he was bare beneath. She played with the metal disk, brushing the firm flesh beneath.

"I was dreaming about rock bands. A girl can't help thinking about guitars like phallic symbols, the way they play with them in front of a crowd."

He chuckled, and she imagined the light in his sleepy brown eyes. Then he sobered. "You were dreaming about other things too. I was about to say fuck it and come in, wake you up. But the music seemed to calm you down. At least, I hope it did."

"It did." She propped her chin on his shoulder and stared down the pleasing terrain of his body, to where he cradled the guitar in his lap. "What should I do, Noah?"

"Go see her tomorrow," he said simply. "The more you want to avoid her, the better it is when you go see her. Doesn't make sense, but that's the way she works."

"I dreamed about you too," she said. "You were being hurt, and I couldn't stop it. Neither could she. And she stood on this mountain, and she looked so alone. It frightened me, seeing her like that, and you... It was like I was the one who could fix it all, but I couldn't move."

He slid an arm around her, resting his other hand on the guitar's face. He didn't say anything. She gazed at his profile. "Noah, why do you have that tattoo? The one that says *Yours Unconditionally*?"

"It was a promise."

"Made to whom?"

"Someone." His expression reminded her of the wistful tune the bard played in her dreams. "I put it there when I didn't belong to anyone, thinking it was a call to the universe. You know, fishing."

He gave her that oddly distant look he sometimes had, as if he were an otherworldly being, tapped into currents she couldn't sense. "I'm still figuring out if it's been answered."

"Do you think you belong to someone now?"

"I belong to Lyda. And to you, because she says I do." He gave the strings a light strum. The music vibrated through her skin.

"What do you think you deserve, Noah?"

"Whatever my Master or Mistress tells me I deserve."

As if he detected the way his answer discomfited her, he lifted a shoulder. "I don't ask too many questions of the universe, Gen. I'm a speck of dust on the eye of an atom in all of it. Whatever happens, happens. Most of the time, what happens are good things." Sliding a knuckle along her cheek, he gave her a look that made her flesh tingle beneath his touch.

"I can't figure out how you do that." She shook her head. "You fluster me, just like Lyda, but in a different way. It's like she comes at me from above, you come from below, and between the two of you, I turn into goo."

"Good thing?"

"Most of the time," she allowed. She wanted to pursue the other topic, but she'd had enough of serious and intense tonight. She wanted to leave that first dream behind. Way behind. "Chloe said she's seen you in full Goth gear. Still have some of the clothes?"

"Like tight shirt and pants, buckled boots, long coat and the eye liner?"

"Dog collar, spiky bracelets?"

"And pewter rings with skulls and bats." He nodded. "Nope, don't have any of that."

She elbowed him. "Dress up for me sometime?"

"Whenever you want. Anything you want." He ran a thumb along her lip.

"I woke up...aroused," she whispered.

"Wet?" he murmured. His thumb passed over the flush in her cheek. "Want me to do anything about that for you?"

"Yeah. But Lyda said no." She caught a strand of his hair, the movement causing others to spill forward over her knuckles. She twisted them around her fingers. "Remind me what happens if we do something she says not to do?"

"It depends. Being disrespectful, a brat topping from the bottom, trying to force a Dom's hand, isn't good for anyone. It's sketchier when your Mistress has set you up, knowing you won't be able to resist getting in trouble. If she thinks we did it to incur punishment in a good way like that, then she'd do something like what she did tonight."

She sighed. "Under the word irresistible in the dictionary, there's a picture of you. She knows it. Sadistic bitch."

His expression reflected fondness, as if Gen had used an endearment. In his world, it probably was. "Maybe she intended for me to get into the 'good' kind of trouble when she offered to let me take you home tonight. But now I feel like I owe her something. I need to clear the air with her."

He nudged her with his elbow. "At least tell me why you woke up hot and bothered."

"Not a chance. You're as bad as she is."

He chuckled again. She was gratified to see regret at her refusal, though, his sexual frustration banked with visible effort. His fingers lingered on her mouth, daring a brief brush on the top of her breast before he brought his hands back to himself. "Well, then. How about I play this phallic symbol for you instead?"

She'd much rather play with his actual phallus. Yet even when she tried to lay it out in her head, she couldn't go there. She'd stepped over some line with Lyda and she felt it, like a knife edge.

So she made him play her some Air Supply instead. The haunting strains of "Sweet Dreams", Noah's pleasant tenor murmuring the words, were just the thing to put her back to sleep.

Yeah, right.

* * * * *

Noah told her Lyda's "Extreme Fit" class was held early in the morning, well before Gen was due for her ten a.m. shift at Tea Leaves. Accordingly, Gen was dressed and ready to go in time to give Noah a cup of coffee when he came into the kitchen with damp hair and a towel wrapped around his waist. He slid an arm around her and pressed a teasing kiss at the corner of her lips. When she gave him the cup, she let her hands wander unimpeded over his back and cup the curves of his terrycloth-covered ass. Giving her a wicked grin, he took his time sliding away. At the doorway, he removed the towel with a flourish and draped it over his shoulder, making her laugh outright as he worked a casual saunter back to the bathroom. When she fired a throw pillow at him, she wished her hallway was an endless treadmill.

Today Noah was headed out to do construction debris removal for a guy who occasionally called him in for that kind of work. Once he was dressed, Gen saw him to the door, watching him stride up to the car of the friend picking him up. As he turned and gave her a nod, she imagined him in that Goth outfit. It took an act of will not to indulge herself in a quick five minute release with her vibrator. Instead she found her purse and keys and headed out to Blood, Sweat and Tears.

Traffic caused her to run a few minutes late, so the class had already started when she arrived. She told herself she didn't have to be nervous about that, since she wasn't there to participate. Even so, she felt like a kid sliding into class past the bell. She slipped into a corner in the back, where a couple chairs had been left against the wall.

Despite her attempt to be unobtrusive, Lyda's gaze flicked to her the moment she hit the door. The woman gave her a spare nod, but didn't pause in barking orders.

"Work it. Even a warm-up requires a hundred percent effort. I better not see anyone dragging their ass this morning, or this is going to be a bitch for all of you. If it's burning, embrace it. If it screams at you, scream back."

Gen had taken various fitness classes over the years, all of which she considered demanding. Gen approached exercise like annual doctor visits—a necessary evil to be dreaded, but she had enough discipline to keep herself trim and healthy. Compared to this, those classes were toddler aerobics. As they swung from the warm-up into high-cardio, Lyda was relentless. No one was allowed to shirk. If a knee was supposed to be lifted, she damn well expected it to bump against the person's chest. She could gauge a ninety degree angle on a squat with barely a glance. Arm movements were supposed to be one hundred percent controlled, maximum resistance on the punches, stretches, pulls.

As awe-inspiring as all that was, watching the instructor was what held Gen's attention. Lyda said she liked Gen's soft places, but Gen found she really liked all of Lyda's not-so-soft places. She wore a tight black tank and mid-thigh exercise shorts with her thick-soled exercise shoes. Her red hair was pulled up in a tail. No makeup, her face all the more striking for the lack of embellishment. The smooth muscles in her arms and legs rippled, her ass absolutely erotic art in motion as she strode back and forth, alternating between brusque direction and performing the same exercises as her students, who were giving it one hundred twenty percent. Maybe because they were exercise fanatics like the woman leading them, but maybe just as much because she scared the shit out of them.

Everything about Lyda should have fed into the "butch" stereotype. She was assertive, bisexual, extremely physical. As commanding as a general. But what struck Gen was how incredibly female Lyda always seemed to her. Maybe part of it was the amazing softness Gen had had the privilege of glimpsing during their intimate encounters. A way she turned her head, a flash in her eye, the curve to her lips. Lyda had no desire to be or act like a man. She was a strong, dominant woman, and Gen realized there was nothing more female than that. Every quality to her, even those usually attributed to men, fit who Lyda was as a woman.

She expected her attention to wander during the forty-five-minute class. Instead, every movement of Lyda's body, every word from that distracting mouth, the delicate lines of her throat as she turned her head, the clench of her fists as she took them into mixed martial arts and boxing moves as part of the routine, just pulled Gen in deeper. It was like being caught in a dream, like last night, only this wasn't a nightmare.

Every once in a while Lyda's gaze would touch upon her, but only enough to feed Gen's hunger. Gen had placed her tote next to her and sat in the chair with her hands in her lap, her legs crossed. She couldn't help wondering what would happen if...

Knowing she was risking deep embarrassment, she adjusted so she was sitting up straight, her back against the chair's straight back. Her feet were now flat on the floor. The lavender T-shirt she wore for Tea Leaves today molded to her curves, a V-neck showing cleavage. Her knit skirt stretched over her hips and stopped at mid-thigh, a comfortable style for casual wear that went well with her rhinestone sandals and showed off her legs. Lyda liked her legs.

This classroom didn't have mirrors. The only one facing her was Lyda, unless she had them do an unexpected spin. But right now they were on the floor doing pushups, as if genuflecting while she stalked through their ranks. Working up her courage, Gen adjusted so her thighs were parted. Not porno style, but a few significant inches. With her back straight and hands resting on the sides of the chair seat, her breasts were lifted. She was putting herself on display for her Mistress, showing deference.

When Lyda noticed, there was no mistaking it. The woman's gaze stopped full on her for a bated breath. Those silver eyes slid over her face, the cheeks Gen knew were flushed, down over her breasts, then to that shadowy place between her knees. Lyda pivoted, barked out a new set of combinations.

It thrilled her, Lyda's cursory acknowledgment of what Gen owed her as Mistress. But then Lyda aimed another look at Gen, lifted her hand, and brought her index and forefingers together, a clear direction to Gen to close her legs.

Swallowing, she did so. When the class launched into a combination that had them turning toward the back, she tried to assume Lyda had done it to protect Gen's modesty, but Gen knew it was more than that. The tightened jaw, the neutral flicker in the eyes, told her one gesture wasn't going to mend whatever she'd done last night. She wanted to fix it, to win back Lyda's approval...

The thought speared her with dismay, brought her up short. She'd wanted her mother's approval for so many things. Ironically, because her mother's expectations for Gen had been so low, she'd had no appreciation for the things that Gen accomplished, the things that mattered to Gen. If she was treating Lyda like some emotional maternal surrogate...

Sure, this had a sexual component to it, but the quagmire of the past could have a lot of different lures. Watching Lyda's unyielding expression, an unwelcome twinge of resentment disrupted Gen's arousal. As the class progressed, uncertainty jumped in as well. She wasn't going to do this to herself. She should leave.

When you most want to avoid her, that's when going to see her helps.

"That's it. Walk it off and get your butts to work. The lazy-assed rest of the population needs your hard-earned tax dollars."

At the good-natured retorts, Lyda grinned, the first time she'd showed warmth. She high-fived several fellow exercise nazis. As they dispersed, her gaze shifted to Gen. The smile disappeared. Tilting her head toward the door on the opposite side of the room, she moved toward it, disappearing from sight without waiting on her.

When Gen trailed after her, she found the door led into a private changing area for the instructors. Locker doors slammed on the other side of the wall, voices murmuring. The connecting door probably led to the public locker room.

"You look like you didn't sleep well," Lyda said. She'd stripped off the T-shirt and sports bra and was bending over a sink as she soaked a washcloth, applied soap to it to wash her upper body. Gen stared at the curve of her back, the bumps of her spine. She knew what women looked like under their clothes. It shouldn't be this fascinating. But this woman...it was. And Lyda wasn't even trying to be provocative.

"I'm sorry about last night. At the end. I'm not sure what I did wrong, but I know I did something. I didn't mean to piss you off."

When Lyda didn't immediately respond, uneasiness filled Gen. Straightening, Lyda met her gaze in the mirror over the sink. As she toweled herself off, her breasts moved with the vigorous motion. Lyda cleaned herself efficiently, every gesture packed with dense energy. Her nipples were dark and tight, the pale curves of her breasts probably damp and cool from the water.

"If you want to be Noah's Domme on a regular basis, he would be open to that transition. Especially if I order it."

She snapped her attention back to Lyda's face. "What?"

Lyda gave her a patient look. "All you have to do is ask, Gen. It's not in his best interest, long term, because you're not a Mistress. You're mostly a soft core sub, one who enjoys being an occasional top under supervision. We could plan some club sessions to keep it interesting for you both. You could send him back to me when you're done with it."

"'It' meaning him, or…?"

"Playing Domme." Lyda sounded so damn matter-of-fact about it.

"Do you categorize everyone, like one of your plants? Figure out the soil, fertilizer and sunlight I need, plant me where you know I'll flourish? Is that what you're doing with him? Finding the place to plant him?"

Setting the towel aside, Lyda turned and propped her hips on the sink. As she unclipped her hair and ran her fingers through it, she demonstrated no self-consciousness about her partial nudity. "Did you come to apologize or start a fight?" She lifted a brow. "Nice submissive posture out there, by the way."

"What do you *want*, Lyda?" Gen struggled to keep it even, rational. "I feel like you want something from me and I can't figure it out…"

"Nothing to figure out, Gen," Lyda said shortly. "When I want something from you, I tell you. You don't have to read my mind. I'm not some Oprah-watching, whiny excuse for a female beating myself up for my past mistakes and looking to blame them on someone else. I own what I have or haven't done with my life."

Anger surged at the direct hit. Gen took a step forward. "You don't treat me like I'm your equal. I don't like it."

"Every choice is yours, Gen." Lyda shrugged. "You don't like being around me, take your ass elsewhere."

"Would you care either way?" Like last night, the moment Lyda had called subdrop, Gen was flooded with too many things defying definition. Her usual penchant for safety, for simplicity, reasserted itself in her consciousness. *Hey, remember me? I keep you from fucking up.* But Lyda overrode that voice.

"Did hearing your husband declare undying love for you change the fact he wiped his shit on you like you were a doormat?" Lyda asked, eyes hard. "I can spout words for you, Gen, but if you can't *feel* the difference between us and that, then walk away. You're too damaged for this."

Just like that. Categorized, boxed and shipped. A red haze clouded her vision, burned her throat, choked her.

She'd slapped Amos once. The derision on his face had paralyzed her, concrete proof that whatever she'd imagined was love had never been that. It had spawned a rage so fierce, she'd picked an iron skillet off the stove and swung. She'd missed his head by a hairsbreadth. The derision had vanished and he'd scampered away like a guinea pig. If she'd connected, she could have killed him. The rage had scared her, but from then onward, she'd understood the term "crime of passion".

The thought flashed through her mind now, because she realized she'd closed the distance between them and actually lifted her hand. The hard quiver that went through her stirred emotions she was afraid to incite with further motion. *Speak, scream. Say something before you do something horrible.*

"It's not damaged. I'm *confused*," Gen snarled. "Give me room to breathe, to figure it out. Or give me something straight out without making it a game, damn you."

Lyda straightened off the sink. The graceful movement brought her toe-to-toe with Gen. Lyda lifted her own hand, manacled Gen's wrist with it. Holding Gen's gaze, she turned her face into Gen's palm, rubbed her temple to it, then pressed her lips to Gen's lifeline. All without breaking eye contact. Something trembled deep inside Gen, something even more wrenching. "Lyda…"

The woman shook her head. She lowered Gen's hand. As she did, she closed the space between their bodies. She bent Gen's arm behind her back so she was fully against Lyda's body, her breasts against hers, Lyda's foot between hers, her thigh insinuating itself between Gen's legs.

Lyda brushed her mouth with her own, a teasing stroke, then another. Gen channeled tension into hunger. She clashed against Lyda's mouth, kissing her hard, her tongue finding the other woman's, dancing with it, tasting, stroking. She bit Lyda's lip and held on, not breaking skin, but trying to convey…something. Lyda let go of her wrist and circled her waist instead, pressing her leg up fully between Gen's legs, cradling one buttock in her hand, digging her nails into Gen's ass as Gen rubbed her pussy against the toned muscle there. With Lyda's arm around her waist, the only place Gen had to put her own was around Lyda's shoulders. She curled her fingers against bare skin, the pulse in her neck, her collarbone.

Lyda took over the kiss, demanding even more from Gen. When the Mistress finally broke it, seizing Gen's hair to pull her back, Gen had her full weight against her leg and Lyda was leaning back against the sink, holding them both there.

"How do you feel, right now, Gen?" It was a harsh demand, Lyda's eyes like flint.

"I'm… I can't think."

"I didn't fucking ask for your head. How do you feel?"

"Right. Exactly right." Gen stared into the woman's face, shocked by the truth of it.

"Yes. This isn't about equality, Gen. It's about what each of us needs, and whether we can provide that for one another. I'm not taking over your checkbook, making you clean my house or ordering you to kiss the bottom of my foot, but there is a vital part of you that needs my control."

Gen pushed away, trying to order her whirling thoughts. "How do I know it's not like the doormat thing? What's the difference? And please don't say I should know."

"But you do." Lyda eyed her. "It's something Marguerite has always seen in you, and why the two of you get along so well, right? It's a different form of what you feel with me, only with her it's more purely service-oriented."

It wasn't the first time Lyda had implied it, but this time Gen saw it clearly enough it came with another minor shock wave.

"Equality is a political idea, Gen," Lyda said. "It has nothing to do with how people care about one another, or what they each need. There is no equality between parent and child, but when it's what it should be, there's no stronger love in the world, right? In times when there was zero equality between men and women, we still have love stories handed down that have become the stuff of legend."

"Where does Noah fit into that?"

"What you felt, when I kissed you? What did you call it?"

"Right," Gen said. "Exactly right."

Lyda's lips curved in one of her knife-blade smiles. "Good description, rabbit. I wanted to put you down right here. Slide my fingers inside your cunt and ass and watch you come apart."

Gen wished she was back within her armspan. If she was, Lyda likely would have done just that. But then that direct gaze became far less friendly. "Why do you turn to Noah when you feel uncertain with me? Do you think he can protect you?"

Gen stepped back at the menace in Lyda's tone. Lyda advanced, taking that ground. "I will tear right through his ass to get to you. It's obvious you had a husband you expected to have enough balls to be in control, and enough of a heart and soul to care about you. But he was weak, selfish, and let you down. I may be selfish at times, but I'm not weak, Gen. Whatever I promise you, I'll deliver. You have to give up control to get where you want to go with this, even though it terrifies you, what I'll do with it."

It did. "Husbands. Two of them."

Lyda blinked, her mouth softening perceptibly. "Oh, Gen."

Gen shook her head. "I don't know if this is a relationship."

"Pull your head out of your ass and figure it out," Lyda said shortly, that lenient moment gone as fast as it had appeared. "Because I'm not going to waste my time telling you things you're not going to believe."

"There are no pictures at your house, not family or friends. But the way you looked at Noah when he was sleeping... I know he matters to you. I think maybe I matter too." Gen took a breath. "I see things in the way you act toward me, different from what I've ever known. And I want even more of whatever it is. It scares me."

Maybe it seemed ridiculous, given how short a timeframe it had been with Noah and Lyda, but with the Dom/sub stuff, things felt as intense and deep as a six-month dating relationship, where these questions would start to be asked.

"Are you getting something you want out of this relationship?" Lyda asked, her face that cool mask.

"Yes."

"Then what the hell does it matter, how I feel? You were quick enough to turn to Noah the other night, rather than both of us. I touched your back and you flinched. Shrank toward him. He was all you wanted."

Gen stared at her as Lyda turned away, found a brush in her bag and began to work on her hair.

She was right. At the time, Gen had focused only on visceral reactions, but Noah had recognized it. He'd even tried to mitigate the damage, but Lyda had shut him down so quickly, charging him to care for Gen.

She'd hurt Lyda's feelings. Plain and simple. Gen had been gripped by that odd sadness, assuming Lyda didn't want to do aftercare, but she hadn't given her a chance to prove otherwise. Maybe the Dom needed the intimacy that aftercare provided as much as the sub. But she'd only let Lyda in for the sex part.

God, she was a self-absorbed idiot. Gen stayed so focused on not taking advantage of Noah, because it seemed so easy to take advantage to him. In reality, it might be more of a danger with Lyda, because she seemed so invulnerable, so in control.

Drawing on her courage, she stepped forward. "I didn't touch Noah last night. Not that way. I felt like something was wrong between you and me. That mattered. I couldn't enjoy him if things weren't right between all of us. You're one of the most self-confident, self-aware women I've ever met."

Since they both knew Marguerite, that was saying a lot. "I don't know if that makes me hate you, want to be more like you or just flat out makes me feel…less. I'm sorry, Lyda. You deserved better from me. Especially after you…I've never felt anything like what you make me feel, you and Noah. Separately, together." She gave a desperate half-laugh. "Noah said you understood how it was for someone figuring it all out. There are times I get swept away in…submitting to you, but I'm not sure that makes me a submissive. I don't know how to make it all make sense, and I feel like I'm making a fool of myself over you both. I'm not sure what to do with it. But I shouldn't have hurt you like that."

Gen shook her head. "You always seem so in control. Even when you're scary, which is most of the time, it feels like you're on top of things. You're right, I've felt safe with M, because of that. She gives me a place to retreat when I need it, a place that's steady, an anchor. But when I'm in that same kind of place with you, it's different. I never want to leave at all. It's home and the destination, all rolled up in one."

Lyda had set aside the brush and turned back toward her. As Gen's words died away in the echo of the tiled room, Lyda studied her long enough Gen wanted to squirm, to disappear. But then she extended a hand. "Come here."

Gen took the hand. When Lyda pulled Gen close, just like that, things were better. As her arm wrapped over Gen's shoulders, Gen pressed her face against the side of Lyda's, her nose against the moist hair line, inhaling the clean smell of Lyda and soap. Gen let out a shuddering sigh and slid both arms under Lyda's, around her bare back. Her breasts pressed against Gen's, Lyda's puckered nipples noticeable through Gen's thin shirt. It was still a new feeling for her, hugging a woman and getting aroused by that contact, but with Lyda, it was a feeling easy to enjoy.

"I'm so sorry," Gen said.

"Forgiven," Lyda said quietly. She pressed a kiss to Gen's temple, spoke against it, no eye contact between them. "You affect me, Gen. And you are *not* less." She drew back to lock Gen in that penetrating gaze. "You're far more than you realize. You wouldn't have captured my attention otherwise."

Before Gen could respond to that, Lyda tangled her hand in her hair, holding her in place in that way that made things tight inside Gen's stomach. "Some of the strongest women I know enjoy submission during sex, because through surrender, they find themselves again. The confidence, the strength, the belief in their own beauty they lost during the day-to-day grind. But I'm done talking about that right now. You've been staring at my tits like a hungry baby, and you're going to pay for that."

Pushing Gen back, Lyda moved away. She locked both doors, then went to the bench in front of the lockers. She took a seat and dropped a folded towel she'd brought with her on the floor between her spread knees. "Kneel here."

In the right setting and circumstances, all Lyda had to do was use that tone, and Gen responded. Accepting that amazing idea, Gen knelt on the towel, a kindness to her knees against the concrete floor. Lyda's cruelty was planned, never neglectful. Something to think about, because it was probably the reason Gen found her ruthlessness so addictive.

In this position, Lyda's naked breasts were close to Gen's eye level. As she watched, Lyda cupped and fondled them. Gen moistened her lips, her breath shortening.

"I can see this getting you hotter, Gen. Do you want to suck on my nipples?"

Gen nodded. Then jumped as Lyda, quick as a striking snake, slapped her face. A controlled strike, hard enough to snap Gen's head to the right and make her wide-eyed. Yet the woman remained as self-possessed as ever as she returned that offending hand back to the enviable task of stroking her own breasts.

"You don't nod or shake your head to me, Gen, like I'm your equal. Not right now. Now let me ask again. Do you want to suck on my nipples?"

She'd just told herself she found Lyda's cruelty arousing, but the direct evidence of it still startled her. The heat of her handprint flowed straight down Gen's body like a lava burn. Her Mistress had forgiven her and administered a short, sharp punishment. Balance was a key that unlocked desire.

"Yes Mistress." Gen suppressed the desire to put her hand up to her burning cheek. Lyda did it instead, running her fingers along the reddened skin.

"Did Noah put anything on those stripes I left on your back and ass last night?"

"No, ma'am. I did, though."

"He was charged with your aftercare. You'll permit him to do whatever I tell him to do to you in the future, because my orders to him trump yours. Your care, his care, are my responsibility. Always. Understand? You're not the alpha in this pack, Gen."

"Yes Mistress." But she wasn't docile, either. She inched forward on the towel, gazing at those beautiful breasts, so close they had saliva was pooling in her mouth. "Can you come, just from having your nipples sucked?"

Lyda lifted an indifferent brow, but Gen was starting to learn, and enjoy, this game. "Perhaps. Do you want the privilege of giving your Mistress an orgasm, Gen?"

"Yes ma'am."

"Ma'am. I like that." Lyda braced her arms behind her on the bench, then shifted one foot, giving Gen a light thump against the side of her buttock with her thick-soled shoes. "Suck on my breasts, Gen. Let me see how much pleasure a woman's mouth can give me. You have some stiff competition. Noah is very good at this."

"He has the tongue stud," Gen muttered. Lyda chuckled grimly.

"With or without, the man's mouth is blessed by the gods. Now shut up and get to it, before I take a wet towel to that pretty ass."

As Gen moved forward, Lyda slid her hand under her hair, curving around Gen's nape. Gen parted her lips over one ripe nipple. She couldn't resist cupping the full curve, squeezing the firm flesh to push the nipple deeper into her mouth. Lyda's fingernails cut into her skin, encouraging her to take it deeper. She slid closer, arm banding around Lyda's back, fingertips whispering down that sweet valley. So delicate and strong. So beautiful. Lyda unclipped the barrette in Gen's hair, spilling it onto her shoulders. Her Mistress loved her hair, fingers delving into it, pulling.

When Lyda's head tipped back on her shoulders, pushing her breast even further into Gen's mouth, she made a greedy sound in the back of her throat, encouraging her. She was giving her pleasure, and it felt so, so good. Gen slid her thumb beneath the waistband of Lyda's shorts, stroked the dimples just above her ass. Lyda curved a leg around Gen, resting her calf on Gen's backside. Both her arms twined over Gen's shoulders, her thighs pressed against Gen's sides.

"My sweet, lovely girl. Mine."

Gen shivered at the praise. She moved off that nipple, clasped both breasts, holding them together and tonguing the channel of cleavage before taking the other nipple in her mouth and working on making it as tight a point as the other, glistening with the juices from her mouth. She wanted all of it, wanted her mouth everywhere, so she took time to run her tongue over the areola, trace the shape of the full curve. She even pressed her face to the outer curve, inhaling the lingering aroma of Lyda's sweat, the female animal smell of her. She wanted to burrow her face in between her legs, get a taste of the same. Would Lyda let her do that?

When she tried to go in that direction, her hair was pulled sharply, and she was brought back up to Lyda's breasts. Lyda caught her chin, squeezed it.

"You haven't earned eating my pussy, Gen. You promised me an orgasm from sucking my nipples alone. Unless you're bored…?"

"No Mistress," she said fervently, and returned to suckling, getting more and more aroused as Lyda's breath rate increased, her body arching, her hips starting to move in a coital rhythm, thighs flexing and releasing against Gen's hips. She was rubbing herself against Gen's upper body, and it drove Gen to even crazier rhythms, more insistent and wild. Suckle, bite, draw deep, lick, rub her face between Lyda's breasts, let her tongue and lips go everywhere as her Mistress's body movements became faster. Gen had both her hands inside the shorts, was gripping Lyda's ass, kneading the lovely curves to help her move against her, find that orgasm she'd promised.

"Un-unh." In one abrupt move, Lyda shifted off the bench, taking Gen to the floor, full out beneath her. She pressed her knees on either side of Gen's hips, pinning her there, her upper body still above Gen's face. She forced Gen's arms above her head, then kept them there with a look.

"Keep sucking my tits, Gen."

Gravity could be a wonderful thing, because now as she squeezed and licked, the breasts moved against her face with Lyda's response. Gen moaned as Lyda pushed up her skirt and Lyda slid her mound over her own, a nice firm rub of clit against clit, even under panties and exercise shorts.

"You don't get to come," Lyda said, dark intent in her voice. "Only me. I'm going to keep you hot and wet, because that's the state I want you to suffer, all day today."

She wasn't sure how she was going to obey, because as Lyda worked against her, as goal-oriented as she'd been during her workouts, Gen's pussy was getting ready to go. Then Lyda's fingers closed over her throat. She lifted her upper body, those breasts quivering before Gen, out of range of her mouth. Lyda's grip tightened, restricting Gen's air flow enough it pulled her attention away from them.

"You feel. Feel my orgasm and deny your own."

Cruel, as she'd said. But Gen obeyed. Lyda's pubic bone, the distinctive bud of her clit, rubbed against Gen's with the friction of flammable things. Her pussy tingled, waves rushing over it. She ached to climax, wanted to go over so badly…

Lyda started to come, her fingers flexing on Gen's throat, holding her down, using Gen's body to bring pleasure to her own. Her nipples were in tight points, because Gen's mouth had caused that. Gen had also caused her climax. Gen held onto that, fought to contain her own to further please her Mistress.

It was as Noah had said. There was a difference between when Lyda wanted to force Gen to lose control and when she wanted to drive her to the edge of insanity to prove her control over her.

Gen reveled in the uncontrolled surges of that strong, lithe body, the way Lyda pressed herself hard against Gen at the end, so hard Gen could feel Lyda's pussy pulsing with the last vestiges of her release. Her hands were above her head where Lyda had pushed them, fingers opening and closing helplessly, her body open to whatever Lyda wanted from it, a tight bow string.

Lyda slid back, yanking Gen's legs up to her shoulders. Her ass left the ground as Lyda gripped both buttocks and pushed her face between Gen's thighs. She stopped just short of putting her mouth on her pussy, but Gen could feel her breath there, her face obscured by the bunched folds of her knit skirt. Lyda drew in a shuddering breath, inhaling her arousal, and Gen let out a pleading mewl. Lyda pressed her lips to her labia, suckled, a small taste, a lick or two, just sampling. Gen bit back on a scream, her hands tight fists. A bated, excruciating moment later, Lyda lowered her back to the floor, her hands gripping Gen high on the thighs underneath the skirt.

"Open your eyes."

Gen did, though she knew they had to be glazed. She was panting. Every part of her was swollen, tight, needy. How was she going to function at work like this?

Lyda shifted from her knees to the balls of her feet, then rose. Staring down at Gen, her Mistress seemed to be branding every inch of her with her eyes. Gen saw herself as Lyda must be seeing her, skirt rucked up her thighs, her own nipples taut points against her thin bra and shirt. Lips parted, cheeks flushed, eyes wild.

Reaching down at last, Lyda clasped Gen's hand and pulled her to her feet. Gen swayed, but Lyda steadied her, cupping her ass with a proprietary hand as she held onto the side of Gen's neck with the other.

"Breathe deep. Steady. Get it under control. It all belongs to your Mistress, so you're going to learn how to bottle it, uncap it when I say. Eventually, you'll come from a simple one-word command from my lips."

Gen believed it. She had one hand latched in Lyda's waistband, thumb frenetically stroking a small couple inches of skin above it. When she touched her navel, Gen dropped her gaze to that. It was beautiful, like all of Lyda. A delicate indentation she'd like to tease with her tongue, a precursor to moving down to a lower orifice. She swayed again.

"Breathe."

It was helping. Her body was still throbbing, but she didn't feel like whining like a puppy for a treat. Not quite as much.

Lyda pushed her down on the bench. "Legs spread. Assume that position you did on the chair out there, trying to distract me."

"I was trying to please you."

Lyda made a noncommittal sound. Turning away to her locker, she left Gen complying with the order as she pulled out a silver gray blouse and lacy black bra. She shimmied out of the shorts, revealing her pert bottom in a black thong that eliminated panty lines beneath the tailored miniskirt she donned. Dropping a pair of shiny black pumps with silver trim on the floor, she slid her feet into them. No hose, but her legs didn't need them. The silver blouse's silky folds etched out her upper body.

"A little fancy for the nursery."

"I have a client meet this morning. He wants me to design the landscaping for the estate he's building. If I get it, it will be a big account."

"I can't imagine you not getting whatever you want."

Lyda closed the locker, giving her a warm look. Moving back to the mirror and retrieving her brush, she brushed out the thick strands in a rippling wave that completed the professional, mouthwateringly sexy look. Gen's vibrant memory and throbbing pussy was the only evidence that a few moments before Lyda had been in the grips of an orgasm, her cunt pressed against Gen, her breasts in her mouth, the nipples and creamy flesh a pure dessert-before-meal pleasure.

Gen trembled. Holding her legs open kept the swollen flesh from being compressed in a dangerous way, but being spread for her Mistress like this came with a psychological stimulation stronger than an actual touch.

"So what did you think of the class? There's always room for one more."

"Sorry. I gave up my childhood dream of joining the SEALs. But if you start to offer ten-minute cookie breaks in the middle and have a chiropractor standing by…"

Lyda's lips twisted. "So if you had to choose between my whip or my class?"

"The whip. Definitely."

"Couch potato."

"Exercise nazi."

Lyda laughed outright at that. Gen's heart tilted. She'd never flirted with a woman before. "I'd like to ask you something."

"I don't promise answers."

"Have you ever been married?"

"No," Lyda answered. "Came close once. But he wasn't strong enough."

"Will anyone ever be?"

"It doesn't matter. My priorities changed." Putting her brush in her bag, Lyda sat it next to Gen and shifted behind her. She held Gen's barrette between her lips as she combed her fingers through Gen's hair, pulling it back into a smooth twist she clipped against Gen's neck. "I want you to keep your hair up in public except when I'm with you. You take it down only for me."

"I mostly have to keep it tied back anyway. It gets into everything."

It was something to say, covering the fluttery reaction the possessive command elicited.

"Tell me about it." Lyda brushed back a lock of her own lustrous mane. "This mess stays pulled back for everything but client meetings. Else I'm snagging it in vegetation all day long."

"Not just for client meetings." Gen remembered it curtaining her face as Lyda leaned over her in her bedroom. Twisting her upper body, she reached up, wanting to twine fingers in the curls tumbling over Lyda's silk-clad shoulder. Lyda intercepted her, clasping her wrist. "Please," Gen said. "I like touching it. I like touching you."

In her past relationships, Gen hadn't used such a direct communication style, but maybe she was learning from Lyda. She was also learning what aroused Lyda. Her gaze flickered, her mouth softening. She loosened her hold, sliding down Gen's forearm in a caress as Gen stroked the red locks. "This is your actual color."

"Mostly. I tone it up, turn auburn into flame for dramatic effect." Lyda smiled, the effect like sunlight. Gen wanted to bask in it like a lazy cat on a porch, soak it into every part of her.

"I'm feeling too much for the both of you."

"Because you think there's a speed limit to these things, or because you're afraid you're setting yourself up for a crash? Do you think you're in the car alone, Gen?"

Gen's gaze slid up to her. Their faces were close, Lyda's hand on her forearm, hers in Lyda's hair, an intimate connection. Was it possible that Lyda had just implied what she thought she had? As for Noah…was Lyda speaking for them both?

Lyda had made it clear she didn't say what she didn't mean, but Gen wasn't ready to press for confirmation. For now, the tingle spreading through her vitals was enough. Gen changed the subject.

"So you don't want me to let my hair down in front of anyone, but you can let yours down for the whole world to see?" And covet.

"Yep," Lyda said. "There's a different kind of fairness in a Dom/sub relationship."

"Doesn't sound fair at all."

"Isn't that what I just said?" Lyda bent down further, all that intentness brought up close and personal. "Does it bother you, Gen, a man getting pleasure out of looking at me?"

"I think everyone gets pleasure looking at you. But it bothers me to think you could do this with me, and then…"

"Don't piss me off, rabbit. It's a customer meet. I don't plan on fucking him." She touched Gen's lip. "I save that for my pets. Both of them."

Her tone changed to the Mistress who could snap Gen's spine straight and drive a spike of arousal through her. "Look at you, breathing so heavy. Your pussy's just begging for it, isn't it?"

"Yes," Gen whispered.

"Good." Lyda straightened. "Keep it that way. It's mine to enjoy when I choose. Would you like to go to Gatlinburg next weekend?"

Gen blinked. She was so aroused, she wasn't sure she could drive herself safely to work, and Lyda was chatting up weekend plans. "Sure."

Lyda pulled a dollar out of her purse, handed it to her. "There's a drink machine in the hall. Get me a Diet Coke. Hurry back, and we'll talk about it."

Gen rose, movements uncoordinated, but Lyda gave her butt a slap sharp enough to elicit a yelp and narrow glance. It did help her focus enough to go find the drink machine, though. Putting in the dollar with fumbling fingers, Gen retrieved the soda, came back. Lyda was leaning toward the mirror, applying some eye liner, making a perfect presentation of her ass in the snug hold of the skirt. Gen wondered what Lyda would do if she slapped *her* ass.

Lyda met her gaze in the mirror. "Do it, and next time I tie you down, your backside will match my hair."

Occasionally there was an advantage to having an easy-to-read face. When Lyda threatened such a thing, Gen's pulse accelerated, telling her she wanted such a punishment. Gen had never particularly longed for pain as part of sex, but the way Lyda took control of her and Noah, the way she administered discipline, was like discovering an adult love of roller coasters.

Plus—and this was an important component of it—her reaction fed Lyda's pleasure, which in turn escalated Gen's...and so on and so forth. Despite that, she wouldn't be slapping Lyda's ass. There was a right and wrong way to incur discipline at her Mistress's hand, and doing it that way felt like feeding tofu to a cheetah.

Lyda was studying her face. "You're not a brat, Gen," she said softly. "Or a bottom, just seeking to get off by being topped. I like that about you. Very much."

Mutely, Gen offered the Diet Coke. Taking it, Lyda pointed her back to the bench. "Same position. Whenever I command you to sit, you assume that posture. If I make you kneel, your knees stay shoulder width apart, no matter what you're wearing, because if you're on your knees, we're in company that understands what's going on. They know you're under my protection. You're safe, as long as you follow my commands. I want you to think about that, because occasionally I insist on some PDS outside a club. Public Displays of Submission."

When Gen was seated, Lyda turned back to the mirror to finish up her makeup. "Noah invited me to meet his grandmother. She lives in Tampa, but goes up to Gatlinburg to stay with friends for a month in the summer. One of them also has a rental house in town, so Noah's grandmother wants him to come stay there for a few days, do some maintenance on it as thanks for her room and board. I think she also likes to show off her cute grandson. He asked me to go with him. I haven't said yes, but I'm thinking I might. Particularly if you'd like to go too."

She anticipated Lyda's agreement would shock Noah as much as it was taking her off guard. "Does he usually invite his...Dommes to meet his grandmother?"

Lyda gave her an amused look. "You were stumbling over that one, weren't you? You knew 'girlfriend' didn't fit. No, I expect he doesn't." Lyda sobered, studying herself in the mirror. "Which is why I shouldn't go."

"Do you want to go?"

"Yeah, I do. Which worries me." Lyda gave her a rueful look. Such a woman-to-woman exchange was something Gen had as a matter of course with Chloe, and rarely but sometimes with Marguerite. It was the first time she'd experienced it with Lyda.

"How would we introduce ourselves? As his friends?" Gen had a hard time keeping her hands off either one of them. If his grandmother had a sharp eye, or even a single functioning brain cell, it was going to be difficult to keep their relationship under wraps. But people tended to see what they wanted to see, right? Both of her mothers-in-law had thought everything was going great, that their sons were perfect. Until the day they announced the divorces, and then it didn't take too much for them to turn the blame all on Gen. Despite the fact Guy wouldn't have even visited his mother except when Gen nagged him to do it.

"We are his friends, aren't we?" Lyda asked.

Gen didn't know how to respond to that. Chloe was a friend. They shared laughter and jokes, hugged a lot, worked together. They told each other about their lives, their feelings. Yes, Chloe shared more than Gen, but over time, Chloe had earned enough of

Gen's trust that she knew more about Gen's feelings on things than she'd ever anticipated sharing. With Lyda, she felt a desire to share a lot of things, but she hesitated because of Lyda being Lyda. Gen could certainly call her and Noah her friends in front of his grandmother, but did that really fit?

"I asked Noah what he thought he deserved," Gen said instead. "He said whatever his Master or Mistress thinks he deserves."

Lyda pressed her lips together, packed her lipstick away. "It's why most Dominants don't hold onto him. That lack of identity and self-esteem is a harrowing responsibility. In the right circumstances, it seems like a treasure, but it's hazardous to the sub. It's tempting to the worst kind of Doms."

"But not to you?"

Lyda lifted a brow, leaned against the sink, gaze sliding with leisurely pleasure over Gen in her submissive posture. "What do you think?"

Thinking was difficult. But Gen gave it a try. "I think you refuse to let yourself back away from a challenge. And you think you're entitled to his service, because you feel you earn it by what you give back to him."

"I *feel* I earn it?" Lyda gave her an amused look, then sobered again. "Noah 's submission is a beautiful thing, but there's a missing foundation support, like a chair with only three legs. You don't realize a leg is missing until you tip in that direction. The thing is, he's very good at keeping anyone from tipping him in that direction. However, if he's pushed there, a crash happens, and it's not beautiful at all."

Gen's brow furrowed, but Lyda continued, forestalling comment. "Eventually, I hope to get deep enough inside him to help him put in a prosthesis."

"What happens after that?" Gen gazed at her.

"That will be up to him, and me. And maybe you."

Lyda hooked a finger in Gen's shirtfront, beneath the connection between her bra cups. She tugged there, letting her thumb drift over Gen's left nipple. "Nope, no moving. Keep those hands at your sides. You've touched me as much as I'm going to permit right now. Your pussy's needy as a virgin's on her wedding night, isn't it?"

Gen wet her lips. Lyda spoke again, sharp. "You answer me when I ask you a question, Gen."

"Yes Mistress. Yes." Gen bit back a plea as Lyda plucked at her nipple. Gen's fingers dug into her thighs as she tried not to squirm.

"Drop your panties to your ankles, Gen. Don't interrupt what I'm doing."

It wasn't easy in a seated position. It required some awkward wiggling. Lyda moved to the other nipple, making Gen gasp.

"I'll clamp these during one of our sessions. Once they're nice and swollen, I'll pull the clamps off. It's excruciating, but when I have Noah suckle you after you'll love it. Pain and pleasure work that way for you, Gen. Have you noticed?"

"Somewhat. Maybe. Yes." She was certainly experiencing those two elements right now under Lyda's firm fingertips.

"Eyes open. You don't get to hide from me in any way. A hundred percent present when your Mistress is commanding you." Lyda stepped back, taking her hand away. "Pull your skirt up to your waist, and straddle the end of the bench so you can't close your legs. Hips tucked under so your pussy isn't in contact with the wood at all."

Lyda gave her another of those kick-your-ass looks, and Gen moved to do it. She made sure her back was straight, the bench cool against her bare buttocks.

Lyda picked up the soda, still so cold that the metal sides looked frosted. Squatting at the end of the bench, she put the top of the can right up against Gen's cunt.

Fuck. The provocative contrast of aroused heat and relentless cold drove a cry from her, but she made herself stay still because that was what Lyda had ordered.

"You tell me when it's too much, Gen. I decide when to take it away." Lyda propped her other hand on the bench, her tone casual even as her expression was anything but. "And while you're thinking about that, you think about this too. You ever raise a hand to me again, there will be tough consequences."

"Do you mean when I almost slapped you for the doormat comment, or what I was thinking when you were bending over the sink?"

She must be insane to try yanking Lyda's chain, but her state of arousal wasn't helping her judgment. Lyda's eyes glittered, appreciating her fire while also conveying she was more than capable of melting Gen down like candle wax with it.

"Both. Consider me the Old Testament God. I punish for thought as well as deed."

At first, she'd been so hot between her legs, the can felt good. But as Lyda kept holding it flush against her tender flesh, the cold invaded, followed by pain, because that was how the brain warned a person when things became too much. Gen struggled against it, though. Her Mistress was watching, waiting, and she wanted to show her she wouldn't fail her. But oh fuck it was starting to really hurt...

"Beg me, Gen."

"I...can hold out."

"No, you can't." Lyda took it away, gave her thigh a reproving tap. "Begging your Mistress for mercy is a gift to me as well. You don't risk nerve damage just to prove a point. We aren't in competition. You'll figure that out eventually."

Giving her an even look, Lyda straightened. "If nothing else, that'll settle you down enough I don't have to worry about you driving. As for me..." Her fingers slid over the tab top. "I'll have the pleasure of knowing just where this has been as I'm drinking it."

Bringing Gen to her feet with a firm hand on her elbow, Lyda straightened Gen's skirt back down over her hips, not allowing her to do it, and then cupped a hand over Gen's buttock, giving it an admonishing squeeze.

"Going back to this nonsense about you feeling 'less'. The only function of your past is to be the building blocks to your future. Whatever parts of your past are in the way of that, bury them like the dead, accept their loss and move on."

"Is that how you did it?" There was no need to state the obvious—Lyda emanated the self-confidence only a woman who'd accepted all parts of herself could.

"I was born believing the word impossible didn't apply to me. So far, I haven't been proven wrong. Time for you to get to work." Lyda shouldered her purse, flashed her a smile. "I told you I'd keep you safe, and Marguerite will give you the death-stare if you're running late. Even I wouldn't want to be on the receiving end of that."

Chapter Eleven

A case of cold sodas couldn't keep Gen's mind from being like a scrambled egg throughout the workday. Chloe teased her about it, bumping her hip once to knock her out of it. "So is it Mistress Lyda or Noah? Or both?"

Gen made a face at her. "Shoo, annoying fly."

"You look so happy. Crazy batshit freaked out, but happy too. That's good, right?"

Gen chuckled. She couldn't help it. "Yeah, that pretty much describes it."

"Have you ever wanted to kiss Marguerite? With tongue and everything?"

"What?" Gen bobbled the Brown Betty tea pot she was bringing back to the counter. She put it down abruptly, terrified she would break one of Marguerite's collectibles. Part of Tea Leaves' appeal was that the patrons could request service from specific tea sets Marguerite had collected from around the world. While sipping from cups that had graced Victorian parlors, grand Russian dining rooms or Japanese tea houses, they could learn about the set's history, either from Marguerite herself, or from Gen and Chloe, because part of their training included a thorough history of tea.

Fortunately, Marguerite wasn't here right now. Beyond the embarrassment of nearly dropping the pot, Gen would have had to see Marguerite's reaction to the question. Chloe was professional enough to show a certain restraint around customers—and they had a lull in traffic right now—but she was nigh irrepressible with M and Gen.

"Is this the first time you've been involved with a girl? I know it's different, with Lyda being a Mistress, and you really have a three-way thing going, but it feels a little bit like what I've always felt between you and Marguerite."

Gen turned to look at her. Lyda had made her consider the Dom/sub undertones in her relationship to Marguerite, but it surprised her to find Chloe had picked up on it, and connected a sexual element to it as well. Gen felt a moment of alarm. Did she feel…? No. Right?

"It's different." She should stop talking, but except for her own relentless internal monologue, Gen hadn't really sounded it out with a neutral party. And truth, Chloe was her best friend. Her sudden serious look of interest reminded Gen of that.

"Lyda thinks my relationship with M is a symptom of why…it's working with her. For my part, I don't know. I don't know what I am, or if I want to be boxed into a name. Gay or straight, Dom, sub or switch. Even thinking about myself in relation to those labels is new to me, no matter how familiar they feel…deep inside. If that makes sense."

Chloe nodded. "Yeah. It actually does. When I act as Brendan's Mistress, some of it feels familiar, like we all do have some of it in us, some inclinations stronger than others, but… Actually, can I tell you something without making you mad at Lyda?"

Gen's brow raised. "Yes. I think so."

"The first time I met Lyda was at that BDSM carnival Tyler and Marguerite do each year. Lyda saw me with Brendan, and she didn't hold back. She made it clear she thought we'd fail, because I couldn't be what Brendan needed."

That was a little more than Noah had implied. Despite her assurance, Gen felt a spurt of anger on her behalf, especially seeing the shadow cross Chloe's face. It told Gen that Lyda had hurt her feelings and cast doubts on her relationship with Brendan, at least at the time. "That's just stupid. Seeing the two of you together—"

"I know. I know that now. But in a way, it was good to have someone like her question it, because it brought my own worries about it right up to the top to confront them. I wanted Brendan to be happy, and now I know that was what Lyda wanted too. Dommes can be pretty scary-protective of those they care about. As if we haven't noticed." She tipped her head toward Marguerite's empty office.

"I figured out that it didn't matter that I'm not a dyed-in-the-wool Mistress like Marguerite or Lyda. Brendan, the way he treats me, acts toward me, tells me he serves me. That summons the part of me that can give him a more souped-up version of what he needs, when he needs it. And that works for us. How much we love each other is more important than any definition of what either of us is. We can't imagine a day without the other being a part of it. That's why it works. It's fluid, Gen. Don't let anyone make you think it has to fit into a shoebox. You create the box in which it fits, and that box can change in size and shape, depending on what you put into it."

When Chloe put her hand on Gen's, underscoring her earnestness, Gen sighed. "I've been married twice, and I never questioned being in a monogamous relationship with a man. I don't even question it now, because it was what I wanted then, no matter that I made some poor choices. But it was a safe paradigm. Now I'm completely baffled. I can't stop thinking about either one of them. And not just together. It's separate and together. But they're still a package deal in my head, if that makes sense."

"Sounds exciting and fun." Chloe slid around the counter, nudged hips again. "I know you like things to be comfortable, and there's nothing wrong with that, much as I harass you. As long as you're happy. But this seems to make you happy too. In a thrilling, scary way."

Gen looped an arm around her shoulders and squeezed. "Yes. I think it does."

Chloe gave her a sly look. "So have you ever fantasized about Marguerite?"

"No. And I don't suggest you do it, either. Tyler strikes me as the type to be possessive, regardless of gender."

"Well, hot as M is, Tyler's the one I fantasize about. In full color."

"What red-blooded woman doesn't? Might as well stop breathing as try not to do that." Gen said. "Though if you don't share pictures of Brendan naked and tied up on your bed, I'll tell M about that morning you sneaked a glance at Tyler bare-assed in the upstairs bedroom when she was doing her yoga in the garden."

Chloe's eyes widened, then she snorted with laughter. Yanking Gen's ponytail, she escaped from behind the counter to greet and seat some incoming customers.

As Gen started preparing the order she heard Chloe taking, she pushed away guilt. She rarely lied to Chloe, but she wasn't prepared to share that yes, she *had* fantasized about Marguerite.

It wasn't a sweaty sex fantasy, and she didn't fantasize about her boss regularly. Just when random things hit her a certain way. Like the time Marguerite had been sitting at her desk, dressed for a meeting with the bank. She'd been wearing a snug blue skirt with a sheer blouse tucked into it. Her lace-clad breasts had been outlined through the fabric. She'd worn a pair of slender heels. Simple accessories that enhanced the beautiful woman's odd mix of fragility and strength.

Gen had been preparing her morning cup of tea like she always did, but when she moved to bring it to her boss, an erotic vision had taken hold of her imagination. She saw herself in an ancient Far East setting where Marguerite was the lady of the house and Gen the servant. Marguerite sat on folded knees on a cushion, painting graceful black slashes on a curl of parchment. She wore a silk kimono in peacock colors, her hair in a thick bundle on her neck. Gen knelt at Marguerite's side and held the teacup out before her bowed head, holding it steady as if her hands were the table.

Marguerite lifted the cup, sipped, set it back down, paying no attention to her. Until she finished her task. Then she turned, removed the tea from Gen's hands and framed her face in her cool, long-fingered hands. She pressed her lips to Gen's mouth, giving her a teasing touch of tongue before she dismissed her, leaving her aching.

"Gen?"

Gen saw Chloe standing on the other side of the counter, waiting for the order. "You really are in the falling-in-love-zone today," her friend said, low, though her eyes danced with mischief. "Bad as me when I was falling for Brendan. Almost as bad as M falling for Tyler. Though in all fairness, he jerked the rug out from under her and then claimed she was falling for him."

"While that may be accurate, it still had the same results."

The screen door creaked as Tyler entered from the side hallway. Through the open door, Gen saw his black Ferrari, one of several vehicles he drove. From the look on Chloe's face, Gen knew the girl had heard the car purr up the driveway and intended to tease him. Gen was the only one taken unawares.

Neither of them had been exaggerating about Tyler Winterman. It wasn't just his amber tiger eyes and dark, salt-and pepper hair, nor even the powerful, well-dressed body that emanated power and wealth. The man had an authoritative, sexy vibe that said he was an alpha's alpha, which wasn't a bad way to describe his and Marguerite's relationship. His unquestioning love and devotion to their reserved boss only enhanced his appeal. Gen was never surprised to see female customers pause with cups halfway to their mouths or completely forget what they were talking about when he came into the tea room. She'd known he was a Dom for a while, but the way Lyda was grooming her Dom/sub radar, it hit Gen's senses particularly hard today.

"I'm thinking the mega-rich thing saved your ass," Chloe said. He aimed a swat at her backside as she danced out of range. "Hey, that's sexual harassment."

"That only applies if I work here, which I don't. What are you two talking about today?"

Please, dear God, Chloe, don't...

"If Gen fantasizes about kissing Marguerite. I think she does, as red as she blushes when I ask her about it."

Gen groped for casual amusement. "Since I'm seeing Lyda, Chloe is trying to determine if I've had the hots for her and Marguerite all this time."

"Not me." Chloe shook her head. "I think you only go for the true Domme thing. You have a vibe like Brendan on that, but it's a different note. It was really low key until Lyda came around, and now it's a full piano chord."

Please shut up, Chloe. Talking about it in front of Tyler, with customers nearby, was stepping way outside Gen's comfort zone. Gen wondered if there was a hole in the back garden big enough to swallow her up.

"Chloe," Tyler said mildly. "That's enough."

Proving just how good a Master he was, Tyler did the impossible, focusing Chloe with merely a look. Her attention went to Gen's still face, and chagrin captured her pretty features. "I didn't know I was getting on your nerves, honey. I'm sorry."

"You weren't." Gen took a breath. "It's fine. It's probably not going to work out, anyway. I'm not sure why I started down a road I don't understand. When I hit a dead end, I'll feel like I've painted myself into a corner with no way out. The two of them already feel like…I can't breathe without them. And that sounds silly and cliché and young. So it's better if you don't get too into it. Maybe it's best we don't talk about it…so much."

Words were falling out of her mouth she didn't mean to say. Crazy batshit was right, with a nice dose of bipolar thrown in. Grabbing several boxes from the hall that needed to be broken down and put in the storeroom, she fled, giving Tyler an apologetic look.

As she hurried down the path, she tried to corral her emotions. She was a grown woman, but every thought, every beat of her pulse, was centered around Noah and Lyda, evidence of her desire to be with them. Her penchant for safety and clear lines kept her falling back, challenging Lyda, even as she surrendered when the woman looked at her a certain way. She was balanced on a knife edge, with an abyss on one side and a fiery pit on the other, yet she knew she was going to jump, let go of the safety bar. The matter wasn't if, it was when.

"Damn it." She broke the boxes down with passion and shouldered into the storeroom, plopping down on a stool. "I'm so fucked."

"In its literal translation, a good thing. But I expect you meant the pejorative."

Gen started. Marguerite sat on her stool in the corner, separating out the latest India shipment. Her tiny silver spoons were arrayed before her to sample the inventory.

Maybe because of what they'd just been discussing, when Gen looked at her boss, she couldn't tuck it all back into her safe subconscious. It was probably the first time she'd stared at her openly like this, cataloging her effect on Gen's senses. Her moonlight-colored hair was clipped over one shoulder, her lips frosted a pale pink. She wore very little makeup because she needed almost none. Her pale-blue eyes were like a mermaid's eyes, mysterious and tragic, yet hypnotic.

Since getting married, she'd finally gained some weight, because Tyler stayed after her about eating, but she still had an ascetic look that emphasized the fine bone structure in her face, her slender neck and those beautiful hands. Ironically, the starburst-shaped scar on the top of one of them only made them more fascinating.

Gen knew the childhood horror that had created that scar, the past that Marguerite always carried in her eyes and aloof manner. But being with Tyler had made it better, had brought healing to wounds that had bled for years. The scars would always be there, the memories, but Marguerite carried them more easily now. Tyler bore part of the load, helped carry her when she needed it.

Would Gen get to that point with Lyda or Noah? Had her feelings for them unlocked what Gen wanted so badly at this point in her life? Was that what was really scaring her so much? The contentment she'd created for herself had come at a cost. She'd lowered expectations and discovered the pleasure of accepting the little joys, rather than making leaps into the unknown. What she faced with Lyda and Noah was hell and gone from that. It was standing at a canyon edge and wondering, if she stepped out, would a bridge materialize out of thin air to connect her to the other side. And would what waited for her there be worth the risk?

"I think I'm falling in love," she said. "Lyda's the one who scares me the most, from the selfish, is-she-going-to-tear-my-heart-to-bits perspective. But Noah...there's something eluding me there. A different kind of fear, like if I get it wrong, I'd be doing the hurting. I feel his heart, but I think it's an illusion... Can I try something, M?"

She sounded like a manic magpie, but Marguerite didn't seem perturbed. Rising, she came to stand in front of Gen, touching her face. It was a measure of Gen's obvious distress that Marguerite would make physical contact. Or say the words she said now. "It depends on what it is. I won't let you do anything that will hurt yourself."

"Is that what I'm doing with them?"

"Not up front. If it ends in pain, I can't change that. But I can be here, and so can Chloe, if you need us. What is it you want to try?"

"Never mind. God, I can't believe I even started to ask."

"So ask anyway." Marguerite's thumb passed over Gen's lips, an intimate touch that drew her gaze back up to her face.

"Do you think I'm with you because I wanted...a Mistress? And I didn't really realize the sexual part of it, until now, with Lyda?"

Marguerite's lips pursed. "It's possible. There are people who marry the opposite sex and embrace a desire for the same sex years later, when other matters are resolved for them. Once they embrace it, they realize it was who they were all along, but other forms of growth had to happen first. As quickly as this has developed between the three of you, it's a credible idea for you."

"Can I kiss you?"

It was rare she was able to startle Marguerite. Gen waved a frantic hand. "No, I don't mean it like…a pass. Oh, good grief. I'm just trying to figure out…"

"It's not transference, Gen."

Gen let out a relieved breath, glad Marguerite understood so quickly. "I know, but I don't know. There's no one else I can test it with safely. Chloe's right. She's not like you and Lyda. I'm sorry, this is *so* beyond appropriate. I've lost my mind. Just forget it."

"If you do need that from me, you misstated it, Gen." Marguerite studied her. "You don't want to kiss me. You need me to kiss *you*."

Her stomach coiled up like a puppy, not sure whether it wanted to cower or wriggle in anticipation. Gen didn't know what to say. Fortunately, Marguerite did. "Let's make it as representative as possible. Ask me for what you need, Gen."

Marguerite's expression and tone changed, such that Gen was looking at a formidable Mistress, one who compelled men to fall on their knees and kiss the soles of her shoes, just like Lyda had described. She hadn't thought of Marguerite Domming another woman, but that talent for some Dominants apparently had no gender restraint.

God…the idea of being on her knees, kissing Lyda's ankles, the arch of her foot, a delicate curve…

Not something she'd ever fantasized about. Yet Lyda had mentioned it today, and there it was, planted it in her head. Maybe every step along the way *was* a progression. What Gen had never considered before now seemed possible, the rest of the journey needed first to understand its appeal to this newly revealed part of herself.

"Please." She looked at Marguerite as a Mistress, not as her boss, her friend…or as an equal. "Will you kiss me?" She spoke over breath suddenly in short supply. "Will you kiss me, ma'am?"

Marguerite considered her another long moment, then she leaned down, sliding one knuckle beneath Gen's chin to tilt her face up. She held her there another breath, then brushed her mouth across Gen's eyelid, making both eyes close. Those cool, soft lips moved over the bridge of Gen's nose, her cheek, the line of her jaw. Gen trembled hard, her hands closing into knots on her knees. Then Marguerite pressed her lips against Gen's. A slow, wet journey, her mouth moving over Gen's as Gen focused all her senses on that one point of contact and how it emanated to the rest of her.

She was the one who drew back, broke the embrace. She stared up at Marguerite as the woman straightened, withdrawing her touch with kindness, a caress of her cheek. "So…it is her. I definitely felt that *wow, zing* moment when I asked you for it, and waited on your decision, but all I could think about while you were doing it was how this felt not quite right. And not just because you and I don't connect that way."

"You want to belong to her."

"Yeah." Gen rubbed her stomach. "This is so confusing."

"It's not confusing at all. Not if you stop thinking about it so much." Marguerite bent again, this time to drop a kiss on the crown of Gen's head with surprising tenderness. "Go back to work. I have a shipment to sort, and employees wanting me to kiss them are not productive."

"Oh, Tyler's here. Tyler's *here*." Gen blanched. "M, I'm so sorry. Should I have done this? Do I need to apologize to him? I mean he is your Mas…"

She broke it off right there. While Tyler being Marguerite's Master had brought emotional stability to her life, saying it straight out felt like a definite no-go zone.

Marguerite relieved Gen's worries on that score by tilting her head, a pointed gesture. Gen twisted around. Now she really did wish a hole would swallow her up. Tyler was outside the shed. He was sitting on a bench about twenty feet away, checking something on his phone. But his legs were stretched out, his ankles crossed, as if he'd been there awhile. Long enough. Marguerite would have been facing him when she leaned down to kiss Gen. That meant Marguerite could have looked for a permission of her own, if it had been needed.

"He's an irrevocably straight male," Marguerite said dryly. "Giving him the opportunity to watch two women kiss is nothing that requires an apology."

Gen choked on a chuckle. Even so, she wasn't up to exiting the shed where she'd have to pass him, meet that piercing gaze. With a sheepish look at Marguerite, she escaped out the back exit and took a circuitous route back to the main building.

It also gave her some time to think. One thing had become clear. If she wanted to pursue things more deeply with Lyda and Noah, it was time to stop waffling over it. Yes, she'd played it safe to keep her world in balance, but one thing she'd learned over the years. When she did move into new territory, there was no sense in being tentative about it once she was committed. There was control in choosing a course of action, as well as a message she could send to Lyda and Noah.

Up until now, she really had been letting Lyda take all the initiative, but Chloe had given Gen a key. Pursuing a relationship, even if the Dom/sub aspect was a strong element of it, was still a two-way street. Well, three-way, in this case. Lyda's reaction to Gen's withdrawal last night at the club had underscored it. Lyda was a human being with needs and feelings. It wasn't fair for Gen to hang back and make her drag everything out of her.

She would invite Lyda *and* Noah for dinner, have them as her guests. She wanted Lyda to see her home. Since Lyda had expressed reservations about a move as telling as meeting Noah's grandmother, Gen wasn't sure how she'd feel about the idea, but she wasn't going to be a chicken, fearing rejection. Whether or not Lyda accepted the invitation, it would tell her Mistress how Gen felt about their relationship.

Plus, Lyda hadn't said when the Gatlinburg thing was, and Gen didn't want to wait until then to see her and Noah. Actually, she didn't want to wait more than a few hours. Thinking of how fast she could put together a decent dinner, she pulled out her phone and found she already had a text, one that worked her up in all sorts of ways.

Pack an overnight bag and come to my place tonight. I want you and Noah here. Yes or no?

Yes. Though she had a feeling her decision wouldn't improve her focus in the least, she was in better spirits, almost ebullient.

She might even be up to giving Chloe's teasing a spirited challenge. She was certain the imp had a naked picture or two of Brendan on her phone...

* * * * *

Marguerite watched Gen hurry away, then stepped to the doorway where she could see her husband. Tyler had lifted his attention from the phone the moment Gen had disappeared, proving it had been a ruse to avoid embarrassing Gen further. Her Southern gentleman.

He met her gaze. "That was interesting."

"I'll bet." She allowed her lips to curve. "How interesting?"

"Interesting enough I wish I didn't have that meeting with Michael in about thirty minutes. But anticipation is everything."

"Yes, it is."

Rising, he came to her, bracing one foot in its polished loafer on the step into the shed. Sliding an arm around her hips, he brought her close enough to place a kiss in the pocket of her throat. The strength of his arm, the firm press of his lips, conveyed exactly how interesting he had found that kiss. However, the gaze he lifted to her own saw her mixed feelings on the matter. "Still worried about Lyda?"

"This is moving fast beyond infatuation."

"You have to let them figure it out, angel."

She arched a brow. "Because you never push your own agenda on someone or interfere with the natural course of things."

"Of course not. But when the natural course of things can be helped along by my will..." He shrugged. "God does it all the time."

"I'm sure Satan does the same thing."

"Imitation is the best form of flattery."

"I'd like to say I'm surprised you'd compare yourself to God or Lucifer, but that would be a waste of breath."

He brought both feet onto the step, giving him back his height advantage, but she was okay with that, since he wrapped his arms around her, twisting his fingers in the soft stuff of her shirt, teasing the bra strap beneath. As he slid his lips past her ear, he nipped at her throat, making her fingers grip his biceps under the dress shirt he wore. He'd probably left his coat in the Ferrari, but he still bore that rich aftershave smell she loved, that had clung to him when they'd shared a bathroom this morning.

"I have a far better use for your breath."

She smiled against his mouth, let the kiss take her under, relying on his strength to hold her up as her knees weakened, as they always did when he kissed her. Not that she'd ever tell him that.

He already knew.

When he lifted his head, she gave him an amused look, despite the rapid trip of her pulse. "Was that a marking thing? Making sure Gen's kiss isn't the one I carry around for the rest of the day?"

"My wife knows me well." His hand dropped to curve around her buttock, stroke with unapologetic proprietary intent. "Just like she knows tonight I'll tie her to the bed and make her tell me every single thing she felt while she was kissing Gen, until I make her come with my mouth between her legs."

"Sorry. I have to wash my hair tonight. I'm busy."

"I'll wash your hair. Right after I make sure you need a thorough shower." Stepping back down, he pressed his lips to her palm. As he held it there, a silent communication, she touched his hair with her free hand and wondered at the miracle of this never-ending combination of peace and yearning he kept alive in her heart.

"See you soon, angel."

"I love you."

She didn't say it outright too often, infrequently enough his gaze lifted to hers now, his scrutiny telling her he was ensuring she was okay. Then his eyes glowed with pleasure. That made her want to say it over and over again, but she didn't have to. He knew that too.

* * * * *

When Gen arrived at Lyda's house, she didn't see her Escalade, but a quick glance at her phone explained it. She'd missed a follow up text while weaving through traffic.

Running late. Make yourself at home. Wine and beer in fridge. Noah in guesthouse in back.

She had to grin at Lyda, giving her the whereabouts of alcohol and Noah. But with her new resolve about things, Gen found she wasn't in the mood to do any sampling of the latter unless both courses were present, so to speak.

Still, she did want company, and she enjoyed being around Noah, not just for his admirable physical attributes. Instead of going into the house, she circled around it on foot. At last, she would get to see Noah's personal space. As she approached the guest cottage, she noticed the touches that said Noah was in residence. A small wooden boat was propped facedown on a sawhorse, being cleaned, painted or whatever one did to maintain it. A couple buckets and brushes were stacked neatly next to it. Even here, he respected the space Lyda had given him by keeping it clean and orderly.

If she'd gotten in touch with her inner Domme earlier in life, and if her husbands had had a shred of service-orientation to them, Gen reflected she might have obtained a more worthwhile investment out of those relationships.

She scoffed at the likelihood. Noah took genuine pleasure in service, and though she could understand the argument that it benefitted his need to serve and submit, she thought about what Lyda had said, that there was a difference between a bottom, who took pleasure merely from being topped, and a submissive, who had a much more complex give and take. Noah had a lovely form of selflessness. Neither of her husbands had had a shred of that quality.

She must be getting better at reasoning this out. It wasn't making her temples pound anymore.

The screen door was in place, the main door open. However, when she pulled back the screen door, she froze.

The door was splintered around the lock. It had been forced open.

She'd been in Miami when Chloe was attacked at Tea Leaves a couple years before. Everything had been over by the time Gen found out what had happened and returned to town. Marguerite had been in a bad way, convalescing at Tyler's. Chloe was still in the hospital. Tyler was of course absorbed in Marguerite, so by unfortunate chance, Gen had been the first one, after the police, to come back to the tea room.

The first thing she'd seen had been the splintered side door, a temporary latch and broken crime tape on it. When she came inside, she didn't know how long she stood there frozen, staring at broken tea pots, shattered tables and chairs. Blood on the floor where Chloe had been beaten nearly to death after she'd gone toe-to-toe with the man who'd been after Marguerite. The twenty-something who'd always been mistaken for much younger because of her pixie face and joyous outlook on life had fought him with no defensive skills, just courage and determination to protect those she fiercely loved.

Gen could only stand in that aftermath, feeling helpless that she hadn't been there to protect Chloe, no matter how futile they'd all assured her that would have been. The intruder would have likely killed her or hurt her just as badly.

It didn't matter, didn't assuage the guilt at all. She'd thrown herself into cleaning everything up, arranging for the repairs, making sure that when Chloe and Marguerite came back, it would be as close to the way it had been as it could be. She'd cried every moment she'd scrubbed that blood off the floor. Regardless of the number of pieces, she'd glued every broken cup and tea pot back together. It didn't matter that they couldn't be used anymore. She knew what they meant to Marguerite.

All that passed through her mind in a flash and then she didn't think. She shoved open the door, calling out his name, hearing the terror in her voice. "*Noah.*"

"Here. I'm back here. Wait there, don't come—"

But she was already hurrying down the short hallway. The guesthouse was basically an open kitchen and living area, with a walled off bedroom and bath, so it was only a few steps. However, as she arrived in the bedroom door, she understood why he'd tried to keep her from coming to him.

His bed was soiled. It looked and smelled like someone had urinated on it. Profusely. She pressed her hand against the framework, the world spinning. She'd also cleaned human urine and feces off the floor of Marguerite's office, left by someone so malevolent he'd marked like a beast the place M loved.

Though none of it had happened to Gen directly, she got a hint now of what it was to experience a post-traumatic episode. Spots marked her vision and she was back in Tea Leaves, scrubbing the floor, sobbing her sorrow and rage.

"Gen, it's all right. Come out here." Noah blocked her view. Nudging her with grim determination back into the front room, he pulled the bedroom door closed behind him. But it wasn't the only thing that had been vandalized. Looking around, she saw a small collection of books had been torn up. Dishes in the kitchen were on the floor, broken.

How was it that monsters like this could hate someone so much, they showed it by destroying everything that belonged to them? Had Noah been here when...

Her gaze snapped up to his face and then swept his body, her hands following, taking inventory. No blood, no torn clothing. He was whole. He was safe. She made herself take a shaky breath, realizing he'd closed his hands on hers, was making a soothing noise.

"Noah, what the hell...who did this?"

"He's already gone."

"He was here while you were here?"

"It's someone I used to know. He came to talk to me, and he got angry. He has anger issues."

"You think?" Gen realized he was shepherding her toward the door.

"I'm going to clean this up. Go on in the house. I'll be there soon."

"*No.*" She planted her feet. "You're going to tell me right now what's going on, who he is, and why I shouldn't call the police. And don't you dare tell me we're not telling Lyda about this."

"I wouldn't do that. I'm going to tell her I need to live somewhere else. It's time for me to move on. He wouldn't hurt her, but this is just...this all belongs to her. He can't destroy things that belong to her."

It was the break in his voice that helped her look beyond her own fear and anger, focus on his misery. As well as the fact his hands were shaking. Not much, but enough to scare her, since he always seemed so placid. Taking a breath, she framed his face. Something in his wandering gaze had her worried he might slip from her fingers and disappear, even while he stood before her.

"Sshh," she said quietly. Firmly. "Look at me, Noah. Look at me."

He was looking at her now, but he wasn't focused. She repeated it, sharp and steady. The relief that gripped her when she saw him tune back in to her made her run her hands down over his shoulders, his arms. "Let's sit down. Let's take a breath."

The house was too small to sit anywhere that wouldn't be in view of the damage, so she drew him out to the front stoop, making him take a seat with her there. He was barefoot. He was lucky he hadn't gotten glass in his heels. She should check that, because his expression told her he might be in a little bit of shock.

"First things first. Did he hurt you?" Gen dialed back the emotions the very thought boiled forth, but she wasn't entirely successful, because Noah gave her a wary look.

"No."

"Not this time." She studied his face, read the truth there. She pushed back the long hair that fell over his shoulder as he leaned forward. "But it's happened before."

"I was his for a while. Then he moved on. And came back. And moved on." Noah shook his head. "It's complicated, Gen."

She could well imagine someone being obsessed with keeping Noah. Hell, she was already pretty tangled up over him. Even the hard-nosed Lyda was protective when it came to Noah. But Gen was putting together pieces. He'd come from New Orleans for the purported reason of taking care of his grandmother. He'd "belonged" to Tyler before Lyda. Lyda had goaded him with the comment about being his babysitter.

"Is he the one who collared you and then let you go?"

She wanted the answer to be no, but when he gave a bare nod, she linked hands with him, let them rest on his knee as she reached up with the other hand, stroked his hair back again. "And you'd let him do it again, because you think once you belong to someone, you've made an unconditional oath. What happens when they conflict, Noah? When Lyda's ownership conflicts with his ownership?"

Noah managed a wry look back toward the open door.

"So you told him no." Gen felt a small spurt of relief.

"I told him I owed Lyda my loyalty until she lets me go. He said he respected that, but he had to punish me for refusing him. That I'm his property."

"So if she let you go, you'd go back to him?"

Noah didn't answer her, just looked at his bare feet. She caught his chin, jerked his face up. A flicker of mutiny went through his gaze, but he held still, let her make him meet her eyes.

"You answer me."

She might not be Lyda or Marguerite, but she'd had years of making hard decisions to regain control of her life, not waiting for it to be handed to her. As a result, she now owned a cherished old beater car, had her carefully tended mortgage and viable dreams of pursuing a full accounting degree, once she paid off the last of the debts her marriages had left her. She'd evolved from being Marguerite's waitress to doing Tea Leaves' books and handling opening and closings. While that might not seem like much to most, it meant something to Gen. She owned her life, and no one would ever take it from her again.

All of that fueled her resolve now, reflected in the hard note in her voice. That flicker in his expression acknowledged it, even though he put his hand up, closed it around her wrist. "I have to, Gen. It's the promise I made."

"To whoever picks you up off the street? Lyda doesn't rate better than a guy who pisses on your sheets to tell you how worthless you are?"

His expression became hunted. "It's not my choice."

"That's total bullshit. You won't make the choice."

"I can't." He pushed himself off the stairs so abruptly it startled her, but not as much as the fevered look in his eyes when he rounded on her. She'd seen Noah's brown eyes reflect deep lake calmness, brief flashes of sexy rebellion, and sometimes a disturbing flow of shadows, here then gone, like clouds passing over the sun. But now those shadows had gathered in full force, threatening a gale.

"I can't," he repeated fiercely. "One person says that makes me a gift, another says I'm damaged and I'm banned from their club." His hands closed into fists. "Someone else tells me I need to be this or that, and *none* of it is supposed to be about me. I'm everything someone needs me to be, until I'm not, and then I can't stop it or change it. I can't think about it. I just *can't*."

The stress of whatever he'd just faced with that invisible Dom had taken him over. He was shouting, though not at her. With his expression so raw and open, she saw something else in his gaze. It wasn't shielding. It was like...

Tea Leaves was in a poor neighborhood, and sometimes Marguerite gave tea and food to the homeless in the area. She had a knack for drawing the ones with mental illnesses that put them out of sync with normal society. When Gen helped her hand out the sandwiches, she saw it in their eyes, a kind of impenetrable block between them and full comprehension of the track from which they'd derailed. They ate what was offered, gave thanks and went on their lost way, sometimes muttering to the voices in their head, sometimes with quiet dignity.

She was stunned to the bone to see such a wall in Noah's eyes, too much like that disconnect to deny it. Gen struggled for something to say, unable to reconcile this with what she knew about him. Yet Lyda had hinted at it, Chloe had puzzled over how to explain it... Everyone seemed to hesitate over explaining him.

"Noah, your value has nothing to do with Lyda, or this asshole, or me or...anything else other than you."

Of all the things she could have said, she'd apparently chosen the wrong one.

Shaking his head, he turned away. His body was rigid, still as a statue, but vibrating like a ticking bomb. She'd risen from the steps, had started to reach for him, when he jerked into motion. He strode toward the upside-down boat. She wondered at his intent, but then cried out as he ripped a concrete rabbit out of the landscaping, descended on the boat and put the statue through the hull with one powerful swing.

"No, no, no, *no.*" He snarled, pounding the boat with every syllable. Gen stood frozen, no idea what to do. Self-preservation told her to stay back. Noah in a fury was far more intimidating. Instead of the gentle man she knew, suddenly he was like any other male who could attack and overpower. Cause harm.

Guy had broken her nose with one punch, proven the strength an angry man could unleash. But she hadn't been afraid. She'd run out the back door, into the street, where their neighbors were out walking dogs, mowing. She'd gone to the nearest one, asked to use the phone and called the police. Divorce papers had been filed within the week. She'd felt rage, betrayal, but she'd refused to feel fear.

She felt fear now, but not on her behalf. This was Noah. Dear, beautiful, sexy Noah, at war with inner demons she'd sensed but now saw in full force, whipping around him in a dervish of uncontrolled and escalating emotion. The boat toppled off the sawhorse and he fell onto his knees, continuing to hammer it with the concrete. When the rabbit broke into several pieces, he reached for the torn planks, regardless of the jutting nails.

"Noah—" She started toward him, her personal safety secondary. Another voice cut across hers like the strike of a lash.

"Noah."

Lyda was coming up the walkway, grim determination in her stride. She wore her usual garb of jeans and nursery T-shirt, but as always, it made her no less intimidating, enough that Noah paused, blinking in confusion. But he was too far into his own head. His lip curled back and eyes refired, a precursor to renewing his attack.

"Noah."

Gen had heard husbands teasingly refer to their wives as "She Who Must Be Obeyed". With Lyda, it wasn't a joke at all. That voice could cut through diamond, let alone the demons clinging to Noah's back.

He jerked, head whipping around, body following. Lyda was reaching out to put a hand on his knotted shoulder. When he seized her arm, Gen bit back alarm, but Lyda didn't move. Her glittering silver eyes stayed on his face.

"Stop it. Now."

Noah stared at her, panting. His body was rigid again, eyes unfocused. Lyda looked toward his grip, her expression cool. "Why are you touching me without permission?"

One at a time, his fingers loosened. Like a tree left broken by a storm, he dropped back onto his heels, back slumped, head down. Lyda studied him, watching the rapid rise and fall of his shoulders, his hands curl and uncurl on his thighs. Only when his breathing had evened out did she touch his head. He flinched, but when he spoke, Gen realized he hadn't anticipated a blow.

"I don't deserve it, Mistress," he mumbled.

"That's my call, not yours." Lyda stretched out her other hand, a subtle gesture to Gen. Gen came forward without hesitation, despite unsteady legs. When Lyda sent her a pointed glance, she understood. *Follow your instincts.* Kneeling next to him, Gen put her arms around his shoulders, used her palm to press his face against her neck.

"Easy," she whispered. "Just relax. Just breathe. I'm sorry. I didn't know the right thing to say. I'm sorry."

"I'm never going to figure it out, Mistress." Noah's voice was muffled.

"Just breathe," Lyda said. "All you have to do is breathe for us. Can you do that?"

"Yes Mistress. I'll do anything for you."

"I know. Be quiet now. No words. Just breathe."

* * * * *

Lyda forbade Noah to go back into the guest house. When he'd hesitated, obviously torn about leaving her with the damage there, Lyda had given him a look that could have withered daisies. "In the house," she said. "My room."

He followed her, Gen trailing behind. She had an idea of what Lyda intended, but had no idea how she was going to accomplish it, since the molecules around Noah were still jittering like a pending big-bang event.

When they arrived in the bedroom, Lyda pointed toward the open door of the cage. "All clothes off. You're in there until I say otherwise."

His stubborn look appeared. Lyda had obviously handled this situation before, but the volatility surrounding the two made Gen's gut clench. Lyda stepped forward, met him toe-to-toe, despite the fact he was a few inches taller than her. "Are you defying your Mistress, Noah?"

He shook his head, and looked entirely miserable. Lyda touched his face. He closed his eyes as she caressed his jaw, his lips. His body swayed toward her and he sank to his knees. He kept his back straight, but head bowed, only inches separating his forehead from her abdomen. While she didn't close that distance, her touch was gentle.

"I'm glad you want to take responsibility for the guesthouse. But right now, you need to serve your Mistress. I want you to calm down and find your center again." Her tone firmed. "Clean up your space on your own time."

That hit the right chord. Though his attitude was too close to despair for Gen's liking, after a few more tense moments, he pulled off his T-shirt, removed his jeans and underwear. He folded them neatly as he always did and placed them next to the cage. His meticulous care brought a lump to Gen's throat. From the stillness in Lyda's expression, she thought the woman might be feeling some strong emotion herself.

He went back to his knees and slid tiredly onto the mattress inside the cage. Lyda bent, locked the door. "I have some things to do," she told Gen. "Sit with him. No talking. Come to me when he's asleep."

Noah had turned on his side, facing away from them, his back rounded, knees drawn up. Lyda met Gen's gaze and mouthed, "Peacefully asleep."

Gen nodded and lowered herself to the floor beside the cage. A mandate not to talk was probably a good idea, since it seemed like her words had been the straw to set off his rage. But when she'd held him, he'd leaned into her.

Maybe words really weren't what were needed. Gen lay down on her side outside the cage, slid up close to it and put her hand through, resting it on his hip. She also threaded one leg through, pressing her toes against the bottom of his curved foot. Without the bars, she could have spooned with him.

She caressed his rib cage, felt him breathe in and out. Kneading his muscles, stroking his bare spine with her knuckles, gliding over the rise of his buttocks, she felt driven by a not-incongruous mix of maternal feelings with those of a protective lover. She watched his shoulders as closely as Lyda would, so she saw when they began to ease, his head sinking deeper into the pillow. Eventually his even breath told her he slept. Peacefully. Remarkable after the display of strife, but maybe when that broken part of his mind was torn open, exhaustion overwhelmed him more quickly.

Unfortunately the aftermath didn't have the same effect on her. She was rattled to the core. Both by the incident itself — Noah being attacked, his reaction to it — and how this might change how she felt about being part of all of this. She needed information, answers.

When fifteen minutes had passed and his rest seemed untroubled, she went to find Lyda. Though Gen was reluctant to leave him alone, she was pretty sure Lyda wouldn't have told her to leave him when he was peacefully asleep unless she was sure he'd be safe. Being trusted to determine what "peacefully" meant indicated Lyda trusted her judgment on Noah's care. Gen already knew a good Mistress didn't do that lightly. While a part of her wanted to react to the knowledge in a way similar to how she'd felt when M let her do the books for Tea Leaves, she was too fragile to feel much about that.

Lyda was sitting on the back stoop, studying the sunset. When Gen sat down next to her, the woman gave her a nod, offered her a sip from her glass of wine. Gen took it, their fingers overlapping before Lyda relinquished it and Gen took a healthy swallow. Then she put it back in her hand.

"There's more on the table there." Lyda gestured toward the screened porch behind her. "And another glass. Or you can keep sharing mine and we'll refill as needed."

"Like in medieval times, when lords and ladies shared the same trencher. Brendan told Chloe about that. She said it was romantic. I said it was unsanitary."

Lyda looked up at her with those fathomless gray eyes, tilted the glass toward her again. "What do you say now?"

Rather than take it from her hand this time, Gen settled next to her. Brushing a lock of loose hair from her own face, she held it there as Lyda brought the glass to Gen's lips. Gen settled her hand over Lyda's, changing the position of the glass. Lyda's lips had left an imprint on the edge and Gen made sure she put her mouth there, fingers overlapping Lyda's again. Their gazes met, even as Lyda kept tipping the glass. Slow, but intentional, until Gen had several more very generous gulps, the alcohol spreading warmth through her stomach. Then Lyda transferred the glass to Gen's hold.

"Pour us some more. You looked like you needed that."

She thought they both did, so Gen topped the glass and brought it back. There were three steps to the stoop and Lyda sat on the top one. Gen sat on the one just below her, the woman's thigh pressed against her upper arm. Lyda shifted, lifting one of those flexible legs and bringing it down on Gen's other side, giving her a nudge so she centered herself between Lyda's knees. Gen adjusted onto a hip, propping her back against Lyda's leg so she could look up into her face. "Are you okay?" she asked.

"Yeah. It's always hard, to watch him tear himself apart like that. It hasn't happened in a while. Goddamn Elias."

"Elias?"

Lyda glanced down at her. "Right. Sometimes you feel like such a natural part of this story, I forget you arrived after we were already a few chapters into it."

It was a gratifying and unsettling observation, but Gen put that away to listen.

"Back in New Orleans, Noah belonged to a Master named Elias. Not the worst or best kind of Dom, but Elias had a tendency to get a little carried away with the power aspect of it. Since most healthy subs know how to protect themselves, it was a minor addiction problem, kept in line by that check and balance. Noah was like crack to Elias."

Gen could well imagine.

"When Club Progeny's management recognized the risk, thanks to a couple over-the-top sessions," Lyda continued, "Noah's membership was revoked. He was too big a liability. Remember when I said a sub's first responsibility is to care for herself or himself? Well, Progeny took that shit seriously. As they should."

"Elias wasn't expelled too?"

"Suspended, for a time, because they treated it as one infraction rather than an affliction. Without Noah's proximity, they might have been right, like a drug user staying away from his drug of preference. But they couldn't control what happened outside the club. Elias moved Noah into his house. One night things went so far, he put Noah in the hospital. Couple broken bones, internal hemorrhaging from being kicked."

Gen's fingers had come to rest on Lyda's knee. Now they tightened, horror filling her. "Does that happen often in BDSM?"

"Abuse has no more place in a Dom/sub relationship than any other relationship." The firm set to Lyda's jaw and warning flash in her eyes underscored it. "However, a healthy D/s relationship looks different from a healthy vanilla one, doesn't it? The lines can get confused if the people involved aren't responsible enough."

Gen thought of the night Lyda had switched her. Her ass had been on fire from the punishment, but she'd also never come so hard in her life. Yes, it definitely looked a little different from a vanilla dating scenario.

"D/s brings a lot of things to the top, Gen. It's why it's called Risk Awareness Consensual Kink. Human beings have endless communication problems and weaknesses. Ones they sometimes don't recognize the way they should until it's too late. Fortunately, after that incident, Elias realized his. He cut Noah loose. Too little, too late, to my way of thinking, but I tend to be an unforgiving sort."

Gen wanted to go find the faceless Elias herself and pin him up against a wall with her car. She thought of Noah leaning out over the water, hands gripping the braided nylon lines, holding them taut to keep the boat balanced and flying.

He was strong, healthy. He could defend himself. But he hadn't. She wanted to say she couldn't comprehend it, but she thought of the person she'd once been, the one who thought if she just kept loving her husband and trying to be a good wife, it would work out. Though she'd wised up fairly quickly, a shadow of what she felt then was undeniably connected to what Lyda was describing about Noah.

"On its face, it seemed like Elias backing off resolved things. But that cord was only cut in one direction. Elias didn't tell Noah it was over. He simply stopped visiting him in the hospital, and assumed Noah was as done with it as he was. For all the time he'd spent with Noah, he still didn't get it. Not until Noah was discharged."

Gen shook her head, a futile rejection of what she suspected was coming. "No."

Lyda nodded. "Noah went home. In his mind, that was to Elias. Thank God, Noah wasn't alone when he was discharged. A fellow sub had picked him up, and when Noah made it clear where he was going, that sub texted her Dom." Lyda's lips twisted. "Ironically, he's a hardcore sadist who can dish out pain like a trained interrogator. Yet he understands where the lines are, more than Elias ever will. His sub, who's also his fiancée, is as fiercely cherished as Noah deserves to be."

Gen puzzled over that. "I really have a lot to learn about all this."

"I'd say that goes for all of us." Lyda gave her a fond smile, something that helped loosen the band around Gen's stomach. A little.

"What happened?"

"Ben, the Master she called, met them at Elias' house. He made sure Elias clarified the relationship was over. Elias handed

Noah his things at the door, pretty much threw him out and told him he was done with him. Ordered him to give back his collar."

Lyda passed an absent hand over her hair as she took another swallow of wine, offered the glass to Gen. "Ben was smart enough to know Elias wasn't cured, and distance was the best plan. Which is where we come in. Ben's boss, Matt Kensington, is a friend of Tyler's, and of course Matt's a Master as well. The D/s community is a tightly knit one. Matt contacted Tyler and told him Noah had a grandmother in Tampa. He suggested Tyler talk to her and figure out a way to get Noah down here. The grandmother has some health issues, so it worked without being a lie. Tyler took Noah under his wing when he first arrived, as a service sub, not sexual, but then he introduced him to me. I got intrigued."

Gen looked up into Lyda's bemused face. "Do you regret that?"

"No. He wasn't something I was planning for my life…but he took me by surprise. I find myself unable to let him go. Not because I'm worried about protecting him, though there's that. I like having him around. Have you ever thought about Jesus, Gen?"

Gen blinked at the shift. "Is this where you tell me you're born-again and ask me if I've accepted Him as my savior?"

"No." Lyda gave her a light pinch on her shoulder. "You know how it's supposed to be—that Jesus merely wants you to let him into your heart, where he'll love you unconditionally. He doesn't choose which of us to love—he waits for us to make the choice to love him completely, totally, which allows him to love us completely as well." She lifted a shoulder. "Or something to that effect."

"I've never really thought of it like that."

"I hadn't either, until I started trying to figure out Noah. And I think the key is there, in a far more earthly sense." Lyda's lips curved faintly. "That boy is definitely not Jesus, though he does have some of the sexy rock star thing going on that Jesus has."

Gen bit back a startled chuckle. She also had to suppress a little twinge of horror, probably residual guilt from her mother's Baptist roots. Lyda looked at her, sobering.

"I don't think anyone's ever truly fallen in love with Noah, Gen. They don't look beyond the fact he'll do anything for you, make life easier, do any chore, give you screaming orgasms. Or that he'll take anything you dish out." Her lips tightened and she looked out over the yard. "He has a soft sense of humor, like clouds at sunset, and a mind so sharp he could design aqueducts in Rome. He's generous-hearted, smart and sexy. And when it comes to this, he's totally fucked up in the head, in a way I'm not sure can be fixed."

Though that brought a wave of dismay, Gen was transfixed by Lyda's face, the emotions reined back behind the carefully chosen words. Lyda had said a D/s relationship didn't look like a vanilla relationship. But some things actually did look the same. Marguerite had told Gen once she was a watcher, a listener, and that she always knew more about people than they realized she did.

Only someone truly in love with another could show such poignant sorrow and unmitigated intent in that understanding. So whether or not it was clearly stated, Lyda was in love with Noah, the light and dark of him. And she obviously knew that love could bring as much pain as joy, but the latter would be worth any amount of agony.

It was a feeling Gen had sought for so long. And no matter how she tried to deny it, she was well on her way to finding it with these two. When she looked down, her hand was clasped around Lyda's free one, those fingers linked with hers. As Lyda said, it was like she'd stepped into a story that had just been waiting for her to join it.

"I don't think that tattoo was meant for any asshole Dom who steps into Noah's path, like Elias," Lyda murmured. "It's like an SOS to the Dom he's meant to be with."

"A soul mate."

"I'm too cynical to go that far, but yes, something like that. It's a specific message to a specific person. The irony is, Noah would rescue you or me from a burning building, or lie down across acid so we wouldn't get a single drop on our shoes, but in the end, Gen, it's him who needs saving. From himself. There's a wire that doesn't connect, and if it's possible for that connection to be repaired, it will happen with the person…or people…he's meant to be with. I was arrogant enough to believe I was that person, but the past couple weeks, I'm thinking it might actually take two people, not just one."

The implication rendered Gen silent, keeping her thinking. Lyda didn't say more than that, offering the glass again. When Gen handed it back, she held onto it long enough to put her mouth on Lyda's knuckles. While doing that, she leaned her head against Lyda's breast as the woman bent her head over hers. Taking and giving comfort.

"I didn't want to leave him," Gen said against that curve. She felt the edge of Lyda's bra cup beneath the thin blouse, the flesh it cradled. "It cracked me open, seeing him that way. Odd as it sounds, it happened again when I imagined Elias throwing him out, telling him to give back the collar." She was seeing that uncomprehending look in Noah's eyes, the despair he'd shown before he went postal on the boat.

She closed her eyes. "Which was good, because he was the wrong Dom. But…you're not going to make him leave, right?"

"No," Lyda said. Her lips brushed Gen's temple, her cheek. "As you go along in life, you realize it isn't finding the perfect guy or girl. It's finding the person who's perfect for you, in the sense life would be a lot worse without them. Noah brings a lot into my life. I'm just trying to figure out what that means to him. What I want to teach him is selfish, but true for the relationship to work. I want to be his choice, not just the Mistress who chose him. I have this inner bitch who wants to be told I'm the one."

Gen lifted her head to look at her. "Everyone wants to know they're the one. The only."

"Even if the only means two, not one."

The reassurance gave Gen's heart a lift, enough that she squeezed Lyda's hand. "I'm familiar with your inner bitch. It's not all that inner."

"Nice. I'll remember that, rabbit." Lyda tugged her hair, sighed. "It's a unique thing for me, to find one I want to keep. Not just until it wears out. I'm willing to do whatever it takes to make sure it never does. But how to work around this, confront it head-on, make peace with it…" She shrugged.

"Do you know what caused it?"

Lyda finished the wine, set it aside. When Gen gave the empty glass a quizzical look, she shook her head. "We've both had enough for now. As far as the why… We're a world of broken toys. Sometimes I think whoever made us set us aside in favor of whole, perfect toys elsewhere, and yet the laugh's on them, because we're ten times more fascinating and tougher broken than something that's never been broken at all."

Gen thought about the inner strength she'd discovered after divorce, destitution. Yeah, it could be like that.

"Except for his grandmother, Noah is estranged from his family," Lyda said. "His parents rejected him, his father the head of that particular spear. What I've learned through bits and pieces, because Noah doesn't talk about it much, is his father first thought he was gay, then found out it was 'even worse'. He learned his teenage son was a sexual submissive, a hardcore one, and he found out in a pretty graphic way. My guess is he probably stumbled on him in a Dom/sub session with someone older, maybe a college student already in touch with his inner Dom. Whatever it was, Dad couldn't wrap his mind around it, saw it as a sickness."

Lyda took a breath. "Ben's fiancée did some digging. Marcie does corporate investigations and is damn good at it. Ben says she could find Jimmy Hoffa. Noah's father had him committed to some whacked deprogramming institution at seventeen. Nothing took, of course, because Noah is...Noah." Her lips twisted. "That's the irony. There's this steel core to him that can't be changed. Noah knows what he is, and you can't knock him off that tightrope with a sledgehammer. Not even with enough meds to turn someone into a zombie."

Gen sucked in a breath. Lyda closed her hand alongside her throat, thumb rubbing a soothing caress. "At twenty-one," she continued, "They washed their hands of him. Noah's father signed him out of the institution, handed him a duffle bag of clothes and told him he was dead to them. He was never to come back, call them, what have you."

Gen thought of Noah's duffle. It was old but carefully tended, with a few mended corners reinforced with heavy duty canvas thread, perhaps like that used to stitch boat sails. *Oh God.* It had to be the same one.

The scenario was a mirror of the scene with Elias. Of every Dom who'd ever cut him loose. It was happening again and again...

"The mental institution may have added layers," Lyda said, "but I think it was the betrayal of his family that severed that wire in his head. Or it could have been there from the beginning. Sometimes we're born the way we are."

She brought Gen to sit on the step next to her then, the two of them leaning against the door. Lyda had an arm around Gen's shoulders, fingers caressing the top of her breast. "So that's that. You're now inside our crazy little world. How does dinner sound?"

Lyda had been inside this story for a while, and though the events of the day may have stressed her out, apparently she was ready to turn things in a different direction. When Lyda's thumb teased her nipple, a spiral of arousal disrupted Gen's pensiveness, increasing when Lyda's eyes heated. Despite the turmoil in Gen's mind, her own body was obviously ready to make that same turn. "That's a nice, tight little point there. I think you need the distraction. We all do. But first you're going to need food. Both of you." Lyda kept stroking, tweaking, as Gen did her best not to squirm.

"He's going to need me to be harsh tonight," their Mistress mused. "I'm in the mood to take you along for the same ride, since I've been thinking about you ever since your visit this morning. I want to run you both into the fucking ground."

"So we just...carry on." Gen pushed the response past the anticipatory quake Lyda was causing through word and gesture.

"Forward is the only way you ever get anywhere." Lyda rose. "Do you want to tell me why I have a voicemail from Marguerite, wanting to talk to me about you?"

Oh crap. "I...we can talk about it later. It's nothing, I'm sure. M sees me spending more time with you, and she's a good friend. She's protective." After Gen's agitated display earlier, she was sure Marguerite was going to reinforce more of what she and Lyda had already done the Vulcan mind meld over. Sometimes good friends, especially when one of them was a formidable Domme, could be a pain in the ass. She was sure M wouldn't tell Lyda about the kiss. That was up to Gen. Or Lyda, apparently.

"Hmm. Probably. But that's not why you just turned the color of a tomato." Lyda's eyes had gone to that laser sharpness. "You're lying to me, Gen, which isn't a good idea. Particularly not in my present mood. Didn't I tell you this morning that you always keep your legs open when you're around me, just the two of us?"

Sexual tension spiked right into Gen's emotional quagmire. The woman had an uncanny way of doing that.

Gen opened her knees, pressing her palms against the cool concrete step. Stepping forward, Lyda put a hand right up under the skirt, just as she'd done earlier in the locker room. This time, though, she found her way beneath the panties and pushed two fingers in to the base knuckle without hesitation, making Gen gasp.

"Nice and wet. Just from me playing with your nipple. Or maybe something else has you simmering. Why did you blush, Gen? What happened with Marguerite? Make me ask you once more, you won't like what I'll do next."

"I asked her to kiss me." Gen bit back a cry as Lyda sent a jolt of sensation to her core. Her nipples tingled like they'd been hit with an electric charge. "I was trying…to make sure…it wasn't just any Mistress."

"Hmm. What was the verdict?" Another scissoring of Lyda's fingers made Gen fight not to writhe. Lyda's face was close, but her expression made her as remote as a queen on a throne. The concrete temperature wasn't doing anything to calm Gen's blood, especially when Lyda gave her clit a tug.

"It's you. You make me feel…different." Gen's throat ached. "I would have told you right off, but Noah…"

"Bullshit. You weren't going to tell me. Why?"

Gen yelped at the next wave of sensation. God, what was she doing with her hand? "I didn't know how you'd react. If you'd laugh at me, or withdraw, or…not react at all."

Lyda sighed. "One sub thinks I owe him nothing, that I can back over him with a truck if I want. Another keeps trying to force emotional validation to ensure she's not on quicksand. Some capricious goddess is testing me. Or trying to piss me off."

Withdrawing her fingers, she licked at the pads while Gen tried to get her breath. "Don't you dare close those legs. You stay there and let that cunt that belongs to me throb. We're done with all the overthinking tonight."

She disappeared into the house. Gen had no time to unscramble her thoughts before she returned, holding something behind her back. "Come up here onto the porch. Bend over and hold your ankles. Close your eyes."

The woman's ability to shift gears was as unsettling as the fact Gen was obeying. If she'd had the ability to form coherent words she would have told Lyda the kiss Marguerite had given her had woken a neon sign in her loins, blinking bright and pointing right at Lyda. But maybe she had just told her that, in a different way.

She bent over, gripped her ankles. Lyda tucked the hem of her skirt into the waist band and then pulled Gen's panties to her thighs. Gen made a tiny noise of protest as a dildo was worked into pussy. And not just there. Her fingers clutched her ankles as she realized it was dual-headed. Lyda slid the shorter, lubricated plug into her anus. Gen groaned with frustrated pleasure as Lyda cinched it all into place. Done in a blink, efficient as only a Domme who'd done it plenty of times could be.

"Straighten up slow. There we go." Gen jolted as the two items started to strum with a low level vibration in both orifices, radiating through every erogenous zone.

Stepping back, Lyda leveled that look that said she was the head bitch in charge and dead certain to stay that way. "I'm hungry. You're cooking dinner tonight. You and Noah both."

Chapter Twelve

Lyda had brought home Chinese takeout, but she was as exacting about her food presentation as a gourmet chef. She wanted it on a certain set of plates. The rice had to be aligned at a ten o'clock position from the entrée—and shaped in an oblong pile. The silverware required polishing with a hand towel first.

Tasks that weren't too difficult, except when wearing a vibrator that pushed Gen beyond motor control. She came the first time while shining a fork. She grabbed the cabinet so her knees didn't buckle. Noah shifted against her, using his body to sandwich her between it and him, steady her. She turned her face into his bare chest as she screamed through it.

Thanks to Lyda's equal attention, Noah couldn't use his hands to balance her.

Lyda had made it clear Noah needed a harsher Mistress tonight, and she was more than up to the task. When Lyda released him from the cage, she'd told him brusquely to meet her downstairs in fifteen minutes, and murmured something to him Gen hadn't been able to catch. Whatever it was had caused Noah's gaze to flick over her in an intriguing—and disturbing—way.

However, once he came downstairs, Lyda brought him to the living room and had him kneel, put his forehead to the floor. While Gen watched from the door—holding onto the frame, biting her lip to manage the waves of sensation caused by the vibrator—Lyda pushed a lubricated dildo up his ass as well. The phallus had an additional cock harness piece she secured around the base and neck of his shaft. The collar around the corona contained a bullet vibrator, stimulating the base of the glans in a way sure to steal his coordination.

Making him straighten to his knees, she'd buckled a collar on his throat. With her gaze trained on his lowered eyes, the set mouth, she'd added cuffs to his wrists and attached a spreader bar to them and the collar. Now he was yoked like an oxen. To pick up a cup of wine, a plate, he had to bend his knees and carefully maneuver, or risk the unthinkable infraction of knocking something over or off the counter.

Yes, it was punishment, but Gen soon realized it wasn't humiliation. How exacting and focused he had to be on his movements seemed an extension of the centering effect the cage had provided him. He was intensely aroused in no time, yet emotionally much more like his usual self.

Seeing him naked except for the harness, his natural grace hampered by the spreader bar but requiring a lot of flexing muscle to obey their Mistress's commands, only served to tip Gen closer to another climax. As far as that first one, she didn't know if Lyda had instructed him to hold her up, or he'd just anticipated the need, since even when Noah was being punished, he and Lyda seemed to work together to watch over Gen. The same way she and Lyda did to Noah.

And, point in fact, the way Gen and Noah did for Lyda. Though it might seem like she needed a lot less care than the two of them, Gen's mind was working that issue, and she suspected what they were doing right now fulfilled Lyda's needs, soothing any agitation this day had caused her with the balm of their submission.

Lyda's appearance only added to the lust saturating the environment. She'd changed into another short robe. This one was sheer gray gauze except for the satin ribbon hem and edgings. As the fabric floated around her, she revealed tempting shadows of her naked, inaccessible body. Sitting at the head of her dining room table now, she had a graceful leg hooked over the carved arm of the chair. The loose neckline highlighted the full crescents of her breasts. Occasionally she let her fingers drift down to stroke between her legs. They couldn't see below the table, denied the view.

Gen didn't have to wonder if it was all driving Noah as wild as it was her. He looked like he was carrying a steel piling between his legs, whereas her arousal was free flowing down her thighs, things Lyda noticed and commented upon with crude pleasure, making them both crazier.

Lyda had been right about the whole thinking thing. There was no room in Gen's mind for anything but clumsily coordinating her movements with Noah's, the two of them working together to prepare the food the way Lyda instructed. Just one setting. Lyda wasn't letting them eat first, calmly stating they were her entertainment.

When Gen put the plate before her, her hand trembling under the sensual duress, Lyda motioned to the floor. "Kneel here. Forehead touching the wood floor, ass in the air. Noah, stay where you are."

When Gen complied, Lyda pulled the dual-headed vibrator free, slow and provocative, making Gen moan. "You're close to coming again, aren't you? Shameless girl. And you came the last time without my permission. I obviously need to make it clear who's in charge here."

Gen cried out as a spatula hit her backside. Lyda had pulled the metal utensil out of the pan that had the spring rolls and fried rice in it, so Gen felt the splatter of warm oil and what was probably rice slide down her buttock. The spatula had slats in it that stung like hell. "Now you've made a mess to clean up." Lyda tsked. "Noah, kneel behind her and take care of that."

With her head down, Gen saw him move into place. With his arms bound shoulder height, he had to tighten thigh and stomach muscles in a delicious way to lower himself to the floor, lean over Gen. When his mouth closed over Gen's flesh, she could feel him quivering from the strain. Or maybe that was because of the state Lyda had inflicted on them both. Her breath became more erratic as he licked off the oil, ate the bits of rice. From the sound of a buckle being unfastened, and his sudden jerk, Gen suspected their Mistress had removed his cock harness and dildo also.

"That's plenty. Your tongue is a napkin, not her fucktoy. Not until I say. Go lie on your back on the living room floor."

Lyda curled her hand in Gen's hair, pulling her back up to her knees. She held her so Gen was staring at Noah, watching him kneel and then roll to his hip and back. He managed it with some difficulty, probably due more to the turgid state of his cock than navigating with a spreader bar. He was agile enough to navigate seas rough or calm. If only he could develop that same balance in his head.

Fortunately, Lyda had the right strategy to get them thinking about other things.

"Gen, go straddle his face and take his cock in your mouth. I want to watch him eat your pussy while you go down on him.

You can come whenever you're ready, but he has to wait for me to give him permission. You keep sucking his cock while you climax. Don't let up until I say stop."

Gen gave her a desperate look. "Mistress—"

"I'm not in the mood for talking. Unless you're in pain or you need the bathroom, I only want to hear more of those sexy little moans or pleading whimpers."

Lyda's stare made Gen drop her own gaze to the floor. How on earth had she reached the point where all of this felt so...right? But she'd known it today when she'd kissed Marguerite. She'd reached a turning point. She definitely wasn't as extreme as Noah, but she responded to Lyda in ways that were strangely liberating and overwhelming. This, a session-like moment, felt perfectly right. Just like sitting with Lyda on the stoop, talking like equals about Noah's well-being, had. Was that how it worked, figuring it out over time, the power exchange?

"Do I need Marguerite here to get you to move your ass, Gen?"

Gen started as the spatula hit her thigh. Though she gave Lyda a narrow look for the verbal jab, it was a surreptitious one, and she scampered to do her bidding before Lyda could think of another way to stretch her to breaking. The woman probably had a rack hidden somewhere to make the thought literal.

Lyda wasn't letting her off the hook for that nasty look, though. When Gen glanced her way again, Lyda's expression froze her in place, reminding her she hadn't answered. She dropped her gaze again. "No, ma'am."

"Better. Do what I told you to do."

Gen straddled Noah's face, another little quake going through her at the proximity of his mouth to her pussy, the vivid memory of what he could do with his tongue, and the intent, hungry look in his eyes. She planted her knees on either side of his face, congratulating herself for not landing on him in an uncoordinated heap.

She slowed herself down as she stretched out over his body, aware Lyda wanted to savor the visual. Noah turned his head to nuzzle her inner thigh, making her pussy throb, anticipating. She forced herself not to wiggle, which would be a blatant attempt to direct his mouth to where she wanted it. But Lyda took care of that.

"Don't play with your food, Noah. Eat her pussy, and be ruthless about it. I want her begging for mercy."

Gen was realizing the word "ruthless" was some kind of trigger for Noah, one with a devastating impact on a woman's senses. He immediately turned that clever mouth and tongue stud on Gen in a way that had her fighting to give him a tenth of the screaming roller coaster ride he was giving her. Screaming was the key word there. He took her up to the highest peak in a matter of seconds and pushed her over.

When she was finally gasping through the lingering vibrations of that climax, squirming against his face, she told herself that wasn't so impressive, given how aroused she already was.

But then he did it twice more.

He called the first time a "hummingbird", the second time "rain storm". If she'd had any brain cells left she might have joked at the Kung Fu of it all, but after the third time she was ready to be dubbed Grasshopper and become a slavish devotee to that mouth.

He knew how to back off, calm down those jittering nerve endings, and restart them. He taught her every part of a woman's cunt could be a starting line for a climax, that it didn't begin and end with the clit. He used that knowledge to obey Lyda's demand for ruthlessness. The third orgasm was a hard, punishing torment that made Gen's vision gray. Just as Lyda predicted, it had Gen crying for mercy.

Lyda still made him do it to her one more time.

Gen came down from that one trembling, tears running down her face. Actually "coming down" was a misnomer. She'd started out so depleted, she'd been unable to do anything but press flat against him and moan through the stimulation, beginning to end, her pussy at the mercy of his mouth. Thank God Noah was back to nuzzling her thighs, Lyda at last giving her a break.

She'd tried her best to torment Noah the same way, but her biggest accomplishment had been keeping her mouth moving on him throughout all of it. She'd sucked that thick shaft deep, shrieking like a banshee against his flesh. Though she'd managed not to bite him during the throes of orgasm, she'd scored him, reveling in the way his thighs twitched, hips kicking him deeper into her mouth.

Now she cradled his balls and kneaded them, stroked his perineum. His mouth vibrated against her as he muttered oaths. The tightening of all those lovely muscle groups beneath her, his cock thick as she'd ever felt it, told her that while her oral skills might not have been her best performance, her screaming reactions had more than compensated to keep him heavily aroused. She realized his trembling body was as rigid as his cock. It made her more determined to draw a climax from him, no matter how he struggled to obey his Mistress. Pushing aside exhaustion, she put her oral skills back to work. She tasted his pre-cum and milked it out of him with teasing strokes along the throbbing veins along the shaft.

Just when she was pretty sure Lyda's intent was that he come without permission, and Gen was feeling a visceral pleasure at being part of the conspiracy, Lyda spoke. "Come for us, Noah."

He thrust so hard up into her throat Gen gagged, but she moved with him, riding him like a bucking horse. She wished she could be in two places at once, seeing the way his biceps bunched as the spreader bar held his arms in their locked position, his chest lifting, hips pushing down hard to flatten his ass into the carpet and then rebounding into her mouth again, pumping into her like he would her pussy.

She kept lashing at him well after his seed flooded her mouth, inflicting as much sensual torture as he'd given her, sucking on the corona, nipping it with sharp teeth as he jerked. Distantly she heard Lyda chuckling at them both, but the strain in their Mistress's voice shot triumph through Gen. Was she hot and wet too? Craving their hands, mouths, genitals to bring her release?

If she was, she wasn't ready to give in to it yet. "He's done. Gen, take your mouth off him. Remove his spreader bar. Noah, stay still. No moving."

Though Gen was weak, she was so saturated with the drugging pleasure of it all, she wanted more. Endless amounts of more. It was a Disneyland-Twilight Zone addiction. As she turned to straddle Noah, her wet pussy pressed against his damp cock. She leaned over his face, her breasts bobbing close to his tempting mouth. The puffs of breath puckered her still tight nipples further.

When she unbuckled the cuffs, she saw he was in the same zone she was, his gaze fastened on her breasts as if they were the most important thing in his universe. He wanted to taste, to suckle. She stretched herself even lower, put her nipple damn near against his parted lips, her breasts pressed against his face. She also did a lot of rubbing against him as she freed him from the spreader bar. "No moving," she reminded him.

Lyda chuckled. "Gen, behave, or I'll let Noah spank you. He'll only tolerate so much teasing from another sub, even one I'm commanding. He enjoys making a pretty female ass rosy, almost as much as he likes having it done to him."

Looking down, Gen discovered Noah's gaze glittering with a promise of retribution, a hint of his savagery threaded with thrilling intent.

She slid off him, unnerved enough that she jumped a little when his now-free hands grazed her, but it was only to steady her as she moved onto her knees. She saw that dangerous look now held mischief. It was also more evidence he'd recovered from earlier. Other feelings took over for her then, such that she squeezed his hand. The shift in his eyes acknowledged her emotions, that and his firm grip a quiet message of reassurance. *It's okay. I'm okay. Stop worrying.*

She knew she'd keep worrying about it. He was an oscillating wheel, the broken part of him out of sight, but not gone. However, thanks to Lyda's determination to keep sanity out of reach tonight, Gen was quickly distracted again.

"I'm nowhere near done with you two. I want Gen on her knees and you inside her from behind, Noah. Are you still hard enough to make that happen?"

A quick glance showed him partially erect. He found a condom in the coffee table, rolled it on. Gen moved onto hands and knees, wobbling like a newborn filly. The woman was honestly trying to kill them.

"Put her on her elbows, Noah."

The butterfly tingle in her clit increased to a flock of birds as he curved one large hand around the back of Gen's neck and pushed her down to her elbows, supporting her to avoid a face plant. Putting his pelvis against her bare ass, he fed his cock into her, pushing a little to accommodate his not fully rigid state. Lyda had an answer for that.

"Start squeezing down on him, Gen. Neither of you is allowed to move otherwise, though. You're my performance art, a perfectly still statue of two people fucking, but all the movement inside, working out all those sensitive nerve endings."

Gen obeyed. She closed her cunt muscles over Noah's length. Kept doing it rhythmically. Lyda had a devilish understanding of the way arousal worked between two attracted bodies. As Gen milked him inside but they were both forced to stay still outside, Noah's grip on her hips increased. He started getting hard again in no time. Which stretched her labia, put pressure on her clit, and started to take her up that slope to arousal again as well. Oh God, it felt so good to have him inside of her. She wanted to move. Desperately.

Lyda had been eating throughout, making casual comments about the tastiness of the meal, things that needed to be done at the nursery, the damn meaning of the universe, for all Gen knew. Now she pushed her plate away. "Gen, come here and take this to the kitchen. Refill it."

It was a good thing the woman wasn't in her mind, because having Noah pull out of her resulted in some creative curses. She toddled toward the table, her arousal coursing down her thigh. When she reached across Lyda to take the plate, their Mistress slid one finger up that track and placed it in her mouth, sucking in a way that had Gen almost dropping the plate.

"You're evil," she said.

Lyda's eyes glinted. "No talking."

Gen shut her mouth, went to the kitchen. She refilled the plate as before, remembering the rule about ten o'clock placement and oblong rice shapes. She locked on the guidelines as if the fate of world peace depended on following a Mistress's orders. There was a pleasure to it, a frustration, a sense of security. Everything began and ended with her. Was that another part of it for Noah, for every person who had this kind of craving to submit?

Whatever. She'd save it for her next philosophical discussion with Chloe. And good God, would she have some experiential knowledge to bring to that discussion.

When she returned, Lyda had changed her robe for the one she'd worn the other night. She must have had Noah retrieve it, for he was now kneeling beside her. The transparent gray robe was on the chair next to her.

"Put that on and take a seat there, so Noah's in between us. I want him to see enough flashes of tits and pussy when you move to keep him hard."

Noah wet his lips at that, though Gen noticed Lyda had him staring down at the floor right now. She also had his hands occupied. They were motionless, double-wrapped around his cock, holding the stiffening member in a pointed up position.

"Here, feed him this." Lyda handed Gen a spring roll once she complied with her commands. "Make him eat it from your fingers."

Gen found the experience of feeding him even more absorbing this time. As Noah closed his lips around the roll, his gaze lifted to meet hers. Lyda watched them, her chin resting on her hand as Noah chewed. Gen waited until he swallowed and looked to her for another bite. Lyda kept passing food to her. Sometimes she made Gen eat, taking the food from her hand. In that manner their Mistress fed them, making sure they both ate dinner, sending Gen back to fill the plate once more and then emptying it in the same manner. Gen feeding Noah, Lyda feeding Gen.

On the second plate, Lyda allowed Noah to release his cock, which stood quite well on its own. She didn't give him direction on where to place his hand, so over time, Gen noticed he braced one on the seat of her chair. As she shifted to feed him, she managed to position herself where his knuckles were against the base of her thigh. Lyda didn't prohibit it. She stroked his hair as she had Gen take food from her fingertips.

Whereas the arousal she'd spawned before had been overpowering and strong, this kept a nice sexual hum going, at a resonance Gen could enjoy for hours. Days.

Finally, they were done. Lyda pushed the plate away, sat back. "Noah, kiss Gen."

He rose on his knees, sliding his arm around her waist. Gen barely had time to draw an anticipatory breath before his mouth was on hers. There was something to be said about restraining a man's natural assertiveness. It was like shaking a bottle of soda. He kissed her with a thoroughness that had to be unique, had to be for the two of them alone, her and Lyda.

He belongs to us, Gen thought fervently, staring into his eyes when he pulled back. She'd destroy anyone who tried to hurt him. Lyda would bury the body at her nursery. Use it for fertilizer.

"Missed a piece," Lyda said. He lifted his head, turned his attention to her. She had a piece of egg in her fingertips. He took it from her with such gentleness, it made Gen ache. His attention was fastened on his Mistress's face with a raptness that matched the intensity of Gen's kiss.

"We're going to Gatlinburg with you, Noah. Both of us."

From his startled expression, it was clear Lyda hadn't informed him that she was going, let alone Gen. But he rallied. "Yeah. I mean, yes Mistress."

Surprised, almost boyish pleasure crossed his face. Even Lyda wasn't immune to it, for her mouth firmed as if to hold back her own smile. She caressed his jaw. "Be still," she murmured, gripping his throat when he started to lean forward. Lyda kissed him, teasing his tongue with hers, holding that flesh and blood collar on his neck. It caused something between a moan and a growl from him, those brown eyes showing pinpoints of fire.

When Lyda drew back, she rose from the table. "Wait for me. No talking."

She disappeared down the hallway, going out the back door. Gen glanced at Noah, and was caught by his gaze. It was amazing how full silence could become. By the time Lyda came back, about five minutes later, she was literally lost in everything she saw in his eyes.

Lyda was carrying a book. Stepping out of the shoes she'd donned to go outside, she turned toward the stairs to the second level without stopping. "Follow me. Both of you."

Noah rose, offered Gen his hand. She laced his fingers with her own. She wanted to say so many things to him, but she kept letting her eyes do it. Lyda was right. Words didn't cover certain things. Lifting both her hands to his face, he pressed his mouth against them. Tears pricked her eyes. He nodded as if they'd actually spoken, and then led her in Lyda's wake.

When they reached the doorway of the bedroom, Lyda was standing by the bed. It was the first time Gen had noticed the cage had a two doors in it, the second fitting into the design so seamlessly it would be overlooked except when open, as now. A divider had been added to the cage, a barred insert that turned one cage into two aligned side by side, so Lyda could reach down and touch either of the occupants from the same side of the bed. A mattress had been added to the new compartment and Noah's mattress had been rotated to accommodate the adjustment. Now Gen knew what Noah had been doing those extra minutes alone upstairs.

"In you both go," Lyda said. "And no, it's not time to sleep. Not yet."

Something had changed when she retrieved the book. Though her face was impassive, Gen picked up a tense note in her voice. Noah seemed to as well, but he moved forward at Lyda's command, holding onto Gen's hand until the last moment, as if he knew she needed the reassurance. Gen watched him take his place beneath the bed, then lifted her gaze to Lyda's.

"I know it's not your thing," her Mistress said. Her expression softened slightly. "But for the next few minutes it is. You can leave the door open."

Gen thought it through. That very first night, Lyda had told her she could refuse anything, without repercussions or guilt. Even now, she was waiting on her, not in that impatient way to goad Gen's arousal with a Mistress's demand or threat. She was giving Gen time to determine if this was a hard limit.

Her gaze slid to Noah. He'd shifted to his side, had his head propped on his fist, and was studying her. As her eyes slid down his body, she noticed he had one foot threaded through the bars, into the cage she would be occupying. Intentional or not, the whimsical gesture, the light in his eyes as he saw her notice it, made her realize this was still within her control. She could leave the door open, right?

Noah had said there was a security to sleeping inside of cage. She supposed that depended on whether that cage rested beneath your Mistress's bed, a Mistress whom you trusted to hold your well-being above all other things. By showing that trust, she supposed a sub gave the Mistress a gift in return.

Taking a breath, Gen moved past Lyda. Giving her another quick glance, she knelt and slid into the cage.

The sheets were pale lavender, and the pillow smelled like that same herb, a pleasant, soothing scent. As Gen slid on to it, she slid down far enough her foot touched Noah's. He curled his toes over her arch, a quick caress. "It's okay," he murmured. "I wouldn't let anything hurt you. Neither would Lyda. You're safe with us."

So service-oriented he could be mistaken for a Dom. She saw the proof of it in the wholly reassuring touch and tone, his direct look.

"Who do you serve, Noah?"

Lyda could issue commands, purr like a siren, or cut like a whip with that voice. This was a new note, cold like an officer dressing down a soldier for an infraction that could have gotten him killed. It brought Noah's head up and his full attention upon her.

"You, Mistress," he said quietly. "I serve you."

"I don't believe you." Lyda opened the book, withdrew a folded piece of paper. "This was on the bedside table in the guest cottage."

Lyda opened it with a snap, showing a bold scrawl. "This was why you hadn't pulled off the bedding yet, wasn't it?"

Sleep on these sheets before you wash them. – Your Master

Gen stared at Noah. He'd dropped his gaze to the floor in front of the cage, looking anywhere but at either of them.

"Look at me," Lyda snapped. His head jerked up, though he looked like he'd rather be Perseus looking at Medusa. "You would have done it. Answer me, Noah."

"Yes Mistress." His jaw was rigid. "He told me to do it, and it didn't conflict—"

"His very presence on this property conflicts with your oath to me," Lyda snarled. "And I asked for a goddamn yes or no answer."

"Yes Mistress." Noah repeated. He was back to looking miserable.

With the negative ions charging the air, Gen's current position felt even more exposed. She thought about leaving the cage, but she already knew Lyda channeled her emotions with purpose. She'd ordered them into the cage for a reason. As if underscoring that, Lyda glanced her way. Just a brief flicker, but it helped Gen hold steady. Until Lyda spoke again.

"Gen had to learn a similar lesson tonight, Noah. That if she belongs to me, she doesn't let other women kiss her." Her gaze shifted to Gen. "I'm still not convinced. Until I say otherwise, whenever the clock chimes the quarter hour, no matter what else we're doing, you say 'I'm yours, Mistress'."

"All this, for one kiss," Gen said shakily.

"All this, for allowing another Mistress to touch you without my permission. If you don't want my ownership, all you have to do is say so, right now. I let you out of the cage, we share a glass of wine. You can curl up with me in the bed."

"But it changes things, doesn't it? You want more than that from me. You want me to belong to you, like him."

"Yes, I expect you both to fully belong to me." Gen trembled at the passion in Lyda's gaze, a dragoness roused from her lair. "You wanted Marguerite to kiss you to prove something to yourself. Now you prove something to me. Watch the clock, and be still."

Lyda unlatched Noah's cage, jerked her head at him. "If you want to prove who you serve, Noah, serve your Mistress now. Get out here."

* * * * *

The man had his insubordinate moments, but Lyda's anger made him obedient as a disciple of God. Noah was out in a heartbeat, a flexible, quick roll and slide that brought him nearly to Lyda's feet, on his knees. He looked at her with such a yearning expression, Gen felt a hitch in her chest. Everything about him said *Yours, Mistress.* Yet he'd said he'd go back to Elias if she released him, as if it was as simple as that.

Gen didn't buy it. She'd lay money, whether Noah admitted it or not, that he'd never looked at anyone the way he was looking at Lyda now.

She knew Lyda saw it, because Gen was starting to learn her face, those minute shifts in features. When something moved her and she didn't necessarily want to show it, there was a tightening around her mouth, a quick glitter in her gaze, like a sudden shooting star, her reaction too bright and quick to shadow.

"On your back." Lyda's attention shifted to his cock. "You're going to have to work on getting that a bit harder, aren't you? Do it, while I'm watching you."

Noah stretched out at Lyda's command, one hand curled around his thick shaft. He stroked and squeezed, thumbed his slit, teased his corona. He knew his body well, and it responded to that and Lyda's attention, his buttocks tightening against the carpet as he pushed his cock deeper into his grip. As his gaze moved hungrily over his Mistress's naked form, standing over him, he slid his other hand over the carpet, stopping at the side of her foot. She glanced down at it, then shifted her gaze back to him. Whatever he saw gave him the latitude to move his hand over her foot, curl around the top of it.

"It's nice having him working for me," Lyda said casually. "I can role play sexual harassment scenarios all day. Though I need to have Brendan give him drama lessons. He doesn't do self-righteous helpless indignation." Her lips quirked.

It took Gen a moment to catch up, realize Lyda was talking to her. The two of them had her mesmerized. "Look at that cock," Lyda purred. "Getting nice and hard for me."

She straddled him, going gracefully to her knees. Moving his hand out of the way with an imperious nudge, she wrapped her own around his jutting cock.

"Hands above your head, Noah. I'm in charge here."

Lyda sank to the hilt upon him smoothly, showing how well their bodies knew one another. She let out a little hum at the sensation, her thighs tightening around his hips, ass flattening against the tops of his thighs as she bore down, took him as deep as she could. Noah's face went rigid with pleasure and concentration, his knuckles pushing into the carpet. Gen's pussy gave an unmistakable twinge of longing.

The clock began to chime. "I'm yours, Mistress." It was a soft plea. When Lyda looked her way, Gen hoped she saw that she meant it. Maybe not just in the heat of a session like this, but other times as well. She'd gotten into a cage for her. Jesus.

Lyda extended a hand. "Come here, rabbit. Bring that footstool by my bed."

Noah reflected avid pleasure at the command. They were good at that. Gen never felt forgotten or ignored, even when Lyda was spinning things up between her and Noah specifically. Like a three-member cast. They might have different timing for entering or exiting the scene, but all three were still part of the play.

When she brought her the carved wooden stool, Lyda put it down, showing her that it was wide enough to bracket Noah's lower chest, right in front of Lyda's knees, and tall enough it cleared him by a mere couple of inches. The implication made Gen swallow on a dry throat, particularly when Lyda gripped Gen's hand with a fierceness that conveyed the arousal Lyda was experiencing, impaled on Noah. "Watch," Lyda said.

She must have tightened her internal muscles, because a groan slipped from his lips. Lyda rose on her knees, his cock sliding slowly from her cunt. Gen looked at that joining point, fascinated as Lyda reached the head, then reversed, coming back down just as slow, using a palm braced on the stool to control her descent. Noah's hips jerked, his whole body contracting in a mouthwatering way to stay still.

Lyda did it again, her gaze fastened on his face. Gen watched them both, aching. She squeezed Lyda's hand in unspoken need.

"I think she wants to play too," Lyda said, breathless. "Come here, Gen."

She guided Gen to straddle Noah, Gen facing Lyda. Bringing her down on the stool in front of her, Lyda cupped Gen's ass in both hands and directed Gen's legs over her own. Then she had Gen slide forward so her pussy came flush against Lyda's lower abdomen, her inner thighs against Lyda's sides, her heels pressed to the outside of Noah's legs. They were close enough Lyda's breasts dragged a teasing course up Gen's stomach, then pressed into her own bosom. Anything Gen might say was caught in a gasp.

Nudging her head back, Lyda kissed her throat, then bit. Gen wound her arms around Lyda's shoulders, fingers tangling in her hair. Lyda's arms bound low around her back and hips in answer, holding her close, face pressed into her throat. "That's my girl. Hang on for the ride."

Another rise and fall, Lyda moving against Gen's body, lifting her with the movement. Gen had a hysterical, lust-induced vision of a carousel horse, only this was a much different ride from when she was a child. As Lyda lifted and lowered her body, Gen's clit rubbed against her tight lower abdomen, her legs locking around Lyda's body to increase the sensation. Lyda's nipples slid across Gen's curves, then came in direct contact with her own taut peaks. It wrenched a moan from her throat. Lyda murmured against her, licked and bit her throat again. Then she closed her mouth on one of those aching points.

Gen made another throaty sound as Lyda suckled her, nipped sharp enough to make her jump, her pussy cream. She'd be marking Lyda with that fluid. It would roll down, join the lubrication Lyda and Noah were producing from their own arousal. She realized then that Lyda didn't have him using a condom. Gen envied that direct contact.

As Lyda kept working herself on his cock, her breath a rush against Gen's throat, Noah's hands slid onto Gen's hips, overlapping Lyda's.

"I can take both of you," he said, his voice rough with lust. "Let me feel her against me, Mistress. If that pleases you."

"You please me, Noah. You both do." Lyda eased Gen back to her feet. Gen moved the stool and then, at Lyda's direction, she sank back down. The brief brush of her wet pussy again Lyda's stomach made her shudder, but Lyda had a steadying hold on her, bringing her all the way back down so her ass rested on Noah's stomach, her legs curved around Lyda and heels resting behind her, between Noah's spread knees.

She noticed Lyda kept a firm grip on her ass. "Bet you wish you could rub your pussy against that nice washboard of his, don't you, Gen? I'll let you come that way sometime. Would you like that?"

She nodded, then remembered. "Yes ma'am."

"Lean back and arch your body toward me."

She felt Noah's hands curve around her upper arms, so she could rely on his strength to follow his Mistress's direction. Whenever he touched her, she trusted him with anything. She was getting there with Lyda as well. Dropping her head back, knowing her hair would be brushing his chest and throat, it made her smile when he caught a strand in his mouth and tugged. Then her gaze went back to Lyda to see what her Mistress would demand next, and more serious emotions took over once more.

Lyda was fucking him again. Her toned thighs flexed as she took Noah deep, squeezed him as she rose almost to the glans, then went back down, her cunt making that enthralling sucking noise. Gen wanted to put her hand to her own pussy, stroke. Noah's thighs trembled, hips jerking even harder at his Mistress's order of self-restraint. With him making those small bucks of motion under her, feeling the flex of his fingers on her biceps, it was clear to Gen how much he wanted to thrust up, fuck his

Mistress as intensely as she was doing to him. Gen was ready to beg for all of them.

Lyda put her hands on Gen's hips then. "How flexible are you? Tell me if this is too much of a strain."

She eased Gen up into more of an arch, her thigh muscles elongating as Lyda pushed her into a position where her pussy was tilted up at a higher angle, more accessible to her Mistress. This time when Lyda slid up Noah's cock, her clit brushed Gen's, and Gen understood what she was wanting. The searing pleasure of it helped her be even more flexible.

She arched further, and, despite the strain, bumped against Lyda's pussy again. Noah helped, pushing her even closer, and Gen made a soft cry.

"Give us both a lap dance," Lyda's voice was thick, her eyes glowing. "Rub your ass against his stomach, then bring your pussy back to mime."

She did it, orbiting between those two points. Noah's hands again flexed on her in convulsive response as Lyda closed in on her own climax. Gen couldn't create enough friction to reach climax herself, but she realized she was flying simply from servicing both of them. Her climax wasn't the point. The clock chimed again.

"I'm yours, Mistress."

"All of you? Cunt, heart? Mind?"

"Yes," Gen gasped.

Watching her Mistress's face, Gen felt a bond with Noah, knowing they were both working to give Lyda a climax as intense as what she'd given them. Beyond that, they had a selfish shared desire, wanting their Mistress to come, knowing they were the cause. For just an instance, she imagined herself with a tattoo that said "Yours" as well, only she had no confusion about exactly who she would mean.

Lyda moved her hands from Gen's hips to her breasts, squeezing them, then slid down again, scraping her nails over Gen's clit before she cupped Gen's buttocks once more, ensuring more prolonged contact between their centers.

"There you go. Work that little pussy against me. Let me feel how much you want to be fucked again."

Gen ground against her, teased Noah with the slide of her buttocks over his stomach. Another climax finally started to unfurl inside her.

"Ah...that's it..." Lyda bounced hard on Noah's loins, her breasts quivering, fingers bruising Gen's flesh where she held onto her. A flush swept up from her loins and across her sternum and throat. "Now, Noah..."

At the strangled cry, Noah thrust up, deep and hard. It detonated Gen's own climax. Lyda kept rising and falling, fucking Noah, teasing them both with how damn good she felt. She was a visual feast, every movement, the quiver of her breasts, the lengths of her thighs, the column of her throat...

"Mistress..." Gen made a helpless noise and Lyda seized her nape, bringing her up to her mouth and pulling her from Noah's hands. Noah shifted his grip down to Gen's hips, giving her the stability she needed as she and Lyda slid off that cliff together, moaning into one another's mouths, a feeling that intensified as Noah let go as well, hips jacking up deeper into his Mistress, the vibration sending an additional shot of response through Gen. It was like everything each one of them did made it more intense for all of them.

It was forever before they slowed. When they finally came to a halt, Lyda had her arms curled around Gen, was putting a teasing kiss at the corner of her mouth. Noah's fingers were embedded in Gen's hips, and she never wanted him to let go. Lyda insisted, though, having other demands to make of them.

Lyda turned Gen around, had her straddle Noah facing him this time, standing on her knees. His hands slid up Gen's thighs, eyes dark and mouth a sensual firm line as he spoke past her to Lyda. "I like it when you're both sitting on me, Mistress.

"We'd eventually squash your internal organs," Lyda said, amused. "You'd die."

"What a way to go. Under two gorgeous, naked women." He smiled then, lazy and wicked. With no warning at all, he jackknifed up, rolled and pinned both women, catching Lyda with a leg thrown over her thigh, an arm around her waist. Gen was sandwiched between as he gathered them close. Lyda propped her head on her hand, ignoring the tangle of limbs, though her hand fell on his shoulder, caressing it.

"You don't get off me, boy, I'll use a zip tie on your ball sac."

Instead, he shifted next to Gen to nuzzle Lyda's breast, then put his lips over it, began to suckle. Lyda's other breast was right in front of Gen. Noah's hand was on her back, exerting a slight pressure, an encouraging and clear message.

It was a sweet pleasure, hearing their Mistress sigh as they each suckled a nipple. Lyda stroked them both, making a little hum as they savored the taste of her, of having their Mistress beneath them. Still in control, but giving them the rare gift of her trust.

As Gen shifted to her throat, tasting her pulse, Noah was moving down Lyda's body. The two of them were devouring her, and Lyda was letting them.

Noah kissed his way over Lyda's abdomen, down her side, working his way to her thighs. Gen lifted up over her, hands braced on either side of Lyda's shoulders. When Lyda's lips parted, eyes glazing, a glance back showed Noah now had his mouth between her legs. A faint hum told Gen he'd engaged that blissful tongue stud.

Gen bent down and covered Lyda's mouth with hers, tongue delving deep. Endless. How many times had they come tonight? Shouldn't they all be exhausted now? But no, it was as if they wanted to explore how many different ways they could bring one another pleasure, how many different crevices and expanses of flesh they could taste with tongue and lips. Lyda broke the kiss, but only so she could push Gen further up, and latch onto her breast anew, take a hard pull as Noah worked between his Mistress's legs. Gen gasped, tightening her fingers in Lyda's hair, looking back to watch. He'd be worrying her clit between her teeth, plunging his tongue deep between those wet folds. He had his hands beneath Lyda's thighs, and her ankles were locked over his back.

Gen slid an exploratory hand down, played between Noah's lips and tongue, over Lyda's clit and labia. The woman nipped the underside of her breast, a rebuke, but one that didn't stop Gen from continuing to flick at her clit, loving the jerks of her hips, her reaction to the jolts of sensation.

"Are you creaming for us, Mistress?" she whispered, looking down to meet Lyda's silver eyes. The response she got was being pulled down for another hard kiss, Lyda gripping her nape as Noah took her over the edge to a moaning, twisting, tornado climax, her hands digging into Gen as it happened. Noah gripped her spread thighs, his knuckles pressing into Gen's legs as he held Lyda still to maximize her pleasure.

When Lyda rolled down that peak, they were all breathing hard. Gen thought it was all incredible, but this last time had been special. Three people enjoying one another, the reins tangled in all their hands, free form, incredibly pleasurable.

Noah sat back on his heels, looking down at both of them. Gen had shifted to her hip, curled up against Lyda's side, held in her arm span. Reaching out, Gen slid a hand down his side. Noah caught it, lifted her knuckles to his mouth. When she brought them back to herself, she could smell Lyda's musk from his lips. Lyda's hand tightened in her hair then.

"He handled the climax, you handle the cleanup, rabbit. You wanted to know how wet I was for you. Go find out up close and personal."

Noah moved out of the way and Gen was pushed between Lyda's legs. She did exactly as bade, tenderly licking the crevices, collecting the climax, savoring the taste and scent. Lyda made a pleased murmur. When Gen lifted her head, she saw Noah was stretched out behind Lyda, his head propped on his fist again while Lyda had her head on his thigh, watching Gen as Noah stroked her hair with his other hand. She looked sleepy, their Mistress.

"Time for bed," Lyda said, confirming it. Noah eased her head to the floor and rose. He switched off the lamp and then, to Gen's surprise—and maybe Lyda's—he bent and picked Lyda up, carrying her to the bed. Lyda linked her arms around his neck, and held when he lowered her there. He stayed close, not pulling back until she brushed a kiss over his mouth and let him go.

"Gen," she said. "Come to me."

Gen slid into Lyda's embrace. Then, another surprise, Lyda brought Noah into the mix. He slid in behind Lyda, the two of them holding onto their Mistress in a new tangle of limbs, mouths close enough to brush lips, breath warm against flesh.

"Sleep," Lyda ordered. "Everyone. I won't be able to function tomorrow if I've spent the night being fucked to death. Or fucking my pets to death."

Too late. Gen felt like a limp noodle. She hoped feeling returned to her extremities soon. Aspirin was going to be in order for muscles that hadn't been used since...ever.

"Noah." Lyda's profile was a silhouette in the darkened bedroom as she looked behind her. "You'll clean up that mess in my guest house tomorrow. And that note doesn't exist. If you forget that, I'll take a strip off your hide."

"Yes Mistress."

Quiet descended. As her eyes adjusted to the dimness thrown by the nightlight by the dresser, Gen could tell Noah was staring into the darkness over Lyda's head with a look she didn't like at all.

Gen curved her hand over his forearm, draped over Lyda's side. A little bite with her nails attracted his attention. "Stay with us," she mouthed. She meant all of it. Not just his person, but everything, his mind, his heart...his soul.

A look of resignation crossed his face, but he nodded. "I want to," he murmured. "But it's not about what I want."

Lyda said nothing, her eyes closed. But her hand tightened on Gen's, a silent message.

Leave it alone. For now.

Chapter Thirteen

ಜಾ

Gen had never been to Gatlinburg. As they wound along the scenic highway that offered panoramic views of the Great Smoky Mountains, Gen coaxed them into stopping on the pull-off lanes more than once so she could gape and snap a few pictures with her phone, even though it wouldn't capture how awe-inspiring it was.

Then she saw a chainsaw carver who had rows of wooden bears set up on the roadside. "I want one," she pronounced. Noah grinned and Lyda rolled her eyes, but they stopped. And after a critical look at the craftsmanship, Lyda had bought a couple herself. She even talked to the artist about supplying wholesale to the nursery.

Gen earned a speculative look from Lyda when she decided against buying one, but the smallest bear offered was eighty dollars. It would cut too deeply into her vacation budget. She told them she'd decided having a picture of one was better and snapped a quick shot before getting back into the car.

They'd left Tampa before dawn. Lyda had taken the backseat, spreading out her paperwork and balancing her laptop on her knees. When she started muttering to herself in a way Gen recognized from Marguerite's adversarial relationship with her own accounting software, Gen began asking questions. Before long, the computer had been transferred to her lap and she was helping Lyda catch up with her books, to the woman's obvious relief.

"Do you do this for Marguerite too?" Lyda asked. "If she does, I hope she pays you well for it."

"I do," Gen said, with no little pride. "She used to do it, and now she trusts me with pretty much all of it. I even did her taxes last year. I don't have a degree yet, but—"

"You should hire out your services," Lyda said bluntly. "I know at least five other businesses who'd love to have someone handle their books rather than doing it themselves. If you ever want to hang out your own shingle, let me know."

"Oh, well... I love working at Tea Leaves, but I can always use more money." She figured she could do it at night, or on her days not working at Tea Leaves.

Lyda frowned. "Doesn't Marguerite pay you enough?"

"Absolutely," Gen said hastily, horrified at the vision of Lyda deriding Marguerite about her pay scale. "But there's only so much you can reasonably pay someone to wait tables and run a counter in a tea shop, given the profit margins. I love it there, though, and I don't want to leave."

"You're not a big spender, Gen. Do you have a lot of fixed costs?"

"No." When Lyda continued to stare at her, and she felt Noah glance her way, Gen bit back a sigh. She could say she didn't want to talk about it, but they were getting to the point it was best to put certain things on the table. "I'm in debt, thanks to my second husband. I've paid off a lot of it. In another year, I'll be clear, but getting clear sooner would be great. So if you're serious about those businesses, I'll be thrilled."

"I'm surprised Marguerite didn't loan you the money to get out from under all that." This time, there was no reproof in the tone, at least not toward Marguerite. Which told Gen that Lyda knew M enough to know she would have offered.

"I wanted to fix it myself. This is my private business."

"Because it makes you ashamed? Sounds to me like you should be proud as hell about it." Lyda leaned between the seats, bracing her hand on Noah's headrest. "Plenty of people make mistakes and get into a hole, and look for everyone else to bail them out. Government, family, friends. You picked up your own shovel, even when that hole wasn't all your doing."

Gen set her jaw. "Yes. I did."

"Then don't let questions about it embarrass you."

She sat back. Noah gave Gen a wink and squeezed her hand. "We better stop for gas," he said. "And I need a snack."

"When do you not?" Lyda said dryly.

"I need a restroom break," Gen added quickly, earning a conspiratorial grin from Noah. Truth, she could use a snack as well. When they pulled into the station, she asked her two companions if she could bring them anything from inside the store. Noah called out a request from the pump to bring him Cheetos and a Dr Pepper. Lyda was quick to lean out the window and correct him, telling Gen to bring him a bottle of water and a granola bar. Noah made a gagging noise that had Gen grinning.

Lyda rolled her eyes. "Fine, then. Bring him that junk. When he becomes a diabetic, I'll get a chance at needle play. I'm sure you can inject insulin into someone's privates."

"Cheetos and a bottle of water," he compromised, crossing his eyes. Gen laughed at both of them. At the convenience store doorway, she stopped to look back. Noah had the gas pumping, but apparently had decided to prove just how healthy he was. He was standing in front of Lyda's window, doing a stripper dance, gyrating his hips and then turning to rotate his very fine ass in a way that had the woman pumping gas behind them gawping. Lyda looked toward Gen, and rolled her eyes again. "Get his damn Dr Pepper and Cheetos before I strap him to the top of the car," she called out the window. But Gen saw her reach through the other window, give him a quick chest stroke and admonishing flick, gestures of affection.

They'd all done a lot of touching throughout the trip. Occasionally, while Noah was driving, Lyda would slide forward, stroke his hair or Gen's. Gen would hold Noah's hand or him hers. After that night, sharing a bed together, things had just grown more...connected. It had been like an official starting point, the moment where it was clear a relationship was happening, growing. Lyda of course still had her more reserved "Mistress" moments, and Gen saw flashes of that unsettling side of Noah, but overall, Gen was optimistic about the turn things seemed to be taking.

Gen had hosted the dinner at her house for them. She'd shown Lyda the craft room and the back garden, as well as how good a job Noah had done on the floor and walls. Before that night, he'd come back and done the painting. She loved the fresh paint smell, which made it seem like she was in a brand-new house. Lyda had given her a couple azaleas to plant around the walkway he'd also helped her build out of some spare brick left over from a construction site.

Gen had been so nervous that night, but once they were both there, the way they settled in, piled on her couch together to watch a movie after dinner... She had a scrapbook building in her mind, not only of the amazing, erotic experiences she'd had with them both over the past several weeks, but other equally significant things. Like Lyda pulling her down on the carpet of Gen's small living room and showing her an array of horrible exercises to work her abs and glutes. Noah, escaping to the kitchen to bring them big dishes of ice cream scooped over warm brownies to save her. Then later, Lyda had put melted ice cream on Noah's bare stomach, Gen licking it off as Lyda teased her pussy with knowledgeable fingers, her other hand working Noah's cock...

Gen tuned back in to the present, a smile quivering on her lips. Yes, things were going well. When it was like this, a three-way relationship wasn't as complicated as it seemed.

It was the first time in a long while Gen had taken a vacation that was more than a day here or there, so it was even more exciting to be taking one with two people starting to mean so much to her. She hadn't really shared how much, since those feelings were advancing at a pace that scared the crap out of her, but it was still really nice to be here with them.

Once back on the road, they arrived in Gatlinburg within the hour. Noah had warned her the town was a gaudy midway carnival set in the midst of all that natural beauty. Regardless, Gen found herself enchanted by it as Noah did the slow stop-and-go traffic down the main strip in the Escalade, past T-shirt shops, fudge stores, Ripley's Believe it or Not and the Hard Rock Café.

"Hey, there's a tacky place." Noah pointed it out.

Chloe had told her to bring back the tackiest souvenir she could find. Gen saw a couple suitably horrible candidates in the store window Noah had indicated. "We'll go back later," Lyda interjected before another spontaneous stop could happen. "We're almost there. I want to get settled."

They turned off the main drive and started up a steep incline, a winding road that took them into neighborhoods dug into the sides of the mountains surrounding the town. They passed a gate to a resort community, and Noah nodded. "That's where Dot is staying with her friends. She said to come see her early evening. Fair warning, she likes to take walks after dinner, and this is probably the only day we'll get a pass." He glanced at Gen. "She thinks eight miles is a nice outing. And she'll give you grief if you get out of breath. Never mind the fact she's in a power wheelchair."

Gen chuckled. "I have walking shoes. I notice you didn't give Lyda that warning."

Noah stroked Gen's leg with his long fingers, then left them there, curved intimately over her inner thigh. "Don't feel bad. SuperMistress back there can wear me out too. She's Xena Warrior Princess."

"Oh God. That makes me Gabrielle, doesn't it?"

"You're cute, short and have good tits," Lyda agreed. "Plus that really nice soft ass. But you're still coming back to my class one day. I particularly like the cool down period in the locker room."

"Nothing cooling about it," Gen retorted, though she got a little breathless, remembering it.

"You should have gotten video," Noah complained.

"Don't pout," Lyda said. "You'll get plenty of girl-girl action this weekend, unless you piss me off and I decide to put out your eyes with a hot poker." She packed up her laptop, tucked the folders into the case. "Barring a few panicked phone calls from Eric, that should take care of work. This looks like our place coming up."

Gen turned her attention to the cottage they'd be occupying for the next few days. A creek gurgled in front of it, the bubbling water and shiny dark rocks flashing with sun sparkles. A short bridge over the creek provided pedestrian access to the cottage from the street.

"I love it," Gen said, beaming at Noah.

Noah parked the car on the other side of the road. "It has one bedroom with a queen and a sleeper couch, so three people can be comfortable. Only one bath, but there's also an outdoor shower in back." He turned, handed the key to Lyda. "If you want, you can look it over while I bring in our stuff."

"I think you purposefully waited to tell me about the one bath until we arrived," Lyda said, though the humor in her voice told Gen she was teasing. Gen slid out of her side as Noah opened Lyda's door. If Gen had waited, he'd have offered the courtesy to both of them, because when they'd stopped for lunch, he'd done just that, opening the door for Lyda and circling around to Gen's side to open her door while she'd been fishing a brush out of her purse to freshen up.

He'd said people had called him a treasure. After traveling with him half a day, she thought he was a luxury. Taking responsibility for bringing in their luggage was only part of it. From pumping gas and driving, to verifying the air temperature they wanted in the car, he never seemed to tire of doing things to make the journey more pleasant for the two women. When Noah was in the convenience store restroom, she'd expressed concern about taking advantage of it. Lyda had shaken her head.

"You won't. You're too much of a service sub yourself. I doubt you'll ever feel truly comfortable having him do all the stuff for you he likes to do for me. But don't deny him the opportunity needlessly. Serving us nourishes his soul." She'd glanced up, seeing Noah returning from the convenience store. A light smile played around her lips as she saw he was carrying a bobble head cat Gen had seen by the cash register and remarked was really cute. "The man can't be trusted with his own petty cash."

She glanced at Gen then. "There's a mutual benefit to it between Dom and a service sub, but the Dom keeps in mind where the line is between taking advantage and fulfilling a mutual need for it. Follow my lead on it, and you'll be fine."

So, despite a twinge of guilt at leaving him with the luggage, Gen followed Lyda across the bridge to the cottage. They stopped halfway across, Gen pointing out a frog sitting on one of the rocks, staring at them with fixed expression. Lyda laid her hand on her back as they looked together, sliding her palm down to Gen's hip, a casual caress like lovers did. "Thanks for saying that, about how I should be proud of myself." Gen lifted a shoulder. "I am, you know, but you saying it made me feel special."

"You are special." Lyda leaned forward, kissed her mouth, her hand tightening on Gen's hip, thumb catching in the back pocket of her jeans.

"So are you. Actually, you're extraordinary. Which is part of why it meant so much to hear you say it." Gen dared to touch her Mistress's face. Lyda stilled as Gen stroked the distinct cheek bone. When she moved up, Lyda closed her eyes, let her tease her lashes.

"I really want to kiss you right now," Gen said.

"I just kissed you."

"I mean a really hot, scandalize-the-neighbors, make-Noah-hard and make-both-of-us-wet kiss." Where had this wanton side come from? Where was the "safe" Gen?

Who cared?

Lyda's eyes opened, so close to hers. "Are you waiting for permission?"

"Yes." Gen wondered how Lyda did that, put as much strength into her gaze as she had in the grip of her hands. "Because that turns you on. I like knowing I can get you worked up. That makes me feel pretty special too."

"Uh-huh." Lyda continued to study her for another protracted moment. One breath, two breaths. Gen took another step closer, so they were right up against one another. Lyda was wearing boots with block heels today, giving her a height advantage over Gen in her canvas sneakers.

"Do it," Lyda said, her voice getting that cool tone that sent shivers all the way down Gen's tailbone to spread out like an upside-down butterfly through her buttocks.

Gen slid her fingers along Lyda's neck, under her hair. Full, lips-on-lips, mouths opening, tongues tangling, pushing against each other, delving deep. Lyda snagged her belt loop with her thumb to bring Gen's pelvis against hers, initiating a nice, firm stroke of mound against mound. Then she gripped Gen's ass, increasing the pressure of that friction. Gen lifted up on her toes so her nipples made direct contact with Lyda's, both of them getting tighter and harder. It was still different to her, feeling that female mirror of her own responses, but that surge of pleasure, knowing she had the ability to increase someone else's desire, that was the same, male or female.

As Lyda pushed Gen against the bridge railing, her leg insinuating between both of Gen's, Noah slid behind them, bearing suitcases. He paused long enough to drop a kiss on Lyda's shoulder, close to her neck where the T-shirt she was wearing bared soft skin. Gen caught his silky hair, giving it a tug. It had fallen over his shoulder so she was able to pull the tie loose, send it all spilling forward. She glimpsed a brown eye full of heat beneath the fine strands before he shook it back and continued on his appointed task to carry things inside.

It was going to be a damn good vacation.

*****

The inside was small but charming, embellished with touches that reflected the mountain surroundings. A fake bearskin rug made of stuffed animal plush had a whimsical black bear's head and felt claws that jutted out of the fuzzy black feet. Gen loved the feel of it on her bare feet when she slipped out of her shoes. Noah put Lyda's suitcase in the bedroom, his and Gen's belongings in a corner next to the sleeper sofa. It was an automatic assumption that their Mistress would take the bed, inviting them into it at her discretion.

Such subtleties were things Gen now accepted as much as he did. Lyda was making a circle of the place, and appeared as pleased as Gen with their accommodations. She also appeared to be considering something. As she moved toward her bedroom, Lyda picked up the bear rug, took it with her. Gen saw there was another one in there as well, a brown bear. Lyda picked it up also and then spread both on the bed, running her hands over them.

Gen glanced left at the sound of a zipper opening. Noah was kneeling next to one of the totes, withdrawing a smaller bag. He stayed on one knee as Lyda straightened from the bed. Gen keyed into the anticipatory air, the conspiracy that seemed to be humming between her companions. She curled her bare toes into the wood floor, noticing Lyda's mouth was still swollen from their kiss.

"What do you have there, Noah?" Lyda asked, arching a brow.

He removed a strap-on with a clitoral stimulator. The phallus was larger than the ones Lyda had used before. At the base was a bulb that would stretch a woman's gateway, and inside it were metal beads Gen expected reacted to vibration and increased the sensation to the outer labia.

"And just what do you intend to do with that?" Lyda cocked a hip, sliding a hand into her back jeans pocket. The position thrust out her breasts, the curve of her hip tempting touch.

"I want to see you fuck Gen with this," Noah said, dark eyes glowing. "And I want to fuck her up the ass."

That grabbed Gen's attention as effectively as his hand closing over her throat. Maybe literally, since the unexpected fervor with which he delivered the request—like a bear's growl—took away any coherent response.

Lyda tucked her tongue in her cheek. Her tone was as casual as if she and Noah were discussing where to move nursery stock. "It was all that talk of how soft and pretty it is, wasn't it?"

He nodded as Gen bit her lip, her cheeks flushing as his bright gaze swiveled back to her. "You want to give her a paddling too, don't you?" Lyda continued. "She was teasing you at dinner the other night, pushing her tits into your face. I did warn her. You think our naughty girl deserves a punishment?"

Noah gave an even more emphatic nod, enough that trepidation trickled through the thick arousal swirling in Gen's vitals. Lyda's gaze turned to her then. "I approve."

And she was apparently ready to get right down to it, because before Gen could digest the direction things were taking, their Mistress had tugged her shirt out of her jeans and stripped it off, leaving both Gen and Noah staring.

Lyda typically wore black cotton bras and bikinis. They were sexy but serviceable. Yet when she took off her T-shirt, pushed down her jeans, she'd revealed red panties that matched a red bra with lots of sheer fabric and lace, a sinful look against her tanned skin. As she strode over to Noah, she unclipped her flame-colored hair and shook it out. She stopped in front of him, spreading her legs, buttocks tightening from the pose. She was magnificent, queenly...irresistible female power.

"Put it on me, Noah."

He put a kiss on her thigh first, a reverent homage and thanks for the pleasure of that outfit. "I thought my pets might enjoy seeing me wear something different," she mused.

"I enjoy you in everything or nothing, Mistress. But thank God for diversity."

Gen's humor was swamped by other feelings as Noah put the harness on Lyda from his kneeling position. He adjusted the straps around her thighs, waist and between her buttocks, but Gen could feel the enormous effort it took him not to let his hands linger. She knew her eyes did.

Lyda ran her fingers through his long hair again as he finished, a tactile approval. "You bought chocolate topping at that general store for the ice cream tonight. Get it. And find something to protect the floor."

Going to the grocery bags he'd left on the kitchen table, he retrieved the chocolate sauce and found a faded hand towel under the sink. As he returned to Lyda, breaking the seal on the chocolate, Lyda's attention came back to Gen's like a hawk zeroing in on prey. "Strip, Gen. Everything."

Gen looked between the two of them. Noah had gone back to one knee, still subservient to Lyda, but the look in his eyes was capable of making this rabbit want to be caught. There was simply no choice but to obey. As she unbuttoned her shirt, she felt the cool indoor air on her breasts, her navel, a contrast to the temperature she felt from across the room.

"I'm not the only one who's been shopping," Lyda purred.

"It was on sale," Gen said, inexplicably flustered under their combined regard. If she'd known the way they'd be looking at her now, she was pretty sure she would have paid more for the outfit, even if it had required her to skimp on groceries.

It had been a long, long time since she'd worn something this sexy under her clothes. The bra had low cups, so low the fringe of lace tickled the areolae. The underwires made her generous breasts even more noticeable. She'd seen Noah's eyes drift to them more than once during the drive. Though he'd probably wondered why she looked a little more substantial than usual, he'd been too much of a gentleman to ask. Though not too much of one to appreciate it.

The bra was a pale green enhanced by her eyes, with tiny lavender bows to cover the functional connection between shoulder straps and cups. The Brazilian panties matched the style, a brief scrap of silk over the triangle of her sex. She'd shaved thoroughly, since Lyda preferred her smooth.

When Lyda rotated her finger, Gen turned so she could see the back. The reverent oath Noah breathed was worth a month of no groceries.

The back of the panties was a triangle of lacing marked by tiny eyelets, the lavender bow at the top dimple between her buttocks begging to be tugged free. Especially by a lover who intended to fuck her up the ass. Realizing how appropriate her choice had been, she quaked with pleasure and nerves.

"Turn back around."

When Gen complied, she was undone by Lyda's expression, the words she spoke. "Every day you give me more reasons to be pleased you're mine, Gen."

Their Mistress glanced at Noah. Flicking his ear playfully, she drew his attention back to her. "Put some of that chocolate sauce on my dick and suck it off. You want the right to fuck my other pet, you have to prove how much."

The crude, masculine words fit Lyda's mood of the moment and only made Gen more aroused. "And you better not get a drop on my pretty red panties," Lyda added.

Noah drizzled the chocolate on the head and top part of the shaft of the dildo. Then, before it could start to drip, he set the bottle aside and put his mouth wholly over the phallus. He took it in with no hesitation, showing it wasn't the first time he'd done it. Was he just as good at giving head as going down on a woman's cunt? Gen imagined what it might feel like to a man, that vibrating tongue stud sliding along the sensitive glans. Since that brought her an image of the hated Elias, she pushed it away.

"That's my boy." Lyda stroked the long skeins of his brown hair through her fingers as he licked and sucked. "Yeah, you're getting all hard, thinking about spanking her pretty ass, pounding into it. Aren't you?"

He made an agreeable noise. The way he was moving his head, the force he was using, was obviously rubbing the base of the strap-on against Lyda. Rotating her hips, she drove herself deeper into his mouth until she had it in to the hilt. Slowly she pulled herself free, tightening her fingers in his hair to hold him still.

"Put more sauce on it." Her attention shifted. "Your turn, Gen. Get over here and drop to your knees. Noah will lube you up while you prove if you can suck me just as good as he can."

Noah took Gen's hand to ease her down to her knees, his normal courtesy, though the press of his hand, that light in his eyes, reminded her he was going to spank the shit out of her and fuck her. And it all turned her on.

He put more chocolate sauce on the dildo, then gestured, a nonverbal warning to move quickly before it dripped. The dildo jutted forward, shaped true to life and feeling that way as well as Lyda thrust it between Gen's lips. She tasted the chocolate, closed her mouth fully around the shaft. It was unbelievably erotic, the mix of messages. Those delicate lace red panties, the fragrant smell of Lyda's pussy and chocolate, the forceful thrust of a cock into her throat.

Noah's hands coursed over her buttocks, cupping and squeezing, a mute command for her to rise off her heels, balance herself against Lyda's bare thighs. He nudged the edge of the panties aside and inserted the tip of the lube into her, squirted. He followed it up with his fingers, a sure, decisive penetration that had Gen's pussy dripping as she thought of how he was going to put himself inside her here. Lyda was going to allow it, order it, while fucking Gen face-to-face.

She'd had two-men fantasies before. She'd never considered the erotic possibilities of a male-female combination, but those ideas were spinning through her mind now.

Lyda drew the dildo from between her lips. Noah kept teasing Gen's rim, fingers still thrusting into her. His thumb slid down, pressed into her pussy and she moaned again, fingers flexing against Lyda's thighs.

"She's going to be a nice, tight fuck for you, Noah." Lyda probed the bra cups, catching Gen's nipples in a pinch between thumbs and forefingers. "There are clamps and a chain in that tote bag, but right now I want the pleasure. Is that tight enough to hurt?""

"Yes Mistress." Gen gasped as Lyda exerted upward pressure.

"On your feet."

Gen managed it with the rough tug. Lyda used that same nearly painful grip to pull her into the bedroom, position her at the foot board. Gen's buttocks rubbed against one another, letting her feel the slippery lube Noah had applied so generously. When Lyda let go of her, her nipples tingled. The Mistress moved away to stretch out on the bed in front of Gen. She held herself on her elbows, her hair cascading down to the pillows. The strapped-on phallus jutted upward, one of Lyda's knees bent and rocking idly as Gen stared at her, hungry. There was dampness on the crotch of her Mistress's panties.

"Brace your hands on the bed on either side of my right foot, Gen. Put your mouth on the top of it and keep it there. Ass up. Don't lower it."

She heard Noah behind her. He ran his palm along her buttock, toyed with the lavender bow. She trembled when he pulled it loose. His fingers played down the seam of her ass as the lacings parted.

"Legs apart."

She adjusted, and the barely there garment drifted down her thighs. Noah removed it with deceptively gentle hands. A moment later she jerked as he gave her a hard smack, making her ass cheek wobble and nerves sing.

That wasn't the only thing the force of his blow made wobble. She saw her Mistress's eyes rivet on her breasts, nipples jutting over the lace edge of her bra in her supplicant position.

His next swat was directly on her pussy. She made a soft cry, her lips working against Lyda's foot. Her gaze flicked up to see their Mistress studying her reaction as well as Noah's, outside of Gen's view.

"He's meaner than he looks, isn't he? Are you ever going to try to take advantage of him again when it's not by my direct order, Gen?"

She thought of him on the floor, his hands bound on the spreader bar, the way he'd looked at her. "Maybe," she admitted, panting. "He's hard to resist teasing."

"An honest answer. Sounds like you'll have the chance to punish her again, Noah."

"Good." His voice was full of male satisfaction. He smacked her again, and Gen felt her pussy throb. She wanted him to hit it, hit her ass again. She wanted it to sting, get lost in this. She was lifting her ass higher, sending that message, and he obliged. He kept going, began to do it faster, more consistently, until she was crying out, quivering at the pain. The more he did it, the more fervently she pressed her mouth to their Mistress's foot. When Lyda's foot shifted, her leg rocking so her hips rolled open wider, Gen put her mouth on the arch, then the sole.

"Oh…" It was starting to hurt a lot, the accumulation of the impacts, but just like when Lyda punished her, the more it hurt, the more she seemed to want. When he finally did stop, her fingers dug into the cover and she whimpered, as if she wanted him to keep going.

"Look at me, Gen."

She was sniffling, a little teary, a catharsis she was learning came with punishments. Lyda gave her a tender look, then crooked a finger at her. "Come here."

Noah's hands gripped her waist as he lifted Gen's trembling body over the footboard. She crawled forward, kept coming until she was straddling Lyda's hips. She didn't make a move to take that phallus inside her, though. That was her Mistress's call. Again, she earned that look of approval that made everything worth it. Lyda settled her hands on Gen's hips and then, showing her own finesse with a strap-on, she began to lower Gen onto it.

She'd been right. It was thicker than the last one. Lyda worked it into her slow, though, controlling her descent. When Gen was in to the hilt, Lyda laid her head back on the mattress, eyes half-lidded and mouth curved in a sensual way that made Gen want to taste her, touch her. But her Mistress was in the mood to be cruel.

"Lace your hands on the back of your head, Gen. You totally belong to us right now. We're the ones taking."

It made her feel even more vulnerable. Noah put his knee on the bed, shifted behind her. As he fitted the head of his cock to her opening, his thumbs parting her buttocks, she made an uncertain noise.

"Sshh," Lyda said, holding her gaze. "Do you want to please us?"

"Yes. Yes."

"Then trust us. Push against him."

She did, and he started to make headway, no pun intended. Noah wrapped an arm around her waist, his strong biceps contracting against the side of her breast. It burned a little, but she breathed through it.

"Squeeze down on me, Gen."

As she did, Noah groaned, and she realized the same motion squeezed his cock inside her. Lyda's eyes sparked. "You see how much pleasure you give both of us?"

"She's too tight, Mistress."

"Relax," Lyda crooned at her, cupping one of Gen's breasts and stroking the nipple above the lace. "He's not going to push. He'll go as slow as you need him to go. Think about how it feels, all those tiny nerves around your rim and inside, quivering, eager. I know it hurts some. Let's see what we can do about that."

Lyda made an adjustment beneath them, her knuckles brushing Gen's labia, and then the strap-on was vibrating, those tiny beads caressing and massaging Gen's opening, the two-way clitoral stimulator pressed in just the right place.

She held Lyda's eyes, held onto her voice, Noah's hands stroking her sides, his mouth brushing her neck. Gen let out a little whimper as Noah made it all the way in.

Lyda's face was suffused with pleasure, her gaze coursing down over Gen's quivering breasts in the pretty bra. She captured one to play with and Noah caught the other, two different types of touches, tearing her into two equally pleasurable sides, a harlequin of response.

Their hands dropped back down to Gen's hips, Noah's hands overlapping Lyda's. The two of them started so gradually, it was a rhythmic motion like two children daydreaming on a seesaw. The slippery movement of his cock inside Gen did start to feel more pleasurable, less painful, though enough of that burn stayed to make it provocative, to keep Gen cognizant of that arousing sense of serving their needs, no matter her own discomfort. It turned her on so freaking much she couldn't even wrap her mind around it.

Holy God, that stimulator. As Lyda began to be more insistent about pushing up inside her, a climax roared up on Gen so quickly, she didn't expect it. Her fingers knotted against the back of her head. "I can't...Mistress...I'm going to come."

"Yes, you are. And there's not a damn thing you can do to stop it."

Lyda made it sound like the threat it was. Gen had never had a climax while being impaled both vaginally and anally before. Throw the vibration into it, the stimulation to her nipples and breasts, and it was like being shot off into orbit. And the stimulation didn't abate. It got more intense, the two of them ramping up the force of their thrusts, so the speed and force of the rocket just kept increasing.

She screamed, long and loud, no hope that a babbling creek would cloak the sound. She wouldn't have been surprised if her climax echoed through the mountains. She begged, pleaded and screamed some more as she spun out of that orbit, control lost, spiraling toward impact. It was almost too much, a torment, but they refused to heed her pleas for mercy. That impact hit and the feeling just kept going, plowing deep beyond her pussy and ass, into her very soul, shattering it.

She had a shred of cognizance left when the two of them followed her. Lyda's face tightened, her eyes getting that lovely glazed look. Vaguely, Gen heard her order Noah to let go. His arm around her nearly cut off her breath, but it was a blissful asphyxiation as they both hammered into her for the full measure of satisfaction. Their harsh groans, pleasurable cries, gasping breaths, kept her captured in a post-climactic miasma, taking her with them, as far out over the mountains and into the sky as they wanted to go. Soaring, soaring, soaring.

She'd never blacked out during sex. When she became aware again, Noah had pulled free and disposed of his condom. He was laying her down on Lyda, Lyda's arms winding around Gen to hold her secure against her body. The strap-on was still inside Gen, but Noah took care of that as well, unbuckling it and pulling it free of them both, causing them to make twin sounds of pleasure at the friction. Gen pressed herself against Lyda's mound, absorbing a ricochet of aftershock. Lyda responded with a teasing little hip rotation and bump that made Gen moan again.

During their lovemaking, the cavitation of their three bodies had left them in a diagonal stretch across the bed. When she rested her head on Lyda's shoulder, she saw Noah wrap his hand around Gen's foot, pressed against Lyda's shin. He bent, pressed a gentle kiss to Gen's buttock, teasing it with his tongue. Then he nuzzled Lyda's knee, kissed it the same way.

She drifted some more, soothed by his caresses. When she tuned in again, he had a damp cloth between her buttocks, something that soothed. Lyda stroked her head.

"Nicely done, rabbit," she murmured. "You're our sweet little fucktoy. We're never letting you go."

It showed how fried her brain was that she accepted that as the best of compliments, a stirring one at that. She was happy with it. She was happy with any designation from Lyda that started with "our", even if it was just playful aftercare. She closed her eyes, and wanted nothing more than to be theirs.

* * * * *

She wasn't sure how Lyda felt about it, but Gen was nervous about how Noah's grandmother would perceive their relationship. There were older female patrons at Tea Leaves who had the detection powers of CIA operatives. If they chose not to comment about something, it had to do with traditional manners and courtesy, not stupidity. They came from an era when sexual matters were behind closed doors, not aired on Dr. Phil like a laundry list.

People were getting more accustomed to same-sex partners, so the chemistry between her and Lyda might pass without comment, but Gen wasn't sure there was any way to disguise that chemistry was a three-way connection. Noah seemed unconcerned about the matter, but since it was clear Noah could be a few sandwiches shy of a picnic on certain subjects, that wasn't necessarily reassuring.

No more time to worry over it, though, since they were even now walking up the road of the resort where his grandmother was staying. What would happen would happen. Gen just didn't want to do anything that would give Noah problems with the one family member who still accepted him. Glancing over at Lyda, she looked a little too dispassionate, her way of covering tension, but Lyda had made it clear she didn't really do families, that this situation with Noah was an exception.

It made sense. How would you introduce a woman who was your Mistress, with a capital M, to your family? You couldn't, so from the get-go the relationship would be referenced in vague generalities. And "vague generality" didn't apply to Lyda at all.

As they turned up the driveway, Gen saw the subject of her worries was already on the lookout for them. Dorothy "Dot" Wilder was a heavyset woman with bright blue eyes and a dandelion-style puff of white hair around her round face. Her hands were gnarled from bad arthritis, her legs bent with the same, explaining why she used the motorized wheelchair. Noah had said she could walk with the aid of a walker, but her back was badly twisted as well.

Those were momentary impressions, however. When Dot saw them, the expression on her face could only be described as pure joy. All the smiling lines on her face turned her eyes into cheerful crescents. "There's my beautiful grandson. Mona, come out here and see Noah. He's here."

When Gen saw the look on Noah's face, a bright reflection of the love on Dorothy's, her worries evaporated. Especially when Dot's gaze swept over the two women, a quick sizing up. It wouldn't matter what missteps she or Lyda might make. She saw the unbreakable history between these two. More importantly, she saw everything she needed to know in his grandmother's eyes. Love, understanding, sorrow, happiness. Dot was the guardian at the gate, the one family member who stood for the child within Noah, the child that stayed inside every adult, either nurtured by love or handicapped by a lack of love.

It made Gen's heart hurt, seeing the connection between them, so strong as a result of how weak it was with others. *Well, the joke's on you*, she thought. Because any parent with a heart would want their child to look at them the way he was looking at Dot. Actually, anyone at all would want Noah to look at them with such devotion.

Gen stilled inside, realizing she had seen that look on Noah's face before. It didn't have the same sensual overtones, of course, but in some of his intense moments with her or Lyda, his heart had been right there for them to see. To take.

When Noah glanced at Lyda, she gave him a light shove. "Your grandmother is top dog here," she said, with a strained smile that suggested his expression had broken Lyda's heart a little as well. "When she says jump, you leap."

Noah kissed her hand, and then he was striding across the wooden bridge and up the steps to hop on the porch and kneel by his grandmother, whom he enveloped in a huge hug.

Lyda linked arms with Gen, both of them studying the two, giving them a minute. "So she lives in Tampa the rest of the year?" Gen asked.

"Yeah. Even when he moved in with me, he went to see her a couple days a week. It does him a lot of good. I hadn't met her before now, though." At Gen's glance, Lyda grimaced. "Yeah, I'm a hardass, I know it. But you two forced me into a weak moment, so here I am."

Lyda tempered it with a wry look, but when she put pressure on Gen's arm, it was clear she wanted Gen right with her when they stepped onto the porch. She *was* nervous. Yeah, in a Lyda kind of way, which was more like aggressive tension, ready for a fight, and there was no fight to be had here. Despite her initial worry over how displays of affection would be interpreted, Gen put her hand over Lyda's. Her Mistress's fingers were cold.

"It's okay," she said. "She's going to think you're amazing, the way we all do."

"I suck at families," Lyda said, keeping a smile on her face, barely moving her lips.

"Not from where I'm standing. Seems like you're working toward creating one out of the three of us. And doing a pretty good job of it."

That won a startled look. "Don't freak me out, rabbit."

"Nice to know you have a freak-out button."

"Remember I also have a whip."

In truth, Gen hadn't realized anything had the capacity to spook their Mistress, but that idea—her, Noah and Lyda forming a family—apparently did. Lyda never lacked for courage, though. She took a breath and they'd crossed the bridge, though Gen squeezed her hand once more before Lyda gently pushed her forward, so she preceded her. As Gen went up the narrow set of steps that led up to the back porch of the bungalow, Lyda following, Noah rose, his hand still in his grandmother's grasp.

"I told her I just saw her three weeks ago," he said. "I'm not back from Afghanistan or anything."

"Don't sass your grandmother," Dorothy scolded. "Every morning I wake up is one more morning I'm surprised I'm not dead. So when I see you, it's like *I'm* coming from Afghanistan."

Yep, just as blunt as the women at the tea room. Gen liked her already, even as the shrewd blue eyes pinned her like a hawk. "Introduce me to your friends, Noah."

"This is Lyda Coltrane, my boss at the nursery, and Genevieve Wisner, a good friend. She goes by Gen."

It surprised Gen that Noah knew her full name, let alone introduced her by it. He must have gotten it from Chloe, which made her wonder what else her coworker had told him about her. Probably best that she didn't ask.

Dorothy extended a gnarled hand to Lyda. "Gently, girl. Fingers are a mess."

Lyda gave her the lightest of squeezes. "All the work I do at the nursery, my hands often ache at night. What do you use for yours?"

"Oh, I've tried all sorts of remedies. I'll give you a few ideas while you're here. If I'd done some of them earlier, I would have been better off. But I hope you won't face that. Look at how tall and lovely you are." She turned to Gen. "And where do you work?"

"Tea Leaves, ma'am."

"Of course. Laura Smith's niece had her bridal shower there. Laura told me it was a delightful place. I'll have to go. Maybe Noah will bring me one day."

"We'd be delighted to have you."

"Good. I'll be coming. And I'm Dot, not ma'am. There's wine, bourbon and some fruity cocktail makings inside. Noah, make us ladies a drink. Mona's lying down watching the news right now. I have no idea why, because she and I are going to be long dead before anything happening in the world affects us, but she thinks by watching it she can control things. Ask her what she wants, and then bring us ours."

"You're not supposed to have alcohol with your prescriptions."

She bumped his leg with her closed fist. "I'm eighty-four years old. If I want to have a pretty strawberry daiquiri with a scoop of ice cream, then that's what I'll be having. I don't think St. Peter's told a single person they can't get into heaven because they didn't follow their doctor's advice. Else it'd be as empty up there as a church on discount day at the casino."

Gen choked on a laugh. Noah rolled his eyes, but he bent, pressed his cheek to hers, winning a *tsk* and a light swat. "Don't mess up my hair. I just had it done this morning."

Noah straightened, keeping a hand on her shoulder. "What can I get you?" he asked Gen and Lyda.

"One of those fruity drinks sounds good," Gen said.

"A dry white," Lyda said. "Toss a cherry into it if you have one."

"We don't go anywhere without maraschinos," Dorothy assured her. As Noah disappeared into the house she looked over her shoulder at him, then glanced back at the two women. Gen had watched him leave as well, though for different reasons. Too late, she realized she shouldn't be ogling Dorothy's grandson, but the woman gave her an amused look. "He's always been a looker, coming and going. When he takes me to see my friends at the senior center, I have to beat those horny old women off him with a cane. Some of them read those cougar romances and get ideas. And I know my grandson. He'd worry about hurting the feelings of Imelda Marcos." She squinted. "I bet neither of you have any idea who that is."

Gen didn't but Lyda did, obviously better-educated on political history. Gen shifted uncomfortably, winning a curious look from her Mistress, but Dorothy fortunately distracted them with two questions. "So which of you is with him? Or hoping to be?"

Given Lyda's moment of trepidation at the bridge, Gen was ready to jump in with a vague but diplomatic answer. She should have known their Mistress was at her best in the face of a challenge. Lyda met Dot's gaze. "The way I answer that depends on how much you know about your grandson, regardless of what he thinks you know."

Gen managed not to let her jaw drop. Dorothy gave Lyda an assessing look. "I know enough to know you're in charge." Her gaze went to Gen. "Of both of them, her and my grandson?"

"As long as they're willing to let me be in charge. That's the way it works. At least, that's what I'm trying to teach him. That it's all his choice."

Dorothy was silent for a moment. "How's that going?"

"Better some days. Worse on others. I'm figuring him out, enough to know some things might not get figured out."

"Yes." Dot gave a brittle smile. "I don't know how much of that came from nature versus nurture. I do know there was a time I wanted to kill his father, and my stupid daughter with him. Anyone who spends any time with that boy can feel how special he is, how generous his heart."

Gen nodded without even having to think about it. Dot's gaze slid to her, the smile getting a little easier, though it was tinged with the past. "His father crushed him, you know. He could have just left it at 'I can't accept your lifestyle and get out', but oh no, that wasn't enough. Art went after him with everything. Told a seventeen-year-old boy someone should cut off his privates because Noah was obviously more of a sniveling woman than a real man. I expect he was trying to shame Noah into being what he wanted him to be."

The hardening of Lyda's expression told Gen she hadn't heard those specifics. Anger flooded her as well. Seeing it in their faces, Dot nodded, her jaw firming.

"Any other man would have simply walked out, not let his father keep hammering at him like that, but Noah doesn't leave a conversation until he's excused. Especially from someone he deems as being in authority, no matter how that person is treating him. So he just sat there, my daughter on the sidelines, while Art raged at him. And when Noah didn't respond, he started hitting him, trying to get him to act like a man. Noah never raised a hand in his own defense, not even to ward him off." She met Lyda's gaze. "You know some of that."

Lyda shook her head. "Not those details. I knew his father rejected him."

"That bastard." Dorothy's eyes went cold as ice. "Noah took care of me when I broke my hip. Lifted this fat body of mine more times than I could count, handled everything around the house. Boy's lean, but strong as an ox. And most don't know this, but he can fight. He has a rage button when you hit it, and while he'll never turn his fists on a living thing, I've seen him take it out with an axe and firewood, or punch a bag I put in the backyard for him for just that purpose. From the way he hit it, I knew somewhere along the way, someone taught him how to fight. He could have put Art on his ass at any time, but in Noah's mind, that's not what being a man's about."

"It's about taking care of the one who loves you," Lyda said quietly.

"Exactly." Dorothy inclined her head. "So however long you decide to be with him, I hope you'll remember what a treasure he is."

She didn't assume forever. Apparently his grandmother was a realist about her grandson and knew his relationships didn't last. When footsteps heralded Noah's return, Dorothy's face smoothed out. She gave Gen a wink, Lyda another direct look. "I'm blunt and up front, because I could die in my sleep. I don't believe in putting off what needs to be said. I also don't need a lot of time to see the forest for the trees. You two are the first he's ever brought to meet me, so I know you're important. Pivotal."

After that astounding statement, which had Gen and Lyda exchanging a look, Dot tilted her head, raised her voice. "Did you put one of those little umbrellas in it?"

"Of course I did. It's like a fully stocked tiki bar in there." Noah emerged from the house. Flipping a tray from beneath the arm of her wheelchair, he tightened it into position, putting the drink where she could lean forward and sip through the straw. "I gave Mona her mojito. And a cup of Cheese Nips." When he grimaced, Dorothy bumped his hip with her gnarled fist.

"It's no different at the end than it is at the beginning. You're back to diapers, and your taste buds want what's good, not the damn food pyramid. Why don't I have any Cheese Nips? And a Twinkie. The yellow kind, not the chocolate."

"Good God," he said. Noah handed Lyda's wine to her, the red cherry a cheerful accent to the white-gold color. He looked at Gen. "I'm bringing yours next."

"I wouldn't mind a handful of Cheese Nips if there's enough to go around. Have to keep myself soft, you know."

His eyes sparked humor at her, and Lyda tugged her hair. "Ow," Gen admonished. Dorothy gazed at them as Noah went back inside.

"I want to like you two," she decided. "I hope you won't give me reasons not to."

"I wouldn't hurt Noah for the world," Gen said. If Dot and Lyda were going to be blunt, she was going to join the party. Marguerite wasn't one to beat around the bush, after all, and— Lord in heaven—Chloe mowed right through. When Dot did come to Tea Leaves, she and the irrepressible girl would be fast friends in a heartbeat.

"You haven't been together long enough to know for certain, no matter what you tell me, but do you think you're in love with him?"

Those Cheese Nips hadn't taken very long. About the time Dot asked the question, Noah returned with two snack cups of the bright orange crackers and a Twinkie in hand, as well as Gen's drink. He'd given her a paper umbrella too. As he put Dot's snacks on her tray, he shot Gen a look that told her he was accustomed to his grandmother's lack of social restraint and he'd rescue her with a tactful comment if necessary. His mouth was opening, probably to do just that.

"Yes," she said. "I am."

Those expressive eyes locked onto her face. She hadn't planned on saying it here, like this, but it had come out, just like that. What concerned her wasn't the environment, however, but his transfixed reaction. Had no one ever told him...

Oh God. No one ever had.

Lyda had said no one had ever fallen in love with Noah. Gen had assumed that meant there'd been those who'd said it to him but, like her first two husbands, they hadn't really known what that meant. Or lived up to what it was supposed to mean. Apparently she was the first person who'd ever said it, outside of family.

Dorothy touched him gently. "She's waiting for her drink, boy."

He started as if out of a sleep. Gen took the glass from him, along with the Cheese Nips. Regardless of their audience, she touched his face. She gave him a searching look. "It's okay," she mouthed, because his body blocked her from Dot. Lyda touched his other arm. He looked between them.

"Sit down next to your grandmother," Lyda said in a quiet, firm tone.

The command seemed to knock him back on his axis, but as he sank down on the ramp next to Dot, his gaze remained on Gen, his thoughts obviously a confused snarl. Dot laid a deformed hand on his shoulder, stroked the hair at his temple.

"You keep hanging out with them," she said. "I think they're pretty good for you."

* * * * *

They left Dorothy with plans to meet the following night for the walk Noah had warned them about. As they walked down the hill, Noah was quiet. So was Gen.

His reaction to her declaration had shifted things off the third member of their relationship, such that Lyda had never been required to answer the same question. But Lyda kept her own counsel on emotions that strong, and wasn't likely to be called out on them until she was good and ready. Gen wasn't sure if Lyda was the type of person who would say it at all. If she felt it, she'd probably express it a different way.

Would she be the type to show a permanent commitment with a collar? The way he'd reacted to Gen saying she was in love with him made her wonder if a gesture like that from Lyda might help resolve some of Noah's "choice" issues. Lyda had made it clear she preferred action to words, and that probably applied to symbols as well. But Noah might be worth a different strategy, right? Or Gen could be using pop psychology on a deeply rooted psychosis, a recipe for disaster.

"Chairlift," Lyda said, pointing at it. "We'll have dinner afterward."

Gen tuned in to the distant contraption. Wires strung between towering poles funneled the colorful chairs up and down the mountain backdrop for the town. When they'd been sitting with Dorothy, they'd watched the continuous loop, people carried up to the overlook and down again.

"Um...I'm not great with heights."

"You'll be with us, rabbit," Lyda said, unconcerned. "You'll be fine."

"So when the cable snaps, you'll use your super-Domme powers to fly us out of harm's way. Or Noah will parasail us safely to the ground with his shirt."

"Absolutely," Lyda responded. "Don't be such a girl."

"I am a girl. So are you."

"Thank God," Noah said. Gen glanced his way. It was his first attempt at levity since they'd left Dot's. Meeting Lyda's gaze, Gen saw the veiled message there. *We need to loosen him up a little.*

Fine. But a chairlift? She'd said she was in love with him. She wasn't sure if she was *that* in love with him.

"I'll do it if you both hold my hand the whole way. That includes you," she said to Lyda. "No playing the Domme card."

"Pussy."

"Yeah, I have one. You seem to like it."

Noah snorted. Lyda narrowed her eyes, though Gen saw her lips quiver. "Watch yourself. That cable isn't the only thing that can snap on your ass."

They returned to their cottage, retrieved the car and drove down the hill, working through the main strip traffic to get to a parking area for the ride, which Noah pointed out was called Sky Lift. Gen found she preferred the generic term of chairlift, since "Sky Lift" only emphasized she was leaving solid earth to ride it.

After they paid for their ride, they hit another snag. "Only two adults per chair," the operator said, with apologetic courtesy.

Standing at the base, staring up the side of the mountain, Gen was all for using that as her escape card, letting Lyda and Noah go without her. She'd provide moral support with her feet on the ground. Lyda slid her arm through Noah's. "Can't you tell he's our child? His ass, superior though it is, probably isn't wider than a twelve-year-old's."

The operator gave a nervous chuckle, as flustered by Lyda's beauty as anything else with testosterone, but shook his head. "As much as I'd like to let you all go up all together, logistically it doesn't work. I can put one of you in the chair right ahead or behind, though. Whichever you prefer."

"All right," Lyda said. "The two of them will go up in one."

"You promised," Gen said. It was irrational, since she understood what the operator was saying, but she truly was afraid of heights. What she'd been able to joke about on the walk to the cottage was no longer amusing as she looked up the steep reality of the mountain, the tiny size of the chairlift all the way at the top. The idea of getting in one of the chairs without Lyda's commanding presence was a deal-breaker.

She winced, braced for Lyda to give her that "suck it up and don't be a pussy" look. The woman had no phobias at all, though family meets were clearly a weak point.

Lyda didn't react as she feared. Which was a shame, because if her Mistress had been catty or cruel, Gen could have said *piss off* and escaped death-by-plummet.

"Yes, I did." Lyda took her hand. "I'm going to hold it until I put you on the lift, and then Noah's going to take over. I'll be right behind you. On the way back down, I'll switch and ride with you. Noah wants to ride with you first."

Noah would never assert his will over Lyda's, but apparently they'd worked it out while Gen had been pondering whether whining like a four-year-old would help. Stepping closer, he slid an arm around Gen's waist, giving her the look that made her happy butterflies start competing with the other more fearful kind.

"And when you ride with me, you'll hold my hand." She wasn't letting Lyda out of that. She didn't care how petulant she sounded.

"I said I would."

Gen's further protests were overridden as her two companions nudged her in line to catch the next seat of the continuously in motion ride. When the operator warned them it was time for Noah and Gen to step onto the platform, Lyda kissed Gen warmly, right there in front of an astounded operator and watching families. She ignored the fact that one set of parents turned their children away as if they'd done something obscene, her gaze staying on Gen's face. "Right behind you. The three of us together, we can handle anything. Right?"

When Gen nodded, Lyda turned her attention to Noah. "You take care of her."

"Always, Mistress. I'll always take care of both of you."

"I'm going to hold you to that." Lyda brushed his jaw with intimate fingers, increasing the vertical lift of the operator's brows.

"They're going to flip right over his head and get lost down the back collar of his shirt," Lyda whispered in Gen's ear. She let out a startled giggle as Lyda released her hand, pushing her forward. Noah tugged Gen onto the platform. She had the *oh shit, I'm not doing this* moment, then they were sitting down, the chair rocking as they started upward. Gen's head was on a swivel, pressing her chin into Noah's shoulder to see Lyda take the chair a few feet behind them.

She closed her eyes, trying to enjoy the sensation of Noah's throat against her cheek and temple, trying to pretend she wasn't getting further from the ground. Trying to ignore all the vibrations and jerks of the creaky chair. He tapped her cheek. "Hey. Look at me."

She cracked an eye. His hand was tangled with hers on her thigh. "Okay?" he said.

"Okay." Good God, her voice quavered. "She's right. I'm such a wimp."

"You work for Marguerite. Plus I've seen you stand up to Lyda. You're no such thing. Jesus, your fingers are like ice." He rubbed them. "You really don't get too high above the ground. You're going up the side of a mountain, you know. And there's a great view at the top. Will you say it again?"

She gasped, clamping his arm in a death grip as the chair jolted, passing beneath a pole. "Really normal," he promised her.

"See up there? There's a piece of metal that holds the lines taut, so when the chair rolls over that metal, it makes things get a little more bumpy. That's all."

She forced herself to look at it, then rolled her eyes downward to focus on the view. It was pretty, Gatlinburg at twilight, the sunlight soft on the trees. "On the way down, if it's dark, all the lights are really gorgeous," he added.

"What did you ask me?"

He looked straight ahead. "Nothing."

"Noah." She summoned enough bravery to detach her fingers and touch the firm line of his mouth. "I'm in love with you. With each of you and both of you. And I'm so glad you wanted me to say it again." She paused when he said nothing, just kept looking straight ahead. "Is it okay that I'm in love with you?"

He gave a precise nod, a movement as careful as she'd be if she thought a single twitch would drop the bottom out of the chairlift. She jerked as they passed under another pole, the ride rocking. His gaze returned to her, both hands covering hers on his knee. "It's all right," he said. "Have you told Lyda? That you're in love with her too?"

"You're great at distracting conversation topics," she said, and earned a smile. "I'm too chicken," she admitted. "I'm not sure if it's something she wants or needs to hear."

"But you thought it was something I might want or need to hear?"

The neutral note made her draw back. "If you don't want me to say something like that..."

"Do you really feel that way?" His eyes were everywhere but on her face.

"Noah, I need you to look at me. Don't leave me alone up here."

His gaze snapped back to her in an instant. "You're not. I'm right here. It's okay."

It was amazing, how he could be so uncertain of one part of his head, and yet one hundred percent in tune with it when it came to caring for her. As Lyda had said, it was a heartrending dilemma for someone who loved him. Yet it made her answer to his question easy.

"I wouldn't have said it if I didn't. It's been a long time since I've said it to anyone."

He considered that, his visage troubled. "Yet you said it to me, even knowing I can't...that I'm not...that it doesn't work for me that way."

"Doesn't it?" For a brief moment, her conviction on that was important enough to forget her fear of heights, to make her touch his face again. "I don't believe that, Noah. I don't care what anyone has said to me about it, even you. Just because it might feel or look a different way, doesn't mean it isn't the same thing."

Noah didn't say anything to that, but he did stretch his arm across the back of her chair and take a firmer grip on her hand. Completely in the now and wholly protective, the Noah she knew...and loved.

"Okay," he said at last, so quiet she almost missed the word. "I don't know about that, but I do know you should tell her, Gen. You're the bravest of the three of us."

If he'd told her she had horns sprouting out of her head, she couldn't have been more stunned. Then they went under another of those damn poles. She could swear the chair shuddered more ominously.

"Do you know they have synchronous lightning bug displays around here?"

She choked on a laugh, both sets of fingers clamped around his while he slid his arm off the back of the seat onto her shoulders. "You made that up."

"I did not. The Tennessee synchronous lightning bugs are world famous. This is only one of two places in the whole world you can see it happen."

"So what do they do? Flash 'buzz off, tourists' in Morse code?"

"No." He grinned, appreciating her. "During their mating season, bunches of them congregate nearby, in Elkmont. The males fly around and flash, and the females watch and respond by blinking back. Sometimes the males all flash at once, sometimes it's in wave patterns, sometimes they don't synchronize at all. It's like watching those programmable Christmas lights, in a way. RVs have to reserve camping passes during that time of year, it's so popular.

"Why do they do it? The bugs."

"Competition between the males is the theory. They figure if they all flash together, a girl bug can compare flashes and decide who she likes."

"So for lightning bug males, it's the size of the flash, for human males..."

"Kind of cuts down on the whole human superiority thing when you figure out most species are the same about things," he said, eyes twinkling. "And the bugs have never divulged whether it's the size of the flash. It could be how many times they can flash, stamina, rhythmic ability, that kind of thing."

She chuckled and managed to bite back the whimper, mostly, when the wire vibrated because the two teenage idiots in the lift ahead rocked their car. On purpose.

She looked back to verify Lyda's presence. While Lyda was taking time to enjoy the view, their Mistress met Gen's gaze, showing she was keeping an eye on her. Had Lyda put Noah and Gen together first to clear the air? Like most things Lyda proposed, it had worked. Noah's acceptance of the truth Gen had spoken in front of his grandmother was settling into a quiet, powerful thing between them, something that altered how he acted toward her. Since it was new for him, that difference was tentative, exploratory. But it was a good thing. She felt it in the clasp of his hand, his bemused looks at her.

Gen now knew the unsettling truth that Lyda could put her into an eager submissive role with a look or a word, yet it was a state that made Gen want to call Lyda hers right back, a two-way street. Surely Noah had that desire somewhere deep down inside, buried by the horrible behavior of his family. Everyone wanted someone who belonged to them, in all the ways that comforted in the middle of the night, that made the yawn of the future not so lonely or frightening. Someone with whom to share experiences, successes and failures, tears and laughter.

Once on the overlook, the three of them pressed hip to hip, Lyda on one side of Gen, Noah on the other, as they took turns peering through the viewfinders. Her fear of heights had to do with dangling at a high elevation, not standing on terra firma looking down the mountain, so as they walked along the deck, Gen enjoyed seeing Gatlinburg transform from garish saloon girl into a mysterious beauty. The buildings softened into silhouettes, lights twinkling across them like a carpet of stars.

When Gen's stomach growled, Noah rubbed his as if it had made the offending noise. Lyda chuckled but admitted she was hungry too, so it was time to seek out dinner. However, when they returned to the lift and it appeared as if Lyda was going to follow the same seating arrangement, Gen gave her a reproachful look.

"You said you'd hold my hand on the way back."

Noah grinned at Lyda. "You did, Mistress."

"Big babies, the both of you."

Despite the fond deprecation, Gen thought Lyda was pleased Gen hadn't accepted the idea of returning with Noah. Unfortunately, the good feeling about that wasn't enough to keep her mind away from a sudden, serious problem. As they positioned themselves on the platform, Gen looked out in front of them.

She'd expected things might go better, with it getting dark and her heading down. Unfortunately, it wasn't dark enough. Instead of staring at a mountainside as she had going up, she was looking out over a lot of open space. Like a million stories of open space.

"Lyda..." The panic in her voice caused an undignified squeak.

"Sit." Lyda had her arm, had her pushed into the seat, and then they were airborne. Gen's heart rabbited, her lungs squeezing down to the size of the furry mammal's.

"Gen. Breathe. One breath, two breaths..."

Maybe Noah would have been the better choice on the downward run, his fingers more resilient against Gen's bone-breaking grip. Lyda transferred Gen's grip to her thigh, covering her hand with her own, but she put an arm around Gen as bolstering as Noah's. "Put your face into my neck and close your eyes."

Gen pressed against her side, obeyed. "There," Lyda murmured. "Keep breathing. In. Out. It's all right. My little control freak."

"Pot. Kettle."

"You can't be too afraid if you're being feisty."

"I react to terror with aggression."

Lyda brushed a kiss over her temple. "We're all afraid of something. Being able to get past it shows courage. It's beautiful.

Open just one eye, and look at the city lights. Keep your head where it is. I'm right here." She rubbed Gen's upper arm briskly, squeezed it. "You're all right. I'm not going to let anything happen to you, am I?"

Gen opened the one eye, saw the pretty lights spread out before them. Now that the sun had set, it was getting darker fast, which helped. She didn't want to move, but she wanted to show Lyda she could be brave. "I...I think I can lift my head. Is that okay?"

"Yes. Go ahead. Good girl." Lyda stroked Gen's fingers. "If you can manage it, look back at Noah and assure him he shouldn't scale the cable like a monkey to come help. God save us, he'd do it."

Startled, Gen looked back. Even in semidarkness, she read the deep concern in Noah's expression. The need to reassure someone else helped. She gave him a nod, a wave of her hand. He smiled in return, settled back. He made a nice distraction, long legs relaxed in a splayed knee posture, his arm along the back of the other empty seat, his hand holding onto the chain above the outside frame. His hair fluttered across his brow.

Gen drew a breath, faced front again, looked at Gatlinburg. "I'm in love with you too, you know. I don't know if that's okay with you or not, but I want to say it, in case it changes anything...for all of us."

Lyda kept stroking her upper arm. A little slower, more methodical. Gen didn't look toward her, but she was already petrified, so she might as well go for all of it.

Gen cleared her throat. "Chloe told me there are subs at The Zone who would follow Marguerite into hellfire. They think that Domme-groupie thing is the same thing as love, the same as what Tyler feels for her. But it's not. I don't think this is that. Maybe it could be, but..."

"You're not the groupie kind. Just leave it there, rabbit."

"Okay." All things in their own time. For now, it was enough. Gen was a grown woman. Whatever Lyda was thinking, Gen was responsible for handling her own feelings. Unlike the heights thing, she wouldn't ask anyone to pick up the slack on that if Lyda didn't ever feel the same way. It was going to be okay.

Really.

Chapter Fourteen

ଔ

They walked around Gatlinburg after dinner. Gen picked up souvenirs for Marguerite and Chloe, and some caramel popcorn for her and Noah to enjoy at the cottage later, despite Lyda's unnatural aversion to junk food. Gen observed she would probably melt like the Wicked Witch of the West if she indulged in a bite. The observation earned her an evil eye and Lyda nabbing some popcorn to prove her wrong.

When they prepared for bed that night, Lyda ordered them both into it naked, though she wore a T-shirt and panties. Putting Noah in the middle, she laid her head on his left shoulder as Gen put hers on his right. He had his arms around them, an indirect restraint that kept his hands out of the way while Lyda played with him. Gen propped on an elbow, stroking his chest, his throat, her own getting tight at how he lifted his chin to let her put her fingers around it, a light collaring as Lyda gripped the base of his cock. He had his hand curved around Gen's hip, forbidden by Lyda from fondling either woman's ass. Yet through the pressure of his palm, Gen felt his desire as vividly as she saw the hardening of his cock under Lyda's skillful touch.

Lyda had made them leave it at that, though. In time, she'd taken her hand from him, linked it with Gen's fingers on his chest, and they'd all fallen asleep that way, Noah stroking a line down Gen's back, her upper arm.

At some point, she must have turned on her side, since she tended to sleep facing outward. When she opened her eyes, she saw it was just past two in the morning, and the bed was moving in a rhythmic sway, like a boat on lazy waters.

Already anticipating what she would see, Gen slowly shifted to her back and to the other side. It put her only a handspan from her other bed partners. Gen folded her hands under her cheek, drinking in the sight of Noah, his gaze trained on Lyda's face, his body stretched out beneath her as he gripped the headboard. Their Mistress was riding him deep and slow.

Their tiredness and Lyda allowing only a little bit of play before settling them to sleep had kept simmering libidos manageable. With sex saturating the air and seeing what she was seeing, Gen was aware of every place the sheets touched her bare skin.

Lyda hadn't removed any clothes. She'd pulled the crotch of the panties aside to sink down on him. Under the T-shirt, her nipples and sway of her unbound breasts were on delectable display. She'd dropped her head back on her shoulders and her hair was loose, caressing her shoulders. When her chin lowered, the glaze of her eyes said she was lost in pleasure, but not so much she couldn't issue another command.

"Push the blanket down and play with yourself, Gen," she whispered. "Cup those pretty tits, put your fingers inside your cunt."

As Gen complied and shifted to her back, Lyda spoke again. "You're not allowed to look at her," she told Noah. "But you feel what she's doing, the movement of her body... He's getting harder inside of me, Gen. Harder than when I told him you'd wake up wet. Even asleep, you knew what we were doing. Show him, Gen. Prove to him I was right."

Gen found his long-fingered hand, already releasing the headboard. Rubbing his calloused palm over her wet pussy, she pushed two of his fingers into a curved dip inside of her. Noah's breath left him in a gratifying near-growl.

"Good. Put his hand back now. My pets don't get to play with one another unless I say so. After you make me come, I'll blindfold you, Noah. Let you eat both of our pussies, see if you can tell them apart. You don't come until I'm satisfied."

She lived up to that threat, riding Noah until she came. By the time she was there, Noah's body had that delicious, all-over straining, hard-muscled look to it, his face taut. As she climaxed, Lyda hoarsely commanded Gen to do the same. She was more than ready, her fingers furiously tugging at her clit, stroking her labia. She was distantly aware of Noah's frustrated groan, then his whisper, goading her on. "Love...hearing you both...come. Fuck..."

By the time she came down, gasping, Lyda was shifting off Noah. Despite the fact she'd just climaxed, Gen gave his cock a covetous look, swollen up hard and thick, the head glistening with Lyda's juices. Once again, he wasn't wearing a condom. She wanted the pleasure of riding him bareback, using the slickness left by Lyda's body.

But they were at Lyda's mercy, their desires secondary. Lyda pulled off her T-shirt, giving them both a view of pale breasts as she draped it over Noah's face, teasing his lips through the fabric before folding it back and tying it around his head.

Their desires might be secondary to hers, but sometimes they aligned. Pleasure surged through Gen when Lyda shifted her attention back to her. "Can you ride him without a condom, Gen? He's safe."

Gen nodded, moved by the trust they were both showing in her. But when Gen took Lyda's place and Lyda straddled his face, planting her knees above his shoulders, lust took the upper hand.

Gen groaned at the excruciating sensation, pushing Noah's engorged shaft into her post-climactic tissues. She worked her way down, her arousal refueled by the idea she and Lyda were marking him together. He was totally theirs, every gorgeous inch.

Lyda gripped the headboard, fingers overlapping his. She brought her pussy down on his mouth, the curves of her ass pressing high against his chest. She glanced over her shoulder at Gen, her eyes gleaming.

"Put your hands on my waist, Gen, and don't take them away. We ride this horse together."

Gen obeyed, thumbs sliding over the rise of Lyda's buttocks, just inside the elastic waistband of her panties. As Lyda began to rotate her pussy against Noah's mouth, her body shuddering at whatever incredible thing he was doing with his lips and tongue, Gen began to rise and fall, taking full pleasure from every inch of his steel cock. Because she'd recently climaxed, she took it nice and slow, building her arousal again. It was clear Noah was in an agonized state of near orgasm. He groaned against Lyda's pussy, his hips bucking against Gen. Gen drank in the sight of stomach muscles rippling, biceps quivering, the beauty of Lyda's body doing its sinuous dance over his mouth.

"Such a good boy," Lyda rasped. "Holding out until you've pleasured us."

Despite his faithful intentions, some things were beyond even a trained submissive's control. Gen expected Lyda knew exactly how much strain that rope could take. Because their Mistress enjoyed punishment too, she delighted in forcing it to snap. Gen felt it all the way to her womb when Noah lost the battle, coming with a hoarse, muffled shout, his hips plunging and pulling back, making Gen spasm right into a spinning climax. Lyda tightened down on him, coming again, either because she'd been that close or the situation was just too much for anyone to resist.

When they slowed down at last, and Lyda ordered her to slide off their "mount", Gen saw she'd left fingerprints in Lyda's sides. As they nestled back into the sheets, this time Lyda was between them. Noah kissed one side of those fingermarks, Gen the other, and they each took a turn at cleaning their Mistress's pussy with their mouths. They worked around one another, Gen laying kisses on her thighs while Noah tongued her labia. They fell asleep with Gen's head on her breast, and Noah's on her stomach, his arm slung across Lyda's thighs, hand curled on Gen's hip. Lyda murmured to them both, an incoherent lullaby of words that told them they'd pleased her well.

* * * * *

Gen woke to sunlight streaming through the window. It was nearly eight o'clock, and she was alone. Despite the warmth of the bed, she decided she'd rather risk the cool early air of a morning in the mountains than be without Noah and Lyda. Donning robe and slippers, she made a quick trip to the bathroom and then headed for the smell of coffee. Thinking of last night, she wondered if it would ever get old, the endless sensual pleasure the two of them wove around her.

The erotic sight awaiting her in the kitchen suggested a giant *no*.

Lyda sat at the kitchen table. She wore nothing but one of her enticing robes and a wicked pair of four-inch stilettos. She'd dropped one to the floor and had her supple leg stretched out, her bare foot braced on the opposite chair. The other foot, still in the shoe, was pressed against Noah's genitals. He was beneath the table, arms cuffed to the base, knees bent outward to touch the floor, an incredibly vulnerable pose, especially with the toe of the shoe pinning his cock down against his pelvis, the spike heel stabbing into his nest of testicles.

He was blindfolded, and there was dried semen on his belly, his chest. She'd obviously made him come at least once this morning. Gen wished she wasn't such a deep sleeper, but a ball gag, buckled so the ball depressed his tongue and the straps cut into the corners of his mouth, suggested it wouldn't have made a difference. He wore a real blindfold this morning, the black eye patches pressed tight against his eyes so not even light would get through.

"There's a fresh pot of coffee." Lyda set aside the local paper and gave her an all-about-morning-sex appraisal. "Freshen my cup, and then get on your hands and knees, straddling him."

Gen moved to do as ordered. When she brought Lyda the cup, Lyda caught her robe tie. "Lose the robe. I want to see gooseflesh before I warm you up."

Gen removed it. "Your knees outside his rib cage," Lyda continued. "Elbows pressed into the floor above his head, so your breasts are in his face. Forehead down."

As Gen moved to take the prescribed position, Lyda caught the side of her neck, holding her still for a mind-numbing kiss. Gen kept her fingers closed at her sides. She was starting to learn too, wasn't she? To be trained, like Noah. She could tell what mood held their Mistress right now. A desire to be totally in control.

"Nice." Lyda hummed against her lips. "You brushed before you came to the kitchen. Girls are nice like that."

Lyda gave her cheek a quick pinch, then put pressure on her shoulder, sending her in the direction of her will. When the position put Noah's mouth in her cleavage, Gen quivered. Even more when their Mistress slipped her foot back in the other shoe and braced that heel on the round part of Gen's ass, applying biting pressure. If his grunt and indrawn breath were any indication, she'd put the other one back in its harrowing position on Noah's testicles.

She'd never stayed in such a state of constant arousal as she did with these two. It was like their Mistress kept her simmering in her dreams, and waking opened the furnace doors. Noah's cock twitched, increasing the heat.

For the next eternity of minutes, Lyda enjoyed her coffee and the paper. Gen listened to her turn the pages, make comments about local happenings that required no answers from her or Noah. Their focus was on how crazy she was making them. Noah's breath rasped against Gen's breasts, and Gen's pussy dripped on Noah's abdomen. She knew because Lyda told her so and tsked. Gen bit back a cry as Lyda shifted the pointed heel in between her buttocks to tease her rim, threatening to shove it in there if Gen was going to make such a mess.

Gen could smell the musk of Noah's earlier climax, knew her pussy had marked that area. She wanted to rub herself against it. But they stayed motionless as possible while hungering for their Mistress and each other. In her position, Gen knew her breath must be teasing his closed lids through the fabric of the blindfold.

At length, Lyda set the paper aside again, and scraped back the chair. "Wash out my cup and start a fresh pot of coffee, Gen. Then release Noah and both of you join me in the shower. Time to scrub one another clean."

Gen didn't think she'd ever handled two tasks so quickly. It was a miracle she did it without breaking any glassware. Then she knelt by Noah. She removed the blindfold first. She wanted to see him stare up at her with his mouth stretched by the gag, hands tied. Helpless to her, in a sense. The look in his eyes made her nipples get even tighter, and when his gaze flicked to them, her breath caught. She unbuckled the gag next, guiding it out of his mouth. Saliva came with it of course, but she didn't care, pulling a napkin from the holder on the table to pat his lips, stroke the impressions the straps had left there. More arousal trickled down her thighs.

"Untie me," he said, staring up at her with fevered eyes.

"Say please," she whispered. He bit her finger and made her smile, even as her chest felt tight.

"Please."

Releasing the cuffs from the base, she backed out from under the table. As he emerged, he reached to unwrap the cuffs from his wrists, but she stopped him. Aware of the weight of his gaze on her bowed head, she did it, putting the cuffs on the table before she wrapped her hands around his wrists, rubbing them.

"Gen," he said. Nothing else, just so much feeling in that word. In love. She was in love with him. So in love. And not just him.

As if summoned by the thought, the imperious voice echoed down the hall. "I know my pets are *not* dragging their asses. There's probably only twenty freaking minutes of hot water in this hillbilly backwoods."

Noah's eyes sparkled at her. Joining hands, they hurried for the bathroom.

Lyda was putting shower products in the stall. Noah glanced at Gen. In the grip of a shared arousal, it was as if they were of one mind. He sank to his knees at Lyda's right knee, Gen at her left. Noah put his mouth on her thigh, one hand clasping the back of Lyda's knee. Gen rubbed her cheek against her other thigh, wanting to go higher, so Noah took the lead, guiding her. He nibbled Lyda's right buttock, ran his tongue along the crease between it and her thigh. Lyda leaned over to test the water, adjusting her stance so Noah could place his mouth between her thighs. Encouraged by Lyda's hand on her head, the shift of her body sideways, Gen slid forward to close her mouth over Lyda's clit in front while Noah's mouth teased her labia and perineum, her rim, from behind.

Lyda made a noise of approval and swayed. Noah's hands went to her hips, steadying her, and Gen placed hers on Lyda's thighs, closing her eyes in sheer bliss as Lyda's fingers tightened in her hair, her other arm reaching back to do the same to Noah, directing the two of them to nibble, nip and tongue-fuck her, alternatively, until she was making lovely, long moans, her body writhing between them.

"Stop," she commanded breathlessly, tightening her fingers to draw them back. She gave them a slumberous, sexy look, then stepped into the shower. Turning, she moved to the back wall. Then she beckoned to them to join her.

The next twenty minutes were playful, joyous fun. Lyda soaped Gen's breasts, running her fingers in all crevices, doing the same to Noah, then letting them do it to her, so that they were all exploring, kissing, fondling. Then Lyda changed back to a demanding Mistress, shoving Gen against the tile and plunging her fingers into her, worrying her clit with her thumb. At her command, Noah pressed up behind Lyda, slid an arm around her waist, bent his knees and impaled his Mistress on his cock.

"Cup your breasts for us, Gen," Lyda said with hoarse demand. "Play with your nipples while I enjoy your cunt."

Gen did, until she was crying out for mercy, to be allowed to come. Lyda let her go only after she did. Noah fell shortly thereafter, their cries and moans echoing through the shower and making Gen want to start all over.

* * * * *

Such over-the-top sexual intensity could easily bespell a person, make her believe she was feeling deeper emotions. So over the next several days, Gen tested the theory, and was happy to find she enjoyed the nonsexual things the three of them did together as much. She savored every new thing she learned about them. Yes, the Dom/sub thing was always a pleasant undercurrent, but it was part of who Lyda and Noah were. A part she realized she liked very much, in or out of bed.

That second day, they did a lot of shopping and sightseeing. She and Noah bought Lyda a T-shirt that said Badass Bitch. She retaliated by buying them bright red Dr. Seuss shirts that said *Thing 1* and *Thing 2* and making them wear them. They sampled fudge, wandered wide-eyed through Ripley's Believe It or Not, and went hiking in the National Park. Noah coaxed Gen into letting him piggyback her for short stints to give her tired feet a rest. It was charming and sweet, and not at all a hardship to rest against his back, her cheek against his shoulder. Lyda's hand occasionally brushed her back or hip. Then there was dinner and the nightly walk with Dot, followed by more bedtime pleasures.

The next day, they went driving around outside of Gatlinburg to explore antique shops, dusty stores piled to the ceiling with paperbacks, and places run by local artisans. When they found a craft supply store, they had to drag Gen out of there at closing time. Lyda promised she could return later…if she was good. The sensual threat set off all sorts of fantasies in Gen's head, while probably scandalizing the shopkeeper.

When they returned to the cabin, Lyda left Noah and Gen to their own devices for dinner, opting for an energy bar and a run. She told Noah she'd catch up to them on the walk with Dot.

"How far does she run?" Gen asked Noah as they went across the bridge to retrieve Dorothy. He grinned.

"Do you really want an answer to that?"

"Let me guess. She found out how far Army Rangers can run, called them a bunch of pussies and doubled it."

"Tripled it, more likely." He had his arm around her, hand tucked into the back pocket of her jeans. "I've told her if she wasn't so beautiful she'd be totally butch. She told me she has no problem being both."

"No, she doesn't." Gen sighed.

Dorothy met them at the door on her walker. She spent a certain amount of time each day using it so her muscles wouldn't atrophy. Gen watched, quietly charmed by Noah's gentleness as he helped Dot into her scooter, then held open the screen door so she could motor down the ramp.

Gen's affection for Noah's grandmother had strengthened into adoration over the past few days. It was fueled by her merciless teasing of Noah, always tempered with a tender love in her eyes and touch. Noah was obviously nourished by the relationship, and that alone would have made Gen love the old woman. Studying them together, Gen realized it was the most relaxed she'd seen him, even when he was with her and Lyda.

"There she comes." Noah nodded. At the base of the steep hill they were going down, Lyda was coming up, moving at a steady pace. Sweat dampened the T-shirt between her breasts, the running shorts clinging to her hips and toned thighs, her thick tail of hair swinging over her shoulders. She had on her earbuds, listening to the player she had strapped to her arm.

"Heavy metal," Noah said. "She runs to old school stuff. AC/DC, Aerosmith. If you ever want to really piss her off, slide some Guns and Roses or Poison into the mix. She considers them rock wannabes." Since he was behind Dot, he rubbed his backside with a grimace, pantomiming an awkward gait, as if he'd had rebar shoved up his ass. Gen hid a smile.

"I never swung that way," Dorothy remarked, "but she is a cool drink of water, isn't she? Makes you feel all fluttery. She's sort of beyond your reach, like bumping into Grace Kelly or Greta Garbo." She lifted a hand to draw Noah parallel to her. "Stop walking behind me making faces, boy. I'll box your ears."

"Yes ma'am." He squeezed her hand. Dorothy looked back at Lyda. "But she makes me think about what Rita Hayworth said. 'They go to sleep with Gilda, but they wake up with me.' She needs things, just like we all do."

"Sometimes I'm not so sure," Gen said. "She's as self-contained as an island. If you erode one shore, she'll just add on to the back side."

"So take a boat out to her. Kings or garbage men, we all need love. To be needed and accepted for who we are, deep inside. That's the way you solve every problem, and find out what's important, and what's not."

She held Gen's gaze long enough for Gen to realize the woman was trying to say something that covered more than just Lyda. Noah touched Dot's shoulder. "Don't be a busybody," he said mildly.

His grandmother looked up at him. "Just saying the truth, my boy," she said. "The truth your heart knows."

Lyda reached them then. As she ran in place, she removed the earbuds, tucking them into the armband. "I love running here," she told Dot.

"Of course you do," Gen said. "There are ninety degree inclines everywhere."

"Maybe it's what I have waiting at the top of the hill." Lyda crooked an arm around her neck, pulling her in for a kiss, surrounding Gen with the scent of sweaty woman. Thinking of how hard Lyda pushed her body and Dot's warning about arthritis, Gen decided she'd learn how to give Lyda massages. Rub lotion into every inch of her skin. Maybe she and Noah could take a class together so they could do it at the same time. There was plenty of that lithe body to share.

It was the thought a person had when she intended to be with someone for a long time. This weekend had made it easier to fall into that mode of thinking, the three of them working so well together, but vacations could be like that. The quick shadow in Noah's gaze at his grandmother's pointed comment warned against that. As did the other things Gen knew about Lyda—or didn't know, as the case might be. *Take a boat out to her...*

She realized then she hadn't been self-conscious about Lyda kissing her. True, it was just a press of lips to lips, not a knee-weakening tongue invasion, but it had been a lovers' kiss.

Dorothy was pointing something out to Noah. She'd seen it, Gen was sure, but it didn't seem to offend her. Lyda's expression told Gen she'd noticed her lack of self-consciousness. And liked it.

Gen slid a finger along Lyda's collarbone, collecting perspiration. "I'm going to learn how to give massages," she said. "Then I can make your muscles feel better after your hard workouts. I'll also feed you ice cream."

Lyda gave her one of her sultry looks. She did a few more cool down circles around them at a trot, until Dorothy told her she was making her dizzy and Lyda dropped to a walk next to them.

It was one of the nicest trips Gen could remember having…ever.

* * * * *

Lyda took the wheel on the first leg of the return trip. Gen was in the front with her, Noah in the back, stretched out on the seat, sleeping. Gen turned on her hip to study him. He had his long legs bent, one foot braced on the floorboards, the other knee leaning against the seatback. His arm was over his eyes, the other loose across his chest. He hadn't taken many extra naps here, his sleep less disturbed. Except for last night.

About three a.m. she'd woken to find Lyda and her alone in the bed. When she'd lifted her upper body to peer over Lyda, she'd seen him through the window, sitting on the back porch swing in darkness. His head was tilted, listening to the evening sounds. Making sure the covers were tucked around the soundly sleeping Lyda, Gen picked up his pillow and the throw at the end of the bed and took them out to the porch.

Noah studied her with his dark eyes, saying nothing, but he made room for her. She propped the pillow against his thigh, lay down on her hip. As he stroked her hair, she curled her hands around his thigh.

"You should be in bed," he murmured. "It's more comfortable."

"I want you to know I'm right here. We both are. Even if she sleeps like the dead."

"She always has," Noah glanced through the window, into the darkened room. "She says it's why she'd be a terrible mother."

"What do you think her mother was like?"

"I thought she might be like Lyda, terrifying, but I was wrong. She doesn't talk much about her family, but one time she said, 'I make them uncomfortable, because I'm so different.' She says they have the Christmas-card-once-a-year, contact-me-if-someone-dies kind of relationship."

"That's sad. But I get it." Gen couldn't say her relationship with her own mother was much different. Their phone calls usually petered out after ten minutes, and they'd started spending holidays separately back in her twenties.

They were three people without close family ties, and perhaps because all of them were aware of what they were missing, they sought it elsewhere. She grazed his chin, stroking the sandpaper stubble. "Whether she says it or not, or we mean it the same way, we love you, Noah."

Their eyes held forever, it seemed. Rather than struggling for the right thing to say, like she'd done the day at the guesthouse and chosen so wrongly, she let her feelings be guided by that penetrating look. Following the map it laid out inside her heart, she didn't analyze the words that came to her lips, just spoke them.

"You're a treasure. You're also a pain in the ass. You're beautiful, sexy, frustrating. You're sad, broken. Strong, amazing. All those things separated out might mean different things, but all together, woven into one special soul? That's a gift."

She touched his mouth again. "I don't want you to say anything. The words are for you. You do with them what you will. We'll simply love you."

Settling her head on his thigh again, she closed her eyes. After a time, he stroked her once more, his feet keeping the porch swing moving in a cradle rock. She fell asleep that way, vaguely aware of when he carried her back to bed, tucked her in between him and Lyda and curled close behind her.

Coming back to the present, Gen thought about how he was with them, with his grandmother, and how he'd reacted to Elias. Last night, the words she'd spoken had been pure feeling, but she knew they were right. What purpose they'd serve, she didn't know. But she hoped it was like looking at the concept for a collage, sorting through paper choices, seeing the picture form until that *click* moment when she knew how it was going to work.

The thought reminded her she had some magazines to flip through, but she turned back to Lyda, intending to ask if she wanted her to read an article, play some music or initiate conversation, doing her part as the person riding shotgun.

Instead, in a blink of the universe, she saw Lyda's expression change, her lips draw back, her body going rigid. Then she wrenched the wheel to the right.

The world exploded.

There was the impact, the flash of the car hitting them. The Escalade was spinning out of control, hitting the guard rail—oh God—going through the guard rail. The nose of the car dipped like at the top of a roller coaster.

Screaming, air pushing through the lungs…pain, crashing metal…Gen head hit something hard, blood in her eyes…

Please, no.

Silence.

Gen opened her eyes. Things were rocking, back, forth, back, forth…a seesaw. It was like she was on a seesaw, vertical, facing down. She needed to throw up, but she was wheezing, a hard pressure against her chest. Her forehead was itching. What a crazy thing to annoy her right now.

"Gen. *Gen.* I need your help." Noah's voice. Urgent, imperative. "Look at me. Look toward my voice."

Her head turned before her eyes opened, and she fought the desire to throw up. She was looking up at him. How was that possible?

"*Gen.*"

Noah had never snapped at her, as demanding as Lyda, his eyes hard as stone. Why wasn't Lyda saying anything? "I…I can't seem to move."

"Wiggle your fingers and toes."

She did, relieved to feel those. A similar look crossed Noah's face, seeing her do it.

"You're wearing your seat belt and the car's on its side on a slope. Keep looking at me. Don't look away. I'm your focal point."

Dazed, she tried to look away, get her bearings, but he made that sharp noise. He even lifted an arm toward her, carefully. He had one hand wrapped around the chicken strap, elbow hooked around the seat back, one foot braced on the back of the driver's seat. She could see sky through the back window. Their various luggage items seemed to be clustered at odd places in the oddly angled car, like one of those funny skewed perspective paintings.

"Gen."

She forced herself to focus again, and he nodded in approval.

"You're going to go out my window." He pointed above himself and she saw it was broken, jagged pieces of glass forming teeth around the opening. She saw trees, smelled forest. As well as burning metal, smoke. "When I say go, I'm going to unbuckle you, give you a lift up there, all right? But you have to hold onto the seat so you don't fall forward, and try to help me, move this way and come right to me, okay?"

She was starting to realize what was happening, understand the slight rocking motion of the car. She knew now why he didn't want her looking toward the front of the car. She swallowed, hard. "Noah, what if...shouldn't we wait..."

"We can't. It will be too late." Though he spoke calmly, his brown eyes were brilliant and intent. "You remember that day Chloe got hurt? I know you wish you'd been there. That you could have helped and protected her. This is your chance to do that, Gen. You're going to save all three of us. Okay?"

"Okay." She wasn't sure of any of it, but then the car groaned, the seesawing abruptly becoming more pronounced.

"*Now.* Hold onto the seat." With the sharp command and a curse, Noah leaned forward, his pocket knife already out to slice through the seat belt. Gen's arms were too shaky, and she lost her grip, but Noah grabbed her arm. She was able to seize it with the other hand as well, and he pulled her up into the back seat. "Move slow and steady. Be still. Be still now."

He held Gen against him with a rigid-as-steel arm. He made that harsh noise to keep her motionless, both their weights pressed to the seat like glue, against gravity. Slowly...so slowly, the seesawing went back to a more gentle motion again.

"Okay." Noah let out a breath and lifted his head, directing her attention to where the broken out window beckoned. Then he looked back down at her. "Out of the two of us, I'm the only one who has the upper body strength to pull her free, lift her up to you. I'll push and you'll pull her through. Okay? I know your arms are shaking, but you have to find the adrenaline, Gen. You have to be strong enough. Understand?"

His dark gaze bored into her face. Though she sensed she was in shock, possibly concussed, things were becoming clearer and his message got through. "Okay. Yes. I will."

"I know you will." He pressed a quick kiss to her forehead. "Once you're out there, move back as far as you can to counterbalance."

She noticed he had blood on his neck, running down into his shirt from his hairline. She wasn't the only one shaking. "Everything working good enough to do this?" he asked. "Anything feel broken?"

It wasn't like they had a lot of options if anything was. He'd just made that clear. Maybe he was just giving her that extra second to let adrenaline juice her up even further. Kudos to the powers-that-be for providing that perk in life-or-death situations. But now that some clarity was returning, she had to look for Lyda. She had to, even when Noah tried to stop her. She looked toward the driver's seat. And bit back a cry.

Her beautiful hair was a mass of blood. She was draped over the steering wheel like a ragdoll, face turned away. She wasn't moving. "Noah."

"She's alive. I refuse to believe anything else." He set his jaw. "We just do this. No talking about that."

"Okay." She bit back the fear, fought the fuzziness in her brain that could kill them all. "What do I need to do again?"

"I'm going to give you a boost out that window. We'll try to do it smooth. Fast, but not too fast. Once you're up there, move back as much as you can to help us counterbalance. Once we're steady again, I'll cut Lyda loose and push her up through the window. You pull, and we'll get her out of there. Move both of you toward the back, so I have a clear track out the window. All right?"

"But...why not just get out and open her door?"

"Her door was the main impact point. It's dented and probably not able to open. And there are other reasons. No time to explain. Here, use this towel to grab the edge of the window, since it has broken glass. Ready?"

Noah touched her face, held her gaze. She thought there'd never been a shorter or longer moment in her life than right now, seeing the steel nerve in those brown eyes, the deep fear, but not for himself. "If the car falls anyway, there's nothing anyone could have done to stop that," he said. "If it starts to fall, you jump off the rear wheel."

"No." A different kind of fear flooded her. "No. We just do it together and see what happens. We just do it. Stop talking about things like that."

He stared into her eyes. "Okay."

She nodded. "I'm ready."

"*Go.*" He boosted her up before she could say anything else. She gritted her teeth, scrambled out the window, cutting herself on the glass in her haste, even with the protection of the towel. Stomach muscles she didn't know she had helped her through that opening and she scrambled for the back tire. The car was wedged loosely between a stand of slender trees and perched on a jutting layer of rock, explaining the instability. She had a harrowing impression of the steep side of the mountain.

Forest covering the slopes had slowed the vehicle, but it wasn't thick enough. Where it thickened was in the deep ravine about a hundred feet below them. A rushing wide creek cut through it, showing the depth of the drop over the edge of those rocks. The car would pitch straight down amid the tall pines, speared by or destroying them on its crashing descent.

The car teetered forward and she scrambled even beyond the wheel, onto the gas tank, not an advisable idea she was sure, but she wasn't concerned about that. "No, no, no," she gritted. *Come back this way, come back this way.* Her flight instinct told her to get off the car, get clear, but she denied it. *No. I won't leave them. I won't leave them. And you're not taking them with you. Come on.*

If her heart rate had been harnessed to the back bumper, she could have pulled them all the way to the highway above. As it was, the car sluggishly stabilized again.

"Gen." Noah's voice was muffled. "Okay?"

"Okay."

"Are you ready?"

"Give me just a sec." Taking a deep breath, she looked up, hoping to see a team of emergency responders with helicopters and sturdy chains, a crane. The road had been busy enough, plenty of people had seen the accident. But it was likely only minutes had passed. "Noah?"

"Yeah?"

She held onto his voice as the most wonderful sound in the world. "You better get your ass out of there with her, or I will *never* forgive you. Neither will she. It will be worse than when you put Guns and Roses on her player. Far worse."

She thought she heard a chuckle. "I love you, Gen." Quieter, that time. Her heart twisted. *No. Don't you do that. You're not saying goodbye, not to either one of us.*

"Ready."

She'd thought that moment inside the car with him had been the longest and shortest moment of her life. She'd been wrong. The car's sudden pitch, Lyda's limp body thrust through the window, Gen grabbing her under the armpits and hauling her up and back with every ounce of strength she had, that was it. The car started to slide.

"No!"

Noah had pushed Lyda's weight into Gen's arms hard enough that it unbalanced her, sent them both toppling off the car. The rear bottom wheel rolled against her thigh. As she spun away from it, trying to protect Lyda, she and Lyda were sliding, following in the car's wake against a slick bed of leaves. Gen's shin slammed against rock and she wedged her foot in a crevice, ignoring the bolt of pain through her ankle as it took the shock. The move brought them to a halt. The car didn't stop moving. It was groaning, metal shrieking.

"*Noah!*" she screamed. Lyda's blood was soaking Gen's neck and shirt, her body a dead weight pinning Gen down, adding to the feeling of suffocation. "No, no, no..."

She lost time then, as if an angel of mercy was sparing her the agony of the truth. She was looking up into a man's face, an emergency responder, his serious face taking up her vision. "Noah! No, no, no..."

She smelled smoke again, the kind of smoke that came with fire. She couldn't stop crying, hurting, dying inside. She gripped Lyda so hard, the EMTs had to pry her fingers away, give her a shot, and then everything was lost, whirling away.

* * * * *

Something is wrong inside his head...I don't think it will ever be fixed...

Love. That's when you figure out what's important and what's not.

She's an island. You take a boat out to her...

The car going over, smoke and fire...

Gen came out of the nightmare, a cry strangling her. Something yanked against her arm, a stabbing pain, and then someone was holding her arm, someone else holding the rest of her. Marguerite. Marguerite's scent, her strength, wrapped around her.

"It's all right, Gen. Sssh...calm down. You're safe. You're in the hospital."

Chloe was holding her arm, where the IV needle and tape had pulled. She circled Gen with her free arm, eyes welling with tears. "It's okay, Gen. We're here."

Gen steadied, trying to breathe, trying to calm down. *Just breathe. Don't go beyond that. Don't go there.* Beyond breathing was thinking, and a pain waited there she didn't want to feel. It would be beyond what she could endure.

"Lyda and Noah are both alive."

Gen's head snapped up so quickly Marguerite might have gotten her chin rapped if she hadn't anticipated her. Leave it to Marguerite to avoid any cliffhanging drama, just a quiet statement of fact, bringing the spinning world back to rights. "Oh God." Gen pressed her forehead into M's collarbone. "Thank you. Thank you."

"Though I'm sure God was there, you and Noah had a lot to do with it as well, according to the EMTs and eyewitnesses."

"Mostly Noah." It was coming back in harrowing pieces, including that horrifying image of Lyda's twisted body, the bloody face and hair. "When you say they're both alive...what does that mean? Are they okay?"

Marguerite eased a hip onto the bed so Gen could keep holding her. Chloe was cross-legged behind Gen, both as close as possible. Gen needed them that close. The room was whites and blues, medicine and disinfectant. She didn't want that reality.

"Noah broke a couple ribs, dislocated his shoulder. He kicked out the back window and caught hold of the rocks as the car went into the ravine. Tore up his hands pretty good on the rocks and the things inside the car, but the EMT who pulled him back over said it was one of the most impressive things he'd ever seen. Beyond all three of you getting out of the car alive, that is."

"I think he hates he missed catching it on his phone for YouTube," Chloe interjected.

They were trying to ground her, but now she only remembered that final second in the car, when Noah had met her gaze. He'd known the car wouldn't maintain stability when Lyda was cut free. He'd pushed Gen to follow his direction, and she'd let him. Guilt and shame swamped her, even knowing she'd been too disoriented to think straight. He'd been the only one in the position to do that, and he'd been prepared to sacrifice his life to save theirs. But he'd fought to live. Whether for them or himself, it didn't matter. He was alive.

"Lyda?" Dread filled her as Marguerite's face became more somber than usual.

"She has a skull fracture and other broken bones. Do you know what happened?"

Gen shook her head. While Noah's look was permanently engraved in her brain, the key moment was fuzzy. "I was looking at Noah, sleeping in the back. All I saw when I turned was Lyda's face. A flash of another car."

"You were on a sharp curve and the other driver was texting and crossed the line. Lyda took the brunt of the impact on the driver's side when she pulled the wheel to the right, but her deceleration when most people would have accelerated to avoid impact may have been what saved all of you. You went off the road, but the car tipped after it took out the guard rail, rather than shooting out into open space."

Only one thing was important. "How is she? Is she awake, talking?"

Marguerite shook her head. "But the swelling in her brain is already going down," Chloe added quickly. "The nurses say that's good."

She thought of Lyda, so strong and beautiful, running up the hill, making teasing circles around them. "No."

"They can't guarantee anything with head trauma, but once she wakes up, they'll be able to tell more. I think she's just resting up." M touched her face, gave her a steadying look. "You know Lyda's very particular about how she presents herself."

"I know. I know." Gen's voice was thickening. "If I'd lost them…"

"You didn't." Marguerite's arms were around her again. "You didn't, Gen."

"First it was you and Chloe, and now this…" She lifted her head, looked at Chloe. "Did you tell Noah how I felt…about nearly losing you?"

"Yes," the girl said simply. "In a way. He was as curious about you as you were about him. I told him you were the wonderful type of person who felt bad because you weren't there, even though it wasn't something you could control."

"I can't stand the thought of losing you. Either of you. It was so terrible. You're my family. All of you." Chloe and Marguerite, Lyda and Noah, all of them rolled together.

Chloe's eyes filled with tears again, and the three of them held one another. "You didn't lose us, and you didn't lose them," Marguerite murmured against Gen's hair. "Most importantly to us, we didn't lose you. You're our family too, dear heart."

Gen cried then. Not just because Chloe was crying, or because Gen was the type of person who cried in such situations, but because Marguerite was crying too, silent tears dampening Gen's temple where the woman pressed her jaw against her.

They stayed that way for a while, then a nurse came in and discovered Gen was awake. Which meant she had to be prodded and poked. It turned out her injuries had been miraculously minor, the concussion the main cause of concern, but apparently they'd already done the diagnostics needed to verify no obvious serious brain trauma. Being awake and responsive to questions helped upgrade her status even further. Even so, the doctor made it clear she was going to be kept for at least one night's observation and gave Gen a list of symptoms she was to report to the nurse immediately if they occurred.

It was clear Marguerite and Chloe were taking careful note of that list. She'd wanted them to stay close, so through it all, Marguerite remained at the door, Chloe in the guest chair. Tyler arrived and stood behind Marguerite. His amber-colored eyes brightened, seeing Gen awake. She managed a smile, her eyes filling again when he pressed his lips to his fingers and turned them in her direction.

The more awake she became, though, the more impatient she grew. She needed out of this bed. She needed to go to Noah, to Lyda. Tyler would know where they were. That was probably where he'd been, getting a status report. As soon as the last nurse cleared the room, Gen was putting her feet over the side of the bed and looking for a robe.

Marguerite and Chloe didn't chide her, didn't try to stop her, but Marguerite did insist on a wheelchair. When Tyler disappeared and reappeared with one, she wanted to hold onto them all over again and never let them go. But as much as she wanted that, her arms needed to be around two other people even more.

Marguerite glanced at her husband. "You found that pretty fast. Please tell me you didn't dump a patient out of it."

"He said he was fully capable of walking, and that a true gentleman never denied a lady a chair." Tyler gave Gen a wink.

Their banter should have made her feel better, but the undercurrent of seriousness told her it wasn't because things were rosy.

"Lyda is in the ICU, so she has restricted visiting hours," Tyler said as they rolled down the hall. "Only two people at a time. We won't be able to get you in to see her for about another hour. You can see Noah now." He paused, and Gen sensed a look passing between him and Marguerite behind her. "He needs to see you. He's been having some trouble."

"Trouble?" Gen looked up at Marguerite.

"He refused to stay in the bed, refused to be away from either one of you. They had to sedate and restrain him." Her boss spoke carefully. "They moved him to a psychiatric unit when his agitation disrupted other patients. Tyler arranged for Brendan to stay in the room with him, but you can help calm him down some. If you're up for that."

"Yes. Definitely." It made her all the more anxious to see him. When they arrived at the psychiatric wing, seeing the buzzer on the locked door, the nurses' desk like a guard station, made her nauseous again. "He can't be in here, Tyler. He's not crazy."

Tyler put a hand on her shoulder, his strong fingers a soothing caress over sore muscles. "I know that, Gen. It's to protect him. He has injuries that need care, bed rest, and this is the best place for those they can't keep in bed in the normal ways."

He squatted next to the chair, laced his fingers with hers. "Brendan or I have been with him at all times in there. You know I wouldn't let anything happen to him."

"I know." The reassurance was nice, but she knew the words were more than that. He was preparing her for what she was going to see.

Only one person was allowed to go with her, and she chose Marguerite, because she sensed she needed the person with her who was most like Lyda. As they were buzzed in and Marguerite rolled her down the hall, Gen could barely keep herself in her chair. She could empathize with Noah. But she also knew enough about him to know why it was different as well. Tyler had expected her to understand the situation without excess explanation and she did. She accepted that as a privilege, not an obligation.

His door was open. While there was a protective mesh on the window, it did allow sunlight into the room, making it more cheerful. A TV was on, low volume. She paid no attention to it. She had only one focus.

Why did everyone look so pale in the hospital? He was a sailor, a man who worked for a nursery out in the Florida sun, and he looked pallid. And hospital gowns always made everyone look so horribly fragile. His hands were bandaged, and his face had a multitude of cuts. Someone had brushed his hair and clipped it out of his face, but right now the usually appealing look just made him look thin and strained.

Brendan rose from the guest chair as Marguerite rolled her in. "Hey there," he said with effusive warmth. "Noah, you have a visitor."

Noah's eyes blinked open. From his disorientation, she could tell he'd been drugged. Suddenly she was so angry she could barely speak. Why didn't they understand? They could have set him up in Gen's room, if Lyda was too injured. That was all he needed. Of course, as Tyler said, Noah had to have a bed for his injuries, and the rooms were private singles. There was probably some kind of hospital policy that couldn't be circumvented, even by two formidable forces like Marguerite and Tyler. They'd made sure he wasn't alone, though, that he'd had Brendan.

Her freaking out wasn't going to help Noah in the slightest. Marguerite had wheeled her up to his bedside. When she closed her hand over his, his grip turned, bandaged fingers clamped around hers. They'd been torn up by glass and rocks, isn't that what they'd said? Holding onto her so tightly must hurt, but he didn't ease up in the least. A metal clank drew her gaze down to his wrist.

Though the three-inch-wide cuff appeared to be a comfortable fleece-lined leather, hooked to a manacle on the bed rails, it still twisted something hard in her gut to see him restrained by them. "So I see you figured out a way to get a nurse to slap cuffs on you," she said in an unsteady voice. "Lyda is going to be pretty pissed about that."

Struggling through that drugged fog, he reached out with the other hand, only to find it brought up short by the cuff that held it to the opposite rail. When he yanked against it, confused frustration filling his face, she was pushing herself out of the chair. Fuck the hospital. She unbuckled the cuffs. His thrashing had dislodged the blankets and shown her his ankles were cuffed as well, but right now she ignored those and leaned over him. As Brendan steadied her swaying body, she focused on making sure Noah didn't try to rise toward her. The gown was pulled to the side enough she could see the bandaged ribs.

She pressed against him, holding him. "You asshole," she muttered against his temple. "You knew the damn car was going to fall."

His arms slid around her, clumsy, uncoordinated but tight as a vise. When he spoke against her ear, a mere whisper, she choked on a sob.

"I know you'd do anything for us. I know that." She pressed her palm against his face, her forehead now against his as she gazed into his brown eyes. "You're going to have to do something for us now, okay? I hate this. I hate seeing you like this. You're going to let the nurse move you to a normal room."

Her voice strengthened. She channeled that inner Domme Lyda had helped her discover. It felt quite natural, fueled by the strength of her emotions. And even better, she saw it penetrate that haze on Noah's senses like nothing else would, except a command from Lyda herself.

"We're going to try to get you as close to my room as we can. But you have to stay in your bed, listen to all the nurses the way you listen to Lyda. Because that's how we need you to take care of us right now. I've only got a concussion and some scrapes, so I'll come be with you as much as possible, and we'll get phones and text one another so you'll feel like I'm right there with you. Okay? We have to pull it together so we can take care of Lyda. She's going to need us to take care of her, and you know how much she's going to hate that. She's going to be a pain in the ass. We're going to wish we pushed her off that mountain. Tell me you understand."

In response, he pressed his forehead harder against hers. "Sorry." His tongue was thick, but she shook her head, tears dropping onto his face.

"There is utterly *nothing* to be sorry about it. You saved our lives, Noah. But if you'd gone down with that car" — her eyes locked with his — "you would have killed us. We love you, you moron. You're special to us. One of a kind. Irreplaceable."

Did he understand what that meant? How much it meant?

His lips curved, but there was pain in his gaze, such tiredness. She nuzzled his face, pressed her lips to his, tasting him, savoring him, trying not to press too hard because his bottom lip had a cut on it. He didn't care, shifting his hand to the back of her head, holding her fast, making the kiss fierce, needy. She refused to think it would have meant the same to him, whether he'd saved them or Elias or any faceless Domme who claimed him. She didn't want to think about the fact he didn't know how to choose anyone, which might mean he didn't know how to love anyone.

No. That was wrong. He knew how to love. Even if it wasn't the way that normal people loved, that didn't matter.

In such a situation, things like that became a lot less important. Just like Dot had said.

* * * * *

Marguerite and Tyler hadn't known Dorothy's contact info in Gatlinburg. Once Gen provided that, Chloe called her, glad to tell her Noah was okay in the same sentence she had to tell her he'd been in a car accident. As soon as he took care of getting Noah moved, Tyler went to retrieve her so she could come see her grandson.

Gen wouldn't be surprised if he'd contacted the trustees personally, or donated a new wing. Regardless of how he did it, the staff was convinced Noah could now be trusted not to escape his bed. When Dot arrived, he was no longer in the psych wing.

Marguerite accompanied her into the ICU the first time she saw Lyda. The sight made Gen cry all over again. They'd shaved her beautiful flame-colored hair and she had a terrifying line of staples for one head wound. She had bruising on her arms and more cuts, some of which had been stitched. Her left leg had a compound fracture and her right arm had also been broken. But the nurse was reassuring.

"She's a hell of a fighter. The brain swelling is going down way faster than we expected."

Gen swallowed. "Is that..." She nodded to a tube that ran into Lyda's head, with a metal attachment piece that made Gen's skin crawl just looking at it.

"Yes." The nurse put a hand on her shoulder. "That's an intracranial pressure monitor. That's how we know how well she's doing, and it helped drain off excess fluid from the trauma. I know it looks scary, but it's one of the good guys. It's helping her."

Gen tried to smile, couldn't. "Her vitals are strong," the nurse said. "The surgeon said her heart is one of the healthiest he's ever seen in his life."

"She's a fitness nut," Gen managed. "She does those insanity workout type of things. Eats horrible, healthy things. She treats sugar and pizza like toxic waste."

The nurse squeezed her shoulder again before crossing her arms over her smock and giving the unconscious Lyda a satisfied look. "She's a miracle, that's for sure. But then, from what I hear, you all are. Somebody's going to be knocking on your door to tell your story to one of those true confession magazines."

Gen didn't care about any of that. She lifted a hand, stopped. "Can I...touch her?"

"Sure you can. Just be real careful of all the things attached to her." The nurse stepped back, giving them a semblance of privacy.

Gen closed her hand over Lyda's, pale and limp on the bed. The mere contact with the slim fingers choked Gen with tears. *God. Oh God. Lyda, look at you.*

What had the doctor said? That concussions could come with emotional outbursts, mood swings? Like being in a terrible car crash couldn't do that all by itself, right?

She rose out of her chair, Marguerite moving close for support as Gen leaned over to carefully touch Lyda's cheek, her cracked lips. It almost broke her down all the way then, being so close to that beloved visage, seeing it so slack and unaware.

Don't be such a girl.

She could hear Lyda saying it, imagine the glint in her silver eyes.

"Noah's okay," Gen said, clearing her throat with determined effort. "I know you want a full report. I can take care of him and me until you can, so you don't need to worry about that. Tyler or Brendan will be with him when I'm not. Brendan's barely left his side. I didn't realize they were such good friends. I don't know anywhere near all the things that I want to know about both of you."

Taking a shaky breath, she touched her Mistress's jaw, felt the reassuring pulse. "That car hit us where you would take the most damage. No one's going to tell me that was dumb luck. You're so damn heroic, just like him. I want you both to work on that. Would it kill either of you to be Joe and Jane Average? Like me. Nothing wrong with the occasional pizza or being afraid of heights. It would be a lot easier on my nerves if the two of you realized that. I can't lose you. Not now or ever. I know you think it's the stress talking, but I'm in love with you both. Maybe we're only at the beginning of what that means, but it doesn't make it less true."

She baptized Lyda with a few more tears, wiping them off her face gently. Then she kissed her cheek, holding the pressure there a long, yearning moment. "I have to go now, because they only let us visit for a little while, but you wake up soon, okay? We both need you. That's the way this works. Maybe Noah and I can visit together next shift. I know you won't feel all right until you see him. He really is okay. As beautiful as ever. The nurses are already fighting to give him a sponge bath. He'll be the cleanest patient in the whole hospital."

Marguerite made a meaningful noise. Gen lifted her head. M gestured to the nurse, who was tapping her watch with kind but firm purpose. "Okay." Gen glanced back down at Lyda. "You rest and get all better. The world can't run without you."

She leaned down once more, pressed her lips to Lyda's mouth. "I love you," she whispered. "Just wake up, so you can tell me and Noah if you want to love us back. Either way, we need you to wake up."

Chapter Fifteen

Lyda woke up two days later. When Gen and Noah were discharged, they stayed at the Gatlinburg guesthouse. Dot's friend had cleared its schedule and made it available to them as long as they needed it. As soon as Lyda was moved out of the ICU, one or both of them was always in Lyda's room, taking shifts to help care for her as she got stronger. Three weeks later, after endless tests, the neurosurgeon confirmed there'd been no permanent brain damage and Lyda was cleared to return home, transferred to the care of a Tampa area physician during her recuperation.

As Gen had predicted, Lyda was a horrible patient. Irritable and unpredictable as a wounded cat, Lyda was on the hit list of every nurse on the floor by the time she was discharged. Gen suspected they threw a party when Lyda was wheeled out the door, even though she and Noah had done their best to smooth over her prickly moments.

It was ironic that a woman who made Gen and Noah do things large and small when she was at full strength was so impatient having things done for her when she was helpless to do them for herself. But Gen understood it, and not just because she valued her own independence, or because she'd seen the same qualities in Marguerite. When Lyda told Noah to bring her coffee, or had Gen prepare her dinner, that was a mutual pleasure. Lyda enjoying her powers as a Domme also satisfied Noah's craving to be submissive, and encouraged Gen's fascination with exploring how far it all went for her. Having to actually rely on someone for help? An entirely different matter.

Throughout all of it, Noah was predictably tolerant, enduring any tantrum or the sharpest cut from Lyda's tongue, for that was his way. But Gen wasn't built of the same stuff, and the time came when she'd had enough.

It happened the day Lyda refused to take any pain medication, despite the fact she was in such distress she was trembling, her limbs jerking in a way even their formidable Mistress couldn't control.

A red haze crossed Gen's gaze, and before she could stop herself, she slammed the bottled water down on a table. "I get it. You're the World's Most Invincible Bitch. But could you pull your head out of your egocentric ass long enough to realize how much it hurts us to see you in pain?"

Lyda was on a day bed they'd set up on the outside porch, so she could enjoy the landscaping of her backyard instead of staring at the four walls or enduring hours of daytime television on the couch. Gen stabbed a finger toward the nursery, where she knew Noah was supervising the other employees, tending the stock.

"The guy that doesn't sleep because of his own demons has done nothing but bust his ass for you since you woke up. Oh, after saving your life, by the way. And just because you know he'll take any level of shit from you does *not* give you the right to shovel it on his head because you can't spring up like goddamn Lazarus from the dead. What difference is there between Elias kicking him physically and you doing it emotionally, just because both of you know he'll take it?"

Lyda's face whitened at that. Gen didn't bother to curse when she saw Noah appear at the opening to the porch, choosing that inopportune moment to check in and see if they needed anything. But she was on a roll. She wasn't stopping now. Emotions erupted like lava from a volcano, accumulated from the first day Lyda had woken up and it had started to look like she was going to be okay. As long as she cared for herself properly, that is.

"If you can't have the decency to do that, then think about this." Gen leaned over, inches between their two angry faces. "You can't start moving around the way you want until you're better. These pills will help with that. Listening to the doctors will help. God forbid, listening to us peons will help. You want to stay in this bed even longer, you want to get worse, ignore them and ignore us and keep doing everything your way. Because it's all about you anyway, right?"

Noah laid his hands on her shoulders, but she shrugged him off, stabbed another finger at Lyda. "You don't care how scared we were of losing you. It never occurs to you that we hover too much because we wake up ten times a night, having a nightmare about you slumped over that goddamn steering wheel, not knowing if you were alive or dead. If any of us were going to live through it."

Lyda stared at her. She was still pale, but spots of color were high in her cheeks. Clearing his throat, Noah lifted the bottle of water from the side table. His other hand stayed on Gen's lower back, fingers stroking, sending a simple message. *Easy. It's okay.* She was shaking, tears threatening.

Lyda pressed her lips together, then she shook her head at Noah. As he lowered the water, she lifted her unbroken arm. "Come here, fierce rabbit."

Gen wasn't sure she was in the mood, but then Lyda's eyes did that thing they hadn't done since she'd woken up. She got that Mistress look, and a million things speared through Gen, breaking her to pieces and putting her together at the same time.

"I said come here."

Gen closed the distance, stepped into that armspan. Then she was sitting on the edge of the bed, her upper body curled against Lyda's, because she'd pulled her down so Gen was lying against her breast. Lyda wrapped her arm around her back, rubbed Gen's hip. "It's okay," Lyda soothed.

Her chin brushed Gen's temple as she gestured Noah close as well. When he knelt next to the bed, laying his hand on Gen's leg, Lyda ran her knuckles along his cheek. He gripped her hand, pressed his lips to it. Lyda's eyes became suspiciously bright. "My pets," she murmured. "My friends." Her gaze shifted to Gen, back to Noah. "My family. I'm sorry. I'm very bad at this."

"Understatement," Gen said. "Selfish bitch." Her arms tightened around Lyda as she said it. Lyda pressed a kiss to the crown of her head.

"I warned you about that at the beginning, didn't I? Now, you said something about it being time to take my pills."

Gen pulled it together, though it took a couple deep breaths. Swiping at her wet cheeks, she rose and retrieved the meds. Noah unscrewed the water bottle. Lyda held out her hand for the pills, as imperious as a queen who'd demanded them all along.

Gen placed them in her palm. Lyda swallowed them, then opened her mouth wide, as if suggesting Gen would want to verify she'd taken them. Eyes narrowing, Gen made a point to bend down as if she was looking. Lyda snapped her jaw shut, gaze sparking. But Gen saw the haze of weariness take her features. Sitting up for a half hour could still wear her out, so an intense fight like that, short as it was, had drained her. Gen felt a twinge of guilt, but given that it had seemed to clear the air somewhat and her point about Noah had been received loud and clear, she couldn't really regret it.

When Lyda slid down gingerly, adjusting her body to accommodate all her aches and pains, Gen arranged the blankets around her, putting pillows where she knew it would help her to be propped.

"I snore when I'm on my back," Lyda muttered.

"Like a freight train," Gen agreed. "It keeps us from having to use a baby monitor. We can hear you in the kitchen."

Lyda shut her eyes, ignoring her. Gen glanced at Noah and stopped, catching a serious look on his face hard to decipher, but unsettling in its intensity. Before she could delve into that, he'd turned and left, headed back to the nursery. Lyda's hand settled on her arm, squeezed.

"Fierce rabbit," their Mistress said. A few moments later, she was asleep.

* * * * *

That was the turning point. Lyda improved even faster from there forward, especially when Noah planted the brilliant idea of treating her road to full recovery like workout and diet goals. Though her broken and battered body wasn't quite as willing to cooperate with Lyda's manic exercise zeal, the change in focus did give their Mistress a pseudo-sense of control of her healing process. It toned down some of her irritation.

Since their argument, Lyda had also treated Noah with such gentle courtesy Gen almost suggested she backtrack a bit into bitch territory, since she sensed it was kind of freaking him out. Or maybe that was whatever was preoccupying him since that day. She tried to get him to talk about it, but he shook his head, told her it was fine.

She wasn't Lyda. She couldn't make him talk when he didn't want to do so, and Gen had seen the dark terrain inside Noah even Lyda couldn't infiltrate. She knew Lyda wasn't yet strong enough to delve into that realm, no matter what Lyda thought. So

Gen had to settle for hoping that, whatever was going on, it didn't fall in that territory.

They stayed busy enough she couldn't turn her full attention to it, regardless. In addition to Lyda's care, she and Noah were running the nursery. As she gained strength, Lyda gave them instructions on this or that from a wheelchair or crutches, but it still made for busy days. Marguerite had hired a part-time girl to cover at Tea Leaves, a Zone submissive who was a friend of Chloe's. Gen felt guilty about it only as long as it took for Marguerite to set her straight.

"Lyda and Noah need you right now. Family comes first. Your job is here, if and when you want it. Always."

If and when. Working at the nursery, Gen started to have an idea of why M had put it that way. As she did the books and she and Noah worked to cover things, it was as if she'd always worked there. She liked learning about plants. Though he'd told her of his horticulture studies, she was still surprised how much Noah knew about it, how much he'd enhanced his knowledge with Lyda's, and so she learned from him as well.

Once Lyda was strong enough to motor around in her all-terrain wheelchair, Gen particularly liked looking out the office window to see her directing Noah and her other employees in daily tasks.

As their Mistress's body started to recover fully, so did her intuition. Several times Gen caught Lyda watching Noah the same way Gen did, with pensive consideration. Or maybe she wasn't thinking about what was going on with Noah as much as with herself, because once or twice Gen had caught their Mistress looking at her that way as well. Which could be a good or not-so-good thing.

Because she wasn't sure she was ready to know which, Gen didn't push it. But she knew the day would come when it couldn't be avoided anymore. She had a feeling that wreck had been a turning point for all of them.

* * * * *

It was midafternoon. Noah and the others were out on deliveries and job sites. Gen was watering the potted plants around Lyda's patio. Lyda was at the patio table, working on some orders. Gen watched her in the corner of her eye. She now had a short crop of red hair. Still not long enough to have any style to it, but it enhanced the sculpted beauty of Lyda's face, the strong character there, the slope of cheek and piercing strength of her gaze, which rose as Gen spoke.

"Noah said Mr. Bergais really liked the oleanders. He misses you delivering them, though, and hopes you'll be back on your feet soon." Setting the watering can aside, Gen came to sit on the patio edge. Though Lyda used a cane more now, she and Gen had a deal that she used the all-terrain chair to move over the uneven ground in the backyard and nursery, so she was pulled up to the patio table in it. Gen's position put her right by the foot. Reaching out, Gen fingered the petal on a spray of lilies, but that wasn't what she wanted to touch. Lyda was out of the cast, her leg bearing two oblong scars from the compound fracture. Since Lyda was wearing shorts, Gen thought about reaching out, tracing those scars. Touching the skin around them.

"He's a nice man. One of my first customers." Lyda put her hand on the side of Gen's face, let her knuckle trail down to her lips. Wondering if Lyda had picked up on her thought, Gen looked up at her. The rest of her stilled for a different reason.

Lyda wasn't given to a lot of affectionate gestures before the accident, but she'd started to do more of them since. Perhaps as a substitute for sex, or maybe because of the change in their relationship. But as nice as that possibility was, the way she was touching Gen now wasn't driven by affection.

Lyda studied her. "I've been watching Noah dig, haul water and sweat in his jeans, sometimes with the T-shirt, sometimes without. Just now, I felt like eating you alive when you were on all fours, pulling up weeds around my petunias. Noah's been watching you with that same kind of hunger. He's also tried his best not to look down my shirt when I'm in this chair, as if somehow he's required to stop showing sexual desire for his Mistress until she says he can switch it back on again." Her lips curved in a tight smile. "It pissed me off, but I get he was trying to be considerate, so don't fuzz up, rabbit. He hasn't been touching you, has he? You've been switching out sleeping in the guesthouse, one of you on the couch, watching over me."

"It seemed the way it should be. Didn't seem right, if you weren't a part of it. If you didn't say it was okay." The air around them was getting that still, dense feeling to it, the way it did when sexual desire started to limit oxygen. Gen told herself this was too soon, not to push it. Then her Mistress made it clear that she'd recovered enough that it was no longer Gen's call to make.

"My body may not be up to it yet, but I want to watch you together," Lyda said. "Tonight. After dinner."

Gen had been so stressed and busy, she hadn't let herself give much thought to sex, but as Lyda catalogued how Gen and Noah had been inciting her desire, a door in her own mind opened, surprising her with the pictures her own brain had been storing about every opportunity missed.

Like the day last week she'd come to talk to Noah in the guesthouse, and he'd been making himself breakfast. He was just out of the shower, clad in nothing but a towel... Then there was this week, helping Lyda with a bra that clasped in back, since the broken arm still didn't move so well for such things. Standing over her shoulder, Gen had watched Lyda adjust her breasts in the cups, her shorn hair soft under Gen's fingers as she dared a quick stroke. She'd wanted to lean forward, press her lips to the side of Lyda's throat, let her fingers drop even lower, follow those curves, play in the cleavage, cradle her breasts, explore the soft nipples until they weren't soft anymore... She wanted to feel Noah press his firm body against Gen's...

"You're glazing over just thinking about it. Aren't you?" Lyda asked. Gen's chest tightened, heart overwhelmed and eyes stinging at that familiar sultry purr. "I'm goddamned glad I'm not the only one. Answer your Mistress."

"Yes." Gen shifted onto her knees as Lyda slid a hand along her face, under her hair, and brought her up, right to her mouth.

Gen groaned, her hands clasping Lyda's arm, the other touching Lyda's face, stroking over the new growth of her lovely, lovely hair as Lyda coaxed open her lips and teased her with her tongue. Gen's whole body drew in a shuddering breath, making it obvious how much desire she'd been tamping down as things were getting closer back to normal.

"I want to touch you everywhere," she said against Lyda's mouth.

"We'll see about that. If that's what you want, you better dress for it. Convince me. Both of you. And I want to go out to dinner. Joseph's."

"Italian?" Gen's brows lifted, making Lyda smile. With her pixie hairstyle, the gesture enhanced the size and depth of her gray eyes.

"Yes. Pasta. Bread. Maybe even dessert."

Gen reached out as if to take her temperature and Lyda swatted her hand away. Gen grinned. "Just checking. Was afraid you were delusional."

"My skull was fractured, but my brain was not affected," Lyda retorted.

"Because your head was too hard to break. Doesn't mean it didn't rattle something around in there."

Lyda pushed the chair back. "Just for that, you'll help me bathe and dress tonight."

* * * * *

Though Gen had been doing that for a while, with Noah's help when Lyda wasn't able to support her own weight, it was clear tonight was going to be different. Lyda didn't require her help as a recovering accident patient. She was commanding Gen's service, a Mistress who knew the power of giving her submissives access to every inch of her body with no permission to take pleasure from it, except for the intense arousal that denial provided.

When Noah had returned home, Lyda had wasted no time telling him the same thing she'd told Gen. When they'd heard the truck return, heard him talking to the other men, Lyda had called out his name. A few moments later he'd appeared around the corner. He'd been sweaty and dirty, looking as delectably rugged and masculine as Lyda had described. As he pulled off his work gloves, glancing expectantly toward Gen, Lyda's cool voice drew his gaze. "You'll be attending me tonight, Noah," she said. "Do you understand?"

"Yes Mistress."

It had only taken the tone of Lyda's voice, and Gen saw a potent flash of that same fire in Noah's eyes, banked for far too long. Gen felt an answering surge in her own desires. The three of them were going to set the backyard on fire just by thinking of all they wanted from each other. What they'd been wanting from each other. Because that was tied up with deeper, emotional yearnings, it was possible it might just turn them all to ash when fully unleashed. She didn't think any of them cared.

"You'll finish up by six and join us in the bathroom," Lyda had said, and that was that.

Now it was 6:10, and they were in the bathroom. Lyda had ordered Noah to sit on the commode outside the large Jacuzzi tub in his shorts only. In the same breath she'd commanded Gen to strip. Noah was allowed to give her a steadying hand as she stepped into the tub to kneel between Lyda's legs, but then he had to keep his hands to himself. Their Mistress sat on a shower stool in the steaming water. At Lyda's nod, Gen took up the soap and began to wash the long legs under his avid gaze.

Her limbs had lost muscle tone these past weeks, but Lyda was recovering some of it, with her adherence to the rehab schedule and the water aerobics regimen the doctor was permitting her. Though Lyda grumbled about being part of the old lady water brigade, Gen thought she was actually enjoying it. Now.

Lyda had met many challenges in her life, but dealing with a body incapable of what she demanded from it had not been one of them. The morning of the third class, she hadn't felt well, but she'd insisted on going. Inevitably, she started to feel nauseous and barely made it to the side of the pool. She couldn't make it out in time, but Gen was already ready with the airsickness bag. Lyda lost her breakfast and stood there shivering, her head down. That was when Gen heard a muttered "Fuck" and realized tears were running down her Mistress's face. Lyda had her head bowed to hide them, shoulders clenched like a fist, her anger at her own weakness.

That was when several of the elderly women in the class came over. One of them put a hand on Lyda's back, another touching her shorn hair. "It's all right, honey... You're doing great... Don't you worry about it. We won't tell you how many of us with our weak bladders pee right here in this pool whenever we cough or sneeze. It's a good thing they use lots of chlorine."

Lyda managed a half chuckle, half snort at that, but the tears kept coming. Gen knew it was prescription meds and physical exhaustion, but that didn't matter to Lyda. Afraid her Mistress might drown herself rather than show weakness, Gen was down on her knees on the edge of the pool, folding her arms around her.

Of course, proving her theory, that just made Lyda stiffen like a board. The women exchanged a look, a message sent and received.

"All right then." One gave Lyda a brisk pat. "If you're all done here, come back over and join us. We're trying an Isadora Duncan move today and you're going to be the center of the flower. Think you're up to standing still?"

Lyda used her forearm to swipe impatiently at the tears. "Don't baby me."

"Baby you? Honey, I was a combat nurse in Vietnam. If you think a little vomiting's going to get you out of this, you have another think coming. When new nurses fainted, I just threw water in their faces and barked at them to get their asses up off the ground."

Lyda gave Gen's hand a squeeze to tell her she was okay and went back into the class. Over the subsequent weeks, the women never stopped encouraging her in their practical way. Over time it was clear Lyda was both deeply moved by their compassion and quietly humbled by it, a new look for her. Some of the women brought things to Gen to help "fatten her up". One day, reading a magazine and waiting for Lyda to finish, Gen was amused to see one of the ladies point to her and whisper to her friend, "I'm pretty sure she's with her, Brigitte. As in *with* her."

You bet your ass, she'd thought, surprised by how strongly she meant it. *But wouldn't you be surprised if you knew that wasn't all of it?* She had a spurt of devilish intent, imagining Noah coming to a class with them.

Tuning back into the present, because there was no place she'd rather be when Lyda was naked, wet and slippery with soap, she worked her way up her legs.

"Be mindful of our audience, rabbit." Lyda gazed down at her, reflecting the sensual mischief Gen had just been experiencing.

As Lyda spread her legs and grasped the shower bar, Gen washed between her legs...very thoroughly. Slow rotations, teasing the labia with her fingers, rubbing over the clit as Lyda sighed. Gen wasn't sure she was strong enough for an orgasm, but she could obviously enjoy arousal.

The bruising on Noah's ribs had disappeared, but he'd had a nasty, deep gash caused by the broken glass of the rear window raking down his back as the car dropped from around him. The stitches had been removed, but the scar would be permanent. She'd noticed it had bisected *Yours Unconditionally*, taking out the "un". She wasn't sure if he'd noticed that, but she'd been far more concerned with how close that gash had come to cutting through his spine.

Noah had been shirtless around Lyda a few times, especially on the nights he'd taken his turn on the master bedroom couch where he could watch over her, but Gen wasn't sure if Lyda had marked the change, either. Tonight was the first time since the accident that any of them would be indulging in slow, leisurely...noticing.

She wanted to touch every inch of Lyda, not just the parts Noah might find more fascinating to see her touch. The good thing was that she could please all of them, at her own pace. So she took her time working up to Lyda's breasts. Once there, she cupped them, spreading her fingers out over their shape, noting the weight, the color of the nipples, the areolae, the track of her breastbone up to her throat. She noticed every wound, though all had healed well enough the stitches were gone.

She flattened her palms onto her shoulders, slid her thumbs into the crevices of collarbone, over the base of the throat, her nape, then she was close, sliding her hands down Lyda's back, along her shoulder blades as Lyda put an arm around her, fingers stroking Gen's hip. She brought her down for a brush of lips.

"You've gotten possessive on me."

It was then Gen realized she'd started murmuring as she stroked Lyda's body. Two words. Repeated at the same floating pace of the steam swirling around them.

"Mine. Ours."

Lyda didn't seem offended. More bemused. Gen turned her attention to the right arm, now healed enough to be brace free. She soaped it to slickness, taking care with every individual finger, elbow, armpit, the beating pulse of her wrist.

"You're putting Noah into a trance," Lyda observed with a light smile, though her eyes were serious.

Gen paused, resting her hand and the soap on Lyda's thigh to twist around. He was sitting on the closed commode lid, back straight, hands on his thighs. The lust in his expression was eclipsed by a yearning that matched what Gen was feeling as she savored every inch of their Mistress.

"I need someone to do my feet while you do my back. Don't you think?" Lyda glanced down at her.

"Definitely," Gen said. Lyda gave her an affectionate caress.

"My pets are never selfish. They're always willing to share with one another. I like that. Noah, take off your clothes and come join us. Do my feet."

Noah slid off the boxers, the only thing he'd been wearing in anticipation of his own shower. He had to work the waistband over his erection, which they watched in appreciation. Gen angled the spray so she could move around to wash Lyda's back while he took her place. Kneeling between Lyda's feet, he took a second bar of soap from the basket to work on the arches and heels, massaging them so the woman leaned back, head cradled on Gen's breasts, eyes half closed in bliss as he worked magic.

As Gen slid against her Mistress' soap-slick skin, Lyda reached back, gripping her buttock so Gen rubbed her mound against her lower back. "Nice," Lyda said in a throaty voice. Gen worked soap up her neck, behind her ears, inside the delicate shells. Then Lyda tipped back her head and Gen angled the spray to wet her short hair.

"Only need about a drop of shampoo for that," Lyda observed, eyes closed, water droplets running over her cheeks, her lips. Gen wanted to suck every bead off them, but worked the shampoo into the baby soft thatch instead.

"I love the color. It has even more gold in it, like fire light."

"Stop at my knees, Noah." Lyda tapped his hand as Noah's fingers started drifting up her thighs. "You don't get that until later. And only if you're very, very good. Do you think he knows how to be that good, Gen?"

"Well, he is male, and not entirely housetrained." When she shot him a teasing look, he gave her a deliberately not-housetrained expression. "Though he does look like he did when he wanted to spank me."

"I'll bet." Lyda reached out blind, found his face. Noah nuzzled her, closing his fingers over her wrist to apply the talents of his tongue to her palm. A tremor of arousal went through Lyda, echoed in Gen's own body. But her Mistress wasn't going to let them control things tonight. As soon as Gen finished rinsing her hair, Lyda drew her hand back and prodded Noah with her toe, setting him back as she straightened.

"That's enough of that. Gen, help me dress. Noah, take our place in the shower and then go get your things out of the guesthouse. You can get dressed in the guest bath." Her gaze met his. "From now on, I want you both staying in the house."

His face had that hard-to-read expression, but he nodded. "Yes Mistress."

Lyda gave them a sweeping look. "Remember, when you're deciding what to wear tonight, I expect proof that my pets want their Mistress."

Wanting Lyda was as inevitable as wanting air to breathe. A feeling that became more agonizing for Gen when they'd left the shower and Lyda decided her foundation garments for the night would be a black corset and sheer black panties that hinted at the folds of her sex. The tiny sparkles sprinkled over the fabric enhanced the tempting look. After his shower, Noah was called to help with the lacing. Gen had helped Lyda into the short black skirt that went under it, so their Mistress stood unsteadily in just that, holding onto Gen's hands, while Noah arranged the ties in back.

Watch this, Lyda mouthed, giving Gen a wink.

Gen had seen Chloe lace up a corset before, and though the girl knew what she was doing, it was a pull, adjust, pull adjust, tie-off process that could take a few minutes. Apparently, Noah put all the adjustment into the front end of the process, his brow creased, his eyes intent as he worked. When he finally said "Ready?" Lyda met Gen's gaze and tightened her grip on Gen's hands.

Noah pulled the corset tight in one, smooth pull that nipped in Lyda's waist, pushed her breasts upward, and gave her hips that appealing flare.

The breath that left Lyda from the expert adjustment was no more about the hold of the corset than the one that left Gen, just watching it. Lyda gave her a knowing, amused look. "Any thoughts about what you want to wear tonight?"

If she owned a corset, that question would have been answered in a heartbeat. But Lyda had a solution. And a mandate.

"There's a waist cincher in the bottom drawer of my lingerie chest. It will fit you. Have Noah put that on you first. It's soft enough to wear under your clothes, and he loves the look. It will make his cock so hard he'll be trying to figure out what he can wear tonight without embarrassing himself. Won't you?" She reached behind her to caress Noah's face. When he pressed a kiss to her bare shoulder, she put her temple against his jaw before shrugging him away with casual indifference. It was entirely deceptive, since Gen saw anything but apathy in Lyda's eyes as she sent him off to get dressed.

Lyda glanced in the mirror, frowned. "Fuck. I look like a scarecrow."

"No, you don't. You need to put on ten more pounds, but you look way healthier now than you did a few weeks ago. I promise."

Lyda gave her a wry look. "Are you reassuring your Mistress?"

"Sometimes she gets insecure too. Rare as a lightning strike, but it can happen."

Lyda snorted. Gen brought her the bolero jacket she wanted to wear over the corset, and then they accessorized with silver earrings and necklace with a tiny diamond pendant. Gen hadn't been giving Lyda empty praise. Yes, she was still too thin and pale, but she was getting healthier. A few weeks ago she *had* looked like a scarecrow. Now she was an ethereal Fae queen, fragile and yet mesmerizing, inspiring protectiveness and a desire to be as close to her as possible. She wouldn't share that, though. Lyda would laugh at her.

When she noticed Lyda looking a little drained from the shower, she coaxed her to sit on the edge of the bed.

"Shoes are a challenge." Lyda stared in the closet. "I want to wear heels, but the doctor says the left leg needs to be about six months stronger. Barbarian."

"Well, he's probably thinking more about protecting your leg than what you should wear to dinner."

"That's what happens when a man sees you vomiting and bleeding and your head shaved." Lyda gave a mock shudder. "I have no power over him."

"Not true." Moving to the closet, Gen studied the racks of shoes. "Noah saw all of those things, and he couldn't wait to be at your feet tonight. But then, when someone loves you, you always have power over them, for good or bad."

When Lyda got quiet, Gen bit her lip. "I know he hasn't said it, but I think it's true." Based on what she was starting to believe love was, she was getting pretty convinced that saying the words weren't what made it real to the parties involved.

"You didn't say anything wrong, Gen." Lyda grimaced as she shifted on the bed. The crash had wrenched her back and neck, sometimes bringing painful twinges. Gen had learned not to make a big deal out of them, but she made a mental note to suggest a pain killer to Lyda before they left. She knew their Mistress wanted tonight to be pleasurable. The trick was going to be getting her not to overdo so she had the energy to do what she wished. While that would be to Gen and Noah's benefit, Gen wasn't really thinking about the selfish side of things. She thought they all needed it tonight.

"How about the black flats with the quarter-inch heel?" Lyda sighed. "At least they give my feet a nice shape, and they're rubber-soled."

"What if we use the transport chair tonight, and you can wear these?" Gen lifted the black spike heels Lyda had been eyeing as her preferred choice to show off her legs, scars or no.

"I'm not clueless, Gen."

Gen blinked innocently, said nothing. Lyda's lips quirked. "All right, rabbit. But the only reason I'm agreeing is I want the reason I collapse tonight to be because of what I do to you and Noah."

"And we appreciate your agreeable nature, rare though it is."

"Little bitch. Come here."

Gen brought the shoes. When Lyda extended a foot with royal haughtiness, Gen bent over to slip it on. Then she snapped up straight and fast at the hard, sharp pinch on her bare ass. Nothing wrong with the strength in her Mistress's fingers. "*Ow.*"

"You deserved it," Lyda said. Her gaze slid over Gen, lingered. "I like having a naked servant. I may keep you like this more often." She ran a finger down the inside of Gen's thigh. "It turns you on as well, doesn't it?"

"Yes ma'am." Breathlessness returned as Lyda's finger slid higher, teased her pussy, just a tantalizing touch before she drew away.

"All right. Get me settled in the living room so I can take a little predinner rest while you make yourself pretty for me."

Once she had Lyda on the couch, Gen found the waist cincher, slipped on a robe and went to find Noah. He'd dried his hair and brushed it to silk, catching it on his shoulders with a bronze clip. Slacks and a dress shirt were an appealing look on him. When she sidled up to him, he was tying a thin silk black tie. His light spice cologne teased her senses, along with the rest of the package.

Lyda obviously wanted to heighten sexual tension between them, so teasing touches and lots of innuendo should be okay. At least that was Gen's logic as she cupped him through the slacks, earning a startled look that became heated as she stroked her way up a cock that was immediately attentive to her. "I need help with the waist cincher."

"I'm here to help." His tone promised some very unhelpful distraction.

She'd said beneath Gen's clothes, so Gen took off the robe and stood in front of the guestroom bed, her back to him. As he approached, the currents of air he disturbed sent a shiver through her. His hands landed on her shoulders, caressing. Did he recognize the proprietary message he sent through that grip? She wasn't going to point it out, not wanting to break the sensual hope it created.

"Watching you serve her naked made me crazy as it made her."

"I think that was her plan. I didn't mind it either." When he pressed a kiss to her nape, she drew a shuddering breath. "Waist cincher."

"So you said." He took it from her, turned her to hook the front. He started from the bottom and worked up, the heel of his hand brushing her lower abdomen. When he reached the top, his knuckles were grazing the lower curve of her breasts.

"She wants to drive us insane tonight," he said conversationally.

"It's working."

"Hell, yeah." His lips curved. "But I'm concerned she's not up for it."

"We'll take it easy. Follow her lead. And our own."

When she met his gaze, he nodded. They would care for their Mistress however she needed care. They'd make it work.

He turned her then, started making his adjustments. "Hold onto the bedpost," he said. "How tight do you want it?"

"As tight as you want it."

A muffled chuckle, and a muttered, "Yep, completely crazy," had Gen smiling. But she noticed he also hadn't done what he usually did, deferred to her or Lyda, refusing to acknowledge his own wants.

Then all thought disappeared as she experienced firsthand what Lyda had. *Oh...my.* Their Mistress might be a Domme, but no woman in her right mind could be unaffected by that smooth flow of motion that gave her both the sense of instant restraint at a strong man's hands and a heightened awareness of all her curves. Then there was how tempting the resulting display would be to a man's appreciative gaze. Noah settled his hands on her waist, smoothing over it, checking the fit. She rotated her ass against the front of his slacks and purred, finding his cock straining beneath the fabric.

"Hope you're wearing a jacket. Or you're going to scare women and children. Well, maybe just the children."

"Your ass really needs a handprint to go with that pinch Lyda gave you."

"I'll tell Mom."

He snorted, then his mouth brushed her throat again. Cupping her bare breasts, he pushed his cock against her ass. "God," she whispered. "I want you both so much. I was so afraid...I'd never have that again."

When he pressed his face hard into her hair, she had the impression he'd closed his eyes, caught up in the same emotions she was. Gen had come to his bedside in the hospital as often as needed, touching base with him until he was discharged. Then they'd worked together to care for Lyda. When Gen faltered in worries about their Mistress, he'd been right by her side, helping, letting her lean on him, saying the right things at the right time. There was nothing weak about this man. Just broken in a few places, and they all had that, didn't they?

"Go get dressed," he said roughly, pushing her toward the door.

She was surprised, but when she turned to look at him, he was back at the mirror, working on the tie. As she watched him, he slanted her a glance, and the gaze that slid over her body, naked except for the form-fitting waist cincher, was molten steel.

"If you don't, I'm going to fuck you on all fours like a damn animal, and we're both going to be in a lot of trouble."

She fled.

She chose a cute little black dress whose lined bodice didn't require a bra, and thong panties with a cotton crotch that didn't have a prayer of absorbing her arousal.

When they emerged to take Lyda to dinner, her expression told them she was pleased. As she reached out with both hands, they came to her, forming a circle. Lyda gazed at them. "Mine," she murmured. "My beautiful pets."

They had a wonderful time at the restaurant. It was obviously a celebration of what lay behind them, possibly what lay ahead. Lyda ordered a pasta dish and gelato for dessert, even taking a bite of the chocolate cake Gen ordered and the cannoli Noah wanted. Gen noticed they often caught the intrigued attention of the patrons, probably because Lyda was liberal with her touches, caressing Gen's hair, touching her cheek, laying her palm high on Noah's thigh. Playing footsie with them beneath the table. What they all wanted was the sweet touch of cream in their after-dinner coffee, the steam rising off it like the sexual current running between them.

Finally, Lyda handed her credit card to Noah, giving him a burning look. "Pay for our dinner, Noah. It's time to go home."

Moments later, they were in the car, him driving. Lyda had Gen sit in the back with her, and she quickly discovered her Mistress was not in the mood to be patient. Lyda pulled her over, fingers delving into her hair and destroying the swept-up style as she took over Gen's mouth. Gen moaned against her lips, and gripped Lyda's waist, wanting the body beneath the corset.

"Eyes on the road, Noah," Lyda ordered against Gen's skin. "You listen to us get hot and bothered. You don't get to look until you have us safely home."

"Yes Mistress." But his voice was raw with the thrilling edge of male impatience.

Lyda put her hand beneath Gen's skirt, and Gen gasped as Lyda broke the elastic of the thong's leg opening with one fierce jerk, causing her no constriction as she pressed her fingers beneath it into Gen's soaking pussy. "Ah, there she is. I just shoved four fingers into her cunt, and all she did was tremble, Noah. She wants to be fucked so badly she's hurting for it. But so am I. What do we do about that?"

It was a rhetorical question, one Lyda already had plans to answer, Gen was sure. Which was good, because Noah had all he could do not to run them off the road. Lyda obviously had no post-traumatic issues about being in a car tonight. And with her fingers scissoring up inside her, Gen had no brain cells to answer the question, either.

Lyda wrapped her fingers around Gen's throat, pushing her back against the car seat and tipping her head back so she was staring at the ceiling. Lyda stroked her pounding pulse, held her collared. "Spread your legs as far as they'll go, Gen. Be shameless for me."

When she obeyed, Lyda pushed up under the clit hood, causing an uncomfortable and overwhelming sensation. "Such a sensitive bundle of nerves. You can torture a girl like this, make her feel so aroused yet so overstimulated, it's pain and pleasure at once. Do you want more, Gen?"

"Yes." Gen squeaked as the dual sensations ramped up. "Yes Mistress."

"Better. I'm feeling tyrannical tonight. I've been out of control too long. Who's in charge, Gen? Who owns you?"

"You, Mistress."

"Good." Those fingers stroked, plucked, while Gen writhed, pinned by that hold on her throat. "Noah, she's so beautiful, her legs spread out like that, pretty little skirt pushed up. I can't wait to strip her down to that waist cincher. Do it now, Gen."

Gen pulled the dress over her head, getting rid of it, gasping as Lyda kept her fingers working between her legs. Lyda ripped the side of the thong, finishing the job, leaving Gen in the waist cincher, heels and jewelry.

"Don't speed, Noah. We might have a policeman joining our threesome if he saw Gen like this."

Gen managed to speak. "I don't think Noah is into sharing that way."

Lyda noticed Noah's set jaw, his grip on the wheel. "My pets share with each other, but nobody else." Reaching over the seat, she flicked Noah's neck. "I like that too."

* * * * *

When they pulled into the drive, Gen had lost her mind to full-blown lust. Lyda had kept stroking and teasing her cunt, and the stimulation of that, added to her provocatively naked body in the waist cincher, was enough to have her ready to do anything Lyda wanted, even if it involved farm animals.

When she made that observation, Lyda gave a sexy chuckle. "Don't think I want to share you that way, either, rabbit. She needs to be carried, Noah. Her legs are shaking."

The terrain to the door wasn't smooth. It also wasn't designed for the light transport chair. So when Lyda reached for the cane that had recently replaced her crutches, Gen's glazed eyes met Noah's in the mirror. Lyda anticipated them.

"I can and will do this," she said. "Bring her inside, Noah."

Noah paused. Though they both realized proving herself was important to Lyda, protecting her was equally important to them. So Noah scooped Gen up and brought her to the door as Lyda bid, but he did it fast. By the time Lyda was out of the car and had taken the first step or two with the cane, he was back by her side.

She'd removed the heels, held them hooked on one finger, so he took them from her with gentle courtesy, keeping his gaze on her progress. Lyda kept her eyes on Gen, waiting for them in an outfit designed for one thing—to encourage lots of hot, over-the-top sex. Gen already had the door open.

When they stepped inside, Lyda moved past them, toward the living room. Dropping the keys she'd taken from Gen onto the side table, she dropped into a wing-backed chair. As she placed the cane at her side, Noah and Gen came to her, hand in hand. They sank to their knees before her that way. Gen remembered the first time she'd knelt to Lyda, struggling with what it meant. Now it was pure instinct and desire.

"I'll watch the two of you first." Lyda's voice was low, the command unmistakable, running a thrill up Gen's spine. "Noah, she's yours right now. All yours. You fuck her exactly the way you've been wanting since you laced her up tonight. And Gen...when you don't think you can hold back anymore, you ask *him* for permission."

Lyda had never placed that power in Noah's hands. Gen sensed his surprise, his flicker of uncertainty. But then his gaze slid over to her. Giving him a look under her lashes she intended to be a sexual challenge, bringing him right to the end of a frayed leash, she tipped forward, sank onto her elbows, leaving her hips high in the air. She adjusted her knees wide, the points of her heels facing upward. Adding to the whole erotic quotient, she wrapped both her hands around Lyda's right ankle, her forehead against the tip of Lyda's shoe. She was at both their mercy.

Noah's hand slid along her calf, caressed the muscle. Taking hold of her foot, he slid off one heel, then the other. As she shivered, he teased her ankle with light caresses. Her pussy got wetter.

"She's dripping on the carpet, Mistress."

"Take care of the mess you've made, then."

Gen heard him slip the buckle of his belt, the whisper of the zipper of the slacks parting. Then his hands were on her ass.

"Beg him, Gen."

"Please, Noah. Please fuck me."

He parted her buttocks, played with her rim, then his thumbs dipped into that vat of wetness between her legs. "Please..." She moaned as he rubbed. She knew he was hard as a rock. Knew he was tormenting her further, getting off on it. She gripped Lyda's ankle, trying not to cut off circulation.

Noah straightened, shifting his grip to her hair. His fingers tightened into a scalp-pulling hold as he slowly, slowly brought her head up until she was staring into Lyda's intent expression. She had that faintly cruel, queen-on-her-throne look, feeding off Gen's denial, her frustrated arousal, like a drug available only to royalty.

"She's dying for your cock, Noah. Do it."

Gen screamed as Noah shoved into her all at once, a hard thrust that stretched her unused tissues. It hurt but it felt so, so good. He kept the hold on her hair, forcing her to stare into Lyda's face, so their Mistress could see every expression as he let loose just as she'd given him permission to do. He fucked Gen like a man who'd been nursing a hard-on for weeks, dreaming about the women who were within arm's reach but inaccessible. He fucked her in a way that said it went beyond that, that the need and cravings building all these weeks had as much to do with confirming they were alive, connected, together, still part of him, as anything else.

Similar emotions unfolded in her as he kept going, became even more savage, perhaps fighting the demons inside him that said he wasn't allowed to feel that way. It was as if he was trying to fuck them into silence. When he let go of her hair and covered her, wrapping his arm around her chest, forcing her back down to her elbows as if they were both genuflecting to Lyda while he hammered Gen's cunt before her, Gen kept one hand on Lyda's ankle but gripped his forearm, digging in her nails.

"I'm here...we're here..." It was like the *Mine, ours*, wasn't it? The same message. Her clit was throbbing, and each time his testicles slapped against it, she thrummed with the intensity. She wanted to come. Wanted to come for him, for Lyda. Yet...

"Help...Noah, please..."

"God, yes," he muttered.

It wasn't a surprise to her that he understood, even with the two of them shaking, so close to that edge. When he pulled back out, she even made a heartfelt whimper that was echoed by a violent clench in her pussy. She was so close to climax.

Noah rose on his knees behind her. Gen could only imagine the delicious picture he made, cock stiff, glistening with her juices. His hand slid from her hair, up the slope of her back, to rest on her hip. "We want to give our Mistress pleasure first," he said.

Gen lifted her head to see Lyda lick her lips, gaze shifting between the two of them. "What if that's not what I want? You think I'll let my cunt run the show any more than I'll let the two of you run it?"

"No Mistress." Noah shook his head. "We just... It needs to be...all of us. Together."

"Together," Gen whispered, pressing her lips against Lyda's ankle.

Chapter Sixteen

Lyda bent forward, touching Gen's back. Gen thought she also reached out, grazed Noah's face, or perhaps the slope of his chest, rising and falling with his exertions, the sexual fervor driving him.

"All right," their Mistress said. "But you two better not think this is going to become a habit. Tuck yourself back into those slacks and take Gen to my bed, Noah. On her back. Make her comfortable, because we're going to use her hard."

Gen straightened at that delicious threat, crooking her arm around Noah's neck as he scooped her off the floor. She could have walked, but now that they'd gained Lyda's acquiescence, they wanted to follow everything she demanded. He laid her on the bed, stepped back, those intent eyes resting on her as they waited on their Mistress, making her way down the hall. When she came into the bedroom, she moved to the edge of the bed. Just like Noah, she lingered on Gen's breasts and hips, her sex, all enhanced by the waist cincher. Gen felt like a visual feast, the two of them devouring her.

"I may make you walk around in one of those all the time," Lyda observed. "I don't think Noah would object. But I'd have to keep his cock in a chastity cage to teach him to deal with it without a perpetual hard-on. Can't have his brains in his cock all the time."

"I'm not seeing the downside," Gen responded breathlessly, her gaze sliding down Noah to the sizeable object of the discussion, straining beneath the slacks.

"Hmm." Lyda pivoted toward Noah. "I want my corset off."

Noah helped Lyda slide off the bolero jacket, then unhooked the corset. Since Lyda's back was to Gen, she saw the garment loosen. When he peeled it off her body, Lyda slid her arms under his and stepped into him. Gen noticed her left ankle was trembling, but Noah did too, his arms circling their Mistress in response, holding her up. Other than that, he remained still as her hands roved across his back, down, and took what seemed to be a very firm grip on his ass.

"I'd forgotten how very nice it is to touch you," Lyda said. Noah put his face into her throat, pressing his lips there. Lyda tilted her head, giving him access, and she stroked his hair, releasing the clasp so the glory of that russet mane spilled across his shoulders. Then her hands were between them, loosening his tie, stripping it out of its knot and letting it lie along either panel of his shirt as she unbuttoned it. Gen had seen Noah's bare chest plenty of times, but watching Lyda revealing it an inch at a time made it a whole new experience. Lyda caught both ends of the tie, twisted and held them against his throat, her knuckles pressed into his flesh beneath it.

"You knew you wouldn't survive if you got us out of the car first."

If Noah was startled by the abrupt shift, he rallied fast, jaw tightening. "No, I didn't know. I hoped I would live. But your lives were more important to me than mine."

Lyda brushed her knuckles up his throat, to his jaw. "That's the first time you've done that," she observed, a husky whisper. "In the past, you would have simply said our lives were more important than yours."

His eyes flickered, puzzled. Gen had caught it as well, though. Those two words "to me" were actually quite significant. A man might give his life for a stranger because of moment of conscience, a selfless act. Whereas a person sacrificed his life for a loved one because there was simply no other choice, that very personal, unique connection of love trumping any other consideration of personal value. Because that person being saved was theirs. Their personal, unique person, to watch over, to sacrifice oneself for.

To the person saved, it might not really matter why the person had done it, but in this case, the distinction was extremely important to the two people saved. Gen didn't want to put too much into it, but Lyda pointing it out suggested a further cause for hope, for the future they had together.

With her usual intuition, though, Lyda left it there. She'd turned to other matters. Letting the tie drop to the floor, she pushed his shirt off, hands caressing the roundest part of his shoulders, the muscle groups in his arms, wandering over his pectorals, down to his abdomen to unhook his slacks. "You dressed up for me, didn't you?"

"Yes Mistress."

"Did you put cologne on your balls?" She pressed her bare breasts against his chest then and pushed his slacks down herself, cupping his ass anew. Noah's eyes closed, his hands gripping her waist. Gen savored the beautiful, vulnerable pose.

"Yes," he said.

"Tease. Take the rest of it off."

Lyda stepped back as he complied. While he did, she tugged down the zipper of her skirt, wiggled out of it, let it drop. The swatch of panties followed. Now only Gen wore anything, but the way they both turned to her, their avid gazes drinking in the way she was cinched in the middle like a wrapped piece of candy, she thought Lyda might actually not ever let her wear anything else in the house.

Noah lifted Lyda onto the bed. When she was on it on all fours, she gave him a teasing look over her shoulder. His grimace of near pain amused her as she slid between Gen's legs like a female cat stalking dinner. She dropped a kiss on Gen's mound, making her quiver, then eased her weight fully onto her, pressing her palms on either side of her shoulders.

It speared Gen with desire, longing and a love so strong, tears stung her eyes.

"Look at me, Gen. Let me see what you're thinking."

She lifted her lashes. She started to reach up, but Lyda shook her head. "Un-unh. Over your head. I want to see you stretched out under me, all mine, legs spread, arms out of the way. Full submission, baby girl. Prove who your Mistress is. Say it."

"You," Gen managed, her throat thick. "Yours." Lyda's gaze softened, and then she slid her pussy against Gen's, a welcome, a renewal, a reacquaintance. Gen shuddered, and Lyda did it again. Gen tilted her hips up, bringing wetness against wetness. Lyda bent, put her mouth on Gen's breast. It pressed her knees into the bed between Gen's and likely tilted up Lyda's hips, if Noah's suppressed groan was any indication.

"Noah, why is my pussy empty? Your cock is supposed to be in it."

If he could have leaped on the bed, Gen thought he would have. As it was, he was behind Lyda in a blink. As he banded his arm firmly around her waist, his gaze met Gen's over Lyda's shoulder. That hold wasn't incommensurate with his desires, but he knew, as she did, Lyda's right arm wasn't going to bear her own weight for long. They could care for her as she cared for them. As they cared for each other.

"Slow and easy. I want to feel every blissful inch. You move with me as I move with Gen. We'll see how good your coordination is." Lyda gave Gen a wink, though Gen saw the strain around her mouth, evidence of shuddering arousal. "Men tend to be hammer and nail, whereas we girls know the pleasure of taking the winding road." She demonstrated with another lazy rotation against Gen's pussy that had her gasping, lifting up to her Mistress.

She knew when Noah pushed into Lyda that blissful inch at a time, because she saw the tightening of her facial features, the arch of her body, felt the quiver that went through her. Since Noah was standing on his knees behind Lyda, Gen also saw his muscle groups tighten, his absorption in the way being inside his Mistress felt.

Gen dug into the headboard as Lyda kept up that friction between them, using the slickness to intensify it. And Noah, bless his ability to follow a meandering road, figured out the rhythm that brought them together, a mix of hammer and nail thrusting and spirals that built in speed and intent as the three of them created a symphony of shifting bodies, gasping breaths, soft pleas, harsh grunts, muttered oaths. It was the pleasure of making love and fucking at once, of being together and being alive.

"I can't…" Gen had been so close before, and now, the two of them were a force she couldn't resist. "Mistress, please…may I come?"

"What do you think, Noah?" Lyda let out a small moan Gen treasured as Noah punctuated her question with a powerful thrust. He set his teeth to Lyda's throat.

"Yes. Fuck, God. Let her go, Mistress." He shook his head. "Let her go over."

Lyda met Gen's gaze. "A fine distinction, Noah. Go over for us, Gen."

With Lyda stimulating her with every intentional and indirect movement of her body, the latter thanks to Noah's efforts, Gen exploded into the climax. That delicious rush of fluid bathed her labia, spurted against Lyda's cunt. It would slide through those slick folds and pool against Noah's testicles. Gen let the thought add to the searing pleasure of everything that came crashing down on her then. She had only one thing she wanted more.

"Please..." She wailed it as she fell over that cliff's edge. "You...two...come...too."

There would be very few times she'd ever be able to order Lyda around. But this desperate demand was the one exception. Lyda's flesh convulsed against her, her face going rigid with pleasure. But Gen also saw and felt the strain that gripped their Mistress, as she tried so hard to fly...and came up short.

"Noah," Gen gasped.

Noah, as melded to them as if he stood inside both their souls, adjusted the band of his arm and his stance, so he supported even more of Lyda's weight. At the same moment, Gen disobeyed her Mistress. She put her hands against Lyda's shoulders, and lifted her hips, taking over that spiraling motion. It gave Lyda the support her still healing body needed to catch the wave of the climax, ride its power with them.

Linked like that, they tumbled into bliss.

* * * * *

Gen laid a slice of the gourmet Colby cheese blend in the frying egg, checking on the toast in the warmer as she did so. Lyda was reading at the kitchen table and sipping her coffee as she was wont to do when she was first waking up. Even before the accident, Sunday morning was the one day she deviated from her regimented schedule. No exercise on that day, and she allowed herself one indulgence, toasted thick wheat bread she bought from a locally run bakery that made the stuff from scratch. She spread natural blackberry preserves on it. Since having it the first time, Gen wasn't sure why anyone would buy sliced, packaged bread again.

She glanced out the window, where she occasionally glimpsed Noah around the greenhouses. He was doing the minimum necessary daily check on the stock and irrigation. Lyda cared for her more delicate tropical plants like children, tending them so carefully they were delivered to customers without even a blemished leaf.

"Come look at this."

Turning the heat down on the omelet, Gen came to her side. Lyda was considering adding hardscape features to her landscape design offerings, so was perusing an array of images on her tablet. "I searched on erotic statuary."

Gen chuckled. "You're going to start a trend of erotic lawn art in the Tampa area?"

"No. Smartass." Lyda slid an arm around Gen's thighs, knuckles stroking her hip as Gen leaned against her. "This is for my own gardens. I liked some of the things I saw at Tyler's place last time I was there. I don't have his budget, of course."

"There are Saudi princes who wish they had his budget." Gen bent closer to look at the picture on the tablet. "That's...oh. Well."

The piece showed two very handsome, muscular nude males having sex, one pressed down on all fours while the other was buried inside him. A woman was stretched out on her hip on a low brick wall beside them, as if they were copulating in a garden setting. She was naked as well, but in a position and with an expression that said she was in charge of them both. Her foot, dangling off the wall, was brushing against the back and hip of the man on top. Her other hand was tangled in the bottom man's hair, fingers gripped tight.

"It's a J. Martin," Lyda said. "Actually..." She enlarged the picture on the screen. "J. Martin and Thomas Wilder. A collaboration."

"Oh. Wow. Well, it's gorgeous, but you can't afford a J. Martin. Not unless you sacrifice every penny of next year's profits."

"Since when are you an art aficionado?" Lyda scoffed.

Lyda had stumbled this morning getting out of bed and wrenched her still weak ankle, which probably explained why she sounded a little cranky. Or maybe she wasn't cranky. She was just teasing Gen in that edgy way of hers.

That was what Gen told herself, even as that part of her that never reacted well to moments like this curled into a defensive ball.

"Even us trailer park trash occasionally read an article," she said, retreating back to the stove. She was past this stuff. She should be past this stuff.

"Hey."

She lifted her head, found Lyda pinning her with a look. "Where did that come from?"

"Sorry. Knee-jerk reaction. I know you didn't mean it that way. Forget it."

"I won't. Come back here."

"This will burn." She flipped the omelet, turned off the stove. Picking up the hand towel, she shook her head. "I mean it, can we just forget it? I don't know why I said something that dumb."

"Neither do I. Which is why I want to know why." Lyda extended a hand. Still imperious, but something kinder in her expression that had Gen reluctantly coming to her, letting her hand be taken. Lyda reached up, touched her face. "What the hell, rabbit?"

Gen sighed, wishing she could just throw the towel over her head. "It was your tone of voice. I know you were teasing or just irritable. I have this weird trigger about things like that. I *know* you didn't mean it. Old stuff, you know?"

Lyda studied her, then pulled her down to eye level, pushing a lock of hair over Gen's ear, tugging it before she settled her hand on her shoulder, thumb sliding along the base of her throat. "Okay. But it's not the first time I've seen you do that. Despite how accomplished you are, you think because I'm better educated or grew up with more money, that I look down on you."

That grip on her throat tightened. "A Domme cherishes her subs, rabbit. *Cherishes.* They're not here for her to kick around to make her feel more superior. Except Noah, when I'm in a bad mood. Then I have you to kick my ass for that."

Despite the grim humor, Lyda's gaze stayed piercing. "That was your last free pass. You put yourself down in front of me or where I hear about it again, I'll be kicking *your* ass. Got it?"

Gen pressed her lips together, nodded.

"Good girl." Lyda's touch eased to a distracting caress between Gen's breasts, with a quick tug on the connecting point between the cups of her bra, accessible from the vee neckline. "Now, truth. How did you know that about J. Martin? You cut your eyes away when you mentioned an article, and that's what you do when you're not telling the whole truth."

She and Noah should take Lyda to Vegas. They could probably come home capable of affording ten J. Martins. "How about *quid pro quo*?" Gen rallied. "You tell me where you and Marguerite went the other day?"

On Wednesday, Lyda had told Gen and Noah to watch over the nursery business while she ran an errand. She was driving again, but only short trips. One, because she still tired easily and two, despite her great annoyance with herself about it, she was still skittish behind the wheel in heavy traffic. Noah offered to take her, but Lyda declined the offer. "I have a ride."

A half hour later, Marguerite drove into the nursery. While Noah went into the house to let Lyda know she was here, Gen had approached the open window of Marguerite's BMW. The 320i was past its prime, but Marguerite refused to get rid of it, citing the fact she wasn't going to buy a modern BMW that had the same body as any other car on the road. When the engine had reached three hundred thousand miles, Tyler had given her a brand new engine for a Christmas present.

"Hey," Gen said, glad to see her former boss. She stopped by Tea Leaves at least once a week, and she and Chloe met for lunch frequently, but she was still getting used to the idea that Marguerite had already predicted. She was likely not coming back to Tea Leaves. Last week, Lyda had offered her a job officially — assistant manager, underscoring how quickly Gen was learning the business and earning her Mistress's trust in her.

"Congratulations on the promotion," Marguerite said. Gen had of course called Marguerite and Chloe after it happened, so they knew, but it was the first time one of them had seen her in her new capacity.

"Thanks," Gen said. "I haven't screwed up badly enough to be fired, yet."

"You won't. But my offer still stands, Gen. No matter what happens, you will always have a job with me if you want or need it."

Unspoken — If this relationship doesn't work out. Fortunately Gen saw nothing but sincere hope for her in Marguerite's gaze.

With her power of prediction, if Gen had read a warning, she would have been terrified. More terrified than she was already, taking such a large leap into so many unknowns. But her usual caution about such things was something she'd left behind. As nervous as she might be about unknowns, she felt more strongly about backtracking.

Lyda came out of the house, Noah helping her down the stairs before she took over for herself with the cane. Gen spoke to Marguerite, low. "She's leaning on that less all the time, but she still tries to overdo, M. You can tell when she does, because the ankle gets shaky."

Marguerite arched a brow. "I'll take care of her. But I'd advise you not to try to handle a Mistress too much. It tends to piss us off."

Gen grinned. "Like I didn't already know that, working for you as long as I have?"

The flash of surprise in Marguerite's gaze — Gen hadn't been the type to joke about the Dom/sub dynamics before — was replaced by an amused look. "Careful. I might tell her what you said. And ask to bear witness to the consequences."

Gen flushed, though the idea of M being at the club when she, Noah and Lyda were there didn't discomfit her as much as it might have at one time. Inside the Dom/sub world, things tended to get tangled and intertwined, an arousing playground.

Noah helped Lyda into the car. As the two Mistresses drove off, he glanced at her. "Do we know what that's about?"

"Not a clue."

A call to Chloe had revealed nothing further about their errand. When Lyda had returned home, she refused to discuss it further. However, whatever she'd been doing had fueled her in other ways, because that night she'd driven both Gen and Noah to sweaty, replete exhaustion. The next day, she took her first short walk without the cane.

Coming back to the present, Gen suspected all these changes she was making to her life — new relationship, new job — were what had stirred that debris from her past. She'd made those insecurities work for her, driving her further education and attempts to improve herself, but whenever change happened, it made her vulnerable to that baggage. But no more. Lyda was right. She was past that.

"I will not tell you what Marguerite and I were doing," Lyda said. "Fairness has no place in a Mistress-sub relationship. Spill about J. Martin, or I'll eat my breakfast on your stomach and stab you with my fork."

When it came to a battle of wills, on most things, Lyda was going to be the victor, because that was the way it worked — the way Gen needed it to be, truth be told. As Noah had said, the why was better explained through emotion than thought.

"I'll tell you, but you have to swear to keep it to yourself, because it's a giant secret we're not supposed to talk about, since J. Martin doesn't do any public appearances. Tyler and he are good friends. Really good friends. And Tyler also knows Thomas."

"No shit?" Lyda's brows rose. "Would J. Martin give me a discount if I met him at Tyler's?"

Gen gave Lyda a light thwap with the towel. "Geez. You have a one-track mind."

"Which is why I'm a successful businesswoman," Lyda said, unperturbed. "You didn't answer the question."

"If you can get him off by himself, maybe." Pretty certain. The other thing Gen knew, because she'd met Josh at Marguerite's wedding, was that he was a submissive. A hot, distracted, entirely appealing submissive, totally in love with and faithful to his Mistress and wife, Lauren. However, if a Mistress like Lyda got him off by himself, the miniscule business acumen he had about the price of his art would be obliterated under the spell of those riveting eyes. "But while his art broker's around, not a chance. Marcus is more ruthless than even you. And he's Thomas' husband." He was also a Master as formidable as Tyler and beautiful as Lucifer. Even though Marcus was irrevocably gay, he could still make a woman shiver when his gaze turned upon her.

She'd probably share any and all of that with Lyda at some point. Despite her mercenary nature, Lyda could be trusted with a secret. But now Gen's attention was distracted by something different, out the kitchen window.

A man was walking up to the front of the nursery. The gate was locked at the end of the drive, as it always was on their closed days, so he must have left his car there. Lyda had a separate drive to the house for her personal guests. As Noah came out of the greenhouse, apparently seeing the man's approach, it was clear he knew who it was. From the rigidity of his stance, the look in his eyes, and the resulting cold spike through Gen's chest, she guessed pretty quickly herself. Lyda confirmed it, following Gen's gaze out the window.

"Elias."

Gen thought the only reason she beat Lyda to the door was her Mistress's residual limp. She heard Lyda call out to her to wait. She might have listened, but once she came out on the porch, there was no chance of that. As she stepped out, Elias had reached Noah. No words were spoken that she saw. The man punched Noah in the face, hard enough Noah stumbled, went to one knee.

Gen didn't remember leaving the porch, didn't remember closing the ground between them. She was just suddenly in between them, with the shovel she'd retrieved on the way clenched in both hands. Noah hadn't even raised his hands, hadn't even closed them into fists to defend himself.

Gen didn't know enough about fighting to use fists, but she knew enough about dirty self-defense tactics from Marguerite to know how useful a heavy blunt object was. She was vaguely aware of a shout as she swung the shovel toward Elias' head, rage driving every action, muting every rational thought.

She was brought up short, the handle of the shovel caught in a strong, capable hand, another arm wrapped around her waist, hauling her back. Noah. Noah had stopped her swing, was pulling her back. Strong enough to stop her, but unwilling to use any of that strength to protect himself.

"Don't you touch him," she snarled. Elias had taken a self-preserving step back, had gone white enough to give her a spurt of satisfaction. She had a further impression of streaked brown hair, blue eyes. Elias was handsome, strong-looking, possessing the build of a man who'd probably played sports in high school or college. Ten years older than Noah, maybe. He wore slacks and dress shirt, a tie, as if he was on the way to a business meeting. Or, being Sunday, maybe coming from church, an odd thought for the moment. *Hey, I'll stop by after the service on love-my-neighbor and beat up the submissive kid who pissed me off.*

"Gen." Noah said it urgently enough she hesitated. "No. He has the right."

"No, he doesn't," she snapped at him.

"He's a grown man who knows what he's doing," Elias said. He had a voice like a DJ's, smooth and deep. She hated it. Hated him. "Move out of the way."

"Not in this lifetime, you piece of shit."

But Noah put her on her feet, still holding her firmly, and moved her out from between them. "No," Gen resisted him. "Noah."

"This is my choice, Gen."

The words tore through the rage, ripped into her heart. No. They were past this, weren't they? She couldn't accept this, couldn't allow it to destroy every hopeful thought she'd had about their progress together, the three of them, since Gatlinburg. Lyda wouldn't take less than all of him. She couldn't. It didn't matter what she said about Noah and crossed wires. Gen knew her enough now, knew it would eventually break the link that held Noah to them. And that link was vital to all of them.

"It's a stupid choice." She put her hands on his face. "Why can't you see this isn't love? I love you. Lyda loves you. Yeah, she might not have said it, but in the way she acts toward you, treats you… Goddamn it, she loves you. And so do I. I won't stand by and let someone take advantage of you, hurt you like this. Don't you understand that?"

He tried to move her again. She dug in her heels, gripped his arms to hold him. He'd have to drag her. She clung to rage, because otherwise she'd have to bear the horrible truth that the past few weeks had been a false happiness. The unresolved issue was right here, ignored but never gone, patiently waiting to ambush them all. The wall was still behind his eyes, never gone, just obscured by her idealism, which was once again leading her to heartbreak. *Don't do this to me. To us. To Lyda.*

"Can you not understand that you owe it to people who truly love you to love them back? To choose them? There's no greater gift you can give us, than to lay yourself all out there for that one…or two…specific people, and let them know that your heart and soul is unconditionally *theirs*. Not just any asshole who comes along." She was poking a stick right into that rage-trigger, but she didn't care. The alternative was unthinkable.

"You just said it," he said, his chin set, gaze dispassionate. "My choice. Please stand aside, Gen. If you have any regard for me, step aside."

She looked toward the porch. Lyda stood there, leaning on the cane. She had that locked expression Gen knew too well. It cut her heart to ribbons.

"Come here, Gen," Lyda said, holding out a hand. "Come to me."

"No." It was a broken plea. It became even more excruciating when she saw the strain around Lyda's tight mouth, the terrible knowledge in her eyes. *There is a wire crossed in his mind...* Those goddamn, fucking crossed wires.

"Fine. *Fine.*" She thrust away from Noah, turned on him. "You'd sacrifice your life for us, but you won't fucking choose us. You'd break our hearts rather than do that. That's worse than letting us die, Noah. But if that's what your fucked-up brain says to do, then go with him. Don't wait for Lyda to let you go, because if she does let you go, it's because you forced her to let you go. She knows she doesn't deserve to be treated like this by you. Neither of us do."

He was flinching as if she was hitting him with the shovel now, but she wouldn't stop. She had two people in her life to protect, one at her back and one at her front. The one at her front needed to hear the truth of it, even if it never sank into his broken mind. The one behind her might deny ever needing Gen's defense, but Gen had been inside Lyda deeply enough now to know there were parts of their formidable Mistress that were as capable of being hurt and destroyed as anyone else. Especially when she opened herself to love, as she had.

"If he beats you, kills you, that won't be the real tragedy, Noah. It's that he'll eat your soul, because he doesn't really know what it means to love you. To accept you as who you are. You deserve that, you're smarter than this. I spent years of my life figuring it out, years I'll never get back."

She stepped up to him. She knew his body well enough to jerk the shirt up and reach behind him to find it without searching. Her hand landed on that scar, the one that had bifurcated *Yours* and *unconditionally*, and erased the "un". "Love can be given unconditionally, but the recipient should *never* accept it that way. They should spend their lives working for it, because that kind of love deserves to be earned. It has to be. You don't value what you don't have to earn, even if it's a gift."

"Gen." Lyda's voice was quiet, firm. "Come here. Be with me."

Gen stared up into Noah's face. He wasn't looking at her. He was looking at Elias. Despairing, she looked over her shoulder. Elias was staring at him, absorbed in Noah's response. Neither one of them was aware of her anymore. She had no idea who that made her want to hit with the shovel more, Noah or Elias.

Making her feet move was like dragging concrete blocks across the grass, but her heart was the heaviest load of all. She looked toward the only solace capable of keeping her from crumpling. Though Lyda's face was as smooth and dispassionate as it always was in such moments, that mask was no longer opaque to Gen. Beneath it, she saw Lyda's understanding, her compassion…the suffering they shared.

Lyda was an island, yes. A strong, remarkable island reserved in expressing her emotions, but she had them. She was just a different language to learn, as Noah was a different language, as Chloe and Marguerite were different languages. And yet all of those languages had a word for love, for tears, for loss, disappointment and pain.

She mounted the stairs. She wanted the men to go. She didn't want to see what Elias did next or worse, Noah. But she wasn't to be given that reprieve.

"Again," Noah said.

She turned to see he now stood where Gen had stood, where he'd stood before Elias had hit him in the face that first time. Elias arched a brow. "Penance?"

Noah said nothing. Elias landed another direct punch in his face and Noah went down again. She saw the spurt of blood from his mouth as he fell to one knee.

Lyda gripped Gen's arm, held her in place when Gen surged forward. She used enough pressure to push Gen down onto the top stair. "Stop this," Gen begged her. She gripped Lyda's leg, hard. "Call the police. Tell Elias to leave. Please."

Lyda leaned over enough to keep a firm hand on her shoulder. Though she assumed Lyda had heard her, her Mistress kept her attention locked on Noah. When Gen shifted her gaze back toward Noah, she saw he looked toward Lyda when he got up, before he turned back to Elias. Noah spat blood on the ground.

"Again."

Gen bit back a scream of frustration. Lyda sank down in a porch chair, which allowed her hand to stay on Gen's shoulder, holding tight, fingers tangled in Gen's T-shirt collar.

Elias gave him a narrow look. "That's starting to sound like an order, Noah."

When Elias hit him this time, Gen heard a bone crunch. She cried out. Noah staggered backward, but this time he didn't fall. Instead, he shook his head to clear it of the pain and stepped up once more. When he lifted his head, his nose was bleeding. Lyda had her arm banded over Gen's chest, Gen straining against the hold.

Elias was looking a little uneasy, even if the expression was mixed with an unhealthy dose of satisfaction at his display of power. As Lyda had intimated, Noah was his drug of choice. Gen felt sick.

"Noah."

Thank God, Lyda spoke. Her tone bore that severe edge Gen knew meant she was at the end of her tolerance. Glancing up, Gen saw her silver eyes had gone to ice. From his startled glance, it was clear Elias realized she'd included him in her displeasure.

The only one who hadn't changed expression was Noah. Except for the brief, involuntary reaction to pain, he was as dispassionate as Lyda in her most ruthless moment. "Once more," he said softly. "And then it's done."

Though Gen felt like he was speaking to Lyda, he was looking at Elias.

Elias's jaw tightened. "You've asked for punishment before."

"The punishment should fit the crime. That's what you always told me."

"I'll do one more, and that's it. If she's letting you go, then you come back with me to New Orleans as promised. Tonight. I have plans for that bleeding mouth."

Noah said nothing. He waited. Despite the power of that last punch, he didn't even appear to brace himself.

It happened so fast, Gen couldn't follow it. Elias threw the punch, but it never connected. Instead Noah was holding his fist in a tight grip, having caught it like a pitcher snagging a line drive straight from the mound.

Finally, his expression changed.

Dispassion became all about passion. Lips peeled back from his teeth and he twisted the arm, stomping the back of Elias's knee as his former Master's body spun from the force and Noah drove him to his knees. Gen heard a crack and knew she was hearing some portion of Elias's arm break, his hoarse cry confirming it. Noah followed him down to the ground, landing on one knee behind him, holding his head to the dirt, pressing it there. Keeping him still, immobile. A shudder ran through his body, a quiver of energy that Gen saw translated to his calloused palm, the strength he held there, the force. Noah would crush his head with only the power of what boiled inside of him.

"*Noah.*"

Lyda's tone could have pierced a full force gale. Which was what was needed to bring Noah's head up. As his eyes found her, Gen saw that terrible, deadly rage. "Stop," their Mistress said. A simple, not-to-be-disobeyed command.

When Lyda squeezed her shoulder, Gen picked up on the cue. "Noah," she repeated. She put all her feelings into it, everything she'd felt when she'd raged at him before, the same passion for a different purpose. To save him from himself. "Noah."

As the scale teetered, Noah on the verge of a life-altering decision, Gen clung to the memory of Dot's words, how he'd never hurt a living being, and prayed for that to win out against the fury, a lifetime of suppressed anger that now pulsed off him like poisonous radiation.

God help her, if they couldn't stop him, if he crushed Elias's head, she knew she would dig the hole herself to bury the body, cover up that crime, protect Noah. Even knowing, with despair, he'd never allow her to do that.

His gaze shifted between them. After a tense moment, he eased Elias' face off the ground. He stepped away from him, stared at the man in the dirt for another weighted second before he at last moved toward him again. Gen held her breath, but this time Noah eased Elias up, back into a sitting position on his heels. As he steadied him, then helped him to his feet, Noah was as gentle with him as he'd been brutal moments before.

"I'll take you to the hospital," Noah said. "We'll get your arm and my nose fixed at the same time."

Elias was blinking at him like an animal stunned by a glancing blow from a car. "I belong to them now," Noah said. "I choose them. I don't want to be with you again. Now or ever."

Gen's relief was so strong it was dizzying. Lyda's steadying hold was still on her shoulder, so she gripped her fingers, drew strength from the return pressure.

Elias cradled his arm, his brow creased. "Why did you let me hit you?"

"Punishment. For allowing you to mistreat her property. Her guest house, the bed." Noah paused, shifted his gaze to Lyda's. "And me."

* * * * *

Gen wanted to drive them to the hospital. She was terrified this new side of Noah would disappear and he and Elias would disappear together. But Lyda said it had to be this way. That they had to trust.

It told Gen she'd never make a good Mistress. She didn't have the will power to be that hands off. She was a middle ground. Under Lyda's direction, she had a touch of Domme and a lot of submissive. However anyone wanted to define it, it didn't really matter.

Lyda made her come to the nursery office with her. Though they were closed today, Lyda had her work up some invoices, do paperwork with her. It kept them busy, but there wasn't a lot of conversation. Gen nursed a hope laced with fear, because it didn't seem quite finished. It wouldn't feel done until Noah came back. Gen knew they were both listening for Noah's return. Noah carried a cell phone while on deliveries, one that Lyda had insisted he carry. When Lyda let Gen call it, it rang under a stack of papers on top of the file cabinet.

"He's always forgetting it." Lyda sighed. "I've threatened to put a collar on him and lock the cell phone to it like a dog's license tag so he'll remember it."

Gen held his phone in her hand, imagining the warmth of Noah's palm. "Are you worried he won't come back?"

Lyda spun her pen on the desk, a meditative movement. "Yes. But he chose, Gen."

"What if it's a one-time thing, and being alone with Elias, he reverts…"

"What could we do about that? Chain him here?"

"You do have a cage. And you could padlock the emergency exit part of it."

Lyda's lips twitched. "There's a difference between edge play and criminal behavior, rabbit."

"What would you call that out there, between them?"

"Not either one," Lyda said. "Not exactly."

Gen didn't agree with that, but she'd been playing the whole scene in her head, over and over, and a question was burning in her brain. One she shied away from, unsure she wanted it clarified. But she'd ask anyway. "Noah saw himself as taking a punishment for you. And you knew that, stood there and let it happen. Didn't you?"

The troubled look that entered Lyda's gaze eased some of her concerns. "Did you know what he was doing when he was letting Elias punch him?" Gen asked.

"Not exactly. It was how Noah looked at me, before each punch and right after, that made me think…" Lyda shook her head. "I can't explain it, Gen, and you probably won't like my answer. I figured out he was sending me a message. Though I wasn't sure what it was at first, I knew I'd rather Elias beat him to unconsciousness here, in my front yard, where we could get him to a hospital, than have him take him off to a hotel room and leave him to bleed to death."

"Criminal behavior, not edge play."

Lyda nodded. "When you endanger your sub's life, even if that's what he wants you to do, you're not being a responsible human being, let alone a responsible Dom."

"Would you have stopped him?"

"Yes. That last punch, when he broke his nose, was it." A grim smile touched Lyda's lips. "That was all I would tolerate."

Gen didn't know how she'd tolerated any of it. She wondered if she would ever fully understand the tangled dynamics that drove a relationship as intense as the one in which she'd found herself. She hoped she might have time to find out. Lots of time. But she'd never go through something like that again. If Noah came back… When he came back, she'd make that clear to both of them. She'd hit Noah on the head with a shovel and put him in the cage herself if needed.

"I wish you'd let me go to the hospital, if for no other reason than to be with him. I've seen a nose set before. It hurts like hell."

"He had to do this one on his own, from beginning to end. Let's go pull out those fresh cherries you brought home from the Whole Foods market. You and I are going to make a fresh cherry pie. Noah loves my cherry pie."

Gen looked over at her. Lyda was on the office couch, her papers spread out on one of the empty cushions, laptop on the coffee table. "Can I have something I've never asked for from you?"

Lyda gave her a steady look. "If you need it, it's yours."

Holding onto Noah's phone, Gen came to Lyda and slid onto the couch, drawing up her legs so her upper body leaned into Lyda's. Understanding, Lyda wrapped her arms around her, her body adjusting to cradle Gen across her lap, letting her put her head on her shoulder, her face against the side of Gen's.

"We can't lose him," Gen said.

"I know." Lyda held her tighter. "We'll be all right. We're strong women, Gen. We survive everything. Fire, flood, divorce, death. Even broken hearts."

* * * * *

By the time Gen heard a car bumping up the gravel of the residential access drive, they'd made the pie crust from scratch, baked the pie, and set it out on a rack to cool. Looking out the window, she saw one of Tyler's cars, a silver Jaguar sedan.

"I texted him," Lyda explained. "Asked him if he would meet Noah at the hospital. The idiot left his wallet on the dresser, which has his insurance card in it. I wasn't trusting Elias to take care of that. It wasn't his job to take care of it, anyway."

When Gen's expression changed, Lyda gestured. "Go and bring him to me."

Gen practically flew out the door and down the steps.

Noah was getting out of the car stiffly. The cut on his mouth was no longer bleeding, his nose was no longer crooked and he was carrying an ice pack for all of it. His shirt was still stained with dried blood. Gen didn't care. She wrapped herself around him, albeit gently, and cupped his skull in her hands as he bent down to her height, returned the favor of banding his arms around her as well.

"Don't you ever do that again," she scolded.

"What? Choose you? Is it that horrible of a decision?"

She pinched his arm as she slid back down to her feet. "Ow," he said mildly. His expression was tired, but there was a peacefulness there. Not the usual floating Zen peacefulness she'd teased him about before she realized it was a lack of will to decide his own fate. This was something different. As he glanced toward the house, it was disrupted by a trace of nervousness. It made her want to hug him again.

"She's waiting for you," Gen said. "She made a cherry pie."

"Hmm."

Gen looked toward Tyler. He'd gotten out of the car, but stayed on his side, the engine still running. He'd realized this wasn't a time to entertain a guest, even if that guest was the kind who'd drop everything to make a run to the hospital and intervene for a friend. Gen mouthed *thank you* to him. In response, the amber eyes warmed.

"Take care of him."

Nodding, she followed Noah. He'd taken a few steps toward the house and stopped. As the luxury sedan purred away down the drive, Gen gripped his hand.

"So how did you explain things to the hospital staff?" she ventured, hoping to cut his tension. His lips curved, though he winced at the pressure on his lip.

"Told them it was a one-on-one game that got out of hand. We never did say it was basketball, so it wasn't really untrue, all said and done."

"No," she agreed. She wanted to hold him again, the idea of losing him still so close and terrifying. It was like being on that cliff all over again. But she understood he had to make things square with Lyda first.

They went up the porch stairs. He held the door for her with his usual courtesy, and she let her hand slide across his abdomen as she stepped into the kitchen ahead of him. Lyda sat at the table. She'd pinched off a piece of crust and was nibbling at it. She'd had Gen pour her a glass of wine earlier and was still nursing that.

Her leg was elevated on the opposite chair, her other foot braced on the bottom rung. She cocked her head at the sight of him.

"They did a good job setting the nose."

"Yes Mistress. If it's all right to call you that."

"You took three fists to the face for the privilege. A punishment I did not require."

"No Mistress."

Gen leaned against the counter so the field between them was clear. The lingering heat from the oven couldn't compete with the coolness in Lyda's gaze. Gen curled her hands into balls behind her, holding onto the oven handle to keep herself in place. She had to trust their Mistress.

"Why, Noah? What made the difference?" Lyda asked.

"Does it matter?"

"No. I asked to hear the sound of my own voice." Those silver eyes became ice.

He had the grace to flush. Cleared his throat. "That day..." He looked between them both. "On the mountain."

It was something that irrevocably linked them, and one of the main reasons Gen thought Lyda had kept the three of them sleeping together in her large bed ever since she'd recovered enough to make that feasible. No cages or guest beds, because when one of them woke, jerking from that nightmare, as they seemed to take turns doing, the other two were there, to comfort and hold in the middle of the night, confirming that it was the past, not the present.

"When I was hanging onto Gen, hoping the car would stop rocking... When I was pushing you up through the window, I kept having this one thought. If I lost you both, there was no one I'd ever again have in my life like you. No one who felt about me...the way the two of you do. Separately, together."

His brow furrowed. "It took me awhile to figure it all out, Mistress. It was hard."

Gen saw the expression she'd been trying to decipher since the day she'd lambasted Lyda for being such a difficult patient. It was the shadow of his soul, struggling behind that wall inside him, a wall he'd been beating himself against, trying to break through it, figure it out, despite the fact it was against his nature, finding a different path through those dark woods.

"But then, there was this one thing," he said. "Something I couldn't stop thinking, no matter how much I felt like I didn't deserve to think it. I wanted you both. More than I'd ever wanted anything."

He took a deep breath. "Since as long as I can remember, there's always been this place inside myself. Everything point A to point B, no curves, no confusion. No pain. Not really."

Safe. Like Gen's life had been. Every step planned so there'd be no mistakes, no risks. She expected it was why she'd felt an unconscious connection to Noah from the beginning, though she hadn't recognized that link until now. She wanted to step toward him, but held herself back. He wasn't done, his gaze still locked on the judge hearing his case.

"It was a prison," he said. "I didn't control anything that came in, and I couldn't let anything out. I took that choice away from myself because it felt…the way it should be. Or so I thought. But until you and Gen became something different than what I'd known, I didn't realize that belonging to anyone who wanted me, for however long they wanted me, but never having anyone I felt like was mine…it was lonely."

His voice broke, became a little thicker. His gaze dropped to the floor and Gen saw his eyes get a little brighter as well. "I was never enough for…"

Even now, he couldn't say it, the source of that mindless rage and pain. Lyda had suspected it had been the welding on those crossed wires. When the agony fair vibrated from him, Gen knew why Dot had threatened homicide toward her own blood.

"Who I was, it wasn't enough," he said quietly, giving up on naming the faceless offenders. "So it made sense, to accept not having value, not demanding anything for myself. You know?"

Gen's throat was aching, tears threatening, a state exacerbated by seeing the change in Lyda's gaze. Those silver eyes were becoming brighter, more focused, the result of a sheen of tears.

"You are enough for us, Noah," Lyda said. Her voice was strong, harsh. As painful as the grateful, overwhelmed look he threw at her. Believing it. But he had more to say.

"If I lost the two of you, I wouldn't be able to handle the loneliness again. You and Gen, you understand who and what I am, accepted it, but asked for more from me. You asked me to choose for myself. To give that choice, who I am, value."

Lyda pressed her lips together, gave one short nod. A tear spilled down her cheek, a glistening, diamond track. "He *can* be taught," she said, her voice husky. Gen thought she would have brought him to her then, but instead, their Mistress had another demand. "You owe Gen an apology."

He looked toward Gen, raw sincerity etched on his face. "I'm so sorry, Gen. Sorry for making you think that you were going to lose me. I...it felt like I had to take care of Elias, finish that the way it should be finished. But I wish you hadn't had to feel that way, to doubt me, not even for a minute."

Gen bit back a sob, making his eyes darken. He stood there, hands opening and closing helplessly. There'd been plenty of times when he'd initiated contact, for comfort or sex, but she knew now he was waiting on their judgment.

She shifted her gaze to Lyda. That judgment lay in Lyda's hands. Gen and Noah would make their amends a different way, a different time. At the moment, she was just so overwhelmed by the possibilities finally, truly unfolding, she was speechless and immobile, a fly on the wall.

"Come here," Lyda said at last. Noah's gaze turned to her, finding her full attention on him. And her arms lifted and open.

The emotions gripping him were so strong, their usually graceful man stumbled, but he made it to her chair. He sank down on his knees beside it as Lyda wrapped her arm around his shoulders, gripped his T-shirt in both hands. He pressed his face hard into her shoulder, but then she brought his face up, put a kiss on his lips that she made hot, hard and needy. Coming up off his knees, he put his hands to her waist, thumbs pressed hard beneath her breasts as he answered the kiss with everything he could give her.

Watching them, Gen ached down to her soul. Still kissing him, Lyda reached out a hand, and Noah did it in the same moment. Gen was across the kitchen in a blink, kneeling on Lyda's other side.

Their Mistress gathered them both to her, held them close. They exchanged kisses until three mouths were tasting one another, exchanging the sweet taste of wine, cherry pie and promises.

Epilogue

"You know, you've just ensured Marcus is going to keep Josh chained to his side whenever he's at a party where there are Dommes. Greedy Dommes."

At Lyda's look, Gen lifted her hands. "I'm just saying what Marcus said."

"It's not like I wheedled a life-sized statue out of him." Lyda rolled her eyes. "It's going to be a small, eight-inch original, and I'm still paying fifty percent of the asking price, which is exorbitant."

"Yeah, because paying fifty percent for a Van Gogh wouldn't be considered outright robbery," Noah put in. "Again, a quote. Heavy on the sarcasm."

"Insanely handsome gay men tend to be melodramatic," Lyda said, giving him a narrow look. "And vicious."

"I'd tell him you said that," Gen responded, "but I think he's already considering murdering you. At this party. There's plenty of property to bury your body."

"And we're right alongside a tributary that flows out to the Gulf," Noah added.

She and Lyda were strolling arm and arm through Tyler's gardens, Noah trailing after them. It was a short predinner break after spending the last few hours enjoying the casual party of visiting friends. Gen had been a little surprised Lyda had accepted the invitation, since they were in the middle of the pre-Christmas rush that had even cut into their Sundays, but Lyda had said they all deserved a day off.

Wonderful hors d'oeuvres, the company of good friends... Brendan and Chloe were here, as well as Tyler and Marguerite, Violet and Mac. Tyler and Marguerite's visiting friends were Josh, Lauren, Marcus and Thomas. A few weeks ago, feeling guilty, Gen had admitted her slip of the tongue to Marguerite, as well as Lyda's interest in Josh's art, which made her wonder if that was why they'd been invited. For her own part, she had a delicious premonition about why she was now being included in this circle.

It was clear, from the dynamics casually demonstrated during lunch and in the relaxing aftermath, that all the people present had Dominant/submissive relationships and were cognizant of that common bond in the guest list. Even though Chloe had already brought her into the know on what the power distributions were, Gen found she could now tell Dom from sub herself, from those little touches, the way the submissives deferred to their Masters or Mistresses in entirely unique yet somehow similar mannerisms. Like her and Noah to Lyda.

She and Noah mixed and mingled, enjoyed conversations, yet there was always that thread of awareness connecting them to their Mistress. What she needed or wanted from them at any given moment. In this environment, that feeling was heightened, to a point that sexual arousal simmered between them, making them all anticipate getting into the guestroom Tyler had offered them tonight. Or maybe those things would happen earlier, in a less private setting, another unsettling thought.

As the group became more comfortable with one another, she'd seen touches becoming more intimate—and more obvious to everyone else. Conversations started to be laced with murmured commands that were anything but casual. Humorous innuendoes had serious undercurrents. The Doms were feeding off one another's energy, and it was fueling the submissives as well.

"So where do you think this is going?" She confronted it head-on with Noah, albeit in a low voice, as they returned to the group and Lyda left them to talk to Marguerite.

He slid an arm around her and, confirming her feeling about what was happening, the hand that would have curved around her waist an hour ago was much lower now, stroking her hip, her buttock. She pressed against him, lifted up to tease his throat with her lips. "Did she tell you to do this?"

"Not directly." His brown gaze caressed her, making her blood run even warmer, as if he was a fire heating it. "But I'm getting the distinct impression all the Doms are on the same track. Tyler has a dungeon, you know. With top-grade equipment."

Gen felt her eyes widen. "Would Lyda…" At Noah's look, she swallowed. Hard.

All she could think of were the possible uses of that equipment, the things she might see. The scenery alone... Her gaze slid over all of the assembled submissives. Noah, Mac, Josh, Brendan, Thomas. Holy God.

"You could pretend that seeing them all naked appalls you." Noah gave her an aggrieved look, though she saw the humor behind it, and his anticipation as well. Sliding her arms around his waist, she stroked the firm landscape of his abdomen through his shirt.

"I'll imagine what Lyda might let me do to you," she whispered.

Cocking his head, he swept his gaze meaningfully over her throat and breasts, making it clear which submissive he was most interested in seeing naked. She flushed. "Or let you do to me," she allowed, clearing her throat.

A more distinct and imperious cleared throat drew their attention. Lyda was giving them a look, brow raised. Gen lifted both hands clear of Noah in an exaggerated "I wasn't doing anything" gesture that had their Mistress's lips quirking.

"There will be time enough for that," she promised.

Everything tightened up in Gen except her weak knees as Lyda spoke clear enough that everyone at the party could hear. It was tantamount to an open declaration of where they might be headed...publicly.

Lyda's gaze shifted to the assembled, who'd taken seats around the patio where they were sharing afternoon cocktails. With Noah and Gen the only ones now standing in her proximity, Gen realized it felt like they'd stepped onto a stage.

"When Marguerite invited me to this event today," Lyda said, "it was because I told her I was seeking the right time and place to do something I've wanted to do for several months now. She suggested this, and I agreed."

Giving Noah and Gen a significant look, she sat down in a patio chair. She pointed to the space directly in front of her. "Come here," she said.

Even knowing Chloe, Marguerite and Tyler were part of the audience, Gen felt no self-consciousness, which said a good deal about how far she'd come in this journey and her trust of Lyda. She remembered those words...*if I ask for your submission in public, it's because you can trust me to keep you safe*... Now she understood that meant safe physically and emotionally. Safe from humiliation or the wrong kinds of pain.

As such, Gen led herself and Noah to Lyda, taking the lead in them both kneeling before her. Gen was aware of Chloe's intent regard to her immediate left, her friend clasping Brendan's hand as if anticipating something quite wonderful. Butterflies fluttered in Gen's stomach.

Lyda touched Gen's face, caressed Noah's shoulder. "I'm not the nurturing sort. Nor especially sentimental. But once I make a decision, I don't turn back from it, do I?"

They shook their heads. In the corner of her other eye, Gen saw Marcus, his arm stretched behind Thomas. Thomas had leaned forward, but his knee was pressed against Marcus', evidence of that connection between them. Mac stood behind Violet's chair, watching, the large male just as attentive. One more shift of her glance and there was Josh. As always, the artist looked sleepy and somewhat distracted, but right now those gray eyes behind their wire-rimmed glasses were unusually keen. He was sitting on the grass next to the edge of the patio, where Lauren sat in a chair, her legs crossed. He had his hand loosely wrapped around her calf, a possessive gesture that didn't negate the dynamic of Mistress and sub that existed between them. Now that she understood more about those possessive feelings herself, it made sense to her.

She brought her gaze back to Lyda. Behind her stood Tyler and Marguerite. Marguerite sat on a padded bench to Lyda's right, and Tyler stood at her back, his hand resting on her shoulder. Gen noticed how his thumb caressed the base of her throat, the seed pearl choker. Marguerite met her gaze, those pale-blue eyes luminous.

Bringing her full attention back to Lyda, Gen found her Mistress waiting on her. Lyda's expression wasn't impatient or offended. It was as if she wanted Noah and Gen to understand the solemnity of the occasion by absorbing the others' reactions.

"I made a decision, right before you made yours, Noah." Lyda met his gaze. "It's a good thing you went down the right path with Elias, else I would have been wasting my money. And you know how I feel about that."

"Yes Mistress," he ventured. He was obviously as unsure what this was about as Gen, but when Gen's hand crept into his at her side again, he clasped it.

Marguerite drew a small velvet bag from under the cushion next to her, placing it in Lyda's palm when she turned to her. "I'm not much for collaring. And I told you I don't really have a use for marriage. Do you remember?" Lyda's gaze shifted to Gen.

Gen nodded. "I believe in action, not words," Lyda continued. "I don't even particularly believe in symbols, but when presenting a symbol is an act that says a million things words can't...well, that's different."

Gen drew in a breath as Lyda opened the small bag and deposited the contents into her hand. It was a trio of rings. One delicate silver, one a handsome gold, and one a twisted band of both, the thinner silver like a vine weaving around the thick gold. The mixed band and the silver were obviously women's rings, the gold a man's ring.

Lyda met Gen's gaze, shifted between it and Noah's. "By taking them, wearing them, we're promised to each other. Faithful through thick and thin, through car wrecks and laundry, cancer and even poor movie selections."

A ripple of laughter came from around them, but Gen was staring into Lyda's eyes. Despite the wry comment, her eyes were serious, intent, the whole world there. Noah's fingers tightened on hers, hard.

"It means you belong to me, and I will care for you. It means I love you both more than anything. It means I'm in love with you, and I want that love to keep growing until we're as twisted together as the band I'll wear, showing that this promise is made to you both. You're under no obligation to take the rings—"

She and Noah reached for them in one motion. Lyda's hand closed over them, preventing the retrieval, but the smile transformed her face as another murmur ran through the group, reflecting the pleasure and approval in Lyda's eyes. Gen also saw the swell of emotion at their quick response. Following impulse, she kept her hand resting on Lyda's closed one. Noah's overlapped them both, his longer fingers closing over Gen's, fingertips brushing the sides of Lyda's hand.

It was Noah who spoke for them both.

"There's nothing we want more than to belong to you and you alone, Mistress. We love you too." The desire and love in his eyes was unmistakable. "And in truth...I see myself as belonging to you both."

Gen touched his face. "Same goes." She shifted her gaze to Lyda. "We're all yours, Mistress. And, if it's not too presumptuous, we feel like you're ours."

"Doesn't matter if it's presumptuous or not, it's always the way it seems to work." The wry comment came from Violet, echoed by a snort from Marcus.

Lyda looked between her two subs, then nodded to Gen, an unspoken command. Gen withdrew her hand and Lyda opened her fingers. Her Mistress picked up the delicate silver ring, putting the other two to the side for the moment. When she took Gen's hand, slid the band onto her left finger, she met Gen's gaze. "Mine, rabbit."

Then she leaned forward, kissed her forehead, her nose, her mouth. The lingering kiss was followed by a look that said *I-mean-it* on every level. Gen couldn't say anything, her throat closed with emotion.

Lyda picked up the gold band. As she and Noah locked gazes, Gen felt that thickness grow to a sweet ache. While her and Lyda's story had had its ups and downs, this possibility had been far more precarious for Lyda and Noah. Those fears were now gone, no foothold to find when Noah was staring at Lyda as if she was everything.

Lyda pushed the ring over his knuckle. As she did, he turned his hand, captured hers in a very unlike Noah aggressive move...if one didn't know the depth and strength of certain emotions he carried. He pressed his lips to her knuckles, his body bending toward her until his head touched her knees. She doubled over him, tangling her hand in his hair, pressing her lips against his nape, rubbing her cheek there.

"Don't you ever forget," she whispered. Gen glimpsed Lyda's face in a rare, entirely unguarded moment. "Don't break my heart."

When he lifted his head, his expression was raw devotion. "Never. I'll take care of both of you, Mistress. Through everything and anything."

He'd said it before, or things like it, but now it meant even more than before. Gen realized he'd picked up the final band when he bent over Lyda's hand. He looked at Gen. In accord, she supported Lyda's hand as Noah slipped the ring on their Mistress's finger. Then their newly decorated hands were tangled together, a hard knot that conveyed a lot of emotion, including tears, as Noah surged up on his knees and hugged both her and Lyda. He rained kisses on their mouths and necks, kisses they returned as best they could while laughing, since Lyda threatened dire things if he didn't stop slobbering over the two of them like a golden retriever. Lyda's laughter was as welcome to Gen's ears as a spring rain on new flowers.

The popping of a cork brought them back to the present surroundings. Champagne had been brought by Tyler's housekeeper, Sarah, and flutes were being filled, distributed by Brendan. He bent and gave Gen a kiss on the cheek, Noah a quick, hard hug. Chloe drew Gen up for a hug as well.

"I'm so, so happy for you," the girl whispered. "You three look perfect together. I've never seen Noah look happy. Not the real kind. The last-a-lifetime kind."

Gen turned to verify, seeing real peace in his eyes. Happiness, arousal, pleasure, love. She saw it in Lyda's face as well, and suspected it was in her own. She'd worn wedding rings twice before, but neither had felt as right as what she wore now.

After congratulations were given, the patio cleared out with discreet driftings of the other guests into the house or gardens, leaving the three of them to share a private moment. Gen was sitting at Lyda's knee again. Noah was standing, but now he dropped to a knee beside her, kissed both their hands. Lyda stroked his hair, then lifted his chin, kissed his mouth. This kiss was another deep one, a teasing gesture that became even more provocative when he lifted his hands and she made a sharp noise, keeping him in place until she left him in an obviously aroused state. Then she leaned down and did the same to Gen. Lips brushing, tongues tangling, teeth nipping, until Gen was breathing fast and shallow. Lyda eased back, her gaze sweeping over both of them.

"I can take you up to our guestroom now, and we can celebrate alone, privately. Or, I can take you to Tyler's dungeon and we can have our own version of a wedding reception." Her gaze sparked. "Either way, my pets will end up naked and at my mercy, while I give them pain and pleasure according to my desires…and theirs. But I will give them this one choice. Which will it be?"

Gen and Noah exchanged a glance. Noah's teeth flashed in an untamed, sexy smile, but Gen answered the question.

"Why can't we have both?"

Also by Joey W. Hill

eBooks:

Chance of a Lifetime
Choice of Masters
If Wishes Were Horses
Knights of the Board Room: Afterlife
Knights of the Board Room: Board Resolution
Knights of the Board Room: Hostile Takeover
Knights of the Board Room: Willing Sacrifice
Make Her Dreams Come True
Nature of Desire 1: Holding the Cards
Nature of Desire 2: Natural Law
Nature of Desire 3: Ice Queen
Nature of Desire 4: Mirror of My Soul
Nature of Desire 5: Mistress of Redemption
Nature of Desire 6: Rough Canvas
Nature of Desire 7: Branded Sanctuary
Nature of Desire 8: Divine Solace
Snow Angel
Threads of Faith
Virtual Reality

Print Books:
Behind the Mask *(anthology)*
Enchained *(anthology)*
Faith and Dreams
Hot Chances *(anthology)*
If Wishes Were Horses
Knights of the Board Room: Afterlife
Knights of the Board Room: Hostile Takeover
Knights of the Board Room: Willing Sacrifice
Nature of Desire 1: Holding the Cards
Nature of Desire 2: Natural Law
Nature of Desire 3: Ice Queen
Nature of Desire 4: Mirror of My Soul
Nature of Desire 5: Mistress of Redemption
Nature of Desire 6: Rough Canvas
Nature of Desire 7: Branded Sanctuary
Virtual Reality

About Joey W. Hill

I've always had an aversion to reading, watching or hearing interviews of favorite actors, authors, musicians, etc. because so often the real person doesn't measure up to the beauty of the art they produce. Their politics or religion are distasteful, or they're shallow and self-absorbed, a vacuous mophead without a lick of sense. From then on, though I may appreciate their craft or art, it has somehow been tarnished. Therefore, whenever I'm asked to provide personal information about myself for readers, a ball of anxiety forms in my stomach as I think: "Okay, the next couple of paragraphs can change forever the way someone views my stories." Why on earth does a reader want to know about me? It's the story that's important.

So here it is. I've been given more blessings in my life than any one person has a right to have. Despite that, I'm a Type A, borderline obsessive-compulsive paranoiac who worries I will never live up to expectations. I've got more phobias than anyone (including myself) has patience to read about. I can't stand talking on the phone, I dread social commitments, and the idea of living in monastic solitude with my husband and animals, books and writing is as close an idea to paradise as I can imagine. I love chocolate, but with that deeply ingrained, irrational female belief that weight equals worth, I manage to keep it down to a minor addiction. I adore good movies. I'm told I work too much. Every day is spent trying to get through the never ending "to do" list to snatch a few minutes to write.

This is because, despite all these mediocre and typical qualities, for some miraculous reason, these wonderful characters well up out of my soul with stories to tell. When I manage to find enough time to write, sufficient enough that the precious "stillness" required rises up and calms all the competing voices in my head, I can step into their lives, hear what they are saying, what they're feeling, and put it down on paper. It's a magic beyond description, akin to truly believing my husband loves me, winning the trust of an animal who has known only fear or apathy, making a true connection with someone, or knowing for certain I've given a reader a moment of magic through those written words. It's a magic that reassures me there is Someone, far wiser than myself, who knows the permanent path to that garden of stillness, where there is only love, acceptance and a pen waiting for hours and hours of uninterrupted, blissful use.

If only I could finish that darned "to do" list.

I welcome feedback from readers - actually, I thrive on it like a vampire, whether it's good or bad.

∞

The author welcomes comments from readers. You can find her website and email address on her author bio page at www.ellorascave.com.

Tell Us What You Think

We appreciate hearing reader opinions about our books. You can email us at Service@ellorascave.com (when contacting Customer Service, be sure to state the book title and author).

Why an electronic book?

We live in the Information Age—an exciting time in the history of human civilization, in which technology rules supreme and continues to progress in leaps and bounds every minute of every day. For a multitude of reasons, more and more avid literary fans are opting to purchase e-books instead of paper books. The question from those not yet initiated into the world of electronic reading is simply: *Why?*

1. ***Price.*** An electronic title at Ellora's Cave Publishing runs anywhere from 40% to 75% less than the cover price of the exact same title in paperback format. Why? Basic mathematics and cost. It is less expensive to publish an e-book (no paper and printing, no warehousing and shipping) than it is to publish a paperback, so the savings are passed along to the consumer.
2. ***Space.*** Running out of room in your house for your books? That is one worry you will never have with electronic books. For a low one-time cost, you can purchase a handheld device specifically designed for e-reading. Many e-readers have large, convenient screens for viewing. Better yet, hundreds of titles can be stored within your new library—on a single microchip. There are a variety of e-readers from different manufacturers. You can also read e-books on your PC or laptop computer. (Please note that Ellora's Cave does not endorse any specific brands.

You can check our website at www.ellorascave.com for information we make available to new consumers.)

3. *Mobility.* Because your new e-library consists of only a microchip within a small, easily transportable e-reader, your entire cache of books can be taken with you wherever you go.

4. *Personal Viewing Preferences.* Are the words you are currently reading too small? Too large? Too… ANNOYING? Paperback books cannot be modified according to personal preferences, but e-books can.

5. *Instant Gratification.* Is it the middle of the night and all the bookstores near you are closed? Are you tired of waiting days, sometimes weeks, for bookstores to ship the novels you bought? Ellora's Cave Publishing sells instantaneous downloads twenty-four hours a day, seven days a week, every day of the year. Our webstore is never closed. Our e-book delivery system is 100% automated, meaning your order is filled as soon as you pay for it.

Those are a few of the top reasons why electronic books are replacing paperbacks for many avid readers.

As always, Ellora's Cave welcomes your questions and comments. We invite you to email us at Service@ellorascave.com or write to us directly at Ellora's Cave Publishing Inc., 1056 Home Avenue, Akron, OH 44310-3502.

MAKE EACH DAY MORE *EXCITING* WITH OUR

ELLORA'S CAVEMEN CALENDAR

 WWW.ELLORASCAVE.COM

Discover for yourself why readers can't get enough of the multiple award-winning publisher Ellora's Cave. Be sure to visit EC on the web at www.ellorascave.com to find erotic reading experiences that will leave you breathless. You can also find our books at all the major e-tailers (Barnes & Noble, Amazon Kindle, Sony, Kobo, Google, Apple iBookstore, All Romance eBooks, and others).

www.ellorascave.com

CPSIA information can be obtained at www.ICGtesting.com
Printed in the USA
LVOW06s1052270714

396199LV00001B/181/P